SHADE

SHADE

An Anthology

of Fiction by

Gay Men of

African Descent

edited by

BRUCE MORROW and CHARLES H. ROWELL

AVON BOOKS ◆ NEW YORK

Copyright notices for each story appear on page v, which serves as an extension of this copyright page.

SHADE is an original publication of Avon Books. These stories have never before appeared together in book form. These stories are works of fiction. Any similarity to actual persons or events is purely coincidental.

AVON BOOKS
A division of
The Hearst Corporation
1350 Avenue of the Americas
New York, New York 10019

Copyright © 1996 by Bruce Morrow and Charles H. Rowell
Cover photo by Luis "Luna" Ortiz
Published by arrangement with the editors
Library of Congress Catalog Card Number: 95-48795
ISBN: 0-380-78305-3

Library of Congress Cataloging in Publication Data:
Shade : an anthology of fiction by gay men of African descent / edited by Bruce Morrow and Charles H. Rowell.
    p.   cm.
1. Gay men—United States—Fiction. 2. American fiction—Afro-American authors.
3. Gay men's writings, American. 4. Afro-American gays—Fiction. 5. Afro-American men—Fiction. 6. Afro-Americans—Fiction. I. Morrow, Bruce. II. Rowell, Charles H.
PS648.H57S46   1996   95-48795
813.008'09206642—dc20   CIP

First Avon Books Trade Printing: June 1996

AVON TRADEMARK REG. U.S. PAT. OFF. AND IN OTHER COUNTRIES, MARCA REGISTRADA, HECHO EN U.S.A.

Printed in the U.S.A.

OPM   10 9 8 7 6 5 4 3 2 1

To the memory of Melvin Dixon (1951–1993)—
poet, fiction writer, educator, cultural worker

Acknowledgments

This book would not have been possible without the many black gay and lesbian writers and editors who have come before us. Praise be their names.

We are indebted to the following for support, advice, and patience: Charlotte Abbott, Thelma Adams, *African American Review*, Kirk Anthony, Paul Beatty, Don Belton, Silas Burgess III, *Callaloo*, David Cashion, Sarah Chalfant, Andrea Chapin, C. B. Cooke and Glyph Media Group, Steven Corbin, Jordan Davis, Hoang Duong, Chris Eamon, Chris Edgar, Amanda Filipacchi, Tonya Foster, Frederick Douglass Creative Arts Center and the Fellowship for Young African-American Fiction Writers, John E. Fredericks, Ethan Geto, Mark Gevissor, Henry Holt and Company, Hetrick-Martin Institute, Jill Jackson, Glenroy James, Isaac Julien, John Keene, Simon Kilmurry, Iara Lee, Doug Levere, Janice Lowe, Erik Meers, David Moor, The Morrow Family, Yvonne Murphy, Luna Ortiz, Other Countries, Rohn Padmore, Ron Padgett, *Paris Review*, Julie Patton, David Paul, Dale Peck, Darryl Pinckney, Taifa Reid, Robert Reid-Pharr, L&V Schulte-Puccio, Lisa Ross, Shawn Ruff, Deb Schwartz, Nancy Larson Shapiro, David Silverman, Bennett Singer, Bob Stock, Teachers & Writers Collaborative, Charles Wright (both of them), and XAX.

And to Roger Schulte—there is no way I could have pulled this together without you by my side.

—Bruce Morrow

And to Elizabeth Alexander, Finnie Coleman, Percival Everett, Trudier Harris, Mae Henderson, Christine Phillip, and Melvin White—who stood with me as I mounted this project.

—Charles H. Rowell

The world is before you and you need not take it or leave it as it was when you came in.

—JAMES BALDWIN

The bottom line is this: We are Black men who are proudly gay. What we offer is our lives, our love, our visions. We are risin' to the love we all need. We are coming home with our heads held high.

—JOSEPH BEAM

Contents

Introduction: Shade . . .

Samuel R. Delany

It gives relief from the sun.

And when one queen casts it at another—or at a straight heckler—it raises eyebrows and makes the corners of the lips twitch. You might say shade's a subtler form of dishing, a mode of repartee with a black accent whose connotations are more ironic and notably more nuanced than what's usually meant by the largely straight term "dis (as in the verb 'disrespect')."

Like so many terms from gay slang—black, white, and down to camp itself—shade is shot through with the idea of irony; and irony, literary theorist René Welleck tells us, is the aspect of those phrases and rhetorical figures which we are not sure *how* to respond to—where language opens up, through a moment's hesitation, into an explosion of potentialities, some appalling, some unimaginably wonderful, and all of which seize power for the speaker and, however momentary, articulate wildly subversive possibilities.

"He *couldn't* have said what I *thought* he said . . . ?" That, I suppose, is the benchmark response to the casting of shade. Well, the writers here, without exception, *are* saying it.

Here's a wide and rich range of stories by contemporary black gay men. Not all the stories are about being gay—nor even all of them about being black. But there is an energy evident enough here and common to most that should, I believe, make any writer pleased and proud to be of such company. I certainly am.

The history of black gay men writing about ourselves and our situation? The general wisdom over these things has it that the first such tale in the United States was Bruce Nugent's story "Smoke, Lilies, and Jade" that first appeared in the black literary publication *Fire!!* in November 1926. The tale I several times heard Bruce tell when he was in his seventies was that he and *Fire!!*'s editory, Wallace Thurman (both black gay writers, by the bye), were discussing how to assure the magazine's success. Well, if they included stories about shocking and salacious topics, everyone would want to read it. What were the two most scandalous topics they could think of? What about homosexuality and prostitution? But who, then, should write which? According to Bruce, they flipped a coin. Bruce won the assignment to write a gay tale and Thurman won prostitution as his topic.

After that, the field appears fairly bare till Baldwin's *Giovanni's Room* in 1956. Baldwin's narrator is also famous for being tall, blond, and "rather like an arrow." It was only with the more loosely structured *Another Country* in 1962 that Baldwin—working all but alone—could begin dealing with homosexuality as part of the black community. In the late 1980s, a group of energetic, young, black gay male writers got together to form the Other Countries Collective. Along with the Joseph Beam anthologies, *In the Life* (1986) and *Brother to Brother* (1991), the collective signals a formal acknowledgment of black gay writing as a range, a force, a field of endeavor and enterprise, inescapable and unignorable throughout the tapestry of black literary production—a formal acknowledgment that will, doubtless, initiate a search for a past and other precursors (for not only *are* we here, we have been here since black men and women have been writing). But this is the contemporary range, field, and force which *Shade* harvests, develops, and sends outward.

The desire to shock in a homophobic society such as ours has got to be, however minuscule, however necessary, however healthy, a part of the coming-out process. If coming out is where you are, embrace it; use it. It gives strength and, yes, pleasure.

An intriguing aspect to the collection at hand, however, is that it contains so *few* "coming out" stories. Far more in evidence than shock *or* salaciousness is the day to day texture of black gay life—the encounter with cousins and neighbors (watch out for Bil Wright's "Your Mother from Cleveland," who lives *right* next door) and mothers, and sometimes, wives. Some of the writers return to those poignant childhood moments before articulation was necessary or even possible (Larry Duplechan's brilliantly evocative "Zazoo"; Robert E. Penn's gently elegiac "Uncle Eugene"), while others set themselves squarely in the problems of adult life as gay men—a life with its own social forms and unique expression of social pain and triumph (Jaime Manrique's wonderfully rich "Twilight at the Equator"; philosopher K. Anthony Appiah's elegant tale of round robin ribaldry "The Pool"). But so rarely among these stories is "being gay" a matter of confrontation and surveillance by the non-gay world, that, when on occasion it veers in that direction, the sheer, preposterous, glorious gesture with which the confrontation is at once brought about and averted (as in A. Cinqué Hicks's marvelous story "Spice") becomes . . . well, a cast of shade indeed! There's an astonishing amount of hope in these tales, whether it's the personal hope of personal pleasure achieved (as in James Earl Hardy's "Take the 'A' Train") or the resonant hope that strikes the soul's roots in (G. Winston James's "Church"—a tale that suggests even an institution as traditionally homophobic as the black church can, when confronted with truth and humanity, change). There are richly experimental stories (Severo Sarduy's "The Initiation," its language as opulent and glimmering as brocade; John R. Keene, Jr.'s "My Son, My Heart, My Life," its narrative clean as a curl of steel). There are tales of self-deception and self-definition (Charles Harvey's "When Dogs Bark"; Randall Kenan's "Wash Me"). Which is which is indeed a shaded call. There's at least one tale of frightening power (Darieck Scott's "This City of Men") that, with a turn to S&M, simply and scarily casts questions in every direction we might want to look.

Epitomized by John Rechy's *City of Night* and Djuna Barnes's *Nightwood*, the story of gay men and Lesbians has traditionally been played out in the shadowed precincts of James

Thomson's "City of Dreadful Night" ("The City is of Night, perchance of death / But certainly of Night . . ."), controlled by the romantic inversion of night for day and the dark, often unnameable secrets it invites the gay writer to celebrate. The reader will find this collection, however, positively drenched in sunlight. Oh, the night pieces are here (Bennett Capers's eerie "Nobody Gets Hurt"; the late Melvin Dixon's powerful "Red Leaves") but, in such a glaring, solar context, they take on very different values, it seems to me.

Much of the discussion of recent black writing has taken place under the rubric of W. E. B. DuBois's concept of "double consciousness" for black Americans. The sense of a world split into parallel—or, better yet, opposing—cultures is so strong throughout *these* stories, however (as, indeed, it must be in any account of gay life), one begins to wonder if DuBois's notion doesn't apply even more to gay culture than to black—or rather, by the focus on black *gay* life, the split is chiseled deeper, to an abyssal gulf that leaves the virtuoso ability of those who can move back and forth across it an awesome social accomplishment.

These stories celebrate difference—the pain of being different, surely, but also the wonder, the joy, and the truth of difference. They are informative. They are exiting. And they are filled, *filled* with the pleasure of rich, writerly surfaces, wonderfully sharp observations, and extraordinary writerly invention.

Find some shade, sit down, relax—and read . . .

—*Minneapolis*
October 1995

Spice

A. Cinqué Hicks

To make gumbo, you need rice. Mama preferred brown rice. Then you also need an onion, butter, oil, flour, okra, green onions, tomatoes, shrimp and oysters, and an assortment of spices and herbs. Mama liked to keep everything in the refrigerator or in the cabinet until she was ready to use it. The countertop stayed clear that way. People had been making gumbo in our family as far back as anyone living could remember.

Mama was peeling the shrimp. She pulled back the stiff skins, took off their heads and put those aside in a pile.

A light sprinkle of paprika is good for seafood. It helps to counterbalance the pungent fishiness.

She paused, looked up, made a face at the orange I was peeling and went back to her shrimp. "I wish you wouldn't eat right before dinner. Especially *that*." She knew I would eat the orange and then nibble on the rind until it was all gone too.

"I still eat the same way I ate last time you saw me," I answered casually. "It was only three months ago."

"Four months." She kept peeling.

She paused again, pulled a yellow and white checkered dishcloth from the handle on the refrigerator door and wiped off her thin, brown hands. She wore the faded lime green sweatsuit that she wore for her aerobics videos. She'd made a point of never having owned an apron.

The kitchen was a narrow alley of brown speckled tile and

1

cherry-wood cabinets finished to a satin semigloss. The counter-tops were plain cream-colored Formica broken up here and there by irregular atolls of coffee stains, and by the food-crusted utensils Mama was using. Standing at one end as I was then, the other end seemed to move away and flow uninterrupted into the dining room beyond.

The gumbo was simmering. She reached up to the spice rack in the windowsill over the cutting board. Her hand flitted lightly for a few seconds over the glass canisters, and then stopped on the red pepper and pulled it down. She twisted off the cap and shook what seemed like too much into the pot of bubbling food.

She looked up at me, a quick light tugging at her eyelids. "Oh, Alv, did you bring a spice?"

"No," I answered, a little worried. "I was just going to use one of yours."

She shrugged slightly. "Oh, I guess that's okay. The way your grandmother used to do it, you had to bring it from your own house. I think it was part of the point—everyone bringing their own spice for the gumbo. It just had to be from your own kitchen. It was how they did it." She scooped the shrimp into a waiting bowl. "Doesn't matter too much really."

"Well, it's the same idea," I offered. I was finished peeling now and split the orange in half.

"Guess so. Course, we do a lot of things different now than they used to."

I remembered that. I remembered how Gramma said that gumbo was just supposed to be leftovers. You threw everything left over from the week into a big stewpot and let it all cook together. And you didn't serve it to anybody but relatives. Gumbo was just a way of cleaning out the kitchen.

I offered to go buy a spice of my own. "Don't be ridiculous. Use one of mine," she said, flicking her chin towards the spice rack. "I mean really, it's just food."

"Thanks." I took the first bite of orange.

First you make the rice. You do that first because it's so sensitive and you don't want to be in the middle of doing something else and forget about the rice. Likewise, you don't want to be sautéing something delicate like garlic and then be forced to stop because you have to take off the rice right at that moment. So you cook the rice first just to get it out of the way. Mama almost always burned a layer of rice at the bottom of the pot, and the first time I'd made a perfect pot of rice, I turned the heat up while she wasn't looking and let it cook two minutes too long.

She glanced at the clock behind her. Five-thirteen. In the action of the kitchen that night I couldn't hear the ticking of the second hand the way I could years ago when I would come down from the attic at midnight and it was quiet and there was just me and my orange peels. Mama sighed lightly.

"Okay," she said, "I told Cleve and Yvonne six o'clock. Which means they won't be here until six-thirty. In fact, let's say seven o'clock. We're talking about Cleve, after all. So I'm pretty much on schedule." She paused, then went on, "You know they're bringing Angela with them."

"I know. Why wouldn't they?" I immediately hoped I hadn't been too defensive. Cleve had met Mama in college the night their dormitory basement caught fire and everyone came spilling out onto the lawn. Angela was his daughter, and Mama couldn't invite Cleve and Yvonne without expecting that of course they'd bring her if she wanted to come.

"All right, all right. I was just making sure you knew so there wouldn't be any surprises."

"What kind of surprises?" I asked. "You mean like she might ask me if I brought her an engagement ring?"

She went to the pot on the stove again.

"Or maybe Cleve'll ask instead of her," I added. "They really ought to know by now why we never hit it off. Think I should make a scene?"

"Now you know, Alvin," she said wearily. "Nobody makes a scene at *my* dinner unless it's me. You don't have to tell your whole life story at the table." She stirred the pot. "This food is going to be good," she said. She looked at me and raised her eyebrows in a sort of apology.

I gathered up my orange and the rinds in a paper towel and went out to the living room. The picture window looked as though it were opening up, getting bigger and bigger as more light came into the room from the setting sun. The San

Gabriel Mountains reached upward in quiet agitation, dusty and green-brown. The sun had just begun to lose its grip on the sky and fall back behind the mountains in a slow-motion tumble to the other side of the earth. I sat on the sofa that faced the window, freeing up a light cloud of dust.

Of course I knew Angela would be there. They were always dragging her around with them to social events. She was getting to marrying age, after all. We were born the same year. Mama and Yvonne would compare their distended, pregnant bodies, Yvonne two months ahead. I couldn't remember a time before knowing Angela or a time before being vaguely aware that someone had intended for us to wake up one day wanting to be married, to buy a house not too far away, to cook our own steaming pots of food. But we never went to a movie, nor to the ice-skating rink the way Mama suggested every month or so, and Mama hid her disappointment behind the fantasy that I was saving myself from all the other high school girls for the right moment when I would go to Angela, kiss her and softly place a small, velvet-covered box in her upturned palm.

I heard the clatter of silverware thrown into the sink. I took a bite of my orange. It had become warmer since I had peeled it. The citrus, tart-sweet juice felt good going down, felt better in this fading half-light of the sunset than in the full, hard light of the kitchen.

"Alv, you out there?" Mama yelled out from the kitchen. "I'm going to put strawberries in the fruit salad. You can pick them out if you want. Yvonne likes strawberries."

I said that was all right with me.

Almost any fruit salad tastes better with a dash of cinnamon. It mellows out the flavor to a smoother sophistication. A friend of Mama's discovered that one summer, and somehow over the years she'd come to believe it was her own idea.

I pulled myself off the couch, freeing up another, smaller cloud of dust. I went back into the kitchen. My eyes hurt as they readjusted to the light. An onion was sitting on the countertop.

"How much of this do you need?" I asked.

"The whole thing." She was slicing strawberries.

"Diced?"

"Well, leave it in kind of big pieces."

I pulled a knife from the holder. Mama looked at me as if considering whether I could handle the next piece of information.

"Then sauté it up in some butter. And don't leave it in too long."

I peeled off the golden outer layers of skin and started chopping. Slice down. Good, sharp knife, so I don't have to saw back and forth too much. Slice down, slice down, slice down. Two more times. Kind of big pieces, she had said. I stopped to wipe my forehead with the back of my hand, and the blade threw a faint gleam over the cabinet doors. Then cut across the patties. Cut, cut, and again cut.

After you've made the brown roux from the oil and flour, you can add the okra and green onions, the bay leaf, the salt and pepper and Tabasco sauce. Mama used to add the white onion here too, but she liked the stronger taste of onion added later. You cook these for a while, until the okra cooks to pieces, and then the water goes in, along with the liquor drained from the oysters and the fish stock. That cooks for a little while. Basil has a certain wild impertinence that could be good for anything with tomatoes in it, and Mama's gumbo had tomatoes. The right amount would cut through the gumbo like a streak of lightning.

Cut left to right, cut left to right, cut left to right.

Mama scooped the strawberries into the salad bowl. I sliced off a pat of butter and shook it from the knife into a skillet.

"The way Gramma used to tell it," Mama started, "people thought about it all afternoon what spice they would bring. Really I should say *herbs*. Green, leafy things. Not that people really had too many to choose from. I think everyone had the same basic ones. But you know, people might want to bring that one they had that nobody else had." Mama shook her finger for drama. "Plus people were always trying to second-guess what the other people would bring, 'cause nobody wanted to double up on somebody else. But you know, things worked out."

I threw a handful of onions into the skillet, and opened one of the narrow drawers to find a wooden fork. I found it and almost didn't notice the photograph at the bottom of the drawer. The rhythm of the cooking halted absurdly. The photo was the one of me from last summer right after the gay pride march, leaning my head to one side with an exaggerated grin. I had my shirt off, my skin gone from chocolate to the color of coffee grounds in the summer sun. I held up a huge cardboard pink triangle in one hand and a bottle of beer in the other. I couldn't remember who had taken it. Last August when I was here, it had sat propped up against the wall on one of the shelves beside the fireplace, right between a candlestick and an abalone shell turned upside down.

I closed the drawer gently, pretending not to see it. The onions sizzled in the browning butter. I stirred them absently, just enough to keep them from burning.

Mama spoke up, "Then we did it the same way Gramma did, and she did it the same way her parents did. Who knows how long that goes back?"

I ignored her. I could only imagine the spot on the shelf vacant with a barely noticeable area where the photo had formed a little tent and there was slightly less dust. Or maybe she had moved the shell and the candlestick to close up the space. It would look more natural that way. There were other pictures of me, so no one would see anything missing or strange.

"That's enough, Alv," she said. She took the skillet from me and dumped the onions into the big pot.

After the liquid has been boiling for a while, you put in the sautéed onions and tomatoes. Then at the very end you add the shrimp. The shrimp you add in raw. I had caught a snatch of conversation once where Mama was saying over the phone to her sister, "Of course you add them raw. Even when Gramma used fresh stuff, she never cooked the shrimp." You add that in the end and then just let it cook.

Mama wiped her hands on the white and yellow checkered dishrag, took a final glance into the pot, poked it a bit, and then looked at me. "I'm going to go get dressed. The food should be all right, but just check it in about twenty minutes if I don't come back."

"Okay," I answered, my mouth full with the last piece of orange.

She faded back into the dimly lit hallway. At the end of it

on the left a light clicked on and she disappeared into her room. Automatically I opened the refrigerator door. I squatted down. Nothing in there really. The red of the strawberries on the bottom shelf caught my eye. Yvonne liked strawberries. I would pick mine out. Cleve would make a comment about that. "Don't care too much for them strawberries, huh, Alvin?"

"No, not really." I wondered if I'd look up.

When Angela first came, she would be very nice and very charming and would smile at me. And I would smile politely in return and then concentrate fiercely on my plate of gumbo, as if I could find and name all the spices and herbs by looking at it hard enough. By the end of the meal Angela would become restless, thinking. "A waste of time, Daddy. At least if the food was good, I could be glad I came. Maybe listen to Mommy squeeze out a recipe from them. But she won't even do that. I'll go home and write it down this time, never to let you drag me here again and waste my time on him." Those words would be in her empty, close-lipped smile.

I'd look quickly at Angela with her pressed black hair sitting stiffly around her neck. Then I'd consider faking illness, but decide not to. I'd look down, listening to the conversation and maybe dropping in some words like accidental bait. Cleve would take an interest in any casual little thing I said, each time as though it were the one word he'd been waiting to hear all his life. He'd try to find some way to relate my comment to Angela, to put my words all over her like perfume. He would fail. He would try again. He would fail again—all through the dinner.

Yvonne would bring up something in city politics. She would say how much talk there was at work after one of the officers of the Black Business Association came out so strongly in favor of "equal rights for gays in the workplace." She would say, "Hm. We supported him, too. He has good ideas, I guess." Then Cleve would put everything in perspective for everyone, saying something like. "They gotta do what they gotta do. But Lord, thank goodness black folks don't really do that stuff. That's a white thing mostly." Angela would click her tongue, and I'd think about saying something in return, but only shake my head and pick out strawberries.

The refrigerator door closed with a soft *shumpp*. I went back and pulled the photograph out of the drawer. I was standing on the grass and my T-shirt hung from the back pocket of my jeans like a tiny waterfall. A street snaked up the hill back into the distance on the left side. My apartment building was directly behind me, a Victorian-style, blue clapboard building set in claustrophobic narrowness between two others. The windows stuck out most to me, black and inscrutable beneath their white false dormers. The sky was a field of blue-gray behind the building, broken in places with smudges of thicker, heavier gray.

The pot was bubbling, and even though I'd been in the kitchen the whole time, the smell of food began to rise up and hover over me. *This shirt will smell like sweat and gumbo for a while*, I thought.

I replaced the photograph in the drawer.

Mama came back into the kitchen a few minutes later, dressed in a straight blue skirt and a billowy cream-colored blouse. She was running a brush through her short hair with quick, brutal strokes. I suddenly felt underdressed in my jeans. "Okay," she announced, "I don't want to get dirty, so I'll set the table and you finish up with the food. It's not that much to do.

"Turn down the heat on the gumbo and let it simmer. Then turn the oven to three hundred and put the rolls in. No, better not put the rolls in 'til they get here. Then we can pull them out fresh from the oven, all nice and warm." She smiled widely at me. "But turn on the oven now."

Mama was leaning in the doorway with a dreamy emptiness in her face. "Angela doesn't like to cook too much, you know. Like me. But she loves to watch other people cook. That's what Cleve says. Been that way since she was a little girl. She really has come up. Yeah, she's really getting to be a pretty . . . a pretty girl." She mumbled the last few words and moved quickly to the dining room.

"Yeah, she *is* pretty," I said.

"Well, when they come over just be nice to her. Don't make a scene. They are my friends."

I stopped fussing with the package of rolls and looked up at her from the kitchen. She was counting the places at the table.

"Why wouldn't I be nice to her, Mama?"

"I'm just saying . . ."

"No, really, I don't see why I wouldn't be nice to her like I've always been." My voice was getting louder.

"Okay, you'll be nice, Alvin. I believe you. Enough."

I put the package down on the counter and went out to the dining room. Mama stopped dealing out the silverware and stood still to look at me. Her eyes looked like two mild, empty question marks, but then firmed up into solid, black periods. I stood facing her. We could have fit all of our questions and all of our answers into the space that stretched open between us for those few moments. Could have dumped them all in there and hoped that they'd match up like socks out of the laundry.

I finally spoke the one thought I could get a grip on. "I won't flirt with her just to make everyone have a nice time."

"No one's asking you to do that, Alv." A disarming smirk came to her face. "Don't be ridiculous." She went back to setting out the silverware. I went back into the kitchen.

"Besides, you don't have to raise your voice with me," she called from the dining room. "Don't forget who's the mother here." Her grainy voice scoured the air between us. "All I want is for Cleve and Yvonne to have a good—"

"All you want," I interrupted quietly—I never interrupted Mama—"is for me to be good and behave and not tell Cleve and Angela about my last boyfriend, or about how I used to bring guys back here up to the attic and make sure they were gone by morning."

Mama was silent and still, a tiny fossil of the smirk still on her lips. I was suddenly embarrassed by what I had said. I made a little inhaling sound with my lips the way I did whenever I wanted to take back my speech after it was already out, as if somehow I could breathe back in the air that the words were floating on.

But I knew I was right. She would have me go to any length to make the dinner go well. I could say flattering things to Angela. I could speak in soft tones with eyebrows raised. I could touch her in secret when no one was looking and wait until later to run home and pull out the pictures of old lovers from under the bed. That would make Mama happy, the kind of happy that nutmeg is.

The bowl of fruit salad would be passed from person to person and arrive at Cleve next to last. He would heap a couple of spoonfuls onto his plate and then exaggerate a look of disapproval. Then he would say only half-jokingly, "What is this? Black people don't eat this stuff for dessert."

Mama would laugh and say easily, "Fruit salad, Cleve."

Then he'd say, "Don't you have any sweet potato pie?"

She'd say with an annoyed voice, "Cleve," and I'd think about saying, "What about orange rinds, Cleve? Do black people eat orange rinds? You'd be surprised at the things I eat."

Mama came into the kitchen, took down four glasses and went out brusquely. After a few minutes, her voice came to me again over the silence: "Look, if you feel the need to say something to Cleve and Yvonne, then I can't stop you. You're a grown man." She showed her palms and sort of shook her head at the ground. "But tonight you are a guest in my house, with my people coming over, and you need to respect that. That's all. Not everything has to be a drama, you know."

"I won't ruin your dinner," I said, putting a sheet of plastic wrap over the salad.

She sighed heavily. "It's not about the dinner, Alvin. You understand? I'm just saying there's no reason why you can't get along with my friends and make a good impression. You don't even have to get along with them really. All you have to do is eat and be polite to them."

I looked up. There seemed to be an invisible line drawn horizontally across the middle of her face. Above the line, her eyes were bright, opened unnaturally wide. Below the line, the corners of her lips tugged minutely downward, dissatisfied and angry. I'd seen that expression before, years earlier, but I could never see the line until now.

"Why did you hide the picture?" I asked slowly.

"What picture?"

I reached into the drawer and pulled it out again.

"Let me see that," she said, squinting, and stepped forward. She grabbed it from me and let out a soft "oh" of recognition. It was the sound of finding someone's lost key in your pocket that you'd sworn over and over you didn't have. Her eyes ticked from the photo to my face and back again, as though she were trying to verify that I was the one in the picture—to make sure it was really me she owed an explanation to.

She was suddenly glib. "Oh, that wasn't a very good picture of you anyway. Plus I'm looking for a frame for it. It used to just sit up there without a frame, remember?"

I nodded. I took it back and looked at it again. That picture could take Cleve's and Yvonne's entire world and for a second set it on the wrong edge. It wouldn't balance anymore and, like a sideways photograph, the faces would become unrecognizable, distorted and hideous. Maybe Mama was right not to let them see it. Maybe it was best to spare them the task of looking at pictures they wouldn't recognize.

I started to move away. Mama tried to change the mood. "Alvin, you never told me what spice you want to put in." She smiled easily.

"I haven't decided yet. I have to be careful."

"It's not such a big deal really. You can almost pick one blindfolded."

"No. It has to go with everything else, right? You can't just throw any old spices together. Randomly. What if they don't taste good together?"

"Doesn't really matter," she said matter-of-factly. "Gramma always taught me you only use the first three or four that make it into the kitchen. You skip the rest."

"But I thought the point was to put in some of everyone's spice."

"Right. That's the way it's supposed to work. But you have seven, eight, nine people bringing all kinds of crazy herbs and spices, can you imagine what a mess that would be?" She took down a bowl from the high cabinet for the rice. "Gramma always said the cook's gotta maintain some control. That's the real secret. No one needs to know what's in it and what's not. The kitchen does belong to the cook, and she's the one who has to take the blame for bad food in the end. So you kind of pull strings a little bit. *There's* your family tradition." She flicked her eyebrows up.

Black pepper. I wonder if Gramma would ever dare to not use such a brave spice. Or a few cloves.

Mama looked at me uneasily. She took in a breath to say something, let it out, and then stood there in the middle of the kitchen waiting for me to say something. My breathing got a little shallower and I thought I could see her shoulders creep in microscopic jolts upwards. My forehead felt unnaturally tight, heavy. She spoke first in a muffled hush. "Cleve and Yvonne really like you." I didn't answer. She spoke again, this time louder and with the usual graininess. "I'm going to go finish up my face. Change your shirt maybe. They'll be here soon." She disappeared from the kitchen.

I walked over to the steaming gumbo pot. Mama's mother used to fool the people. She was the cook, the one in control. But no one ever had to know that. Year after year, everyone brought their spices and their herbs anyway. That was the tradition. I took the lid off the pot.

Garlic powder? Thyme? Herb de Provence is complex and rich like a poem.

I pulled a pair of scissors from the silverware drawer and cut the first narrow strip off the bottom of the picture. Then I cut this strip into tiny particles, watching them drop quickly and lightly into the gumbo.

There are many substitutions and additions to any gumbo recipe, and Mama had used them all. You can put in crabmeat with everything else. You can leave out the seafood altogether and use chicken parts—my favorite variation. Some like to put in bell peppers, mushrooms, squash. My mother was the first in the family to use filé on a regular basis. But okra really is most common. Sometimes, rarely, Mama will put noodles into the mixture. Cleve wouldn't like it that way—not authentically southern enough. In any case, the whole mixture is served over a bed of hot rice and mixed with all those spices.

I cut another strip and then this one, too, into seeds for the gumbo. They sat on top, making brilliant, violet constellations against the muted red of the food. Tarragon was not as good as this. Rosemary was not. Parsley was not.

I cut a third strip. The little pieces were beginning to double over one another. Almost enough. I cut into the black rectangles of the windows and dropped those pieces in. And I thought there must be so many people you couldn't see behind those windows, dropping one by one into the stew. I could spice all the gumbo in the world, I thought.

Peppercorns are loud and obtrusive, and even if you use them carefully, they will demand everything from you.

Angela would bring chili pepper because you could never go wrong with the free and impulsive hot spices. Cleve would insist on it before they left, and Angela would come to the door with chili pepper in hand, and Mama would say it was so perfect because I liked spicy things and of course it would taste good in gumbo. I imagined Mama kissing her on the cheek.

Later, Mama would have to apologize for the tiny, mysterious seeds that somehow got into the gumbo. She would throw me a sly glance. Some idea would come to her subconsciously. Yvonne would be suspicious. Maybe she would notice the inorganic sharpness of the edges, but she would ignore it and move on as fast as possible to dessert.

I stirred the gumbo and the multicolored particles sank in. The steam continued to rise. A wide spiral formed in the pot. It was almost done now. The sound of a car engine surged up in front of the house. I replaced the lid and feeling the warmth of the kitchen fade behind me, I slipped the last piece of the photograph into my pocket.

Nobody Gets Hurt

Bennett Capers

One

Tonight, when Roy picks me up from my job at Piggly Wiggly, he has this look on his face that tells me something's up. I climb into his rusted Impala and Roy shifts the gear in drive and pulls away fast, making a wide half-circle around a solitary shopping cart. On the freeway, he flips on the radio and starts tapping his skinny fingers to the groove of Janet Jackson singing *and that's the way love goes*. He motions towards the six-pack of wild cherry wine coolers sitting on the car floor and I grab one. It isn't until I've downed half the bottle that he finally speaks. "Cassandra waiting for you?" Under the law, Cassandra is my wife of three weeks. Roy knows as well as I do that she's waiting for me. But that doesn't stop him from asking his next question. "Got time to go for a ride?" He takes his eyes off the road just long enough to look me straight in the face. "Just a ride," he says, though we both know that's not all. And because I can tell myself we're just going for a ride and aren't going to do anything, I say, Sure. I say, I have a little time.

Roy smiles his crazy smile and begins bopping his head to the bass line. Every now and then, he tips his head back, takes a sip of his wine cooler and then pushes the bottle back into the wedge he's widened between the seats and wipes his mouth with the back of his hand. I roll down the window to catch the night breeze.

14

We've been driving twenty, thirty minutes maybe when Roy pulls over on the shoulder of the road and turns off the headlights. He stretches his arm across the back of the seat and turns towards me. I grin. "You said we were just going for a ride." Across the road, a red, white and blue Amoco sign slowly spins on its axis, giving off too much light. I shake my head and say, "You're crazy. Not here." But Roy just keeps staring. I turn and follow his gaze. The gas station, a small cube of a building, sits lonely in the center of the asphalt parking lot. To the left of the station are two gas pumps. From where we're sitting, they look like oversized, unused slot machines. Inside the station, a Pakistani sits at the register, his back to us, one elbow propped up on the counter, his chin resting on the palm of his hand.

I nod towards the station, towards the Pakistani at the cash register. "Your new boyfriend?"

Roy gives me a look and says, "Yeah. Right." Then he stares at the gas station again. I look at the building, the gas pumps, and I'm hit with the silence of this place. It's like someone died out here. Or is dying.

"So? What do you think?" Roy asks.

I shrug. "What do I think about what?"

"This place."

I shrug. "It's a gas station."

Roy scratches his chin. "I'm thinking about you and me robbing this place. It's deserted out here, man. We could come here tomorrow night and hold this place up for every penny it's got."

Roy's never stolen anything before in his life. I look at Roy. "You're bullshitting me, right?"

"We could make a couple of hundred easy."

"I hope for your sake you're joking. And who is this *we*?"

Roy sits there and just smiles and waits. I try to picture Roy, as small and skinny as he is, robbing a gas station. The closest I get is imagining Roy in a cartoon, and even in the cartoon, Bugs Bunny outsmarts him. "You're bullshitting me, right?"

Roy looks from the gas station to me. "Paris, I'm broke."

"You're always broke. You'd think you'd be used to it by

now." I wait for Roy to laugh, but he doesn't. The truth of the matter is, Roy's gone eight months now since the naval ship-yard company he worked for laid everyone off.

I'm about to say something, I don't know what, when Roy slaps me on the back and laughs. He says, "Yeah. I'm bull-shitting you. But it's fun to think about. That money. Paris, I could pay you back all the money I owe you."

We drive around a bit more in silence. Roy opens the last two coolers and hands one to me. By now the cherry wine is warm, but I drink it anyway, enjoying its sweet taste. Roy drives, and I stare out the window. I watch as one moth, and then a second, collide soundlessly, gracefully even, into the front windshield. I raise the cooler to my lips and drink.

I have a bit of a buzz from the cherry wine, and don't even notice that Roy's driven me home. When he turns onto my block, he cuts the headlights off and we coast down the street real slow, in complete darkness. Roy parks the car a hundred yards or so from the house. On either side of us, two-story wooden houses with sloping porches line the street. All of them are badly in need of paint. None has a yard. Though my house is not much, it is the reason Cassandra married me. She married me because of the house, and I married her because of my mother. Now her car is parked in the street next to the house. Except for the yellow porch light, the house is entirely dark. Tonight I'm lucky. She's asleep.

Roy lifts the floor mat and retrieves a long, very much flat-tened joint. He presses the car lighter and then lights the joint with the red coil. When he inhales, his caramel-colored face glows a warm red in the darkness. His face, still a boy's face. Narrow. Smooth. Not even shaving yet. Roy catches me staring at him and grins. He lowers the joint and his face fades into darkness again. He passes the joint to me.

I shake my head. "Cassandra," I say, and Roy knows with-out my having to say it that I don't want Cassandra to smell marijuana on my breath. Knows as well that up until three weeks ago I would have said, "My mother."

Has it been three weeks? It has. My marriage to Cassandra and my mother's death both in the same week, as if seeing me married, seeing that she had found a replacement, someone to watch over me, gave my mother the calm to let go. My mother, clutching her crucifix, had watched us from her bed—the ceremony took place in her bedroom—watched as Reverend Tisdale coughed during his benediction, watched as Roy, the best man, his fingers trembling, handed me my mother's old wedding ring to slide onto Cassandra's waiting finger, watched as I repeated words I was told to say.

Roy pulls a stick of gum out of his pocket. I take the joint. Inhale long and hard. When I try to pass the joint back, Roy shakes his head. "Keep it," he says. I out the joint with the tip of my fingers and stick the roach in my shirt pocket. I tell Roy I better be heading in.

I open the car door and the night air smells of rotting garbage. Roy opens his door as well. He walks around to my side of the car, the side that is deepest in the shadows. Almost instinctively, I think about Cassandra, about the neighbors. I shake my head. "You're crazy. Not here."

Roy keeps walking towards me, until he is so close I can feel his breath against my face. In the near complete darkness, he grins and says, "Stick 'em up." He folds his hand into a fake gun and jabs his finger into the pit of my stomach.

I just look at Roy and laugh. "I'm supposed to pretend you have a gun, right? The power of suggestion, right?"

Roy shakes his head. "So we have a smart aleck here. Just raise your hands in the air. Slow!"

I play along, and we are eleven and thirteen again. He's the drug-dealer gun-toting psychopath cop killer, and I'm Shaft Superfly caught in a bad situation. I raise my hands in the air.

Roy begins patting me down, first checking my jacket, then my pants. He reaches in my back pocket for my wallet.

"This is just an excuse to feel my ass. You're sick, you know that? You'll probably be thinking about my ass when you jerk off tonight."

"Your skinny ass?" He presses his pointed forefinger, his imaginary gun, against my lips and I clench my teeth shut. "I could blow you away if I wanted to." Roy barely manages to keep a straight face when he says this. With his free hand, he fingers my wallet. "Let's see how much you make bagging groceries."

"I don't bag groceries."

"That's right. You got promoted to stockboy, right?"

"Assistant store manager. Don't open my wallet, Roy."

With a flick of his wrist Roy flips the wallet open, and I lunge for it. But Roy is quicker. He holds the wallet out of my reach and waves his make-believe gun in my face. "Uh-uh. You don't want to move. Nobody moves, nobody gets hurt." He opens the wallet slowly and pulls out two tens. When he looks up, he has a big grin on his face. "Lend me a ten."

I lower my hands. "Lend you a ten? You owe me already. You know that, right? Now you want me to lend you more money? You must be high." I shake my head, just as I'd do when we were boys and Roy would try to beg a dollar off me so he could buy *Sports Illustrated* or see *Godzilla vs. King Kong* or *Shaft* or something at the Rolex Theater on King Street. I'd shake my head and Roy would just smile and wait, knowing that I wanted to flip through the pages of *Sports Illustrated* too and that there was no way I'd see a movie and just leave him on the sidewalk, knowing that Roy was Roy after all and I could refuse him nothing. Refusing Roy would be like refusing my mother—it just wasn't going to happen.

He pockets one ten and replaces the other. He hands me my wallet, all the while grinning, his teeth white against his dark face. "Don't worry," he says. "How long have we known each other?"

This is how long I've known Roy: I can't remember a time when I didn't know him. I say, "Too damn long." Then I add, "Since we were kids."

Roy moves towards me. "And don't I always pay you back?" He pulls me into the night shade of the sycamore tree and kisses me hard. But I'm thinking about Cassandra, about the neighbors. I push him away and he stumbles backwards. He flashes me a look of hurt and anger and I hate myself for pushing him. Hate myself but don't know how to say it. I rub my jaw and shove my hands deep into my pockets. I lower my voice. "Not here, okay."

Roy's face doesn't change. I turn away. I stare at a child's broken Big Wheel sitting on the side of the road. At the flicker of light coming from someone's television set. When I look at

Roy again, his face still hasn't changed. I mumble something about it being late and start walking towards my house. I've taken nine, maybe ten steps when I hear Roy's voice right behind me, like he's right behind me hissing in my ear. When I turn, Roy's still standing next to the car, his figure a silhouette in the darkness. "Paris. That gas station we drove by tonight." He pauses, as if waiting for me to respond.

I look at my watch, then at my house, then back to Roy. "Yeah?"

"We're going back there tomorrow night. Right?"

Maybe it's the buzz from the coolers and the pot, but all I do is shrug and turn around. Behind me, there's the scraping sound of metal rubbing against metal as Roy opens and closes his car door, then the sound of the engine running. I make my way to my house. To bed. And to Cassandra.

Two

It's the smell of burning Pop-Tarts that wakes me. That and the sunlight coming through the window bright enough to blind me. I climb out of bed, take a long piss and splash water on my face. When I get to the kitchen, the first thing I see is Roy sitting at the table and reading the comics like he lives here, his black and white Nikes crossed and resting comfortably on the kitchen table. I don't know where Roy got it in his head that just because he drives me to work every day he's entitled to a free meal, but obviously this is what he thinks. The second thing I see is Cassandra, standing on tiptoe on the other side of the kitchen and opening cabinet doors. Three months ago she showed up out of the blue at the front door and I was about to tell her whatever she was selling—Avon, Mary Kay, insurance, whatever—we weren't buying when she thrust a torn piece of newspaper in my hand. Circled in red ink was an ad that said: WANTED: LIVE-IN NURSE FOR DYING WOMAN. Then in normal-sized letters: Age Under 25 Preferred, No Experience Necessary. Below that was the address of this house. I looked at her and said, "What the fuck?" But then my mother called, "Send her in" from her bed, and I knew my mother had placed the ad. And my mother hired her. Now Cassandra pulls out a

Tupperware mixing bowl and lowers her head as she cracks an egg into it. "Morning," I say, and she looks up and smiles nervously and says, "Afternoon."

I go to the fridge for some milk and drink straight out of the carton. When I turn around, there's the rustling of pages and Roy peers at me from above the comics. He mouths, "Sleeping Beauty awakes at last."

I glance at the stack of bills on the table—utilities bills, funeral bills, higher than the day before. I turn back to Roy. "You got that money I lent you?"

Roy just grins sheepishly, like he's still a kid, like he's not twenty-one. I flip on the black-and-white, and there's some guy in a suit talking about unemployment being on the rise. Yeah, tell me something I don't know. On the next channel, another guy is talking about some woman in Union who killed her two children and then made up some story about her car being carjacked by this black man. I'm hoping she gets the electric jump starter cables. I turn the channel until I find *The Price Is Right*.

I pull up a chair and Roy nudges me in the ribs. He leans over and whispers so Cassandra can't hear. "Cassandra got any hose?"

I just look at him. "Any what?"

"Hose. Panty hose. We need some hose to cover our heads. We just can't walk in that gas station with all those security cameras they got now. We need some stockings. We need to be incognito." He nudges me in my side, like I didn't feel it the first time. "Go on. Sneak in her drawer and get us some hose." Roy bends his head closer to mine. "Remember that time we ripped off that record store on King Street? We were professionals." Before I can even say a word Roy's humming the theme song from *Shaft*, poking me in the side again when he gets to the part, *Who is the man who will risk his neck for Brother Man? Shaft! Damn right.*

"You mean back when we were in middle school? You mean that one time we stole a Parliament Funkadelic album?" I remind him that the old man who ran the record store was blind and had only one leg. I mean, how professional did we have to be?

But Roy's not even listening. "Afterwards, we went back to your house and your old lady wasn't home. We fucked like crazy. On your bed. On the washing machine. In the shower. Remember how we broke the shower rod and you made up some lame story to your old lady about practicing your chin-ups? How come we never fuck like that anymore?"

I kick Roy in the ankle and motion towards Cassandra, who's standing practically in hearing distance, her back to us, making little half-circle twisting motions as she scrambles eggs. Only her hair, straightened and sprayed and gelled, stays in place.

I turn back to Roy. I keep my voice low. "All that's behind me. I'm married now."

Roy looks me straight in the eye. "Yeah. I know. I was the best man."

Maybe it's because I think Roy won't go through with it that I slip out of the kitchen, go down the hall to the bedroom and grab a handful of stockings from the bottom drawer in the dresser. When I return, Cassandra is still at the stove. I push the stockings into Roy's hand and he winks a thanks. Then he whispers, "These are clean, right? Because life's not about pulling smelly hose over my face. If I have to do that, the whole thing is off."

Sometimes you just have to ignore him.

Cassandra starts up with the cabinet drawers again, opening several before she finds a spatula, and then comes to the table carrying a frying pan full of what's supposed to be scrambled eggs. She dishes out a heap on my plate, then a heap on Roy's. Roy pierces the eggs with his fork and begins to remove broken bits of eggshell, like he's doing some kind of scientific excavation. By the time he's done, he has enough bits to reconstruct half an eggshell. Which can only mean one thing: the other half is on my plate. The two of us eye the picture of Tony the Tiger on the top of the fridge. Mmm, Frosted Flakes. Cassandra pulls back the tab of a diet Pepsi—all she ever has for breakfast—and takes a sip. She asks, "So what were y'all two lovebirds whispering about earlier?"

Roy almost chokes on his food. But I don't blink an eye. I look at Cassandra and try to figure out if she suspects or not.

She takes another sip of her Pepsi and stares back at me wide-eyed, her twenty-four-hour smile the same as always. I remind myself that this is the same woman who, after three months, can't remember where she keeps the spatula she uses every day. But at the same time I'm thinking, why take chances? I say, "She's crazy, you know that?" I'm talking to Roy, but looking at Cassandra when I say this.

Roy follows my cue. "She's crazy, all right. But baby got back. I envy you, Paris."

Already there's the beginning of a blush on Cassandra's face.

"She got a cute ass, all right. But she's crazy." I'm smiling now, looking at Cassandra.

"Cute? Cute is not the word. She has one of those asses to die for, man. You know, the kind that's out to here, the kind you can grip." Roy makes squeezing, gripping motions with his hands, then a sucking noise with his lips. "Baby, baby."

"You stop, Roy." Cassandra says, but the blush is all there now. She has the same look she had that day I asked her to marry me, kind of surprised, but at the same time like this was something she was expecting all along, something my mother had prepared her for since that day she stood at the front door in her nurse's uniform. She takes another sip from her Pepsi and crosses her legs. I go back to my eggs.

The rest of breakfast we eat in silence. A very old and grey and tired-looking Bob Barker announces prizes on *The Price Is Right*. When the contestants get to rolling the big wheel, I know it's time to leave.

I go over to Cassandra and do something I haven't really done since my wedding day three weeks ago. I go over to Cassandra and kiss her on the lips. Nothing major. Just a little peck. Cassandra seems as surprised as I am when I do this. She touches her fingers to her mouth, as if to seal my kiss there. When I turn around, Roy's eyes are hard, unblinking. He pushes back his chair and says, "Let's go."

Later, in the car, Roy doesn't look at me, he just looks straight ahead and tells me about how when he picks me up from work tonight, we'll drive out to that gas station, that we'll make sure it's empty first, that there's no one around except the Pakistani. There's a rush in his voice as he describes this. "It'll be a piece of cake," Roy says. At a stoplight he pulls a stocking over his head and makes fish lips at me. But I don't laugh. Roy pulls off the stocking mask. Says everything will be fine. That nobody will get hurt.

I say, "I never agreed to help you."

And like that, Roy's face goes still. He grabs the steering wheel tight. Fixes his eyes on the road. He says, his voice low, quiet, "We've always done things together."

I look out the window at the passing traffic. I wait a few seconds, then say again, almost tenderly this time, as if it is his forgiveness I'm seeking, "I never agreed to help you." I'm thinking that I've never refused Roy anything before.

When we pull into Piggly Wiggly, Stacy, one of the cashiers, stares at me from the store window. The cashiers are always wondering why I don't have my own car, why Roy drops me off and picks me up every day. Especially since I could drive Cassandra's car if I wanted to. They never ask me this, but I know this is what they're wondering. I climb out of the car and stick my head just inside the car window.

"Roy," I say. "Don't do anything *stupid* stupid, okay?"

Roy glares at me.

"Roy," I say.

He shifts the car into drive and pulls away fast.

Three

Roy doesn't pick me up from work. I tell myself he's okay, that everything's fine. I sit on the newspaper vending machine and shield my eyes from the headlights of every car that turns in to the Piggly Wiggly parking lot. But none of the cars is the Impala. None of the drivers Roy. I tell myself that Roy's okay. A half hour passes and Stacy the cashier punches out and asks me if I need a ride. Roy is never late. "Yeah," I say. "Yeah."

When I get home, I hear Cassandra in the bedroom, but I don't even bother to say hello. I head straight for the living room and sit on the edge of the doilied couch, flicking the remote back and forth from channel 2 to channel 4 to channel

5, the only stations with local news on. The palms of my hands are sweaty.

On top of the television set, my mother's plaster Jesus stands open armed, looking like a pale hippy on drugs. Crucifixes hang from the walls. The day she asked me to marry Cassandra, my mother was clutching her crucifix. And when I shook my head, she gripped her crucifix tighter and I imagined the imprint it would leave in her palm. "Why not? Cassandra don't have no family. And no place to go when her job here is done. I told her this house could be hers. And you need someone to look after you. So why not?" When I remained silent, my mother clutched the crucifix like it was a rope around her neck. A day later, I walked into her room and said *yes. Okay*.

I keep flipping the channels.

And then there it is. "Earlier this evening a holdup was thwarted at an Amoco station on Sam Rittenberg Road when the clerk fired at the armed robber and the robber fled the scene. Police say the robber is still at large, and ask that anyone with information leading to an arrest call 723-COPS."

Roy.

Before I even have time to organize my thoughts, I've grabbed Cassandra's car keys, I'm thinking I have to find Roy.

I'm heading towards the front door when Cassandra stops me. She blocks the hallway, stretches out each arm until her hands are pressed flat against the walls of the hallway. It's a second before I get it, before I notice that she has on high heels and a tight, peach-colored camisole. She stands with her legs crossed, like a contestant in a beauty pageant, and thrusts her chest slightly forward. She tries to purse her lips. She sticks her forefinger in her mouth and draws it out slowly. She wets her lips with her tongue, leaving her lipstick smeared. "After that kiss this morning, I thought I'd surprise you."

I mutter I have to go and Cassandra touches my arm. She says, "Paris, you can't go on grieving forever. Your mother's dead, Paris. Dead. Before she died, she made me promise that I'd look after you, she told me I'd have to be patient, that she was all you ever had." Cassandra looks at her feet, then looks up at me, fixes her eyes on mine. "I've been patient, Paris. But at some point you gotta realize she's dead." She looks at her feet again. "You've barely touched me since she died."

I say, my voice low, "I never touched you before she died."

We just look at each other. Then her face changes. I remember when I was little, I was given a mutt puppy. It wasn't toilet trained, and I had had it for less than a week when my father said, "No," and drove me and the puppy out to a quiet road in the country. On either side of the road were rows and rows of corn, their stalks bending wildly against the wind. My father didn't even bother to turn off the engine. He set the puppy on the side of the road and drove away, my face pressed against the back window, staring at the stupid little puppy. That's how Cassandra's face is now. Like that puppy's face. And it occurs to me that she loves me, that for her the marriage was never about the house. That this entire time she has loved me. And I feel nothing, absolutely nothing, for her.

For a second, just a second, the points of her heels wobble and I reach out to steady her, but she backs away, doesn't let me touch her. She says, "Half my stockings are missing." She narrows her eyes. "You know anything about it?" Her voice is hard, bitter. "You know anything about my stockings?"

The lies spill out, just as they did when my mother would ask me questions. "Why would I know about your stockings? You think I'm a cross dresser or something?"

I mumble something about having to go and stumble past her towards the front door. When I glance back Cassandra still hasn't moved. She stands with her back pressed against the wall, her arms raised as if shackled, her hands limp, and it occurs to me that this is how the Pakistani must have looked, hands in the air, Roy waving his gun towards the cash register. Then her whole body seems to shake and she screams, "It's Roy, isn't it?" She screams, "Faggot!"

Four

I drive past where Roy lives. I keep looking in my rearview mirror for cop cars, don't slow down because I don't want to look suspicious, just in case. When I don't see Roy's Impala anywhere on his street, I keep driving. I turn on East Bay. I'm

about to head out to Mr. J's, but then I remember how many
people Roy owes money to out there and figure he won't be
there. I check for cops and make a U-turn. The other place
I know Roy to hang out is this place on Meeting Street. When
I get there, the place is smoky and loud and still crowded. I
speak to Suzette, the girl behind the bar. She leans over the bar
when she answers me, her braids brushing against the bar
counter. She says, "No, sugar. Haven't seen Roy for weeks now.
He owe you money, too?"

Back in the car, I head to Mr. J's on Rivers Avenue, not
really thinking Roy is there, but. I get there and push aside the
yellow and black bead curtain, but the place is empty. Just some
man I recognize but can't place listening to the jukebox, listening to Isaac Hayes crooning *and I'll never get over you* and
bopping his Gheri-curled head to the bass line and gyrating his
hips against the jukebox.

Outside, driving again, it's hot and the air that blows
through the rolled-down window is hot and the air conditioner
doesn't work. I'm about to head home when I remember Roy
told me he stopped parking his car on his street a few weeks
back, after some guy working for Andy's Used Cars tried to
repossess it. I drive back to Roy's street. I get there, and no
longer care whether cops are there, hiding in wait or whatever
they do. I take the stairs four at a time to where Roy lives on
the second floor and push open the unlocked door.

Roy lies on his cot-sized bed. Light from a streetlamp filters
through the window, giving Roy a glow almost. With one hand
behind his head, the other on his crotch, he sleeps shirtless but
otherwise fully clothed, his Nikes still on. An old fluorescent
table lamp sits on the floor. The room smells of sleep.

I'm about to wake him, but stop myself midmovement. His
left thigh is wrapped tightly with a bloodstained shirt. There's
blood on the bed as well. The blood is dry.

Roy, I'm thinking. You're a dick.

I reach into my shirt pocket and pull out the last of the
joint from the night before. Inhale deep and hard. I turn the
lamp switch, but nothing happens. I try to remember the last
time I was here. Before my mother got sick, Roy and me would
come here almost every day, would spend hours sometimes just

joking around, or watching TV, or getting lit, not saying a word. This is my first time here since my mother got sick. What little furniture was here then is now gone, and looking at the emptiness, I know Roy's sold it all, electricity's probably been turned off too. Only his cot and his books are left, the books stacked in a corner by the window. *Native Son. Invisible Man. Giovanni's Room.* On the floor next to the books is a gun. I pick it up and run my fingers along its curve. It feels like something perfect, like a warm summer night—like six on a warm summer night. I open the cylinder, and look through six empty circles at Roy. He never even had any bullets. I close the cylinder. Spin it round and round with my thumb.

Roy coughs and rubs his eyes and looks at me. A slow grin appears on his face. He says, "You came." He tries to sit up, but squinches his face in pain. He falls back to the bed. Breathes hard.

I turn away from Roy and stand at the window. Across the street in the park, two guys are playing one on one on the lamplit court. One goes for the layup but misses. I turn back to Roy. I take another hit from the joint. The joint is so short now that it almost burns my lips. I out it against the windowsill. When I exhale, I say, "You're a dick, you know. You could have gotten your stupid ass killed."

Roy grins awkwardly. "I knew you would come."

And like that, I know. That in part, this was all for me. The robbery. To spend time with me. And I want to hit Roy, shake Roy and hit Roy until I knock some sense into his head. But I don't move. I brace the anger rising up in me. "Your stupid ass could be dead right now, you know that?"

Roy nods, grins.

I head into the bathroom and find a towel, hold it under the tap until it's soaked through. When I return, Roy is craning his neck forward. I unknot the bloodstained shirt around his thigh, unfasten the top snap of his jeans. Roy grips the side of the bed, lifts his butt, and grits his teeth as I tug his jeans down. He lets his head loll back against his pillow and smiles weakly. With the damp towel, I dab at his wound, the hardened blood, until the area where the bullet grazed his skin is clean. I take off my own shirt and wrap it around his thigh. Then I clean the trail of blood along his leg. By the time I reach his feet, the towel is the color red. "You could have been hurt worse," I say.

Roy scratches his chin. "Paris," he says. His voice is quiet, like that of a child caught crossing the street without looking both ways, a child too young to believe in death. "Nobody got hurt bad. The guy, he shot at me, but he just nicked me. See." Roy tries to lean up and again he winces in pain. "Nobody got hurt bad."

Inside, I'm thinking about the bullet wound in his thigh. I'm thinking about the Pakistani at the gas station, nearly scared out of his wits. I'm thinking how for years I wished my mother dead, just so she wouldn't find out about Roy and me, and when she died I still lived the life she chose for me. And I'm thinking about Cassandra, hands raised in the air, standing there as if she was the one robbed.

Outside, a siren wails in the distance, approaches, then passes. Not for us. Not this time.

"Paris," Roy says. There's a smallness in his voice that takes me back to when we were just boys, horsing around, playacting Shaft and Superfly and thinking that no matter what, everything would be all right, things would work out fine. "Paris," Roy says.

I move near the bed. "What?"

Roy tilts his head to the side and looks at his leg, then at me. His breath has the sweet-sour smell of day-old milk. In the distance, there's the sound of an approaching garbage truck, and light filters through the window, and I know soon it will be morning. "Hold me," he says.

I sit on the bed. Hold him. Cradle him. Whisper, "Sleep."

Twilight at the Equator

Jaime Manrique

One

Ramón made a looping motion with his cigarette. He dragged without inhaling, and blew ringlets of smoke that the afternoon breeze wafted in the direction of the street. He was one of the most affected human beings I had ever met, and I pictured him perfectly at home in the court of Louis XIV.

I had picked up Ramón after lunch, when my relatives retired to take their siestas. He was the only friend from my adolescence I still kept in touch with. When I had visited Colombia with Ryan, we had spent quite a bit of time with him. Even though Ramón had his own apartment, he still went to his parents' home for lunch, and it was there that I met him. We headed for Barranquilla's shady zoo where we spent the hottest hours of the afternoon strolling under the gigantic rubber trees, meandering from exhibit to exhibit, laughing at the capuchin monkeys gnawing desperately at their tails, grooming and eating each other's ticks, pitching their still moist turds at one another and masturbating gleefully, shooting at the zoo visitors. We marvelled at the kaleidoscopic and tuneful tropical birds and at the multiplicity of lethal vipers. All these provided us with plenty of amusement as we reminisced about the main events of our lives in the years when we hadn't seen each other. Now we were having *frosomales* on the terrace of El Mediterraneo, a Greek ice cream parlor that is a traditional focal point of Barranquilla's social life.

"Yes, Santiago, all signs of contumacy are being systematically squeezed out," Ramón shuddered, opening wide his tawny eyes. "One runs into death every time one turns a corner. For the people who are marked, it must be like living with an AIDS sentence. You made a solomonic decision to stay in gringoland; otherwise, you'd probably be pushing up daisies. Just last year, I was really afraid for Alejo's life." He paused to check out a young man in tight jeans and T-shirt crossing the street. "For myself," Ramón went on, "I gave up being a controvertist a long time ago. Yes," he seethed, frowning and wringing his hands. "I embrace the mediocrity of it all. If this place was the pits before, it's much worse now. It's rotting in a million places. This city is like an organism which didn't get vaccinated when it was born, and now it's riddled with monstrous diseases. Barranquilla is a perfect metaphor for the rest of Colombia. But I embrace the collective peristesia of the national soul. And make no apologies for it."

His pretentious choice of words, which would have sounded unbearable in an American or European, rang authentic with him—a perfect example of Caribbean rococo. I sat there, agape, grateful that his theatricality remained unchanged. What was a wonder to me was how he had managed to thrive despite the belligerent local machismo.

Like a Balanchine dancer, Ramón sprang up from his chair. "Excuse me for a sec, but I must absolutely inspect that beauty," he said, referring to the young man who now stood at the opposite corner, lighting a cigarette and casting smoldering glances in our direction.

I took a spoonful of *frosomal* as Ramón and the young man made contact. For the past few years I had dreamed of this moment when Ramón and I would meet here, enjoying a *frosomal*, which is a kind of vanilla-chocolate milk shake flavored with cherry and pineapple syrup.

The sun was now in the west, descending, lifting the sluggishness of midafternoon. There was considerable traffic; scores of people ambled in and out of the stores, cafés and restaurants that line Calle 72. A languorous breeze swept down the wide street, and the ungainly bushes of four-o'clocks framing the terrace metamorphosed, blooming in one breath, an explosion of scarlet petals and black eyes.

Ramón, looking in my direction, pointed at me with his pinky, as if he were trying to persuade the swarthy young stud to join us. Ramón's maneuvers brought back memories of my past as a gay youth in Barranquilla. In the ninth grade, I developed an intense crush on Pablo, one of my classmates. He was the handsomest boy I knew: gangly and muscular, with black hair and matching eyes, and the features of a young Cary Grant. All the girls were in love with him, including Rosita. Pablo was not intellectual, but he liked American movies and dancing. I liked him because when I was with him I felt enriched by his beauty—the way I would have felt, say, riding in a sports car. He was also very sweet and kind. Often he stayed in my house overnight. Late at night I'd climb in bed with him and then he'd let me do with him whatever I wanted. Because I had already been sexually initiated, I sort of knew what to do. Pablo and I were inseparable.

Then one day he announced that his family was moving to the United States, to Georgia. The month before he left, I tried to commit suicide by jumping from the roof of the school. I thought I was trying to kill myself because I was unhappy with school; it was many years later that it would dawn on me I had tried to kill myself because I was so distraught Pablo was leaving. From Georgia, he wrote to me for a while. Then the letters stopped. Years later, I heard he had been killed in Vietnam. After Pablo left, I answered an ad for a pen pal in a magazine. The man, Adriano, was in his twenties, a teacher, and he lived in Bogotá. We exchanged photos. Although the word *homosexual* was never mentioned, I was aware that we both were. I started falling in love with Adriano. I dreamt of running away to Bogotá to live with him. One day he wrote saying he was coming to Barranquilla to visit me. I panicked. How would I be able to explain this relationship to my mother? I didn't answer Adriano's letter and I never heard from him again.

I wondered if things had changed in the city since I had lived there. In my adolescence, there was only one kind of known homosexual in Barranquilla, *el marica*, the queen. The others (the vast majority) were the *cacorros*, the "straight" men who went to bed with the queens, assuming exclusively the active role. What was considered homosexual was to surrender one's ass. Even then, I wanted an alternative to these clichés. Now I had returned home, afraid of sex with strangers, looking upon each new encounter as a reckless flirting with death. Although Ramón was terrified by the increasing number of AIDS deaths in the city, he still carried on with the promiscuity of the past. He felt fully protected by condoms, and refused to surrender the full expression of his sexuality.

Ramón shook his index finger at the trick, using it like a magic wand to glue the boy to the spot. Then he strutted in my direction.

"*Cariño*," he purred, sitting down. "Isn't he out of Almodóvar? I have to give him a couple thousand pesos, and he'll cooperate. He's shy about meeting you. I'll give you a full report tomorrow. I feel almost guilty about leaving you here all alone, but I know that you'd do the same if you were in my heels. Anyway, I leave you in the best spot in the city for cruising. If you want company, just stay there, looking like the cosmopolitan woman you are, and before you know it, someone will approach you. But wipe that Vivien Leigh look off your face. You look like she did in the last reel of *Streetcar*. We're in the tropics, darling, not in New Orleans. Think Sonia Braga—that's the look that will get you boys here. Anyway, I'll come by to pick you up tomorrow night at ten o'clock American time, I promise. And I'll make it up to you then. I have a nice surprise for you." Ramón pecked me on both cheeks and sashayed down the steps, puffed up like a bird of paradise in heat.

I was too tired to cruise. I paid the check and decided to go back to the apartment. Walking on Calle 72, in a northerly direction, I reached the corner of Avenue Olaya Herrera where I saw, on the grounds of the old soccer stadium, two trucks loaded with armed soldiers.

I went into the park across Calle 72; its grounds were as unkempt as I remembered them, but the leafy almond trees created a cool canopy. Over the years, the park had become dangerous at night, so few people frequented it around dusk.

In my childhood, it was notorious because at night the maids who worked in the neighborhood would use it to rendezvous with their beaus. As a child, I'd come to the park to gather the ripe almonds on the ground. When I had stuffed my pockets with the yellow fruit, I'd search for a hefty stone to smash the fleshy shells and the porous wrapping underneath that hid the tender, tasty nut. Today I spotted black-coated squirrels looking for ripe fruit, digging on the thick carpet of leaves on the sand. Homeless people occupied some of the broken-down cement benches of the park, and a bunch of Boy Scouts were practicing a military drill. The children were aggressive and intent; they seemed more like ferocious midget soldiers than regular Scouts.

Arritoquieta opened the door to my relatives' apartment. She informed me that my aunt and uncle were out but that they would be home for dinner. She offered me a coffee, which I declined. I went into the library. Outside, it was still light, but the room was in semidarkness. I sat on the rocking chair by the window. I was glad to be in the apartment, where I felt safe, and not out alone in the streets. I looked out the window: The carmine sun dove in the Caribbean, creating a widespread hemorrhage in the sky. Transfixed, I watched the violent sunset bleed slowly until darkness began to set in. I became absorbed in the process of day turning into night when little squiggles began to appear over the city, darting back and forth at the speed of lightning. At first I figured it was an optical illusion taking place in my retina, created by the hallucinating palette of the western sky. As the squiggles became more numerous, I realized that they were thousands of bats flying above the red-clay roofs of the houses, the tops of the condos, the spires of the churches, the cathedral and the tallest trees. The bats were out for their nocturnal feeding.

Out of nowhere, a completely forgotten incident from my childhood came back to me. I must have been five and I still couldn't read. A frenzy was created in Barranquilla by a woman who died in a doctor's office during an abortion. Momentarily losing his sanity, the doctor had hacked the woman's body into numerous pieces, stuffed them in a bag, and taken a drive all the way to the sea. Every few hundred yards or so, he dumped a chunk of the corpse on the bushes along the road. I remembered the front-page photographs: One day her decomposed arm; the next, her eyeless head, maggots crawling out of all the orifices. As a child, this incident filled me with such unspeakable horror I never mentioned it to anyone. In fact, I hadn't thought about it since it happened thirty-five years earlier. But as night fell from the Caribbean to the equator, over the Amazonian jungle, above the icy peaks of the volcanoes of the Andes, all the way to Patagonia, to the bleak, glacial regions of Tierra del Fuego, this image, this memory, burst through the fortress of denial with such violence that I sat on the rocking chair in a trance, shivering, sweating a cold sweat.

I could not break the spell until some time later when the tropical sky glowed with shimmering stars the size of planets, and a moon as gigantic and luminous as the midnight sun of arctic summer poised herself in the night sky, not just as a light fixture, a deity to be worshipped, but as an object of desire.

Two

That night Aunt Caty and I were in the living room having coffee and chatting, when I checked my watch and realized it was time to go downstairs to meet Ramón. When I got up to leave, her attitude toward me became maternal, as if I were a youngster, not a grown-up man.

"Please be very careful, Sammy. I hope Ramón is not going to take you to some dangerous place. The thing is, you don't really know Colombia anymore. I'm sure you've heard what the paramilitary groups have been doing to homosexuals," she said.

I reassured her that I wouldn't do anything reckless.

As I waited downstairs for Ramón, salsa music blasted from the neighborhood cantinas. Because it was Friday night, or Cultural Friday, as Barranquilleros call it, the street was bustling with dressed-up people on their way to social gatherings.

I felt uneasy. Although I had tried to play it cool in front of Aunt Caty, I knew perfectly well what she was referring to. Since the late 1980s paramilitary groups had been killing the *desechables*, the homeless, the disabled, the blatantly gay, especially the drag queens. Most of the killings—which were in the hundreds—had taken place in Bogotá, Medellín, Cali. In

Barranquilla there had been a few isolated cases, and not recently. Even so, I was aware that this was not your usual night out with the boys in New York City.

A taxi pulled up next to the curb where I was standing. Ramón was sitting in the backseat with a young man, not the same one I had seen him pick up yesterday in the afternoon. I got in and the taxi took off.

"Santiago, this is Humberto," Ramón said. "He's one of the most fabulous young men in all of Colombia, so I wanted you to meet him. He was dying to meet you, because he's also a writer. And he's read, and memorized, every single comma you've written."

We shook hands. Humberto was very attractive, in his early twenties, and he had an upper lip shaped like a swan in flight that heightened the carnality of his face.

"I admire your writing very much," he said, holding on to my hand. Right away I knew that I could have him for the night, if I wanted to. The only thing that wasn't clear was whether I would have to pay him or not. But I would find that out later.

"We're going to The Godfather III, which I thought would be the most appropriate place to go since we're all such cinematographic queens," Ramón said.

Humberto, who sat in the middle, his body leaning against mine, said, "We call it The Godfather III because of the frequent shoot-outs that take place there."

I wasn't in the mood for high drama. "Couldn't we go someplace less . . . exciting?" I said.

"Darling, it's *the* place to go in Barranquilla," Ramón said with finality. "Besides, the shoot-outs are a thing of the past. Now they have bouncers who check you for weapons as you go in. If you ask me, that's the only reason to go there: to have those hunky men, with their huge orangutan hands, checking you in very very intimate places . . . uhmmmmm," he purred.

We all broke out laughing, yet I couldn't help but be tense about the evening ahead of us. As we chatted merrily about gay life in Barranquilla and New York, always remembering to use English and French words so that the taxi driver wouldn't understand what we were talking about, I noticed that we had entered one of the *barrios populares,* one of Barranquilla's poorer neighborhoods. The taxi stopped in front of a house at the corner of an unpaved street. I paid the driver, and we stood in front of a house with its door and windows shut. From inside the house I could hear salsa music playing. The street was dark, and next to the bar was an empty lot full of smelly garbage.

Ramón rang the bell. The door was opened a crack, and when he was recognized we were let in to an empty room, where two bouncers who looked like heavyweight boxers checked us for weapons. The one checking me put his hand inside my underwear. Ramón made orgasmic sounds as he was searched. When the men were satisfied that we didn't carry weapons, we are admitted.

We crossed a series of dim rooms, where men gathered around tables drinking or making out. Then we entered the patio, where the jukebox was playing salsa music.

High walls surrounded the patio so that the neighbors could not look in. Multicolored papier-mâché lamps provided the suggestive illumination. The floor was inlaid with tiles in Arabian designs, and in the center of the dance floor there was a lighted Moorish fountain. The tables for the customers were placed against the walls of the corridors, and in the back of the patio, under guava trees, tame parrots and macaws pirouetted about. A profusion of red and yellow hibiscus, the kind that opens for the night and dies at dawn, and bougainvillea in bloom, created a carnavalesque garden. We sat at a table, and a barefoot waiter in shorts and wearing a guayabera approached us. Ramón asked for a bottle of rum and Coca-Colas. After he finished taking the order, the waiter asked, "Will there be anything else for the gentlemen?"

Ramón and Humberto exchanged looks. "Yes," said Ramón, "we'll take the Friday Night Special for three. That's all."

When the waiter left, Ramón said to me, "You're probably wondering what the Special is. We'll let it be a surprise. Suffice to say that it is one of those exquisite pleasures that only we third-worlders can enjoy."

A young man was doing salsa moves on the dance floor. He wore tight ripped jeans, sneakers, and a T-shirt draped over his muscular torso. With the exception of the people engaged in conversation, everyone was staring at him. The *salsero* was performing for all of us, so that we could admire his great body and his dancing, but he never, not once, looked up. He danced always looking at his crotch. When the record changed, the dancer joined his friends at a table, and another one replaced him. He, too, danced alone, totally absorbed in the intricacies of his steps.

"Do they always dance by themselves?" I asked.

"Mostly by themselves," said Humberto. "Though sometimes there are two people on the floor, but far apart, with their back to each other."

"Why is that?"

"Darling, have you forgotten?" Ramón said. "Real men don't dance together. These are working-class boys; they aren't gay."

"So why are they here?"

"For money, *cariño*. These boys are not homos. They just do it for money. They dance to advertise their talents and their baskets. If you like what you see, you go to their tables, buy them a drink, and negotiate a price for the night."

"Is this a hustlers' bar?"

"If you want to be that precise, yes. I prefer to think about it this way: they have what I want, and I am willing to pay for it. No, people don't come here looking for love, if that's what you're thinking about."

The waiter approached us with a tray. He set down on the table a bottle of rum, a bucket of ice, two large bottles of Coke, and two dishes, one with a local white cheese and another one with green wedges of mango and lime. "Whenever you're ready for the Friday Night Special, let me know."

"Thanks very much," Ramón said, batting his eyelashes. "You'll hear me meowing when we're ready."

We had a couple of Cuba Libres. Then Ramón said, "Humberto, go with Santiago for the Special. I'll wait here."

I was beginning to suspect what "The Special" was. The waiter led us to a room abutting the dance floor and then closed the door. On a table there was a mirror with long lines of cocaine, cut straws, joints, a pipe, two vials with *basuco* rocks— a very poisonous kind of crack—and syringes.

We sat around the table. Humberto did a couple of lines of cocaine hungrily. Then he pushed the mirror in my direction. I considered it for a moment. Throughout most of the 1980s I had abused cocaine, designer drugs, and finally crack. At the end of my using, I was buying five-dollar vials in the crack houses of Ninth Avenue, behind Port Authority. But when so many of my friends had started dying of AIDS, I decided to lead a cleaner life. It was around that time I met Ryan, who, because he was HIV positive, led a life free of alcohol and drugs. After a while, I realized I no longer needed to get high to have a good time. I declined the cocaine.

"Oh, okay," Humberto said, indifferent to my abstinence. He did another couple of lines, and then lit a joint. Again I shook my head when he offered it, though at one point I had been a connoisseur of Colombian grass. When he lit the joint, because of his proximity, the smoke hit me full on my nostrils and I started getting high. That was all I needed. I didn't want to get any more stoned than that. Yet it was hard to fight the temptation. I knew that if I took a few tokes, a great euphoria would come over me, and I'd instantly develop a bond with Humberto. I didn't want to spoil my chances of going to bed with him that night. But I had learned over the last years that I could have fun without doing drugs, and I wanted to keep it that way. I knew that a toke could lead to a few lines, and then to the crack pipe, and next in line was the syringe. The risk of going back to the life I led at the end of my using, to that bleak hopelessness, was too great. I got up.

"You stay here as long as you want," I said. "I just need to get some air."

I joined Ramón. "Back so soon?" he said, looking surprised.

I sat down. "I'm not in the mood," I said. "I am . . ." As I searched for the right word, it dawned on me: *I'm in mourning* was what I wanted to say. A wave of sadness engulfed me. Being here with Ramón reminded me of the trip Ryan and I had taken to Colombia. Ryan still did not show any symptoms at that time. Although the virus was there, a presence between us, making ours a triangular relationship, Ryan was still healthy, handsome, and we were very much in love with each other.

"I'll go join Humberto," Ramón said. "I think you want to

be alone with your melancholia. You and Great Garbo," he sighed.

I was sipping my drink when Humberto, lit up, returned to the table—his eyes blazed from the cocaine. When a new song was played, he took to the dance floor. Although he danced like the other men, he made it clear—by giving me furtive glances—that he was dancing for me. Now that I could inspect him, I saw how beautiful he was: he had long sensual limbs, and his tight jeans revealed a nice crotch and a shapely ass. He twirled, with feline movements, an invitation to pleasures rare and exquisite. In his gestures there was the promise of total surrender. I was entranced watching him, getting aroused, when Ramón returned to the table.

"I feel like a new woman," Ramón said. "Makeup and drugs . . . and men, that's all I need to be happy." He noticed Humberto on the dance floor. "Uhm, just what I thought. He likes you. You can do with him whatever you want, darling."

"Is he a hustler?"

"No, Santiago, he's a *chico bien*, a boy from a good family, a sophisticointellectual. He's impressed with you because you're a cosmopolitan writer living in New York. Tonight he'll do anything you want. Absolutely free. Compliments of the house."

"I'm horny for him," I admitted. "But I can't take him to my relatives' house."

"Darling," Ramón snorted. "This isn't New York by any means, but here we have divine decadence, pleasures that the Emperors of China never had. As part of the Friday Night Special we have access to a room equipped with everything: condoms for all sizes and tastes, lubricants, whips, chains, torture instruments, whatever you're into. That's why I put up with everything else I hate about this country—because of the divine decadent pleasures."

It was past midnight when Ramón found someone he liked, and they disappeared into one of the cubicles off the dance floor. Left alone with Humberto, I began to talk about more intimate subjects with him. Humberto was a Literature student at Barranquillla's private University. He had already published short stories and essays in Colombian newspapers, and he was working on his first novel. In this respect, he was no different than many of my students in New York who wanted to be writers. Then he told me about his lover, Raúl, who had died of AIDS just last year. Raúl was an older architect, and they had moved in together, which in Barranquilla amounted to a scandal. Humberto's family had cut him off. They had lived together for a short while, and suddenly Raúl developed AIDS pneumonia and died within a year.

As he told me this story, he became human to me. He was more than just a handsome young man—he became a person of depth, someone whose life had been touched by suffering. Moved by his story, I reached over and grabbed his chin. Humberto closed his eyes, and grabbed my hand, squeezing it. The contact of his skin on mine gave me a hard-on. This was no different than going into a bar in Greenwich Village, chatting with a guy, asking him home. Right from the beginning you knew what the outcome would be: you'd have sex, and then you'd get up, exchange phone numbers, and you'd never call each other. I knew that in a few days I would be returning to New York, that Humberto would stay in Barranquilla where his life was, that whatever happened between us would probably have a longer life as a memory. Bluntly I asked, "Would you like to have sex with me?"

"Yes, I'm very attracted to you," he said, taking my hand and nibbling the tips of my fingers.

What happened in bed was a total surprise to me. Perhaps because we both had lost the men we loved to AIDS, perhaps because we had lost them recently, perhaps because we both came from the same culture and had experienced the isolation of a homosexual in a place that denied our existence, perhaps because the tropical night was splendorous, and scented with the sweetness of honeysuckle, perhaps because the night seemed to exist just for the purpose of making love, we surrendered to each other with a passion and a totality that I had never experienced before, not even with Ryan. When we kissed, desperately, avidly, it was as if we were trying to pass back and forth all the secrets in our souls. When I took his cock in my hand, I held it with wonder, for all its perfection, for all its power to give pleasure, to make me forget—for that miraculous instant—all the sadness and pain of life. We made love on the floor, standing up, on the bed, sitting up, biting, squeezing, pumping, fisting, as if this was the last chance to do with one person everything we had learned about the pleasures of the body.

After climaxing, we were embracing when I noticed that he was crying with the same ardor with which he had made love to me. Shaken by the depth of the feelings I had experienced with this stranger, grateful to be alive, grateful to have experienced an ecstasy that had made me appreciate again what a holy instrument the flesh is, I embraced him with all my strength, and cried, too, until we both did it in unison, as if we were part of a chorus, wailing for everything we had loved and lost.

Three

The midmorning sun already fell with a scourging rage. I stood alone on the empty wide beach; the sand under my sneakers baked the soles of my feet. I gazed in the direction of El Barranco de Loba, a couple of miles away. Beyond the beach was a meadow where domestic animals were grazing. In the distance, where the terrain elevates in a gentle hillock, I saw the first house in the town.

I had been walking for a while on the gravel path leading to the village when a man shambled in my direction: he tottered on the trail with a drunken gait. I loped off to the right to let him pass. He was tall and dark, wore a straw hat, torn pants and a shirt opened all the way down to his belly button, but no shoes. When he was just a few feet away from me, the man removed his hat brusquely and placed it on his thigh. "Welcome," he bellowed.

"Good morning," I said, nodding and then staring at my feet, since I didn't want to be engaged by a drunken stranger.

Coming just inches away from me, he placed a hand on my shoulder. I froze and looked up. The man, who was sweating profusely, had an incipient salt-and-pepper beard, and his unfocused hazel eyes were bloodshot and coated by a filmy but gleaming membrane that was half cataract and half glassy veil. He searched my eyes.

"You're Sofía's son," he said. "I was sorry to hear she died." Then he added, "Your grandmother must be so happy about your visit."

I was astonished that this man remembered me, since the last time I had visited El Barranco I had been a young man. But so very few strangers ever visit the town that once you make an appearance, you are never forgotten. The man's breath stank, as if his insides were rotting. But he didn't seem dangerous or hostile. Besides, since he had mentioned my mother by name, I reasoned he had been an old acquaintance of hers.

"*Mamá* Paulina doesn't know I'm coming," I said, and started walking toward the village.

The man followed me. "Oh, she knows you're here," he said. "She's waiting for you."

I did not contradict him. I started feeling agitated as we neared the colossal *ceiba* tree that marks the entrance to the town. A part of me wanted to question this man about how he knew my mother, but I held back. Under the *ceiba* tree a cantina took umbrage; *bolero* music spilled out to greet me. Two men drinking beer were sitting on chairs, reclining against the wall. My companion waved at them.

"*Adiós*, Francisco," they called as we went by.

We walked on a wide street carpeted with verdant turf, and decorated with huge smooth beige stones. The houses rose several feet above the ground on cement platforms. The peasant dwellings are attractive in their simplicity: walls made with whitewashed cow dung, thatched roofs, their windows and doors painted green.

"You see, the town never changes," Francisco commented as we climbed.

El Barranco did look exactly the way I remembered it. The streets were almost deserted; most of the activity concentrated in the patios, which were encircled by walls made of cacti planted close together. Through the cracks in the walls, I saw people cooking, washing, grinding corn, and children playing under the fruit trees. The town's population was primarily black. Walking by my side, Francisco often muttered to himself. We were nearing my grandmother's house when he grabbed my forearm, and forced me to stop. I was about to yank my arm free when he pointed to a house on the left, saying, "That's the house where the murder took place."

"The murder?" I echoed, to make sure that I had understood him.

"The murder took place in that house over fifty years ago, then the family moved away." He let go of my arm and continued walking. Was he delirious? I wondered. And whose family had moved away—mine?

I was sweating and thirsty when we arrived at my grandmother's house. The front door was open. When she saw me, a pretty young girl started screaming, "Lina, Lina (short for *Mamá* Paulina), Sammy is here, Sammy is here."

I climbed the steps to the terrace and Francisco followed me. I entered *Mamá* Paulina's living room, which was cool and shadowy. In the patio, I could hear a bunch of cackling children. "Lina, Lina, Lina," the voices cried in unison. The room contained a red clay *tinaja*, where the drinking water was kept, a small, unpainted table, and two chairs, upholstered with cowhide. A calendar on the walls was the only decoration. There was a door to my left, which opened into the only dormitory; another door opened to the open-air kitchen in the patio. I placed my shoulder bag on the table and took one of the chairs. Francisco stood at the door, grinning. When he heard voices approaching from the patio, he said, "How about a few pesos for a beer, *compañero*?" I was about to reach for my wallet, just to get rid of him, when *Mamá* Lina, followed by half a dozen loquacious children, entered the room. She had a wet towel wrapped around her head, and wore a dress with a black and white pattern; she was barefoot. We embraced. Lina smelled of coconut oil and ripe mangoes. Pulling away from me, she took my face by the chin and she said, "Let me look at you, Santiago." Her eyes were moist, and her facial muscles trembled with emotion. Lina was tall, lean, like a stalk of sugarcane. Even though she was close to ninety and toothless, she seemed hale. The smaller children huddled beside her giggling, pulling her wide skirt, and the oldest—a boy and a girl—stood behind her. They were my black cousins. They looked at me with awe, as if I were from another planet. "Don't forget about me," Francisco said from the door. "Just give me a few pesos for a beer, Santiago."

Noticing Francisco, *Mamá* Lina grabbed the broom near the *tinaja* and marched towards him, motioning as if to sweep him away. "Shoo, shoo, drunk," Lina said, to the delight of the children who broke in riotous laughter, shrieking and skipping and repeating after her, "Shoo, shoo, drunk."

"But, Lina," Francisco protested. "I brought your grandson to you. Let him give me money for a beer."

"Shoo, shoo," she repeated, now fanning his legs with the broom. "Shoo, shoo. Look at him, he's heading back to the cantina. Don't go to the cantina; go to the river and get a fish for your family. Lazy drunk. Don't let my *comadre* Petra do all the work."

Defeated by her attack, and the children's chorus of hilarity and catcalls, a downcast Francisco descended the steps and stumbled away from the house in the scorching sun. Standing on the terrace, the children all chanted, "Shoo, shoo. Lina beat Francisco, Lina beat Francisco."

When Francisco withdrew, Lina addressed the oldest boy, who was in his late teens. "Juvenal, take Santiago's bag to my room, and put it in the trunk. Here is the key. Don't forget to lock it. Etilvia," she addressed the oldest of the girls, a young woman. "Go to the *tienda* and get your cousin a Coca-Cola."

The young people marched off to do their errands; Lina took me by the hand and, followed by the four smaller children, we stepped into the patio. The wood kitchen was under a large straw roof, and here there was another table—where food was prepared—and chairs. We walked past the kitchen, until we arrived at a *ciruela* tree from which a hammock hung. Lina ordered a chair brought for her and offered me the hammock. I did as I was told. Lina's large patio contained custard apple, mango, citrus, and sweetsop and coconut trees, red chillies, and the usual fowls, plus *pisingos*, a local duck. "I have four donkeys and ten pigs; they are feeding by the river now," she informed me as if she were boasting of great riches. I knew that donkeys were prized possessions because they were used to carry water from the river and wood from the forest.

Lina introduced the smaller children to me. "This wee

thing," Lina said with such affection that I could tell she was her favorite, "is Patricia. She's five years old; she's the daughter of Carmen Izquierdo." Carmen was one of my half aunts; she lived in Cartagena, where she worked in a government office. Patricia was extremely pretty. She wore her hair in two pigtails, and looked like she, too, had taken a shower just before I arrived. The other three children were triplets. They were the offspring of Diana Marulanda, another one of Lina's daughters. Diana had lived with Lina all her life, but had died suddenly, of a heart attack, the year before. The triplets were nine years old, and they wore torn shorts, but no shirts or shoes. Like backup singers, they moved in synchronicity, but without uttering a word. They scrutinized me.

My mother was Lina's love child with *Papá* Julián. But after my grandfather married *Mamá* Martha, Lina had given birth to four children by different men. The children's fathers had left, leaving Lina with new mouths to feed. Besides Carmen and Diana, there were two sons. Lina's children had in turn married and reproduced, and, invariably, the mothers and fathers moved away, leaving the children with Lina, until they grew up and moved away. With the exception of Carmen Izquierdo, I had barely had any contact with my half uncles and aunts. Because they were black and poor and uneducated, I was brought up not to consider them as part of my family.

Etilvia returned with a cold bottle of Coca-Cola, which I gulped down. When I finished, I noticed that the children were gazing at me enviously, as if I had just had a great treat, which, to them, it no doubt was.

"Now, children, go get cleaned up so you can take your cousin to see the improvements of the town," Lina said. The children scurried away, jumping and twirling, as excited as if they were going to the circus.

"I want you to see the bridge at El Salto while we make your lunch," Lina said. "Later it will be too hot to walk." She paused, smiling at me tenderly. "I knew I wouldn't die before I saw you again," she murmured. "You've made Lina very happy because you remembered her."

Although she was my grandmother, I hardly knew her. All

my life I had felt closer to my stepgrandmother. Lina was illiterate, and she had lived her ninety years in El Barranco.

"You'd better go back today before it gets dark," she told me. "The guerrillas could kidnap you for a ransom. Just because you came from far away, they may think you have money."

I told her I planned to return to El Banco later that day. "Do you think the guerrillas know I am here?" I asked.

At that moment a band of rowdy parakeets alighted in one of the mango trees. "News travels fast here," she said, pointing to the birds. "The parrots spread it. I bet you they already know."

"Do the guerrillas ever bother you, Lina?"

"Once in a while they come by and take a chicken or a pig. Once they took one of my young *burras*. But here I am, ninety years old. Nobody can bother me anymore." She smiled to herself. "Look at your grandfather; how mean he was to me when he left me to marry your *Mamá* Martha. He used to boast he had a pact with the devil, and he made all that money. Never gave me a penny. And now he's six feet underground, and Lina is still here," she said, proud of her endurance.

Lina seemed as old and as fecund as one of the ancient trees in her yard. I was about to ask her some questions about my mother when I saw the children approaching. They had scrubbed their faces, combed their hair, and were wearing their best clothes, as if they were going to a party or to Sunday church. I got down off the hammock. Patricia approached me and grabbed my hand.

"Take Santiago to see the bridge first," Lina instructed Etilvia and Juvenal. "And make sure you're here by noon. I'm going to make a big *sancocho* for your cousin. I'm going to kill my fattest chicken for my grandson."

The children led the way. Under the punishing sun, we paraded the green streets of El Barranco. They seemed as proud as if they were on a carnival float. We were heading for El Salto (The Fall), the lagoon in the back of the town. In my childhood, I had crossed El Salto on horse, on the way to my grandfather's farm, Tosnován. The trip by horse took an entire day because the path through the forest was narrow, rocky, precipitous. Tosnován was located in mountainous jungle, and the shrill serial chorus of the cicadas, the howls of the monkeys, the burbling of the icy creeks as they spilled from the snowy and unseen peaks of the Cordilleras, the cackle of parrots, parakeets and macaws, the song of tiny birds with neon colors, the roars of the tigers, the hooting of the owls, and the rasping maraca sounds made by the vipers as they brushed the leafy ground, the small iguanas of iridescent green, the red ferocious ants carrying big chunks of vegetable matter, mowing down everything, the snake-long centipedes, and weird-looking, asymmetrical, poisonous spiders—the size of chicken eggs—all these things enchanted and frightened me as a child.

The first time I visited Tosnován, as we approached the farmhouse, I saw the farm children take flight in panic and climb up the mango trees, from which they observed us as we dismounted. My grandfather explained that the children were frightened because, besides their parents, and a handful of farmworkers, they were not used to visitors. A few days went by before the children allowed us to get near them. I was fascinated by their feral state; how they seemed just a step above the wild animals. After I had been there for almost a week, I approached one of the little farm girls. Since she was too shy to initiate conversation, I asked her how old she was. The girl, who was barefoot, her feet encased in a crust of black mud, her long hair down to her shoulders, said, "I was born the last time the parrots nested here." I was thirteen or fourteen years old at the time, and her answer astonished me. Even at that age, I sensed that there was a gap between the two of us that I could not bridge just by talking, no matter how sympathetic I was toward her.

That night I asked my grandfather about the last time the parrots had visited the farm. "The red-beaked parrots come around every seven years," he said. "They're due to nest here again next year." Although I had seen my grandfather many times tell the time of the day by looking at the position of the sun in the sky, it was during that visit to Tosnován that I began to sense how radically dissimilar this world was from the city where I lived during the school year. In my early twenties, when my grandfather's fortune declined and he had to sell the farm, I had felt a great sadness because I realized it was the end of a whole world, a whole way of being and feeling.

I started making conversation with Etilvia. She was tall, fleshy—like a young Sophia Loren painted cinnamon. I asked her if she was in school. "Oh, I finished high school last year. I was the best student in my class; I read all the books in the library," she replied eagerly.

Sensing her quick intelligence, I asked, "Do you want to continue studying?"

"Yes," she said. "But how? The nearest place where I could continue my education would be Cartagena."

There was such finality in the way she said it that I felt an ache in my heart. Cartagena was just two days away by boat, but to her, because of her parents' poverty, it was as far away as another continent. Sensing how trapped she was, I wanted to rescue her from that town; from a life of penury that—at best—included marrying, having many children, her mind going dormant.

"Anyway, it's okay I'm not going to school anymore," she said. "I can see in the daylight, but I can't read at night. My eyes get very fatigued when I read."

"There is a hospital in El Banco," I said. "You should go there before your eyes are ruined."

Etilvia stared at me, with a blank expression. I understood that her parents couldn't afford the boat fare to El Banco, much less the hospital fee. Impulsively I took out my wallet and handed her a bunch of pesos. Etilvia didn't count the bills, she didn't say thank you, either. She rolled the money and gave it to little Patricia to put it in the pocket of her dress. But her eyes twinkled with gratitude.

We arrived at the bridge. It wasn't much of anything, but it did the job: Its cement structure rose over the waters of El Salto. On the other shore, the narrow path had been replaced by a dirt road, which now connected El Barranco to the interior of the country. I was told that, once in a while, a vehicle would come into town from the state of Santander. We stood there admiring the cobalt blue lagoon, which was covered with lotus plants in bloom. Many swamp roosters flew airily from leaf to leaf, picking at the insects that nested in the topaz and ivory blooms. In the distance, a bloated dead dog bobbed in the still waters, and a turkey-size onyx vulture perched on it, picking at the eyes.

Etilvia said, "I like to come here with Mariela, my best friend. When the river is swollen, like now, we dive from the bridge. I wish you could meet Mariela," she added, joy creeping in her voice as she talked about her friend. "Mariela's so wild. She doesn't care about what people think. Lina gets very cross when she finds out we've jumped from the bridge."

"Is it safe?" I asked.

Etilvia smiled. "It's safe if the water is deep. Here, I'll show you."

She climbed the railing and dove into the waters below. I stood there, transfixed by her boldness. The children started screaming happily. For what seemed the longest time, Etilvia remained submerged. When she resurfaced, she called me to join her in. "The water is so cool," she said. Laughing in unison, the triplets jumped in. I squeezed little Patricia's hand, to keep her from joining them.

"I don't want to mess my new dress," she said coquettishly, to set me at ease. "The water is very muddy. It will stain my dress."

Etilvia and the triplets began to play games in the water, screaming and carrying on. I had bathed in this lagoon many years ago with Rosita and my mother and my aunts and their friends. More than thirty years had gone by since that time, but I could almost hear their laughter now, and see their young, pretty olive-skinned bodies in 1950s bathing suits. Why had I come here? I wondered. After so many of my beliefs had crumbled in middle age; after the death of so many of my loved ones, my ideals had been replaced by a spiritual malaise that recently had made me yearn for answers I could not get. And yet, a part of me felt that in a world that rewarded aggression and greed, there was no room for someone searching for a center, for meaning, for a redemption that went beyond the personal, the selfish, the fulfillment of bourgeois needs and wants.

Juvenal, who had been quiet all this time, now stood next to me. He was very black, taller than me, and sturdily built, a living sculpture. He reminded me of African warriors I had seen in photographs.

A shot, followed by a volley of them, rang in the distance, and hundreds of birds, flapping their wings, imbricated the sky.

"It's the guerrillas on the other side of El Salto. Maybe they're hunting. Maybe they've executed a prisoner," Juvenal said matter-of-factly.

"Are they really that close?"

"They swim often on the other side. Sometimes they come into town to talk to the people, or to ask for things. Many of my friends have joined them out of boredom. There's nothing else to do in El Barranco." He paused. Juvenal pulled a leather pouch from his pants pocket and, untying it, dumped the contents on his palm. Sparkling nuggets of gold filled his palm. "I know a place where I get these. After I have a bunch of them, I sell them in El Banco and give the money to Lina. When my mother was alive, she sold corn *bollos*, which she made; but now I have to help Lina feed the children."

"They're beautiful," I said, fingering the resplendent little pieces.

Juvenal smiled and, with parsimony, poured his treasure again in the pouch. "There are many dangerous vipers there,' he said. "Sometimes they attack you. The other day, one of them jumped at me. It went 'ZAZZ, ZAZZ, ZAZZZZ,'" he hissed, baring his snowy teeth. "I had to pull my machete in a hurry and cut his head off."

I flinched.

"Look," Patricia said, "Etilvia and the triplets are drying out."

On the far shore, Etilvia and the boys were sitting on the sand, and shaking their heads to dry their hair.

"I think we'd better call them," I said. "We shouldn't be too late."

After we left El Salto, we went by the cemetery, but didn't go in.

"It's too bad you didn't come next month when my mother's tombstone will be laid," Juvenal said. "I've been saving money so she could have a nice tombstone."

I knew that in these villages the size and the quality of work that went into a tombstone constituted one of the most important status symbols for a family. We continued walking until we came to the edge of the town, then we turned left and soon arrived at the cantina I passed with Francisco on the way to Lina's house. Since I was thirsty and sweating from the blazing sun, I offered to buy them a soda. Perhaps because it was lunch hour, the cantina was empty, although the jukebox continued to blare Mexican *rancheras*. We all ordered Coca-Colas. The bottles that were handed to us were like ice cubes, frosted, the liquid inside half-iced.

The children walked to the terrace facing the river in the distance, and leaned against the wall to drink their Cokes. They drank in silence, relishing every single little sip they took. There was an enraptured look on their faces as they stared at the slow-moving river. A big boat floated by, blowing its horn. The basso melancholy sound was like a magical instrument they listened to with enormous concentration. I thought how, as a child, my mother must have stood by the shores of El Barranco, waiting for the big boats to go by, waiting for their bawling horns that must have sounded to her like the song of sirens inviting her to dream about the world beyond this village.

Sixty years later, I could detect this same yearning in the children's faces. I imagined little Patricia's dreaming of visiting her mother in Cartagena, and wearing very pretty dresses all the time; and Juvenal, dreaming of striking ever richer mines of gold, until he could build a gold mausoleum for his mother; and the triplets, dreaming of a world in which they would each have an individuality and talk to others, not just themselves; and Etilvia dreaming of her eyesight restored, so that she could continue to read, so that she, and her friend Mariela, could go away to a great metropolis, and attend a university and fill their minds with all the knowledge and the culture they were capable of receiving. The intensity of the yearning in these young people's faces pierced my heart with a pain that had no name, a pain that left me wordless. I felt farther away from New York than I had felt since I had started my journey. I wondered if these children, too, would someday journey away from here. And I wondered whether their journey would lead to long lives of quiet fulfillment, or to sadness and tragedy. I wanted my arms to turn into long wings, so that I could shelter them, and fly away with them to a place where we could all live safely, in this moment forever.

Lina's delicious *sancocho* was served for me in the living room. The succulent meats and roots and vegetables were piled on freshly cut banana leaves. Lina and the children gathered silently around me, to watch me eat. Despite my ravenous appetite, I felt uncomfortable. I would have preferred that we all ate together, but that wasn't how Lina wanted it. I ate as much as I could, and when I finished the children brought pewter plates from the kitchen and served themselves. With their plates heaped, they went to the patio to eat under the trees. The children didn't use silverware to eat, and they scooped up the thick soup with bowls made from the fruit of the *totumo* tree.

I realized what a special day this was to them. Although I don't think they ever went hungry, the concept of three meals a day was alien to them. Because of the generosity of the river and the land, there was always some kind of food available. I remembered the stories that Carmen Izquierdo used to tell me back in Barranquilla. There were times of the year when all they had to eat was whatever fruit was in season: *ciruelas,* or guavas or mangoes, plus black coffee, if they were lucky. Food was only plentiful during the months when the Magdalena produced its annual harvest of fish. Then they had bocachicos, *lebranches, lisas, coroncoros,* sardines, and *bagres,* a catfish that grows the size of a big dolphin.

The noon heat had settled upon everything, creating an eerie repose. Not an animal moved, not a bird flew in the sky, even the trees became still, as if to conserve their moisture, I was full, drowsy, lethargic, the tangy taste of cumin and annatto lingering in my mouth. Lina suggested that I go lie in the hammock under the *ciruela* tree. She stayed behind to eat her meal alone.

When I woke up from my nap, I found Lina sitting on a bench next to my hammock and gazing at me. She was puffing a *calilla,* the long, thin cigar that black women, especially fortune-tellers, smoke. She inhaled the way the African *palen-*

queras do, by sticking the lighted end in their mouths. Lina reminded me of an ancient matriarchal sorceress, someone whose wisdom was beyond me, beyond anything I had read in books or could rationally understand.

"Lina's *sancocho* made you sleepy, eh?" She beamed, and sucked powerfully on her *calilla* before she exhaled potent aromatic clouds of smoke.

I nodded. There were so many questions I wanted to ask her, yet I found myself speechless.

"You look like a picture I have of your father," Lina said. "He was a good man to me. He bought me this house when he was living with your mother. If he hadn't done that, Lina would be living in the forest now."

"Did you ever meet my father, Lina?"

"No, he never came to visit, and Lina has never been any place farther than El Banco. But he used to send me sacks of rice and sugar and he always remembered Lina for Christmas. He wasn't like your grandfather, who just took and took from me and from your mother." There was resentment in her voice when she talked about *Papá* Julian. More than sixty years after he had left her to marry *Mamá* Martha, she couldn't forgive him.

I heard myself ask, "Lina, what was the murder that took place down the road? Francisco mentioned it to me this morning."

Lina dragged on her cigar and closed her eyes; a grimace spread over her crinkled face. She pulled out the *calilla*, which was moist with saliva up to its burning tip. Then she spat on the floor. "So Francisco told you?"

"Yes, Lina," I said, pressing her, now that my curiosity had been piqued. "What murder was he talking about?"

"A long time ago," she began, the way one begins a fairy tale, "long before you were born, your grandfather's oldest son, Carlos, your uncle, he killed a boy with a machete. Your grandfather's family had to leave El Barranco. They took your mother with them. That's when they settled upriver in El Banco." She paused and looked away, into the trees. "What was so bad about the murder," she said, now locking her eyes with mine, "was how your grandfather behaved. Because he had money, and the boy's family was poor, your grandfather treated the other family very badly. We didn't have the police here then. We didn't have a jail, either. No one had been murdered in the town before that time. So your uncle went unpunished because your grandfather was rich in cows and land." She paused, lost in thought, trying to remember events that had taken place long ago. "Oh, I go to Church," she said finally. "I hear the priest preach about what's in the Bible, about the sins of the fathers being passed to the sons. Your uncle Carlos never paid for what he did, but I know what happened to that family. I heard about your uncle Migue, the one who's a drunk, and lives in the streets in the market in Barranquilla. And your other uncle, Jessie, who went to Venezuela to work in the diamond mines and was lost in the jungle. I knew all those boys when they were born. They just lived down the street. And they were cursed by what Carlos did." She leaned over and grabbed my arm firmly. "It's good you found out about the murder. It's good you know now what's in your grandfather's blood. I don't want you to suffer like your poor mother and Rosita. That Sofía, she loved your *Papá* Julian more than anything, and they were never nice to her."

I thought about how odd it was that it had taken Rosita's death to make me come back here, to look for answers to the void I felt. It was just an accident that I had run into Francisco, that he had mentioned the murder, that I had been curious enough to ask Lina about it. But it was a coincidence that, in a matter of hours, shed new light on the life I had lived to that point. Now I understood my mother's blind loyalty to her family, as if she had been sworn to secrecy at the risk of her life; now I understood what it was like for Rosita to live with Carlos. I understood, too, that the years I lost to drugs, I had been following patterns that had been established long before I was born; and I understood the horror that lay at the heart of our family's history.

A few hours later, I embraced and kissed Lina as we said goodbye. I took a good look at her, trying to engrave her image on my brain, so that I would never forget it.

"I'm glad that you came before I died," she said. "Now I can die in peace."

"I'll come back again, Lina," I said, "and you'll still be here."

She smiled her toothless smile. "I'll be here under the earth, Santiago. But wherever you go, remember Lina will always be looking after you."

Your Mother from Cleveland

Bil Wright

"Had to sign my Black self the hell out!"

Your Mother from Cleveland came at me from up the block and across the street, bellowing. I didn't have a chance to get any further than the top step of the stoop.

I hadn't seen her for weeks, it was true, but twenty minutes before I was due at my desk forty blocks away was not an ideal time for an explanation. We weren't friends. We were neighbors. Still, it wasn't the first time she'd made me late. Your Mother from Cleveland dropped a shopping bag directly in front of me as a roadblock. Plastic bottles, sample cards of yellow pills and a pair of savagely soiled size fifty-two pajamas spilled out of the bag.

"Got a show on the twenty-fifth at The Red Rug. That's this coming Monday. You better write it down, Baby Louise. I want your face close enough to sit on. Doing my special tribute to Josephine Baker in the first act. Big Maybelle's Big Band Classics in the second. Intern was fightin' me to stay, but a week's worth of bedpans is all Your Mother from Cleveland could bear. Besides, I figured if they could still pick up a pulse after a week, I was pretty convinced I could do my show.

"You know anything about pneumonia? They sure don't tell you anything you could get a hold on. Like how do you get pneumonia in the middle of July? They just kept talkin' about 'bacteria.' I think that's why I didn't listen so good. Even 'pneumonia' don't sound as deadly as 'bacteria.' That's a ugly ass word. Now, you think about a word like 'BACTERIA'— makes your damn skin crawl. Then you think about a word like—'SEQUINS'! Imagine a good-lookin' intern strolling up to the side of your hospital bed, takin' your fleshy black palm in his, leanin' over close enough for you to smell his shower soap an sayin', 'You got Sequins. Too many Sequins. They're all over everything. It's probably the worst case I've seen.' Now how bad could you feel? Even if you thought it was incurable, it couldn't be but so bad to go out from too many Sequins, could it?

"But they weren't sayin' anything that encouraging across town at St. Helena's, up on sixteen, Coleman ward, bed B. They weren't saying anything that made me wanna do a thing but get the hell outta there and get ready for my show. That's all I could think about, baby. Monday night. Your Mother from Cleveland is gonna give the children Festival of Lights. Carnival in Rio and Aida's Fourth Act Finale. All in twenty-two minutes. On a four-by-four platform in the Bronx. If they like this one, they're gonna give me Monday nights for the next couple of months. I'm gonna do what I do better than anybody, an' it sure as hell ain't layin' up on a bed of concrete in St. Helena's.

"We will not do any more masks and plastic gloves. No more bad hairdos in nylon dresses masquerading as professional nurses telling me, 'Don't get your hopes up, Bed B. No tellin' how long you'll be in here.' No! No more four-syllable pneumonias, and I'll be damned if I'll listen to one more announcement that evil 'bacteria' is storm-trooping through my damn lungs. Not while Your Mother from Cleveland still has it in her to give you a show. Don't you even think about not being there, Baby Louise." I winced. I'd only been 'Louis' once, the first time I'd introduced myself to Your Mother. After that, it seemed as if she'd made a point of letting the entire neighborhood hear her calling me "Baby Louise."

Your Mother from Cleveland approached the steps of the crumbling east-side tenement we both called home. Except that she was Leontyne Price laying claim to Egypt at the Met. The only thing louder than her wheezing was the mint jelly green of her raincoat as Your Mother carefully negotiated her way through the front door and down the hall.

I missed Your Mother from Cleveland's show in the Bronx. I'd only seen her perform once, and although I'd made countless promises since then, with all the best intentions, I'd never made good on any of them. The one time I'd traipsed out to Brooklyn Heights on a Wednesday night, Your Mother hadn't gone on until two o'clock in the morning. Despite a tour de force performance from Your Mother, the evening yielded *tres, tres* bitter regrets. The next day, two other night birds in my department called in sick, leaving me to lay out over two hundred display ads single-handedly with a Budweiser hangover and an hour and a half of sleep.

As usual after not going to one of Your Mother's shows, I started tiptoeing past her apartment, hoping I wouldn't run into her. A month later, on my way to work, I noticed a yellow flyer taped to her door. I glanced at it on my way out, sure it was a promotion for yet another performance. And in a way, I suppose it was.

> YOUR MOTHER FROM CLEVELAND
> (1961–1994)
> WILL BE GIVEN A LEGEND'S FAREWELL
> AT GRAPPLER'S MEMORIAL CHAPEL
> 337 WEST 23RD STREET, N.Y.
> SATURDAY 8/31/94 1:00 P.M.

I peeled the tape slowly from the door, careful not to rip the flyer. I had a vague thought that I'd make a copy at the office and replace it. I knew I wanted one for myself, though. Leaving the building, I tripped down the stairs I'd been climbing for two years and looked back in that ridiculous, automatic way, as though the stairs had somehow repositioned themselves since I'd last used them. I stood whimpering like a toddler abandoned in the middle of a department store on Red Tag Day. Then I headed for the subway.

Work was hellish. I spent most of the morning shuffling ads randomly and rolling dust from my desk between my fingers. By afternoon, I'd taken the flyer out of my desk to stare at the picture of Your Mother from Cleveland. Somebody'd spent money on a color Xerox, and it was worth every penny. Your Mother was wearing a gold halter gown that looked like Eartha Kitt in her I Want to Be Evil days. But even Eartha could not possibly have managed the box-hedge Afro with the greased and straightened bangs and Scotch-taped spit curls. "It's my Odetta meets Tammi Terrell sixties tribute," Your Mother had once informed me, and I wondered if she'd stipulated somewhere that she be laid out in it.

The following Saturday morning I took a cross-town bus that let me off about a half block from Grappler's Memorial Chapel. Grappler's had the pulse-quickening distinction of preparing more gay men for burial in the last ten years than any other funeral home in Manhattan. I'm not quite sure what I expected, but it turned out to be as anonymous looking as any other funeral home I'd been in, although there hadn't, thank God, been that many. Sitting at the entrance was a relic who looked like a waxed extra from a B movie about organized crime. He pointed over his shoulder to a staircase.

The room at the top of the stairs was very dark with a soft pink glow. In the center of the room was a sand-colored casket which I assumed held Your Mother, although I couldn't see her very well from the doorway. There were only two other people, grey-haired women in simple black dresses sitting silently in front of the coffin. I wondered if one of them might be Your Mother's mother.

It was a quarter after one already, and I'd cursed myself coming across town for probably getting to Grappler's too late to get a seat. Because of the flyer, I expected that there would be quite a turnout of Your Mother's friends and family. I was so shocked that these two women were the only ones in the room that I stood in the doorway, feeling uneasy about going in at all. I must have stood there for almost ten minutes before a stampede came up the stairs behind me. I cleared the entrance to the room for at least a dozen drag queens of varying shades and sizes, mostly large, wearing every variation of day drag imaginable, from Geoffrey Beene to Buffy's Budget Basement.

As the new mourners filled the room, the two older women got up, stood together for a moment at the coffin, then passed me on their way down the stairs. I went in and found a seat over to the side and towards the back.

I couldn't bring myself to go up very close to Your Mother. I've only been to a couple of these things, ever—and I never get up very close. But what I could see from where I was sitting startled me—a big, bald, cocoa-colored man in a navy blue suit, wrinkled, yellowed white shirt and a hopelessly off-center salmon print bow tie. He looked like a high school science teacher or a midtown accountant; some bifocaled Mr. Brown or Mr. Jackson who'd disappeared into an office building one day and been trapped irrevocably inside—until now.

Eerily, the navy blue suit could easily have been the one hanging in the back of my own closet, the uniform I'd worn from one side of the city to the other trying to find work when I first moved to New York from Chicago. I'd considered wearing it to pay my respects to Your Mother, but it was unmistakably her voice behind me at the door of my closet laughing, "Relax, Baby Louise. The suit's going too damn far." Now I knew I'd heard wrong. Or maybe I hadn't. Either the two women who were there when I first arrived were responsible for how Your Mother was dressed or maybe she'd talked me out of wearing my own suit, knowing she'd already decided on one for herself. In a room full of "Des Sisters De La Drag," as Your Mother called them, all giving you designer mourning cum Auntie Mame cocktail ensembles, Your Mother from Cleveland was serving up tailored and tasteful burial attire—conservative, male drag.

I'd assumed because of the flyer that someone had organized the service, but after almost an hour, nobody seemed to be taking charge. There wasn't a moment's silence in the room, though, as entrances were dished ("Oooh, Miss Sissy, if you're not throwing us Supreme Jackie Kennedy! The veil is on fire, darling, *on fire!*") and exits observed ("You got an appointment, bitch? Is he paying?")

As the din peaked to a shrill cacophony of laughter and pump heels beating the floor for emphasis, I realized that what was going on around me *was* the service. This *was* the Legend's

Farewell the flyer had promised. All of the ceremony that I expected, and perhaps thought only appropriate for a presence as large as Your Mother's, didn't seem to be on anyone else's agenda. I was disappointed, but I definitely didn't have the guts to pay her any kind of tribute myself. And after all, I reminded myself, she wasn't really a friend, she was my neighbor. I barely knew her. I waited a few minutes more and started over to Your Mother to say good-bye.

An elfin-looking man who appeared to be in his early sixties, with a face so deeply flushed it looked more eggplant than red, weaved over to where I was standing. He hung perilously over Your Mother's open coffin towards me.

"This one," he rasped, "was a survivor. This one had a helluva lot of balls. I knew it when I first seen him do a show out at Coney Island. Club called the Plucked Pigeon. I said when I seen what he did, I said, 'Balls.' " He leaned across Your Mother at me. "You know Coney Island?"

"No. No, I don't."

"Clubs out there, ya don't see hardly any coloreds at all. Not without a whole lotta trouble. Whoever booked this kid wasn't doin' him no damn favors. Coney Island ain't no Greenwich Village. It's da last friggin' stop on the line. It's more like the rest of the friggin' world. I thought there'd be hell to pay for a while, that night! But he gave 'em a show an' a half, all right. Colored or no colored.

"Kid reminded me of myself back when I still had it in me to do what I done that night o' Stonewall in sixty-nine. I know you know about Stonewall, don't ya, kid?"

"Well . . . I mean I'm not an expert or anything. But I know about it."

"Well, I am. I am a friggin' expert on it. I'm as much of an expert as you're gonna get." The elf was pretty loud by now, but no louder than the queens around us. I think it was that he was yelling over Your Mother that bothered me. I kept watching the spit fly out of his mouth and into the coffin.

" 'You can kiss our sissy asses!' That's what we told the world in sixty-nine. And this kid right here had the same kinda moxie. No matter what you see in front of ya, he was a survivor."

I looked from the diminutive man with the liver spots freckling his pale, rubbery scalp to Your Mother from Cleveland barely contained by his coffin. I resisted even imagining any kinship between them. Why? The man was earnest enough. Sloppy, repulsive even, but earnest. He'd paid the tribute to Your Mother I didn't have the nerve to. Hadn't I wanted there to be some kind of eulogy? Wasn't the purpose of a eulogy to tie, however clumsily, all of our lives together in some comforting daisy chain of commonality? Hadn't that been what the drunken elf had attempted to do?

The one time I'd seen Your Mother from Cleveland perform, this queen, Demeana Divina from Brooklyn Heights who did Barbra Streisand and Maria Callas, was the headliner. Your Mother from Cleveland was one of seven Guest Stars.

Apparently Demeana had come up with this gospel finale to be performed (read lip-synched) to "Oh Happy Day," originally recorded by The Edwin Hawkins Singers and covered by The Staples Singers with Mavis Staples steam-piping out the lead. The very blond Demeana, of course, was doing Mavis' voice, and the Guest Stars had been assigned the chorus. After all, they were performing on her turf, n'est-ce pas?

As drag divas are wont to do, I suppose, Your Mother missed her chorus cue and entered from the wings directly on Demeana's (i.e., Mavis') opening solo line. She had forgone a finale evening gown like the others and was wearing a white choir robe with a red sequined stole and matching pumps (also sequined). Her wig was a towering Mahalia-meets-Clara-Ward with sausage curls big enough to hide money in. Demeana, in a pink cotton shift, close-cropped yellow Afro wig and checkered bandanna, was beginning to resemble a spastic albino sharecropper mutely mouthing prayers for rain.

Now, Your Mother wasn't lip-synching at all. Your Mother was wailing live harmony off Mavis in a gospel tenor that took me back twenty years to a sissy in the church I grew up in, who would make old people jump over pews when he sang. The crowd rushed Your Mother with dollar bills. In my delirium, I forgot that the only bill I had left was a twenty, which I'd vowed not to spend and should have left at home. I thrust my last twenty into Your Mother's hand and then kissed it passionately, honored that she'd allowed me to do so.

The climax of the number, as if it needed one, was when Your Mother jumped out of her sequined pumps, presumably taken over by "the spirit" in a brilliantly choreographed strut from one end of the stage to the other. Yes, *c'est vrai, c'est vrai.* The evening's curtain calls were fraught with high tension, but Your Mother was glowing unmistakably triumphant, having further established herself in the Firmament of Legendary Drag Artistes.

I wanted to share my memory of that night with the rest of the people in the room with me and Your Mother at Grappler's Memorial Chapel. I wanted to tell them Your Mother from Cleveland's "Oh Happy Day" was as much a moment of theatrical genius as any I'd seen on Broadway in the last five years. I turned to the Stonewall Survivor, but he'd retreated to a darkened corner where he was nursing a small flask. The others were cataloging Your Mother's repertoire, a drag queen's legacy they were greedily dividing up amongst themselves.

I thought about Your Mother's apartment and all of the costumes, makeup and wigs that she must have left. Who'd get the gold halter gown on the memorial flyer, for example, a number that could have supplied the power for the state of Texas?

Hell, Your Mother liked me. I'd bet she'd want me to have something to remember her by. Like the choir robe with the red sequined stole. I supposed the pumps would be too much to hope for. Besides, what would I do with them? You couldn't sit around eating takeout in red sequined pumps, could you? Shit, if they were mine, I could do anything I damn well pleased with them, couldn't I?

I didn't have the nerve, though, to go up to any of the others and stake any kind of claim. I turned back to Your Mother. This time it would really be good-bye. I stared at her smooth, dramatically chiseled face. My eyes traveled down to her hands folded over each other and I remembered how she waved them about as she carried on about any and everything. It was the navy suit that still seemed so odd and uncharacteristic. It was I, I thought, who'd someday be buried in a suit, and no one would think it was strange at all. But Your Mother, I was sure, had changed out of this straightjacket as soon as her soul had taken flight from her body and changed into something . . . well, something *tres, tres* Your Mother.

I tried to imagine what someone like Your Mother would wear in the Great Hereafter as I headed for the staircase. I got halfway down before she stopped me. I could feel her standing behind me, although I didn't dare turn around. I wasn't afraid, but I did get goose bumps on the back of my neck when she spoke. "You better go back up there and get what you want, Baby Louise. Ask and ye shall receive."

Actually, I was no more surprised by Your Mother than I'd ever been. I suppose I was more impressed with how well she seemed to know me and grateful that she didn't hold it against me for missing that last show. I did as I was instructed, thinking that if I was going to ask anything of these queens, though, I'd better be specific. I might have to be tough, maybe even a little ruthless. I might have to do my best Your Mother from Cleveland right there in front of her. I had to have a first, second, and maybe even a third choice. I'd ask for the sequined pumps. And the choir robe with the stole that matched them. If I couldn't have another chance to see Your Mother give the children Festival of Lights, Carnival in Rio and Aida's Fourth Act Finale all in twenty-two minutes, I'd be grateful as hell to have whatever The Legend, Your Mother from Cleveland had left behind.

Damn it, I wanted to slap myself. I was shocked and embarrassed at how badly I wanted the wig. The Mahalia-meets-Clara with the curls big enough to hide dollar bills in. But I'd ask the queens anyway and I knew Your Mother from Cleveland would make sure I received.

"Summertime, and the Living Is Easy . . ."

Reginald Shepherd

I am sitting in the library of Marshall's parents' house reading a book about beauty: another sentimental education. The book isn't mine, but I want it. The house is huge, three floors of rooms tastefully decorated with ormolu clocks and reclining bronze figurines on mantels: things I will never own. I envy Marshall the rows of pristine hardcovers lined up shelf over shelf, dust covers unmarred by the indignities of hasty packing in stolen milk crates, the two circular staircases made of banded Siena marble, one with Venetian cut-glass chandelier, the guest bedrooms and small rooms in the back that were once servants' quarters (now they hire people with my skin to do things and leave). I envy him the luxury of hating it. None of it is mine, not even Marshall.

Marshall is my best friend. We had a brief affair, before we became friends. Marshall would say we slept together, once, twice (we've put all "that stuff" behind us, he says), but I say it's all in how you look at things. Marshall says I am out of touch with reality, but I am the one who grew up in a housing project and he is the one who grew up here; we have different notions of what constitutes reality. He doesn't like me to talk about things like that, his money, for example, but as far as I'm concerned, that is as good a reason as any. Our relationship relies upon a certain degree of mutual annoyance. I am annoyed that Marshall is rich and white and beautiful, and he is annoyed that I constantly remind him of it. He'd like to enjoy his abundance of blessings without feeling it is anything out of the ordinary. He wants to feel normal. I, on the other hand, want him to feel guilty.

The book doesn't say much about any of this, though it does talk about longing. The author finds beauty in strange places: Czechoslovakia and northern Minnesota. The book is about the beauty disease. What the book doesn't say is that beauty costs money.

I am lying in my room, one of the guest bedrooms, listening to the Smiths. It's ninety-five out and muggy, and I want to go swimming, but it's thundering and a deceptively blue plastic tarpaulin covers the pool. So it won't attract lightning, Marshall says. Marshall's parents are vacationing on some Caribbean island (one of the Grenadines, I think, or Guadeloupe) and I have yet to see anyone but a gardener (his skin like mine, like that of the smiling people left behind on that vacation paradise when the tourists have gone home for the season), but this house is full of invisible presences stripping and making beds, stocking the pantries with heat-and-serve meals, and rolling protective tarpaulins over the pool. Marshall is asleep; he finds thunderstorms relaxing. Yet another way in which we're not alike.

Marshall's family has two dogs, some mix of terrier and golden retriever. The family rescued them from the pound as puppies; this house takes in all kinds of waifs.

The dogs are Marshall's excuse for being here; he will take care of them, avoiding an expensive and probably incompetent kennel. Marshall's family have known people whose dogs died in kennels; Bob Barker's cat received a permanent bald spot while in the care of Pets of the Stars. I, on the other hand, have no excuse. Or, Marshall is my excuse. Though the incidence of firstborn sons dying while their parents are on vacation is doubtless lower than that for dogs.

I understand that golden retrievers are among the stupidest of dogs. Marshall told me that as well; he finds it funny. He loves his mutts.

Marshall calls them mutts.

The dogs are afraid of thunder. They are probably afraid of lightning. One of them noses his way into my room, where I am lying on the floor trying to make the most of the air conditioner's artificial breeze, and I take great satisfaction in kicking the door closed. I can hear the dog paw at the door, then stop. It has probably climbed into the bathtub, but the air-conditioning filters out the scratch of nails on porcelain. It rained last night also, and the dog was cowering in the tub after midnight when I went to pee. I yelled at it until it left; I never touch these dogs.

Marshall was far away, dreaming of dusty softball games in spring, or damp soccer matches in fall. I will never do those things.

Life is an affair of places, isn't it? I love it here. There is the pool and there are the books and there are the kinds of food the titled rich are served in Proust, whom I refuse to read. For dessert there is invariably ice cream: kumquat currant, persimmon lime, macadamia poppyseed yam. Marshall is a connoisseur of ice cream, an emperor. There is the central air-conditioning and the home entertainment center that takes up half a wall. There is the VCR and the videotape library (that is what they call it) of all the classic films I have ever promised myself to see, the ones that play Tuesday matinees at revival houses in Somerville. And there is the illusion that I have Marshall to myself.

We go for walks and for drives in the country, to the beach, to town with its three-block-long main street and to the mall ten miles from town, where I wonder whether I am imagining the strange looks we get together (can they be wondering if we are lovers, or adopted brothers?), the lingering glances when I enter a store alone. When I meet their eyes the proprietors always smile and look away. At home Marshall and I play chess and Parcheesi and backgammon and Chinese checkers, and Marshall always wins; he is the one who grew up with hundreds of well-scrubbed friends with whom to play those games. I had black and white TV. I endure the humiliations of losing stoically, since it is I who like to sit for hours watching his face scrunched in concentration. But I always win at Scrabble, and in general I am much the better cheater. We argue about the

economy and whether socialism in one country could work, we
watch music videos with the sound off while I massage his
shoulders, sore from a morning's game of racquetball. We play
old Smiths albums as the soundtrack to *Imitation of Life*. The
remake featuring Lana Turner and a white actress as the tragic
mulatto. Troy Donahue beats up when he discovers the girl he's
been dating is a nigger's daughter. To be honest, I prefer to
hear the dialogue.

I am bored all the time, and luxuriate in my boredom. It's
not often I have the opportunity to lie by a pool for weeks at
a time and ponder the utter pointlessness of life. It's quite pleasant to know that when I wake up near noon (I prefer to read
at night) and can't think of a reason to get out of bed, I don't
have to. My melancholy is as cool as the fresh orange juice I
drink quarts of each day, as warm as the azure skin of the pool
when I break the surface tension with my toe, just playing,
really, not quite ready to commit myself to the colder water
waiting beneath that glittering canopy. I can take all day to
decide. I can postpone decision until the end of the summer,
when my life will begin again.

Marshall is full of plans to improve himself. He is not wondering how he will make September's rent on a stifling apartment with a window opening onto a brick wall. Come fall he
won't have to ask himself each morning how to ignore the
pimply-faced kids with greasy blond hair and Metallica T-shirts
who shout epithets from the playground across the street whenever I come home or leave. It really doesn't matter what they
call out, "Hey, Mike! Hey, Michael Jackson!" or "Get the Vase-
line out of your ass yet?" whether they make fun of my skin
or my clothes or the way I walk: it's one of the only neighborhoods I can afford. Those kids are too old to be hanging around
in playgrounds.

Marshall will not be looking for another job staring at a com-
puter screen for eight hours a day plus an hour's unpaid lunch,
because it pays better than retail and sometimes includes partial
health insurance. He is always proposing rounds of tennis,
squash matches; maybe we can go riding. I tell him I don't feel
like it. I don't know how to do those things, I don't want to
learn how to do those things, I would prefer not to. I'd rather

lie here beside the pool and think about my problems, knowing that for the immediate future I need do nothing about them.

One afternoon Marshall goes on one of his outings without telling me. He knows I hate to be disturbed when I am reading, or sleeping, or masturbating. "Where did you go?" I ask accusingly when he returns, well after dinnertime. "Why didn't you ask me if I wanted to go with you?"

I ask myself, "If Marshall didn't love me, why would he invite me here?" and respond, "If he loved me, he would sleep with me." Marshall always says, "Of course I love you; you're my best friend." We're not speaking the same language at all.

I put on "Parade" by White and Torch, another British duo, moody like all the music I love, and close my eyes, listening. I keep the blinds drawn tight. Wearing nothing but one of Marshall's old Madras shirts, too big for me, I like to pretend I am reclining on a divan in the atrium of a stone house in Marrakech, protected from the desert sun by a maze of fine latticework shutters, lazy dust motes floating on the few stray threads of light that infiltrate the cool enclosure, the silence perturbed only by the singer's thin, almost broken voice, a barely discernible English accent filtered through an adolescence in a provincial Northern town spent listening to American soul music. A boy I like to think is gay (all pretty English pop singers are, you know), whose records no one in America buys but me, singing of love abandoned, false love once imagined to be true. *Looking through your eyes, you won't even notice me.*

When Marshall knocks on the door I don't answer. I don't carry a torch for anyone.

I condescend to Marshall only to keep him in his place. If he were not so wealthy, so handsome, if only he were not so white, I could afford to be kinder. But he is, so it must be understood that I am the more intelligent.

In deference to my host, my obscure object of desire, my muse and nightmare Marshall, shall I describe him, imagine him as if he led some life beyond my desire-filled resentment, my resentful desire? Marshall lifting a tennis racket to test the heft of it before his serve, Marshall tilting a glass of milk to barely parted lips while an unruly curl pokes from beneath the plastic snaps of a backwards blue corduroy baseball cap, or biting into a half-peeled pomegranate, licking the tart juice and a pulp-cased seed from his lower lip with his tongue. Marshall browsing the ethnic snacks section of the local grocer with his Brooks Brothers chinos and untucked pink button-down Oxford, or checking his "goddamn cheap Rolex" with a scratch on the face. Marshall shaking the sweat from his hair after he has come back from running, his grey tank top clinging to the skin that sheathes his sternum and covered with a fine sheen of dust.

By the standards of one who has been the same height since the seventh grade, Marshall is quite tall. He has a slim muscular build, a swimmer's body they call it (in high school he was captain of the team), and a great devotion to keeping fit. Marshall has always been what our college catalogue called a scholar-athlete. He has a thin line of fine hair between his pectorals, and large pink nipples that stand out from his chest. Very sensitive nipples, I recall. He has black curly hair and green eyes and his ears are small and almost translucent. The left side of his mouth doesn't quite match the right, and his face looks a little lopsided when he smiles. I like to see him smile; it makes me hate him less. His teeth are perfectly even, and obscenely white.

I'm sorry I ever started this.

Most of my love goes to the pool, which has been for the past week unwrapped, unrolled, uncovered, revealed in all its hyaline glory. This is an affection Marshall and I share. He does laps; I float.

There is, apparently, someone who cleans the pool. I have never seen him. Marshall is driving through the country and I am lying by the pool reading Jean Rhys. It's comforting to read about the sufferings of the first Mrs. Rochester on an island where people whispered that she must be part black, an island like the one on which Marshall's parents are summering a thousand miles away, with ivory beaches I can see myself lying on if I close my eyes. Jean Rhys smashed up her life and I have no life to smash up, but we both have our islands and that is what matters. Through the speakers I have carried onto the back patio Dionne Warwick insists I make it easy on myself and I am taking her advice.

After all, in a week Kyle will be here.

I'm under no illusions. Kyle's presence will bring discomfort and anxiety. Like everything, I suppose. To Marshall, of course, it will bring someone to sleep with every night.

Kyle and I do not like one another. Kyle dislikes me because I am snide to him and often rude. I dislike Kyle because he is Marshall's lover.

Ever since I have known him, and before, since our freshman year, when he was just a Homeric myth I watched play volleyball on the Green out the windows of the dining common, Marshall has had a succession of boyfriends named Travis or Justin or Shane; I'm sure there must have been a Lance, but I can't recall him just now. With each succeeding one I have simultaneously asked myself, "How could Marshall go out with someone as stupid as Trent?" and "Why couldn't Hugh be interested in *me*?" Few of Marshall's boys (that's what we called them, I and my small band of bookish young men who never got laid, who never thought of sleeping with each other) had IQs larger than their waist sizes, but they all knew how to carry themselves. Marshall was always valiant in praise of their hidden virtues, though as far as anyone could see (and anyone could, even I), their virtues were only too apparent. But then, I can vouch for intellect's lack of allure. One of Marshall's boys was named Cameron; he rowed crew. "Call me Cam," he always said; I never did.

Each had his own distinctive charm. None of the relationships worked out, not for long, but all of those boys did. Trent played rugby, Shane was a wrestler. (Discretion, when required, has always been one of Marshall's virtues. I leave that sort of thing to him.) Late at night in my dorm room, Marshall would ask me what he should do about Skip or Ashley, while I played Echo and the Bunnymen and diffidently rested a damp open palm on his knee while gazing empathetically into his eyes.

Our relationship was not off to an entirely healthy start, but I always gave excellent advice.

Marshall slept late after our talks, and I got up to work the breakfast shift at the snack bar. Cameron always ordered four eggs, and extra butter on his toast.

Kyle is the worst of a bad lot. He and Marshall have been dating for a year.

I'm Marshall's best friend. I'm allowed to say such things. He laughs good-naturedly and agrees.

When Kyle is gone, I will still have Marshall. I don't know if that comforts me.

Kyle has just returned from a month in Europe, a birthday present from his grandmother. At dinner he tells me about his trip; he's trying to open up to me. He wants me to be on his side. He was mugged in Amsterdam, Nice was filthy and noisy, and the water in Marseilles made him sick. I hate people who complain about their trips to Europe. What Kyle doesn't understand is that there is only room for one on my side.

I am floating in the pool listening to Marshall and Kyle argue. It's their main activity when together: that, and having sex. I suspect it's only the fighting that maintains the attraction; the fights make them feel different from one another. Every bout of raised voices and mutual recriminations is followed by a lengthy silence; I keep the air conditioner turned up.

As far as I can tell, they argue about nothing, who's been unfaithful to whom in whose absence, even if only in his unspoken desires the other can read like a Dr. Seuss primer. Did Kyle sleep with Jonathan in Zurich? Was Marshall in Disneyland with Evan on Kyle's birthday? (I tell Kyle he's being silly, why would Marshall do that? I show him the 101 Dalmatians souvenir figurine Marshall gave me, but can't remember when.) Marshall always turns to me for counsel, as he has for years. I eagerly prize out every detail; it makes them seem more real, the two of them. Marshall tells me, "We have our best sex after we've fought. Sometimes we won't speak for almost a week, but still have incredible sex two or three times a day. You don't think that's too weird, do you?" I try to explain to him that healthy relationships are based on more than just sex.

Marshall tells me Kyle is jealous of us. "Sometimes I think he doesn't really understand what friendship is." I tell him he's being hard on Kyle; Kyle can't help being who he is.

I try to imagine them in bed, the ways their bodies fit together: what Marshall's body does to Kyle's, what Kyle's does to Marshall's. At times, I confess, I've listened at the door of Marshall's bedroom, desperate at least to hear. At times I'm sure Marshall must know. At times I think he likes it.

I can imagine the bodies, but never the people. When the shouting stops I decide to swim some laps. I have never swum a lap in my life, but there's a first time for everything.

Downstairs, they are quarrelling again, but I never see either of them anymore. When I'm not in the pool I'm in the library, and when I'm not in the library I am sleeping. Thunder doesn't comfort me, but the calm steady hum of the air conditioner does. I turn it up high, then bury myself in blankets, sinking into a white linen pillow of sleep to a soundtrack of white noise. I read profiles of the hot young writers and actors in the Hip Issue of *Interview* and tributes to Marilyn Monroe and Dr. King in *Life*. I keep myself an informed voter with *Time* and *Newsweek*, and then my fingers slacken and my head lolls back. When I wake up the magazines have slipped between the bed and the wall, or dropped behind the headboard. I don't look for them. There is no shortage of magazines.

This afternoon I am reading, out of sequence because that leaves more room for me, a series of letters I found just after graduation in the room next door to mine. A tall blond boy who people whispered was Edie Sedgwick's cousin, and half-insane, lived there; he should have graduated, too, but he went to Italy instead. Each letter is a tortured demand for love from someone who had spent the year travelling over Europe, and when she returned had given them all back, because she'd decided she was a lesbian. I imagine myself that girl, probably foreign, perhaps even Italian (he'd gone there in search of her ghost), sitting by the cliffs on Corfu or at a sidewalk café in Budapest with a sad smile because all the quotes from Baudelaire in the world could not make me love this man again, could not make me love any man. That boy spent the last month of school throwing knives at the wall we shared, but the letters were beautifully written.

Marshall comes to see me, sitting on the edge of the bed as if I were a sick relative he is obligated to visit once a day. Affecting not to notice the stale smell of semen hanging in the room, he says he worries he's neglecting me. He knows I'll always be here when he knocks. He can indulge me when I sulk.

Sometimes we laugh and he hugs me; sometimes we hold hands. It makes Marshall uncomfortable to know that underneath the covers I am naked.

It seems that Marshall and Kyle are not speaking again. I pretend to be busy packing my clothes and my records and my favorite books from the downstairs library, tokens of this summer of playing house, consolations for my imminent return to life. I can keep myself occupied with this for years. Every night for the past week, Marshall has come to my room to tell me the latest twists of their arguments, to ask me what he should do. Every night I tell him I don't know, I've never had a relationship like theirs, and every night after he leaves I dream of his large pink nipples. Once I dreamt I was kneeling in front of him and he detached his penis and handed it to me, walking away. It was made of wood and very hard and I held it in my hand for a long time before I woke up.

I ask Marshall why he and Kyle can't at least be civil. I tell him it's not fair that the two of them should ruin the last days of the only real vacation I have ever had. I know they're not sleeping together and I'm glad.

All my things are finally packed and I am rewarding myself with a final afternoon in the pool; as I have for almost three months, I am wearing one of Marshall's bathing suits. Kyle is leaving for California this afternoon; he and Marshall have agreed to patch things up before his flight. I allow myself to be carried by the pool's vague eddies; I'm memorizing every movement of the warm, clear water.

I can hear them yelling and then doors slam. A cab honks and before long takes off; Kyle is gone. Marshall is standing on the patio, shading his eyes against the glare. I wave slowly and he waves back. Like in a movie, there is no sound. I don't move. I have to go back in the morning and look for a job, but now I smile and close my eyes, floating on nothing at all, and wish again this place were mine. I feel happier than in months.

Powers That Be

L. Phillip Richardson

FOR JESSE

George transferred a token to another pocket, then slid his hand in again in search of quarters. He knew he had at least two quarters, change he'd received from buying that lousy slice of pizza. *Doughy, greasy, and no fucking cheese hardly. Hell, what do Greeks know about pizza anyway?* He began his search again, raking over the coins. More tokens. Sweat glistened against his brown skin. He was getting hot in the tight space. Then, in the innermost recess of his pocket, stuck in a tattered seam, he felt the outer ridge of a quarter, and its companion beneath it, nestled, hiding, as if for warmth or comfort.

Exactly what he needed now—a little warmth and comfort. Fumbling the two quarters in his hand, he inserted one, then the other, into the slot at the front of the screen. The light went out and he pressed the start button. A porno flick on a tiny screen. It was an orgy, white guys. George didn't watch it. From his jacket pocket he pulled out matches and the vial he'd just purchased with his last five-dollar bill. From another pocket he retrieved a glass pipe. A stem really. His hands were damp as he opened the vial and tapped the crystal into the pipe. Quickly he pulled a lighter from his pocket and began to heat the pipe. Its flickering flame danced before his nostrils as he warmed the bottom of the pipe. He pulled hard, in a short gasp of breath, then again, harder. The smell slowly became less acrid, more sweet, suffusing him with a welcome calm.

On the screen, three or four white guys were all tangled together. A blond was getting fucked. His dark-haired partner, muscled and freaky, was pumping him with a furious in-and-out motion. No rhythm, just mechanical action—like a piston. He was using a rubber and a leather band that snapped tightly around the base of his dick and balls. *Freaks. All of them.* George thought. *Didn't those things hurt?* He leaned back against the door, relaxing with the slow deliberate puffs, in fascination.

The pace of the screwing increased; the dark-haired guy must have been close to orgasm. His head jerked back, his eyes closed, a strained look on his face suggested either pain or pleasure. George stared at the images. The nervousness from his failed job interview was being replaced with a sense of well-being. High energy. *What were cock rings used for anyway? To give more pleasure? Or to keep the dick hard?* He'd never had problems like that—well, maybe, only if he was tense or nervous. Actually, he had something of a reputation in bed.

The guy with the cock ring removed the rubber and was masturbating himself, just as furiously as he'd been fucking. George thought how funny the quick action of the video contrasted with the slow feeling of his high coming on. Then, onscreen, someone began to help the guy jerking off, biting and tonguing the ring that pierced his left nipple. The surrounding area was wet from saliva. Then, all of a sudden, he came, blasting several powerful spurts. The first hit the blond in the face, who, at that moment, was sucking another. The next two splashed his tit. The last couple of shots lacked sufficient energy to fly, becoming webbed in the fingers of the rapidly stroking hand. Another free hand began a cadence of slaps on the blond's ass.

George's hand had drifted to his crotch. He cupped his fingers, feeling the fullness but no real interest. All the white guys seemed to be satisfied; several hands now smeared the come over the blond's chest and stomach. George squeezed his balls, then his dick. Holding himself added to the sense of calm the pipe gave him. Like a boat safely docked, he felt anchored.

The scene dissolved into a lone white boy, playing with a dildo at the crack of his ass. *Fucking freaks.* He pressed the button two or three times, advancing the videos until he came upon a young black guy, nude and sweating, exercising alone. He felt fine now, comforted by the slow, mellow puffs every few seconds. A kind of lazy, peaceful excitation. He squeezed his dick again. A new warmth was there, beneath his fingers. A new need.

He triggered the lighter again, but this time only a small flame erupted for a few seconds, then sputtered and went out. The lighter fluid was all gone. He let it fall to the floor. *Damn cheap lighter.* He made a mental note to get some matches later. For now, George floated on a few more hot drags, half-daydreaming about men, half-surrendering to the ticklish buzzing sensation in his groin. Handsome black men, sexy men, came to mind—like Bill. He was feeling chill now, not nervous like he'd been lately. Chill—like at Keller's last night. It was true: Thursdays were nice there.

Then the screen went blank and the light in the cubicle came on; his quarters had run out. Interrupted, his pleasant reverie faded in the sudden glare. No problem. He leaned forward, out of his relaxed pose against the door; he could feel the dampness beneath his armpits and on his neck. He was dressed too warmly for these close quarters: a baseball cap, a waist-length black leather jacket, over a gray hooded sweatshirt, black jeans over thermal underwear. Much too much for this tight space. But outside, for the long hours, the cold hours, he was ready.

For a second his thoughts went back to this morning, his job interview. He didn't want that stockboy job anyway. Working out in the cold, hauling and unloading boxes. His Aunt Ernestine's husband, Wilson, knew somebody who knew about the inventory job at Walsh Shipping & Packing. It was far, somewhere in Queens. When he met the supervisor, a short Italian-looking man in work clothes, he began to feel uncomfortable. Mr. Picone was expecting him, but when they met, looked George up and down suspiciously. So what if George wasn't dressed up? Neither was Mr. Picone. It was just a stockboy job, hauling shit.

Mr. Picone made him more nervous asking all those questions. No, he didn't finish high school. Yes, he'd worked before, at Burger King. No, not at least a year, just three months. Yes, mostly cleanup: clearing tables, hauling trash, mopping. He mentioned a few other odd jobs, but Mr. Picone knew the rest, or guessed it. Then he began telling George about his duties. *Duties. Don't-ies* really. There were more things he wasn't supposed to do than he could remember. Clock in at 7:45 A.M. and then out again for lunch. Lunch was only thirty minutes, or he'd be docked. Clock back in, and out at 5:00 P.M. Three times late and he'd be out the door. Call an hour before start time if he was going to be absent. Just one absence allowed during the first six months. Too much shit to remember. So, in the end, it didn't work out. But no sweat. It didn't matter because his new friend, Bill, was going to hook him up with something next week.

Now it didn't matter. He felt calm and relaxed again, a kind of relaxed power even. He put the pipe back in his jacket, still warm. He sniffled, and with the back of his hand, wiped his nose. Straightening his clothes a second, he opened the door. As he turned, he kicked the discarded vial into a corner, there next to the useless lighter he'd dropped and forgotten. It was in a wad of spit. *Fuck.* He'd get some matches later. His stomach tightened again. *Damn grease. Lousy pizza.*

He stepped into the narrow corridor, hardly big enough for the small crowd there. Jamaican music from the sound system came wafting back to him. Three sets of greedy eyes quickly surveyed him up and down. Two white guys, Yuppie types day-off slumming, in bombers and jeans, and a gray-haired black man with a Macy's bag. George was attractive, almost six feet tall and slim. His muscular frame suggested an athlete. His face, still smooth, was that of a young man coming into his own. One of George's glances caught one of the white guys on the downstroke at his waist.

George hadn't eaten since the pizza at noon, and it was now almost four o'clock. He decided to eat something and chill until later, maybe get high once more before going home. As he left the main corridor, he glanced at the black attendant, who, at that moment, was removing bubble gum from the floor

with his mop. The reggae music was louder now, more ani-
mated; it seemed the attendant marked time to it scrubbing.
Then he looked up in time to glimpse George's shadow. George
was one of the new faces beginning to blend into the old shuffle
of the steady clientele.

Outside on the street, the white guy who had caught
George's eye came up beside him. It was rush hour and there
was a steady stream of pedestrians.

"Uh . . . What's up?" the guy asked, offhandedly.

George watched the midafternoon traffic clogging the avenue, a circus of inner-city sounds. "I'm cool . . ." he said, meeting the insistent eyes straight on.

"What are you into? You hustling?" George was amused;
a boyish, fanciful smile played across his face. Desire was so
funny.

"My name's Mark . . ." He paused, waiting for George to
introduce himself. Hopeful. A tire screeched and George's gaze
darted to the corner. A taxi was making a sharp turn and the
gray-haired black man with the Macy's bag all of a sudden had
to jump back. "You just hanging out?" Mark asked, anxious,
following George's eyes.

"Yeah . . . Uh, Mark . . . I'm just chilling for now," George
said, shifting away a bit. "Think I'm going to get something to
eat." He turned and walked away.

He chose a nearby Burger King. He got on the shortest line,
but then had to wait longer than most. The woman in front of
him discovered a problem with her order and declared, in a husky
alto voice, that she wasn't having it. The cashier, a teenager with
big fly-girl golden earrings, kept saying, "Sorry, miss . . ." whenever the woman tried to explain. George looked on, entertained.
Then he grew sorry, too. This was Burger King and the lady
couldn't have it her way. *Some shit*. Finally the cashier reordered
a missing item and slid the woman's purchases to the side.
"Next." George's order, large fries and a Coke, was ready before he could assemble his last three dollars. Now only small
change was left of the twenty dollars he'd gotten from Wilson,
through Aunt Ernestine's efforts—for Friday, his *big* day at
Walsh Shipping & Packing. He sat in a corner where the window faced the busy street.

He watched passersby and drenched his fries in catsup. The one good thing about Burger King was their French fries. He ate fry after fry laden with catsup, spilling some on the one napkin he'd received. Then sipped some Coke. It tasted good, not greasy, not too spicy—perfect. Everything went better with Coke, right?

He smiled a bit and thought about his meeting tonight at Keller's with this new guy he liked, Bill. He wondered how it would go, if he'd be nervous again. Not like with Mr. Picone nervous, good nervous, excited like, expectant. Last night he'd gone into Keller's to use the bathroom and, as he moved through the crowd, saw Bill at the bar. A lot of other nice-looking men, too. Bill was a little taller than he was, darker brown. At first he wondered if Bill had modeled at one time. He was handsome in a no-nonsense way, had a bright, easy smile, and eyes that sparkled even in the dim light of the bar. As George passed within inches of him, their eyes met and he hesitated.

"Can you make it?" Bill asked, turning slightly.

"Uh, yeah . . . sure," he replied, surprised.

"Thursdays are always like this, crowded . . . but I like it . . ." Bill continued. "I get to bump into nice people . . . like you . . . I'm Bill," he joked.

George was nervous; then someone behind him jostled him and he bumped into Bill.

"Or have them bump into me . . ." Bill added.

"Oops . . . I'm sorry," George said, looking back to see who had pushed him. "Uh . . . I'm George . . ."

"Nice to *finally* meet you, George . . ." Bill extended his hand, laughing, dragging out the word "finally." George shook hands, quickly, but the feeling was immediate and powerful; holding Bill's hand for a short second had communicated a sense of ease, excitement. Right away he knew he was attracted to Bill.

"You come here often?" Bill went on with interest. "I haven't seen you here before . . ."

"I don't come here much, Bill." Now George's bladder was insistent and made him fidget. "I really only came in—". He was about to say "to take a leak," but then thought better of it. "—to use the bathroom," he continued, masking his nervousness with movement.

"Well, I'll let you go, then . . . but let's talk some more later."

Later turned into two hours, three beers for George, two Scotch and waters for Bill. George bought the first round. As they talked, Bill learned George wasn't working. So after that round, Bill just placed a twenty-dollar bill on the bar.

Over the two hours, George learned that Bill was thirty-one, came to New York from the South after grad school, and liked comic books. When he talked and laughed, he touched George's arm for emphasis. George liked Bill. He felt Bill had a way of seeing inside his words and slang and silences, getting at the truth and humor there most people dismissed. He thought Bill was level where some of his friends were extreme; fun and sensitive, where they were funny and sensational. And Bill was masculine, without the madness he usually discovered in his circle of friends and would-be boyfriends, like LaRon. At one point, George had even become aroused. He felt good.

He revealed facts about himself he didn't often think about. When he talked about his mother and her accident and death, Bill understood. Throughout the story, Bill had let his knuckles rest against George's hand, as they leaned against the bar. It was five years ago; George had been sixteen then, when he came to stay with his mother's sister Ernestine and Wilson, her Jamaican husband. Bill, too, had suffered loss, his younger brother, Donny, a few years ago, in a drowning accident. They paused like this for a long moment, isolated from the constant buzz around them, by this shared heaviness.

"I was at school in Georgia when it happened . . ." Bill added, remembering. "When it was all over, I jumped into my books—in a big way . . . It was my best year in grad school. Do you read much?"

George had been looking down at his beer, twirling it in his fingers, then looked up into the smile. "Yeah . . . mostly comics . . ." He smiled too.

"So did I, in college . . . I wanted to be a writer; I told everybody I was studying Contemporary Literature."

Bill mentioned a job opening a friend had told him about. It was at Metlife, in the Mail and Internal Handling Department. He was a good friend of Bill's, and if he asked, he would pull some strings. "If tomorrow is bad for you, go down on Monday, first thing," Bill said. "I'll set it up with John tomorrow, get an idea about the test for you."

"Test?" George asked, unsure. "I don't know, what kind of test?"

"Don't worry. It's just a basic test, you know, math skills, reading comprehension." George looked skeptical. Then Bill added, "Don't sweat it. You worked all those crazy hours at Burger King, so I know you counted your paycheck. And how many comics did you say you read?" They'd both had a good laugh.

That first meeting had been so smooth and fun they planned to meet again the next night. Bill was seeing a play with a friend after work, but would meet George at Keller's afterwards.

Now George was wondering how it went today with Bill's friend. John was his name. His French fries had grown cold and were mostly uneaten. Worse, they were soggy. He wasn't hungry after all. He took a long and loud last slurp of the Coke. It was 4:55. He didn't want to go home just yet. What he really wanted was another good hit. It was better to do it here than at home or in the neighborhood. Snoops everywhere—especially Wilson. Yes, first get a good hit, then go home to chill, before meeting Bill later. And then what? He left his tray of uneaten fries and headed back to the sex shop.

The near emptiness earlier in the sex shop was now a parade—a silent marching band of spectators. Throughout the bleach-scented corridors, the reggae music was up-tempo; everyone cruised in um-bah umbah steps. George liked this high-energy beat, so unlike the slow wailing ballads Wilson played at home. Amid a volley of stares and half-stares, George noticed the attendant busily dispensing quarters. He jackknifed his way through the parade to a far corner. His favorite cubicles, the last three, had their red lights on, meaning they were occupied. George, in the corner, waited, avoiding the slow parade of men.

One of the guys who had stared at George, a young white guy in sneakers, with thinning hair, followed him back to the corner. The guy wore faded jeans, ripped at the knee. George wondered how the guy tolerated the cold. Really, this was mid-February. He figured the guy hadn't traveled too far from home. Not like that. Getting warm, George started fidgeting.

As he took his hands out of his pockets, he noticed the guy glance down at his crotch, then made a sudden low hissing sound—*Tssss*—like a vent blowing off steam. Several nearby heads turned, first looking at the guy, then at George. He wasn't hard, but with the thermals, George made an impression. For the moment, he became the center of attention, his every move sending waves through the already unsettled ebb and flow of movement. Powerful, silent waves. Watchful, George shifted, fidgety, his lips just barely moving with the song: "Let's get together . . . and be . . . all right." It was a nice thought, the song: "One Love." He wondered if Bill liked reggae.

Then the red light of the last booth went out and a short Hispanic man opened the door. For a second, as the man hesitated in the doorway, they looked at each other; although the man was well dressed in full business attire, he reminded George of Juan Valdez. Without the sombrero and horse. It was his thick moustache. As George moved to enter the cubicle, they slipped past each other without touching.

George closed the door and immediately collected all the scattered change from his pockets. A couple of tokens and three quarters. Some small change. He loaded the quarters into the slot. That would be enough time for a good hit, a good high. He pressed the button and on the screen came the scene with naked white guys; it seemed antiseptic, like the faint freshly mopped smell of the cubicle. He pulled the pipe from his jacket, then went for the lighter. It wasn't there. Then he remembered he'd dropped it into spit and had forgotten to replace it with matches.

Shit!

Sex noises came from his cubicle as he cracked the door to look out. In the corridor, it was still busy, but some of the faces were different. Mark, who had followed George outside earlier, was standing not far away. Several people nearby looked in at George half-hidden by the door. As Mark looked into the partly opened door, he recognized George. George saw him and silently made a match-striking motion with his hands. Puzzled, Mark watched the animation, then reached into his bomber jacket, withdrawing a book of matches. George saw them and signaled with his head for Mark to approach him. Just then a young black effeminate guy slowly made his way to the back and paused in front of Mark. He saw Mark looking at George and George motioning behind the door. He traded glances with them and smiled knowingly, apparently hip to what was going on, then swished away in a flourish of movement. Then, without hesitation, Mark stepped inside the cubicle.

He circled George as they shuffled by each other in the tiny compartment. George motioned again for the matches, lit one quickly and started to heat the pipe. Mark's eyes, surprised and curious, watched the operation for a second, then went downward.

"What's your name?" Mark asked, whispering.

From the side of his mouth came the slow response, "George."

Mark's body blocked most of the light in the cubicle. As George began to smoke, Mark strained to see in the flickering dimness, then reached down and gently grabbed George. At first, as if unawares, George didn't react; then, as the vapors began to take him higher, he directed his gaze at Mark.

"Nah, Mark . . . it's not like that," he said, his voice a raspy baritone whisper.

Mark gently squeezed again. It wasn't hard, but filled his hand comfortably. "Shees! Man, you got a big dick," he said, excited.

For a long moment, George's gaze was fixed on Mark, testing him, measuring him. Through the smoke, his eyes narrowed, locking on Mark's. He dropped his hand.

"George . . . just let me see it," he said, anxiously.

George squinted again, taking a long drag. He looked at Mark's face, half in shadow, half in light, for a long second. When his match went out, he went to strike another. And he heard himself say: "That depends . . ."

"On what?" Mark asked, dubious but interested. "You hustling?"

George heated the pipe again; he was just beginning to feel at ease, to chill again. He noticed, on the screen, a guy giving another a blow job. As he pulled on the pipe, he squinted. "You can blow me . . . for twenty bucks," he said, feeling powerful and in control. Just then he remembered he was low on cash, was broke really.

Suddenly the screen went dark and the ceiling light came on. Hot and sweating beneath his clothes, he stopped smoking. He knew the attendant periodically checked the booths when the videos weren't running. He couldn't afford to get busted. But he'd wanted to get high so bad, wanted it to last, to fly off the mountaintop. Shit. He became edgy. The bright light, the sudden exposure—he was so close. For only seconds, they stared at each other, sharing their need to give in to their desires. Then George, in a hoarse whisper to Mark, urged him to put more quarters in the machine. Mark retrieved some coins from his pocket, loading five or six quarters into the slot. Taking charge, Mark pressed the button.

It got ugly. In the new darkness of the cubicle and with their new familiarity, George started to smoke again. And Mark, more confident now, reached down again; he didn't have twenty dollars and, anyway, didn't do that, he told George. But he still wanted to see George's dick, to see him blast a nut. He offered him five dollars instead, just to play with it; he wanted to see him come. What the hell, George was starting to feel fine; now he'd get there. And besides, he was broke.

Puffing, George leaned back, while Mark, fascinated, pulled it out and stroked him, for a long while. But George never became hard, it just expanded a bit, even when Mark stretched and pulled it. Then, impatient, Mark wanted George to do it, make himself come. It was still no use. When Mark's quarters had finally run out, he didn't want to give George the five dollars he'd promised. So what if George didn't come? They argued in fast whispers for tense seconds. Finally Mark withdrew some folded bills from his front pocket and peeled off two singles, offering them to George. *Two dollars?* There was a moment of silence under the glaring overhead light. Then George, in a swift and measured movement, strong-armed Mark against the screen and took a ten-dollar bill.

What did he think this was—a game?

Later, on the train, heading home to Brooklyn, George thought about it. Mark had tried to rip him off. Tried to get over on him. Just like Mr. Picone. Trying to box him into a corner, then use him. *Do this. Do that.* For chump change. He was nobody's chump—he was a man. He didn't need them anyway. Shit.

He came in and went straight to his room. In the living room he heard soft reggae music playing and Aunt Ernestine talking. She called to him, twice, before he answered. No, he didn't want dinner. She wanted to know why. He didn't answer her. Lying across the single bed in his small bedroom, he was thinking about tonight, about seeing Bill later. Then Wilson appeared at his door. "Eh, boy," he said, in a lilting Jamaican tone, entering the room. "Don't you hear your Aunt Ernestine talking to you?"

"What?"

"You heard me."

George didn't answer, he just stared. Then Aunt Ernestine came up behind Wilson.

"Georgie, aren't you hungry?" she asked, moving in front of Wilson. "We ate already ... Let me fix you a plate."

"No ... I'm not hungry ..." he replied. "I had a snack in the street."

Wilson moved as if to speak, but his aunt continued. "How was your interview, Georgie?" He hated that baby nickname. "Did you get the job?"

"No, Aunt Ernestine ... the man didn't like me ... Made me nervous, anyway."

"Didn't like you?" Wilson chimed in. "Made you nervous? ... I told you to wear a decent shoe and pair of pants."

It was impossible. Wilson became furious and they started arguing again. Finally Aunt Ernestine calmed him down and Wilson went, shaking his head, back to the living room. It was no use. In the end she took Wilson's side. As always. *Why'd she have to go and marry that Jamaican man?* His mother had been right: Aunt Ernestine was always too proper for her own kind. It probably explained why she married so late, never had children of her own. And now she was compensating, always checking up on him. Snooping around. She and Wilson. George wanted to smoke again, bad, but couldn't.

He was pissed. When he got his new job, things would be better. He'd move out. Start seeing Bill regular, maybe. Give up those fast flings. Every weekend the same thing: get high, disco, all those "Oh-George-I-want-you-to-meet-my-friend" friends. Tired. He was tired of crashing in strange apartments, then dodging Aunt Ernestine's questions.

He grabbed a comic book and tried to read. It was Spiderman. George always thought he was like Spiderman: a man who lived in a web. Only Spiderman knew how to use it, escape it.

It was nine-forty. George got cleaned up and began to get dressed. Unlocking his closet, he pulled out a pair of loafers and a pair of navy wool slacks. He'd wear a shirt and the nice sweater he'd got for Christmas from a quick fling. What was his name? LaRon somebody.

When he was ready, he went to ask Aunt Ernestine for some money. She was in the kitchen, cleaning up. Wilson had already left for his night job.

"Twenty dollars?" Aunt Ernestine asked, surprised, turning in midstroke from wiping off the stove. "What happened to the twenty dollars Wilson gave you yesterday?"

George frowned. "I spent it . . . I told you I had eaten in the street." He looked at her, resentment creeping into his voice again. She eyed him, noticing his casual clothing. She knew he was going out again.

"Georgie, I don't have twenty dollars," she said, placatingly. "You should have asked me earlier." She stopped as George frowned again. "Wait, I think I have some small change . . ." She pulled down a canister, opened it, and retrieved two folded five-dollar bills.

"Here, Georgie." She offered him the two fives.

As he took it, he smiled; and his smile immediately blossomed on her face. She didn't like to see him upset. She replaced the canister. "I keep the change from my grocery shopping—my emergency household money, for when Wilson isn't home," she explained. George made a mental note of this. He turned to leave. "Oh, by the way," she said, "your friend Larry called." George stopped and turned back.

"Larry?" He looked puzzled. "I don't know any . . . Oh, you mean LaRon."

"Yes, that's him," she agreed. "Nice boy ... so polite ... Didn't you see the message I left in your room?"

"I thought I asked you not to go messing around in my room!" he said, half-whining, half-hollering. He couldn't take it. He stormed out.

As he walked the long blocks to Keller's, he was still angry. No privacy. No fucking respect. They just didn't understand. None of them. Except Bill. He came real close.

When George entered Keller's, the Friday night crowd was just as lively as yesterday's. Keller's was a mostly black bar in the village, on occasion sprinkled with a handful of white and Latino guys. The merriment around the entrance stopped for a second as several people looked at him, then it resumed. He searched the multitude of faces for Bill's. The jukebox wailed with Whitney Houston; she was singing "You Give Good Love." Then he saw Bill, in the back, at the bar. As George came up to him, Bill saw him, too. A bright smile sprang to Bill's face. George was also smiling. A small group nearby watched with interest as they exchanged smiles.

"Hello, stranger," Bill said, jokingly, glancing at his watch. It was almost eleven o'clock. "I thought you weren't coming ..." He noticed George's outfit. "You look nice ..."

"Well." George laughed at the compliment. "I was reading ... then I fell asleep." He began unzipping his jacket; he was getting warm.

"A comic?" Bill asked, assuming.

"You guessed it—Spiderman." They both laughed. "How was your play?" George asked, with curiosity.

"It was great. It was *Six Degrees of Separation,* about a young black guy who tricks some rich white people for a while, getting over on them ... We really liked it. I told my friend I had to meet you here later, so he came along. He just went to the bathroom."

They continued talking, but George was thirsty, his mouth becoming suddenly dry. He started to order himself a drink, then noticed Bill's was empty. He felt expansive, deciding to treat Bill and his friend to a round. Hell, he had twenty bucks to burn. Then Bill explained that his friend was leaving soon, that he didn't feel well. So George just ordered a beer for himself and a Scotch and water for Bill. As he turned to pay, with the ten he had, he heard Bill saying something to someone nearby. Then, all of a sudden—"You fucking bastard!"

It was Mark from the peep show. Heads turned toward Mark at the outburst. George looked around in time to see Bill's shocked expression. A sudden mixture of surprise and fear welled in George; he stood there, paralyzed. Bill grabbed Mark, who was cursing and reaching for George. Immediately a space opened up around them. Bill tried to restrain Mark; he kept asking what was going on. But it was no use. Mark pushed past Bill and shoved George against the bar. In the soulful cacophony of Keller's, a fight broke out.

The bouncer from the front was trying to get through the crowd. In the roar of the confusion, someone's beer bottle shattered on the floor. Then Mark shouted out that George had ripped him off earlier, in a peep show, that he was a crack fiend.

It was then that George punched Mark in the face. Mark fell backwards into a cigarette machine. Bill went toward Mark, trying to stay between them. Then the bouncer came up behind George and grabbed him; several others joined in, helping to restrain him.

In the end, they had let him go. Several people had said that Mark started it, had pushed George first. Still, they threw George out.

An hour later, George was still trembling. He wanted to smoke real bad again, to get high, be cool again. To chill again. He had spent his last money. He opened the door to his compartment and peeked out; someone from the corridor looked in and saw him. George was half-hidden by the door, his zipper down. He had his dick in his hand, flipping it up and down slowly—almost in time with the reggae music. It was another Marley classic: "Redemption Song."

Church

G. Winston James

Eerie. That's what it was. Eerie walking into that church after all those years. It was like hearing myself say, "Why do I gotta go to church, Mama?" all over again. It was like hoping that it wasn't first Sunday this Sunday and praying that if I had to be there, at least the Gospel Choir would be singing. I felt, walking out of the bright light of the summer morning and into the calm dim of the chapel, that I was stepping into the past. The past of a family and friends and a Jersey town I'd left long ago for a bigger life that could contain this young boy's grown-up dreams.

It was all Black people. Black women mostly. Dressed to the teeth. I'd almost forgotten what it meant to go to a Black Baptist church. This was the place where the well-to-do and the can-hardlies mingled and shook hands with equal pretense. And it was beautiful to see, even when I was a child. Though I never could stand those old women pinching my cheeks and mussing my hair. The church was a place where you could witness the Black family defining itself: the faithful wife, the obedient children, the disappearing older children and the often absent husband. Every Sunday was an experience, though each was painfully similar to the one before it. I'd chosen to leave it all behind, mostly because I thought that too much of anything just couldn't be good for you. And I'd stayed away because I realized I was right.

But here I was coming back. Following behind my mama, as she ushered my niece and nephew to their seats. All I could think as I walked was how the intervening years seem to slip away when you come face-to-face with something you were accustomed to. Some of the backs of the heads were the same today as they were ten years ago. The stained-glass windows were just as stained and no more or less allegorical than they had been when the Pastor had interpreted them for us years before. This was Sunday, all right. So I left my family, as I always did, and sat where I used to sit and talk with my friends, though they weren't there today. Today I would simply go over our old conversations and hope that none of the congregation noticed my lips as they mimed the past.

"Good morning, son!" I felt a hand on my shoulder. "We ain't seen you in such a long time."

"I know," I said. "I've been away, Sister Bailey." She smelled strongly of a perfume applied by hands that had long ago forgotten the meaning of enough.

"Well, you welcome back," she said. She lightly pinched my cheek, then patted my face and looked at me with her head slightly tilted to the side, her white handkerchief dangling from her palm. The wrinkles in her face and her deep-set eyes made me think of gentleness and grandmamas, even though I never knew mine. "Such a handsome boy," she added. "You enjoy the service. OK." She smiled broadly. "The Lord's got a message for us all."

"I will, sister," I said, as I remembered all the sermons I'd slept through when my friends weren't there to keep me company. I thought about Sister Bailey. About how old she was, and how old she had always been. I decided to give the church its due; it had a way of giving some people the what all to keep going on.

It was third Sunday, I believed. I picked up my bulletin and quickly flipped through it just to check if this was the Sunday the Gospel Choir would be singing. Sure enough, it was, and I saw happily that some things just don't change. It wouldn't make a difference what the Reverend had to say, as long as I could feel that music mixing with the marrow of my bones.

Oh yes. Oh yes, I could remember Almetra singing "One Day at A Time, Sweet Jesus." I recalled how Sunday after Sunday it would move me to tears. Singing. Singing. And I could see Grace, born to a name that defined her and guided her to open her mouth in the service of the Lord. She sang. Yes, she did. "God Is." It was "God Is" every time she stood up in front of the choir. Every time she gospelled, "He promised to lead me, never to leave me. He's never ever come short of His word," dear God, she was joined by the chorus and the Holy Spirit as it worked on even the least holy of the holies in the congregation. Yes, this was Church!

But even the most holy of them were hypocrites. No matter how many times the Lord bent them low, and made them holler, "Save me, Jesus! Save me, my God. I'm a sinner," I could still see the flames of self-righteousness licking at their heels. I always thought that I must have been the only one that God didn't give shoes, because I felt the fire. So I walked slowly—so as not to stoke the flame—away.

I was lost in recollection during the processional hymn, so I sort of missed the ushers walking down the center aisle—the way they fanned out as the Preachers climbed those short steps to the altar. We had all sat down again before I came to. And there he was, Reverend Rollins up in the pulpit. He had never been a fiery Preacher—though at times he tried—but he was a well-respected man in the Baptist community and in the city. In his way, he sort of resembled Martin Luther King. It was in the roundness of the face, I think, and the little moustache. I'd always thought that perhaps one person too many had spoken of that resemblance, and that that had left the right Reverend feeling that he had naught to do but to achieve more than he was able to dream. When he entered city politics, and then allowed city politics to enter the church, he lost much of the credibility he had as my Preacher. I found that I would sooner trust him with my vote than with my soul. Unfortunately, I was still too young to vote.

I found myself scanning the congregation and not paying too much attention to what was going on at the front of the chapel. I was trying to locate those schoolmates of mine who had never left our hometown, and who never would for fear that there was something more out there to be taught, let alone learned. In a sense, I was still bitter, because I used to hate them all for fitting in so well. Then I would get angry at myself because I'd learned that hate was a sin. It was many years and many miles before I appreciated the amazing usefulness of the word *dislike*. But now I only watched for them at the edges where our separate worlds slid across one another. And I marvelled at their ability to become an integral part of such an old and oft-forgotten town.

We were more than halfway into the service before I admitted to myself that I really wasn't there. I was doing more wondering and surmising about things than I was doing participating. Even as I came to that realization, I was wondering whether all the "uh-hums" and the "yeses" from the congregation weren't actually these other people inadvertently affirming conclusions they'd come to in their own private wonderings. Speaking responses aloud to questions they had silently been thinking. Then I started asking myself if maybe church wasn't mainly about this: bouncing your own ideas about life, love and religion off the walls and the ceiling of the chapel in hopes that maybe one or two of them will come back and hit you squarely in the face, and maybe make you moan.

When the Deaconess called for the welcome of visitors and announcements, it dawned on me that I had indeed come into church today for a purpose. To be among family. As she stood up in front of the pulpit, it reminded me of the time when the Pastor had stood by my side in that same spot and had asked the church whether they would second and ratify the motion from the Deacon Board to allow me to become a member of the church.

He said, "All in favor say aye." And I bowed my head for fear that he would be answered with a chorus of nays, but he wasn't. I was put on that path that led to baptism in the cool waters in the pool up high at the back of the chapel, above the altar. He'd whispered, "Hold your breath." I did, but not long enough. When he dipped me into the water, I suddenly felt that his strong arms wouldn't be enough to hold me and keep me from drowning in the knee-deep water. I let go and the holy water filled my nostrils and my eyes. He lifted me snorting and gagging to my feet before the congregation. They chanted "Amen" and I breathed. Relieved. Reborn.

"Are there any visitors?" the Deaconess asked. "If so, please stand and state your name."

I rose to my feet. Away so long. Now as a visitor in my own home. "Good morning, Calvary," I said. "My name is Langston Ambrose, and I am a member of this church, though I've been away a long time."

"Well, welcome home," she said. "It's good to see you. All grown-up." She smiled.

"Thank you. I'm very glad to be back."

I was about to take my seat when Reverend Rollins rose to his feet in the pulpit and went to the podium. He dropped his pastorly demeanor for a moment and said, "Langston Ambrose, come here," as he motioned with his arm. Then he said, "Praise the Lord that the lamb never strays far from the fold."

This was actually what I'd expected. To be called to the podium and asked to account for all the years of my absence. I went smiling. I shook his hand, felt his still steely grip, and wondered again what he might be trying to prove with it.

"It's been a long time." He smiled, still holding my right hand and gripping my left arm with his other hand.

"Yes. It has," I replied.

"Now, did you graduate already?" he asked. I sort of chuckled then, hoping that he would remember all the years that had passed, so that I wouldn't have to embarrass him. But he didn't recall, so I said, "Yeah, Pastor Rollins. Ten years ago."

"Ten years!" he exclaimed, grabbing my shoulders as though I were a runaway child that had only just returned home. "Time," he said. "Our young ones are growing up. Praise the Lord." He held me out from him, as if appraising his young son, then asked, "Now, you went to that school in . . ."

"New York," I finished for him. "New York University. I graduated in 1982."

"Amen," came the response from the congregation. For a young black man to go to college, let alone graduate, was a reason for celebration.

"What'd you get your degree in?"

"I earned a bachelors degree in Latin American Studies," I said.

"Well, amen. And what have you been doing?"

"Well, a lot of things, Reverend Rollins," I said, smiling, knowing that he and the rest actually cared. "I worked for a couple of years here and there doing international relief work with people like Save the Children and CARE before setting off to travel on my own. I've, uhmm, even written some books—"

"Praise the Lord," he interrupted. "We've got an author. Heh heh," he laughed. "What kind of books?"

"Books of poetry, a collection of short stories, and one novel." I felt as if I were divulging childhood secrets. There I was confessing publicly from the pulpit about my writing when no one in my family had ever seen any of my work. I'd been writing and being published for a long time, yet it still seemed like such a private act, the fruit of which I shared with particular people at particular times. My parents never could understand why I never shared my writing with them, but I had my reasons. Aside from some of the obvious ones, ever since I was a child, I never really thought they appreciated the things that I did that were art, especially when my particular art tended to be so revealing.

"When are we gonna see these books?" the Reverend asked. "You're gonna give us some copies to put in the church library, aren't you?"

"Sure," I laughed. "I hadn't thought about it," I lied. The fact of the matter was that I knew that it would be a long time before there was room on Calvary's shelves for my books. But standing up there, I thought just maybe.

"So where have you been that you couldn't come to church every once in a while?"

"Well, I've been a lot of places. I've lived in Venezuela, Brazil, Angola, Mozambique, Switzerland and England." I took a deep breath. "I don't stay put much." A few people in the congregation simultaneously "uhmmed."

"Well, no, you don't," the Reverend answered. "You're a man of the world, huh?" He patted my shoulder.

"I guess."

"So how long are you gonna be with us? You back to stay?"

"Yes. I'll be living here for a while."

"That's good. So we'll see more of you."

"I think so."

"What made you decide to come home, Mr. World Traveler?" Reverend Rollins asked. "You seen it all or you just back for a change?"

"Well, not really, Reverend Rollins," I said. I hesitated a moment. "No, I've got a reason. You see, I'm dying. I wanted to come home to die. Ain't no use in dying someplace where only a few people even know your whole name."

In that moment, I tried to recall if I'd ever heard such silence in that church. Tried to remember if I'd ever stood this close to a man and not heard him breathe. For a while I was trapped in the vacuum I'd created. "I've got a kind of cancer," I breathed. "It's eating me up inside. That's why I came home. And in a way that's sort of why I came to church, Reverend Rollins—hoping that you would call me up here. Because I've got something to say."

"That's all right," Sister Bailey crooned. "Tell us."

I looked to Reverend Rollins and he nodded his assent to let me continue. Strangely, I wondered then about the structure of the Church. I couldn't quite figure out where the hierarchy started after the Trinity. Right then I thought that it just had to be the Deaconesses who sat most close to God. But what would Sister Bailey have said if my cancer had been showing all over my face, instead of on my legs and all tied up in my intestines? She probably wouldn't even have dared to touch me, I bet. But there was no point in thinking about it, asking people to accept more than they can fit into their world.

"I've only lived a short time," I began. "But as you've all heard, I've lived a full life. And I'm not afraid to die."

"The Lord is thy shepherd," someone shouted. "Amen. Amen.'

"I don't want to die. Don't get me wrong, Reverend Rollins. I feel like there's still so much to do. So much more to see. But it doesn't do any good to complain, does it?" I tried to laugh. To lighten the mood. "But one thing I've lived with for as long as I can remember has been weighing on me lately. And I've just got to get it out."

"What is it, son?" asked Sister Bailey. She was standing in her place. I thought to myself how beautiful her spirit was and how today she was the church for me.

I had so many things to get off my chest and out into the air that I almost didn't know where to begin. But then I remembered where I was and who all was listening, so I decided to let most of those sleeping dogs lie right where they'd grown so fat over the years. I figured there wouldn't be any use in talking if everyone decided not to listen. So I chose the only thing that was really close to my heart, yet seemingly benign enough that it could tell my story without really touching on the facts of my life.

"It's my love for children, Church," I said. "I've never had any, so I've never had the chance to raise any, but I love them just the same. I see too many of them wasting their lives being angry the wrong way. Being rebellious in a pitiful way."

"I know it," someone said.

"We've got to teach them, Reverend Rollins. We've got to teach them what it means to live. Dying isn't hard. I can tell you that. Hell, I've been doing it for a long time. But, now, living. That's another question."

"Yes. Uh-hum."

"Reverend Rollins, promise me that when you tell the church that they won't know the minute nor the hour, that you let them know that it's not just for God. When you're staring death in the face, you've got to come to terms with yourself and your life before you ever set eyes on God. Tell them that it's all right to go out there and fall and get hurt. God made bones to heal. And tell them that the world is a big place and that there's somewhere out there where they'll be happy, and that they shouldn't stop looking until they find it. Or they shouldn't stop struggling 'til they build it."

I looked over at Pastor Rollins, and was suddenly ashamed for making him "Johnny-on-the-spot" this way. His face said in a thousand ways that this was not what he'd planned for this Sunday's service.

"I'm sorry," I said. "I guess I'm just being selfish, taking up all this time."

"No. You're not," Reverend Rollins said. "You're saying

what you feel like saying. Who am I to say that it's not the Lord speaking through you? I prepared a sermon. It's true. But maybe so did He." Then he turned to the congregation. "Can I hear amen?"

"Amen."

"Can I hear a hallelujah?" he asked.

"Hallelujah!" they yelled. "Hallelujah."

"Thank you, Calvary," I said. "I've seen so much death in my life—you just don't know! Children starving, senseless wars, stupid drugs, AIDS. People just dying all over the place. So young. I've stood by too many bedsides. Listened to too many stories about what they would've done and what they wish they could do. There can't be much worse, Reverend Rollins, than to realize when you're just about to die, that you haven't really lived. So tell them to live."

"God grants them the gift of life," Reverend Rollins said. "It's not for any man to tell God's children how to live."

"I'm sure," I said. "But He also gives them other gifts and talents that they can choose to use productively or not. I'm just asking you to tell them to really use this one." I smiled. "It's probably the most important of all."

He looked at me for a moment. Sizing me up, it seemed. Then he said, "Of course, I'll tell them." I guessed he'd decided that he didn't want a public debate.

"Now, are you really OK?" he asked. "If not, you've got the whole church family to help you."

"Yeah, I'll be OK," I said. "I've just got one regret." As I thought about what I was about to say, a lump formed in my throat. And I stood there in silence, wondering if this was the place to do this.

"What is it, Langston?" the pastor asked.

"I just—" I stopped to fight back a sob.

"That's all right," someone said. "Take your time."

"Well, it's something I guess I never outgrew. I saw my mother cry once. She'd told me to hurry back from playing outside, and I'd said something like 'Ah, Ma' before I went out. When I got back she gathered my brother and one of my sisters and me around her. She lowered her head, then she said softly, 'Do you all hate me too?' Then she cried. One of my sisters had told her she hated her because she corrected her about something. I've felt since that day that maybe if I had said something like 'Of course, Mom. I'll be back,' maybe she wouldn't have had to cry. I promised myself then that I would never hurt my momma again. I never wanted to see her cry again."

I took a few deep breaths as the tears started rolling down my cheeks. "And now I'm gonna die. And my momma's gonna cry." I couldn't hold back the grief. "She's gonna cry. Cry again because of me." I started to sob.

Then I looked up to see her. My momma. Someone was holding her, trying to console her. But she was struggling against them. Fighting to get up, even as my niece and nephew slept on. She cried, "That's my son. That's my baby." And she bolted from her pew and carried all her sixty years running to the front of the chapel. The whole way she was shaking and screaming, "That's my son! Oh, my God, that's my baby. Can't no AIDS just take my baby! Lawd Jesus, I love him too much!"

Before she reached me, the congregation lit up with the Holy Spirit. Two women and some man jumped up from their seats and fell in the aisles, convulsing. They were just shaking and kicking. Some people were screaming, "Praise God!" And others were just wailing.

I heard Sister Bailey try to start up a chorus of "Swing Low Sweet Chariot," but her "coming forth to carry me home" was drowned out by all the hollering. Then as my momma grabbed me up in her arms and pulled me against her breasts, I got lost in my childhood. I think I dreamed that a sweet soprano voice cut through the hysteria—floating from the back of the chapel, from in front of the doors. The voice sang, "One day at a time, sweet Jesus. That's all I'm asking of you." I whispered, "Almetra" because I thought I saw her. She'd just walked into the chapel. In my dream, her voice seemed to attract the Holy Spirit like a magnet. It lifted the holiness from the congregation and it travelled on her every note. Then the Gospel Choir rose up behind me to accompany her.

When my sobs woke me from my dream, the choir was up. They were singing the final verses of "Hush, Somebody's Calling My Name." The music gave the congregation some focus again. As we all recovered and softly sobbed together, Reverend Rollins asked that we stand and pray. And we did. Then he asked the choir to render a selection.

As the choir prepared, my mother and I started for our seats. I felt ashamed. Not because I'd cried in front of a whole bunch of people, but because my momma had loved me enough to declare my affliction when I had been too frightened to do it. While we walked, I looked around at the chapel, and thought to myself, "This is Church." I felt my momma's arm around my waist, and knew, "This is family." I cried my tears, and witnessed, "This is love."

Then I turned around and looked at the altar. I wondered, teary-eyed, those three truths notwithstanding, whether there actually was a God. That's when I saw Grace stepping out from her place in the choir. I thought "God Is." But when she began, she was singing something different. It was "Better Than Blessed." She sang and I thought, "Well, goddamn, what a Black woman can do to a song!"

She sang, "I've got God, the Father above me. And I've got Jesus Christ, His son, walking beside me. I've got the Holy Spirit within me. All of God's angels, all around me. And I am blessed. Better than blessed. Thank you, Lord."

I thought then that she was singing about more than God. Walking with my momma, and crying with my niece and nephew, I knew that she was singing about family. She was singing about the Church family. The Black family. Even in its weakness, it was stronger than all tribulation.

Grace was singing, "I used to complain that I had no shoes, then I saw a man who had no feet to use. And I am blessed. Better than blessed. Thank you, Lord."

I realized that that's just what I was talking about. Realizing how slight most of our limitations really are. Then I found my-self wishing that I could believe in more than just gospel music. I wanted to believe in God because of how good that burning in my heart felt at that moment. So I thought about the verses Grace used to sing. I remembered "God is the joy and the strength of my life." And I wondered if maybe God wasn't whatever made you truly happy in life. Then I looked up at the ceiling of the chapel. I threw my question to the beams. As

Grace was singing, "I am blessed" one more time, my question bounced off the ceiling, fell down and slapped me to the floor. And I cried, "I'm gay! Praise God! Hallelujah!"

And I heard the congregation say, "Amen!"

The Pool

K. Anthony Appiah

*Everybody who can afford the club does afford the club; here, on
the island, we are short on social institutions. But nobody makes an
appearance by the pool until late afternoon. We—we who live here, I
mean—do not swim in the sun's full heat; and, since the pool is ours,
the tourists who risk sunstroke daily on the beaches never visit it. In
the end, I suppose, we all depend on the foreigners who chase our
sun, our beaches, our beautiful brown girls and boys. Traders and
hustlers, restaurateurs and hoteliers, doctors and lawyers, even those
of us who think of ourselves as separate, up in our plantation estates,
depend on the tourists to buoy up the economy. In the end, we are
all epiphytes on the trunk of the holiday trade: those of us who don't
serve our visitors live off those who do. Here, at the club, however,
we can forget about them and pretend that the island belongs only to
us. Now that I am half a foreigner myself, I enjoy my summer afternoon visits. I expect to be alone.*

But a couple of days ago something broke the pattern.

It was very still there by the swimming pool. A bright sun,
the peaceful sounds of the surrounding gardens (the mutter of
insects and birdsong and the wind in the leaves), a single idle
swimmer in the water. I stretched easily as I lay on the tiles,
and looked up, eyes shaded with a lazy hand, to where the
lifeguard sat in his high chair, dozing. Too early yet for most
of the club's members; I was pleased to be almost alone. I didn't

know the boy swimming, but the lifeguard I have always known, the one constant fixture all the years since my first childhood visits to the pool.

"Who's that in the water?"

"Some boy."

"You know him?"

"He's new."

I knew that the lifeguard would not wonder at the question; would think my interest in the swimmer a pretence, a device to establish our desultory conversation. I couldn't ask more and I didn't need to. Even though I had not been to the pool for over a year, he and I must talk only as much as if I had been away for a summer weekend in the hills; it was characteristic, somehow, that he had asked me only, "Where have you been this year?" and then lost interest, when I said I was still in America, still teaching music.

But if the boy was new, it meant he was not the younger brother of one of my friends; "new" meant unconnected, without roots, unimportant in the lifeguard's social scheme. The boy pulled himself out of the water: height around six foot, slim, prettily muscled. As he wiped the towel over his face, I saw that he was handsome . . . beautiful, perhaps. Then, with water glistening on his dark brown skin, he padded along the tiles, towards the changing room, passing within a few feet of my head.

I said, "Hello," trying to sound simply cheerful, raising myself onto my elbows. "You're new."

The boy stopped, smiled, sat on his haunches.

"You aren't?" His accent was not the local variety of English. I couldn't yet place it.

"I've been coming here since I was five . . . since before you were born."

"But not recently."

"No, not for a year. I've been away."

"Glad to be back?"

"Yes."

The boy stretched out beside me, in a motion of such utter surrender that I glanced swiftly, involuntarily, across to the lifeguard, to see if he had noticed; but he only scanned the pool, dispassionate, checking that it really was empty, and then wandered away, as if to escape the disturbance of our conversation.

"I'm Peter. Peter . . ." I stopped. Lying in the sun, dressed only in swimming trunks, a family name seemed silly. And, anyway, family name meant family, and I was beginning to hope—somewhere in a remote region of my consciousness—that this idle chatter would lead to something I'd rather my family not know about.

"Joe," the boy said.

I thought I could now hear the accent the boy was trying to hide.

"American?"

"No, but I've been in the States a few years."

"So have I."

It was at this point that the conversation began to get interesting. Because, instead of inquiring further, the boy said: "I know. I know all about you." And smiled.

I wondered what that was supposed to mean. I saw the boy wanting to tell me what he knew and how he knew it; so I took pleasure in not asking, saying, "Oh," and looking across the pool to where a crow had just settled and was pecking at the grass.

"You're a musician in New York. You live with an actor called Jonathan. Your parents live here. Your father is a big lawyer, a politico. Shall I go on?"

I decided I was not going to fool the boy with a pretended lack of interest. Absurd, I thought, to continue—but fun. And so I stifled an exaggeratedly implausible yawn before I said: "No. Tell me something surprising. You could have read it in the newspapers. I already know all that."

"Jonathan told me 'all that.' "

I had no time to arrange my reaction to the quiet mockery in his repetition of my last phrase; puzzlement drew tight the muscles of my jaw, screwed up my eyes, until, all other possibilities ruled out, I knew (I should have guessed, of course) who I thought this was. I spoke carefully.

"In that case your name isn't Joe; it's got to be Jamie."

It was the boy's turn to look surprised.

"You're wrong."

"If you're not Jamie, why did Jonathan tell you about me?"

"I met him in New York a couple of months ago at a party. I told him I was going to be here this summer; he told me about you because he said you would be here too. He also said you always swam at this club. I've been coming here for a week, waiting for you ... Who's Jamie?"

"Jonathan's lover."

"What does that make you?"

"His roommate."

"If you're his roommate, why don't you know what his boyfriend looks like?"

I laughed. If this is Jamie, I thought, he's a clever boy. "I've been here most of the time since they met; and J. is very secretive about his conquests till he's sure of them."

"I see."

"We'll meet when I get back."

He nodded slightly, and his gaze caught mine and held it, staring me down until I turned away. I lay back and stared up into the empty sky.

For a minute we said nothing. (So many possibilities to consider, I needed time to savor the game.) Then I spoke without looking at him. "Since Jonathan told you everything about me, you knew I would find you irresistibly attractive. You have five seconds to tell me whether you took that into account in deciding to wait here for me." "One ... two ... three ... four ..."

The boy gazed at me languidly, waiting out the fourth second before he said: "Yes."

"And ..."

"Jonathan showed me a picture of you. If we go back to my hotel, we can do what I've been wanting to do since I saw it."

You see, the pool at the club is, for me, the kind of place whose familiarity never fails to please. I can remember so many childhood Sundays, after church; sitting there, by the water; my brother and I splashing about noisily with our friends; my mother handing each of us our sandwiches ("One for Richard ... one for Peter ..."); the tables, with their sunshades of dried palm leaves; the rusting garden chairs; the lifeguard, in T-shirt and swimming trunks, motionless in his high chair.

Richard was six years older than I, and I remember still the reluctance with which I followed him into all those races along the long length of the pool; races he always won. Growing up, for me, meant winning one of those races. One day I would be big enough. Sometimes I thought he might always be bigger than I, might always be, as he had always been, a better swimmer. Now that I can look down at the tabletops, remembered from eye level, and measure in that downward glance my distance from those days, I find reassurance even in the memory of my numberless defeats. The easy idleness of the lifeguard (of course, always the same ageless lifeguard, never surprised at my twice-yearly visits); the rust on the chairs; the same hard odor of the chlorine. All this pleases.

So that when I come here now, home for a holiday, my mother no longer with me (no longer any role for her as manager of the sandwiches), the remembered rush of those long-ago Sundays is part of the calm I feel in this place I possess so securely.

This calm, with the childhood memories that feed it, is, I think, the reason that I, among all my friends, am the only one who finds nothing sexy about swimming and all that surrounds it. Of course, when I come here during the week, there are few people about, and none of them is one of those poolside California beauties, underdressed even in this near naked world, who populate Jonathan's fantasies; but even on Sundays, when all the brightest and best of our island beauties stalk the tiles, rippling in their display, I see them only with my boy's eyes. Their muscles are reminders of Richard's fine fifteen-year-old body, envied but not desired.

Richard has been gone a long while now; there is no other way I can remember him. Since he died, no one in the family—least of all me—has been quite the same. Perhaps it is his ghost policing my desires.

So I still don't really know why, when that boy slipped out of the water, I was prepared for desire. As he padded along by the pool towards me, I thought how good he looked, how healthy, how strong. In short, I thought only what I had thought so many times about my brother. I had asked the lifeguard earlier who he was, and he had said that he did not know. And so I knew he was a tourist. I spoke to Jamie first only out of a sense that I, as a citizen of this little kingdom, should welcome an alien visitor (though curious, too, to know how he had entered our world).

Then, in an instant—it sounds absurd, but it really was an instant—he overthrew a lifetime's tradition of seeing the pool as sexless, and my boy's eyes were man's eyes again.

He didn't wait until we got to the hotel. As I drove down the mountain into town, he trailed his hand gently across my neck, tightening his grip occasionally, like a masseur who has found a point of tension. But there was no system to it, as if he was, in fact, only exercising his own hand. At one point, he reached over and kissed me lightly on the cheek. It seemed foolish to explain to him that everybody here knew me, knew my father (and, though it mattered less, my mother), and that because of that, what he was doing scared the hell out of me. On the island, as I had often heard my father's friends say, "nobody queer." It is part of our official fantasy that the boys on the beaches, who have found that there is more than one way to work in the tourist industry, do not enjoy what they do . . . or have been corrupted by foreigners. For a while, as his hand roamed gently over my shoulders, I tried to relax, to forget about all the people who might see. Then I looked in my rearview mirror and saw one of the crazy old taxis that career about the town rattling towards us at impossible speed. "There's a car behind us; please stop doing that." (Fool, I thought, why has the panic entered your voice?)

"Turn right."

I was too distracted to disobey. We turned down a dirt path, which ran into a field of high sugarcane. I stopped the car. "What is this about?"

"Now there isn't a car behind us."

He took me out of the car, dragging his vast green towel, undressing me as we walked. Then he stretched out the towel and pulled me down to him. Sex, he certainly knew about. With tongue and hands, with all of his beautiful, hard body, he matched and molded my desire to his. All the time, part of me was thinking how strange it was that I had never done this here in the fields before. I remembered the first time I had sex with another boy, at school, far away in England, on the playing fields under a starry sky. And the romance of the memory seemed now something tawdry because I had waited ten years to fuck on the bare earth at home.

After sex (I've never known how to write about it, and the mechanics, after all, are always very much the same) we lay for a while in the sun. I, trying to hide the fact that my ears were tuned to catch the faintest sound of a human approach; he, humming quietly and strumming an invisible accompaniment on the muscles of my belly. After what seemed like hours, I raised myself slowly and pulled on my pants and my shirt. "Maybe we should get back to the hotel."

"Sure. Come back and have a drink in my room."

While the boy showered and dressed, I wandered around his hotel room. The hotel was the best in town (actually, I think we own a large chunk of it); it's reasonably comfortable and fabulously expensive. I opened a drawer by the bed, without interest, and saw in it a small, blue passport. American. It was in the name of James Anderson. I laughed, a sharp laugh. I had been right. This was Jonathan's lover: beautiful, beloved Jamie. Jonathan had never expected him to be faithful, he had told me that as soon as he met Jamie. But Jonathan could not have imagined so elaborate an infidelity.

A quiet knock on the door sent me scurrying into the bathroom. "There's somebody at the door. I'll wait here." The boy forced a smile; his look meant "you're being paranoid.' In a few moments, he returned with a couple of daiquiris. "It was just room service."

I said, "Thank you," held my glass up when Jamie made to clink it in a toast, and took a long sip. Jonathan's lover said: "I lied to you."

"Oh," I said, and then "I know," pointing to the passport on the bed, where I had tossed it.

"Are you angry?"

"Not yet."

"I was going to tell you at once, but somehow, when you said my name first, said that I had to be Jamie, I couldn't. I could hear in your voice that being Jamie meant that I was off limits." Then after a pause, quietly: "Now I feel bad."

"Postcoital depression," I said as if to no one in particular, my gaze wandering to the window and out into the town. Then, drawing a sharp breath, I focused again on the boy and the situation. As the dark eyes engaged earnestly with mine, I saw that the boy wanted, above all, to play out the scene. And then I knew how to play it.

"What are you trying to do? So far you have put my most important friendship at risk, and made me act like a fool in my hometown on an island where gossip spreads like wildfire. Do you plan to ring Jonathan and tell him now, or are you saving that up for later?"

"You are angry."

"No. I really am not. I would like you to think about what you are up to and then give me an explanation of it. And if it makes as little sense as I anticipate, I shall forget the fact that you are so damn gorgeous and walk out."

"I don't see why Jonathan should mind," Jamie said, drawing me back to my last question.

I shrugged my shoulders and turned to look again out of the window. "I would not like to speculate about the exact details of your understanding with Jonathan; but I take it it does not include seducing me."

"It doesn't exclude it. I said I might sleep with someone else here in the islands. Does he ever sleep with you?"

"You mean, for old times' sake? We sleep together, yes; if we're both drunk, or one of us is depressed. But we haven't fucked—if you will pardon the expression—for a couple of years . . . Why am I telling you what you already know?"

"I don't. I've never asked J. about your sex life. And why do you think I'm betraying him? I still want him. I just wanted both of you, I guess. You share your apartment, your car, almost everything else; why can't you share me?"

I said nothing. I was thinking: "How hard it is to untangle why Jonathan and I live together still, long after we have driven desire out of the bond between us. And why should I try to find the language to make our life clear to this manipulative kid who doesn't give a damn about the delicate balance of my life with J.?" Then I thought: "This boy believes sex is its own thing, that it can be kept apart from everything else. Maybe J. told him that to reassure him about me. J. never bothers his boys with the truth." And then I thought: "I have nothing more to say to young James Anderson."

My mind floated free. In a chalet across the gardens I could see a TV flickering, and I wondered, without malice, if the boy had gotten this idea from a soap opera. Outside it was getting dark, most of the lights of the town were now lit. It would still be very hot out there, out of the air-conditioning; and it was too late to go back to the club for a swim. I had lost interest in this conversation; was enjoying the sense of being at home in my own place. The atmosphere of my childhood, the shapes, the smells, the warmth surrounded me in the town, out there; all I had to do was walk out into it. Jamie moved up and put a hand on my shoulder from behind, so that I turned sharply around, leaving his hand hanging, for a second, in the air. There was no threat in my gesture, only surprise at the broken chain of association; but Jamie flinched, worried for an instant. I thought: "I really don't want to play anymore." When I spoke again I tried to keep the distance out of my voice.

"Do you know where Jonathan is?"

"In Connecticut."

"Good, you know the number. Call him and ask *him* about sharing. And explain how the issue arose, would you? I don't want him blaming me."

The boy took his shirt off, and then his shorts. "I met J. five weeks ago. I'm ahead with him. You and I have a month to even things out. Then we'll discuss what's next. Okay?"

I chuckled, watching James Anderson now from infinitely far away, as if this were a humorous episode in the life of a stranger. I began to summon the little energy I needed to resist the naked body, gathering the impetus for farewell and departure.

"Crude bribery. It's not a good idea. I get too much of a kick from resisting temptation ... Jonathan should have told you that. It's the Presbyterian upbringing. Look, I'm going home. I'll call Jonathan. I'll tell him what's happened. I'll see you at twelve-thirty tomorrow for lunch at the Palace Restaurant. If you want something to do with that overcharged body of yours this evening, I saw a good-looking white American boy looking you over when you came in. Maybe you could persuade him you're a native. He's probably looking for experience, so you'll be doing him a favor ... And thanks"—by now I was smiling pleasantly—"for the drink."

"If you go now, I promise I won't see either of you again."

"It won't work, kid. And anyway, what you need you can get from the quiet American."

When I flipped open the drawer by the bed, idly, and found his passport, I thought, at first, only how awful this would be for Jonathan. Here I was, his closest friend, his only family, and I had been taken to bed by his lover. Altruism lasted a moment. My next thought was what a fool I had been, how easily taken in; picked up in the innocent sanctuary of my childhood afternoons. And then I was amused by the scene of melodrama that I imagined (and later knew) had led Jamie to such an elaborate dissimulation. By the time he returned with the daiquiris, I was back lamenting the loss of my innocence. "In this of all places, at home ..."

I knew that I had to call Jonathan now, or the delay would imply guilt or complicity. But I didn't know what tack to take on the phone to him. I tried to tell him, as simply as I could manage, what had happened. I suppose I must have sounded very confused. I wondered, above all (all right, it *was* silly), whether he would believe I was innocent, the dupe in this idiotic episode. It was faintly humiliating, too, to have to tell a story in which I was the creature of Jamie's whim. And J. (damn him!) said only: "He *is* tediously physical, isn't he?" performing, for the moment, his light comedy aesthete.

I suppose I should have known that J. would find it simply amusing. Everybody always says they know that affairs will end. It is easier than admitting you hope (you dream) they will not. But he only says it because he believes it, because he has no such dream. Sometimes I feel responsible: if he didn't have me, he might have to give more to these men who give him what his body wants. But there's not much to be done about it, in the end. I mean, I don't think I could live without him.

* * *

Jamie, stripped to the buff, threatening that he would get out of our lives if I didn't stay and fornicate: there was a sight to remember. I didn't know if he'd come to lunch the next day as I'd asked him to. To his credit, he didn't. And, master of the situation to the last, he sent the American to keep the appointment for him. The boy arrived on the dot at twelve-thirty and loped over diffidently to my table.

"Dr. Clarke?" he said, all nervous formality.

"If we're being proper, it's Professor Clarke. I teach music at a university, but I don't have a Ph.D."

He nodded slowly as if taking in an important piece of news but then proceeded undeterred.

"Jamie sent me, with a message."

"Yes?"

"He said he always keeps his promises."

I acknowledged this with a raised eyebrow, and surveyed the boy, standing there, taut and serious, moving his weight from one foot to the other.

"What did he promise you?"

"He said you'd give me lunch."

"Why should I?"

"He said you noticed me and that meant you thought I was sexy."

I smiled—well, who wouldn't have been charmed by such frankness?—and summoned a waiter. "Shall we order wine?"

His name was Michael.

After the meal, I asked him about his encounter with Jamie. "May I ask how he persuaded you to be his Mercury?" I had eaten little and drunk a great deal of the wine and I was drifting into a comfortable postprandial prosiness. We had talked almost entirely about music, about which Mike seemed eminently well informed. The American had also had his share of the three bottles on the table, and was finally beginning to relax. But he was obviously losing the gist of what I was saying. I was too drunk to appear solicitous; I had stopped even pretending that I expected him to contribute more than his attention, so the boy simply let the words wash over him. When he realized that he had been asked a question, he recovered it, decided he did not know what to answer, and said in puzzlement: "Mercury?"

"Messenger of the gods." (I know I smirked at my own joke.)

"Oh." Mike breathed the word out, as if in relief at the resolution of a deep mystery, and then smiled quickly to show he appreciated the ironies. "He picked me up in the bar at the hotel . . . Hey, was that really your idea?"

"Yup, I hope you appreciate it."

"I didn't go with him."

"Go with him? You mean you did not fornicate?"

"I don't think you should say that word so loud here."

"Well," I said, whispering theatrically behind my hand, eyes scanning the restaurant in a pantomime of wild suspicion, "did you or did you not make the beast with two backs?"

"We did not."

"Then, I repeat, how were you co-opted as messenger?"

"He told me he'd just broken up with his lover, and that he wanted someone to take him a message. He said he knew you thought I was cute, because you talked about me, and that I'd get lunch with someone who knew the island if I came."

"That's it?"

"No. Not exactly." He was sheepish now. "You see, I heard you play last fall at college. I wanted to meet you."

Everybody has ulterior motives, I thought. Nobody here is honest. Then I looked into the boy's eyes, dragging a bright smile from my drunken imagination, miming a creative intensity: "And did my music move you?"

"Peter, I don't want to talk about your music when we're drunk. Let's go to the beach, lie in the sun and sleep, and we'll talk about it when we wake up."

I thought only: Why not? "May I make a condition?"

Mike nodded, smiling.

"That you will come back to my house for supper with my parents, and listen to me play."

He nodded again.

My mother tried hard not to show her unease in the presence of this stranger. She knew that her son had said that the young man was a fan of his; someone who had heard him play. It seemed to her, I am sure, less than sufficient reason to bring him home to dinner. My father, silent and mild as always, beamed over the table at all of us, with no sign that he shared her worry. So, as the meal progressed, she unloosened. I could see her thinking, "This Mike has good manners; seems to feel genuinely privileged to be here." He charmed her with his silences, and his quiet appreciation of her house and his welcome. She was delighted, too, that this stranger was enough to make me settle, after the meal, at the piano. I had gotten out of the way of playing for my parents, and I could see what pleasure my mother took in this unexpected performance.

"Well. I think that's enough. Mother, why don't we put Mike in the spare room? I don't feel like driving, and it's late to call a cab."

Before she assented, Mike mouthed a formulaic "I'm sure it would be too much trouble," and I silenced him. "It will take only a minute to put sheets on the bed. Stay, we should like you to."

My mother looked over at her husband. And he, unconscious of her questioning, smiled at her, and said only: "Yes." He was talking to Mike, man to man. "The driver's gone to his family for the weekend." Then, to my mother: "Darling, why don't we make up the spare room? I suspect we should all like to go to bed." My eyes chased from my father to my mother, and caught an instantaneous widening of her eyes: and the small thrill of adrenaline became amusement, as I realized that she too was wondering whether Father's words were innocent or secretly mocking.

"I'll see to all that," I said, and kissed each of my parents as they moved to leave the room. And Mike inserted his thanks among our good night wishes.

This morning I woke early, excited at the prospect of the new day. I had enjoyed the sense of control as I installed Mike in the spare room, embraced him without desire, and put him to bed. I wondered if he had expected me to stay, if he had wanted me to. It didn't matter; there was time enough for that. As I fell asleep, I had planned the day ahead. Breakfast with my parents; a morning drive around the island, up in the lushness of the hills; lunch at the Golden Island restaurant. And all the time talk of music. Innocent, gentle, sexless pastimes. After Jamie, I wanted to rediscover aimless flirtation; to remind myself that the fun was in not wanting any more than the fun, was in thinking of anything else as a bonus.

Then, at the end of it all, and cleansed by the day, we could spend what was left of the afternoon together (with the lifeguard) at the pool.

This City of Men

Darieck Scott

Dear Danielle,

Kansas City International Airport. Return of the Native—of a sort, for I was (am) no native really, only a past sojourner in these parts, returned after an absence of twelve years for reasons of irony more than anything else. As the automated door slid open and I glanced around for the shuttle to take me to the rental car, I thought the slant of the horizon looked familiar. And though I had forgotten that this part of Missouri is rather hilly, my body did seem to recall the dip down toward the traffic light as I drove through Platte City (a town, actually, very small, and devolved from beige to sullen gray) on the way to the state line, and to Leavenworth.

Except for these physical recollections—which, because they stood in the here and now, made my remembered images even more dim—I could recall little that was specific. The name, the sights of Leavenworth, such as they were and are, had become in my absence mere proxies for misery: two miserable high school years of friendlessness and quiet, nameless dread. But perhaps the problem was that the town itself has changed not at all in the years since I graduated and my family left, that it is a mausoleum, requiring no independent memory to preserve its past. Everything is the same. The army base. The prison.

Eric.

But everything has changed about him.

117

Or has it?

But just one more gate to traverse, before I get to Eric, just to set the tone (it tantalizes me, too, to procrastinate this way, but you know me, and, hopefully, have learned to be patient):

The Missouri River travels along the border of Kansas and Missouri proper, rounding a bend and rolling serenely through a wide ravine just outside the town's eastern limits. Nothing stands along the banks here, only the bridge, the dirt and the trees. One imagines, looking down upon the water, European explorers in small boats, peering up into the dark and dangerous woods with little spyglasses held to their eyes, while the people for whom Kansas and its many towns would later be named followed along under tree cover, themselves pondering danger and impending darkness. But the river must have been higher, faster—bolder—then. Now, in this season at least, it is slow and sedate, and from a modest height looks like a long shallow pond in movement.

This is where my thoughts wandered, as I drove toward the bridge along the ponderous arc of an empty two-lane highway. And then I felt, just as I reached the bridge and saw clearly the scattered, dark-windowed homes uphill from the river's edge, a small flutter. A twitch. It was—do not recoil—my (the language is best at conveying its meaning in these matters when at its most stark, so:) cock. I didn't—*wouldn't*—acknowledge it then, though I will now. I can't remember now what I told myself; I likely ascribed the movement to a contraction of abdominal muscles engaged in digestion, perhaps, like Ebenezer Scrooge proposing the undigested-food hypothesis to Jacob Marley's ghost. But that was I-then, and this is I-now.

Now I know better.

There: Now, it's not my intention to confuse you, Danielle, though I know I have. But remember that evening, at Green's on the Marina, when you said (quoting Joan Didion, I believe) that we tell ourselves stories in order to live? I'm trying to make what's happened one of mine. And I'm hoping that you'll bear with me, and understand.

I am a homosexual. Surely you guessed it, when you read Eric's name? Even if you did, the shock is probably no less; I'm saying it now because I don't want you to dread it as my story unfolds, to know it without consenting to know. I would apologize, but I can't. I didn't choose it. I knew about it (*it;* already I cannot bear to name it, and must rub it away, elide it beneath the most impersonal of pronouns)—I knew when I met you, yes. When I proposed to you, surely. You no less than I can now thank the gods that you turned me down, but did you *know,* the way you knew when you read Eric's name? I don't expect you to write back, but I wonder.

I discovered what I had long refused to know sophomore year in college. My roommate was a football player, a halfback who was never around because he was being courted by professional scouts and preferred the company of his fellow athletes to the rest of us in the dorm. One night I came home late from a screw-your-roommate party and he was there. I think I smelled them before the door was fully open. The light from the hallway fell slantwise across their bodies in the pitch black room. I saw his huge butt, its thick curly black hair bristling in the crack, wildly bouncing up and down, and heard the two of them breathing like running hogs. His asshole—I do apologize for this, but I want to be clear; I don't want to leave you with any illusions—clenched and unclenched with a mesmerizing power. I couldn't see her at all, but I knew I wanted what she was getting. And just as promptly I shut the door, and left, and decided I wouldn't get what she got, that I wouldn't even seek it. I would be honest with myself, I decided. I would not forget, would not call myself bisexual, would not *slip* on drunken nights as I *happened* to go to a gay bar. I would face it. But I wouldn't do it. You understand, I think; you can guess the reasons—your father was as sternly Catholic as my own. And then there are the sexual standards we black men must meet—because we are not permitted to be men anywhere else, we must at least be men in the bedroom, etc.—though I hardly need tell you that.

And Eric.

I write that, knowing that his name, too, at this place in my story, is a trick of reconstructed memory. He is significant, true, but to what extent, then as now, he was (is) only a trigger, perhaps a vessel in which I bottled a part of myself, I cannot say. I do wonder whether and how things would have been different here, had things been different between us then. I wonder what meaning this town, this wretched little patch of earth that I've held tight-fisted in my memory as the quintessence of what is contemptible in my life and in the world—I wonder what meaning it would have had. And I wonder if Andy Brent assigning me to this case merely hastened a transformation that was inevitable, and I would have had to return here eventually, anyway.

But Eric: It's an effort, I find, to describe him. My words are so spare when I try to *think* of Eric—embellishment, nuance, metaphor, eloquence, disappear as into a hungry black vacuum, and my voice becomes as laconic and laden as the air on an August Sunday afternoon. I can describe only what it means not to be able to describe; I describe only the difference between the me without him, and the me that is now. Oh, he takes me, Eric does. He takes me and I am left dry, bland, malleable, like sand on an exile's desert isle. He takes me and I am left: Wanting.

No, this is not a love story. It is a story of evil.

Eric is in prison.

I picked up the phone book in the hotel room the second night that I was in town. I had to send out for it because, as the pale and hopelessly adolescent bellhop explained, the previous occupant (I surveyed the dust on the table rammed into the corner against the shabby window: when had *he* been here? five years ago?) must have made off with the room's copy. He handed me the slim volume, white and yellow pages combined, revealing a spray of red acne blotches on the underside of his arm as he did so. His was not the sort of presence in which I usually become flustered, but I felt the blood rise in my face as the boy smiled apologetically and backed out of the room. I was embarrassed, you see.

I had felt no sense of urgency when I first contemplated returning to Leavenworth, about Eric or anyone. I had no wish to contact any of my former classmates (nor, I am sure, would they have any desire to come into contact with me). Indeed, driving to the offices of White & Weinberg to meet with opposing counsel that very morning, I saw someone on the sidewalk I'd run track with; he looked my way and I glared in the opposite direction. But when the bellhop handed me the phone book, it became clear what I was doing—frighteningly clear, like the sudden resolution of a shapeless shadow into the distinct features of a malformed brute raising a butcher knife above your head. (Melodrama, you'll say. Yet I swear to you that this whole matter has played in precisely that fashion.) I was lonely, I said aloud; there was nothing playing at the town's one movie theater but something I had seen weeks ago; I had finished preparing for the next day's depositions—those were my excuses.

I was calling Eric.

Or his father, rather, who has the same name. The phone book says Eric Reede without a senior or a junior, so the man who answered when I called thought I wanted to speak to him. I told him that I was a friend from high school, that we had been in Spanish class together junior year. I said, "Do you remember me, Haze?" using his nickname. I spoke with a presumptuousness that, as I think of it now, must have been my way of flirting.

"Oh, you mean my son," Eric, Sr., said. I was embarrassed, and fell completely silent.

"He's in prison, you know," he said tentatively.

Again, I said nothing.

"You never heard?"

"No"—I tried now to speak in a professional, detached manner—"no, I haven't been in contact since we graduated high school. I live in San Francisco now." As if that explained anything.

"Oh," he said. Evidently it didn't. "Well, you wanna talk to him, you gotta call his lawyer. He don't see nobody but his lawyer these days. Jeff Weinberg, you can look it up. Eric won't see you, though. Just wants to see his lawyer."

"I am a lawyer," I said.

"Oh!" this evidently did explain something. I imagined that he sighed—it seemed that his silence became less wary, anyway—and so I asked, "I hope you don't mind my asking, but— where is Eric in prison, and what for?"

"Right here, in the Leavenworth federal pen," he said.

"And *why*, well, if you ain't heard, they say he *raped* a boy—I don't like to say *boy*; Eric wasn't but two years older—but they say he did that to a young man on the army post, on federal property, see what I'm sayin', which is why he's in the Leavenworth pen. But you know that, you're a lawyer."

It will be odd to you—it is odd to me—but the moment (I describe this conversation to you because of the moment)—it lived in me, Danielle. I felt a pulsing, breathing, kicking space explode into being inside me as Eric, Sr., spoke. I didn't reply, or gasp, or tremble. But I twitched; I twitched again, down there.

"Course, I don't believe it," Eric, Sr., said.

I did.

That's what I mean, when I say this is a story of evil.

Notes on Eric:

As I said, we were in Spanish class together, junior year. We sat at tables rather than in rows—Mrs. Astorbrook maintained the view that students learn languages best in conversation with one another rather than with the teacher. Eric sat next to me. He missed the first two days of class, and arrived late on the third, smelling as if he had just come from gym class without showering. (This was my story for him. He didn't explain, so I didn't find out, nor did he ever return to class in such a deliciously fulsome state. It's likely that I was titillated, rather than revolted as I pretended to be; the girl on my right and I traded wrinkled-nose faces when Eric sat down.) We didn't talk at first. Mostly we listened to Mrs. Astorbrook. But Eric smiled at me when the bell rang, and asked me for the missed assignments. Something about his smile—I ascribe lasciviousness to it now, but surely it was something different. I gave him the assignments, in any case, and was rather happy to do so, and then forgot about him, until that night at the football game.

I had left the bleachers and passed back through the ticket gate on the way to the parking lot. It was halftime, and colder than I'd expected. And since I was new to town, I didn't know anyone, so I was likely despondent, fearing that I would never make friends, never belong—the all too common run of nightmarish insecurities that comprise the cultural bludgeoning we conceal behind that clinician's term *adolescence*.

Eric came up to me, and he didn't seem to be feeling any of that. He was walking in my direction, smiling again, if not lasciviously, then conspiratorially at least, exuding an ease and familiarity with which I would not have been able to greet my best friend, if I had had one. He wore a long-sleeved thermal T-shirt under an open checkered shirt (a look I associated with white boys—and they excited me, too, I must say now), tucked into the town's one pair of button-fly Levi's 501s (everyone else—I swear—wore boot-cut zip-ups or Wranglers). The billowing shirt gave him a broad-shouldered, narrow-waist look. There was a bulge in his right pocket.

"Hey, Jules! You leavin'?" He punch-touched my shoulder, as men and boys do.

"Well, yeah," I said—or something in a casual tone, grateful to be swept into his conviviality. "It's cold. And we're losing anyway."

"Don't go away yet, man. Stay with me and hang out. I'll warm you up."

He reached into his pocket and drew out a small, copper pipe, short-stemmed and wide-cupped, with a fine wire grating in its mouth. "Why 'on't you come and help me fire this up?" His eyes were seductively hooded.

We got stoned that night, and infrequently over the rest of the year. I never proposed these assignations; I lacked all confidence that anyone would want to spend time with me unless as a last resort, and so waited, impatiently, the junior high school girl with ugly knees and braces in her mouth, for occasions of last resort. For reasons at which I might guess (or, truth be told, which I might wish), Eric kept coming back, and during and after stoned stupor he would talk to me, almost confessionally, about matters that concerned him. I was privileged to be only the second person he told about his first experience of sexual intercourse, for example. I remember that my head rolled slowly forward from the soporific cushion of a beaten faded blue couch in his basement bedroom when he told me. I couldn't speak, as hashish rendered me dumb rather than chatty like Eric, but my face tried to register the surprise I felt. Eric smiled. "She's a white girl," he told me, and watched with satisfaction as my mouth opened. "She was crazy, she wanted it so bad," he whispered. Several days later I stood in the cafeteria lunch line behind him and her. She remarked that whatever was passing for meat that day didn't look very tasty, to which Eric loudly replied, "Want me to put some sperm on it?" The white guys behind us (not to mention the girl, whose name and face I cannot recall) were, as you might imagine, less than amused. But I relished the moment—for reasons that require very little speculation now, but then were cloaked behind Eldridge Cleaver–like exultation about one of *us* having taken one of *their* women.

I saw Eric less frequently senior year. He didn't take Spanish II, or any of the other precollegiate track courses where I was often one of two, at most three, black faces. I saw him in the hallway, lined up against the walls with his fellow athletes, and nodded, as men and boys do. He and his new girlfriend had become very close, I was told.

I've said nothing about his looks, in part because I believe it is their meaning rather than their actuality that's important to the story. Yet again, however, in searching for meaning I am reduced to the kinds of breathless description one might easily find in a teenage girl's love novel—or in pornography. Eric had a farm boy's lanky physique, I would say, the deceptive power of its modest musculature honed by sweaty tussles on wrestling mats after school. I think you can imagine the rest—how his legs and buttocks looked in his worn 501s, and other such salacious trivia.

About his color I can say more, I fear. His skin was (and is) very dark, poised just at the edge of ebony, finely dusky and suede-smooth even to the eye. You understand, Danielle, don't you? His skin was the kind of skin we say we most admire in our people—though, as we've rather guiltily discussed, we rarely date anyone of that complexion. There is a compelling sensuality to the color, a *physicality*. A sexual potency. I know where such descriptions originate, of course. Remember what you once said, that sometimes you think that the way you're attracted to black men like that is through the worst of racist stereotypes, of you and of them? You as the wanton woman of color who wants it all night, and he as the big, mean, monstrously endowed and insatiable, slavering buck? Eric isn't big, but he's six feet or so, with broad, powerful shoulders.

So you understand, I think, part of the (perniciously conceived and guiltily repressed) meaning Eric has for me.

Eric Reede is in prison for sexually assaulting a male minor, two years his junior, at the boy's home, which was on federal property. So Jeff Weinberg, Esquire, echoed Eric, Sr., as we drove from the courthouse downtown to the prison on the town's outskirts. Weinberg, founding partner of White & Weinberg—coincidentally the very firm that represents the plaintiffs suing the corporation my firm is defending—agreed to help me see Eric without further question once I told him that the two of us were old friends. "It's important that Eric not become a one-man freak show," he told me, by way of apology for his initial suspicion. He said that he was Eric's friend, too, though he had only come to know him during the trial, and related to me the tale of Eric's unspeakable deeds with blunt stoicism and occasional unblinking eye-to-eye contact, as if to say, *Man to man, between friends, we both understand how to speak about and react to these untidy matters, right?* He intended quite the opposite, but his presence and comfortable *male* demeanor shamed me.

Eric may have been drunk, Weinberg said, but then again he may not have been. The "boy"—Todd Stoffen, a name that, when Weinberg said it, I felt some dim connection to—was probably a homosexual, but as there was no evidence of prior acts, and laws prevented Weinberg from probing the matter too vigorously, and the prosecution managed to present over objection testimony that Todd had dated several girls and had a wonderful time at his junior high prom, etc.—that may not have been true, either. It is undeniable, however, that at approximately four in the afternoon of a Tuesday in July, Eric entered the Stoffen home, apparently at Todd's behest, and, for whatever reason—Weinberg used precisely that phrase and shrugged: "for whatever reason"—punched and kicked and wrestled Todd "into submission," and then "literally" dragged him up the stairway and into Mr. and Mrs. Stoffen's bedroom, where he lashed him with twine to the posts of the Stoffens' Victorian antique bed, and anally and orally "sodomized" him.

"The whole thing must have taken about thirty-five, forty minutes," Weinberg said, and stopped.

Weinberg drives a sleek red European convertible, a diamond among the Leavenworth rough of Trans Ams and Firebirds and Ford trucks. A short, Superman curl of brown hair blew back from the top of his forehead in the wind as he talked to me, and I chose to focus upon it, in an effort to appear wholly unconcerned with the rest of the story. The clarity of my memory of his curl—I can see its individual strands, the minuscule S-tail at its end—suggests something of my state: I was experiencing a kind of tunnel vision, like an accident victim's disoriented focus upon the sight of fuzzy dice, dangling behind the windshield of the approaching car just before it strikes her. I was breathless.

Weinberg made no effort to rescue me. "He brought the twine with him," he continued. "So evidence of premeditation was there. The worst part was the, the *ejaculate*," he stumbled, staring up into a green traffic light. "When the general's wife came home—must've been as short as five minutes after Eric left—she found it smeared all over Stoffen's forehead, cheeks, and lips." He shook his head. "Eric must've had a lot to blow!"

I fear this tale must now become truly lurid and macabre, because Weinberg, quite uproariously, in fact, laughed. I didn't—but I laugh now, as I write this to you—I twitched.

(There is a scene from an all-male pornographic video I've just received in the mail—its name escapes me; I ordered several—in which the star makes his penis "speak" by contracting his well-exercised abdominal muscles so that it lifts and bounces, in a way that calls to mind the *boiinnnng!* sound that would spring from the panels of Archie comics when Archie or Reggie saw Veronica. This repulses you, I know. But I can't restrain myself now. You have become my mother-confessor, distasteful though it may be to both of us. I am taking you, one step by one and later three by three and then over tall buildings in single bounds into what you might call my particular hell. I don't know if *I* call it hell, or whether one day I will feel justified in doing so. It is, I confess, a place where magazines torn from plastic bags scatter the dust of the hotel room floor beneath my bed. It is, if you will, a place of sin.

And I must walk you there with me now, my dear. You must follow as I recount, because I must, the labor and birth of—*this*, whatever we choose to call it. There are two metaphors here, you see: one of journey, one of birth. The journey is for you, a narrative straight-line path with signposts and sights and historical trivia. The birth is mine, the Rosemary's Baby metaphor for what I feel: a deep and terrifying physical evolution.)

The Fort Leavenworth prison is massive and imposing, as one expects (though I did not remember) a federal prison to be. With its rotunda dome and gleaming white paint, and its position atop a low hill overlooking the ripple of valleys that house the greater part of the town, it looks like a state capitol rather than a penitentiary, or like a patrician palace of ancient Rome, towering above the hovels of the plebeians. Indeed the only other building of such majesty is the courthouse, which pales in comparison. To complete this law-and-order trinity there is, of course, the army base itself, Fort Leavenworth, a green and sprawling country club miniature town which is the site for the War College, and where, every year, officers the rank of major arrive to be schooled in Clausewitz and other masters of the art. The open gates of the fort are a two-minute drive, west to east, from the gates of the prison. Together, the War College and the penitentiary are the town's distinguishing features (the courthouse fades, like the Holy Ghost), colossi of federal power bestriding the supine and meek local body. No doubt they provide the greater part of local jobs, as well—twin patriarchs, one might say, tall, grim, strong and solidly male. Women here disappear into their vital and invisible helpmeet roles: wife, mother, teacher, nurse, secretary.

It is in this city of men that Eric grew to what we may charitably call his adulthood.

(I have enclosed for your perusal a few copies, randomly selected, of homosexual pornographic magazines. They're the kind with fantasy experiences detailed in letters, so you needn't worry about offensive photographs. Just note one thing: the frequent reoccurrence of military and prison themes.)

"It's racism that put me in here, man," was the first thing he said to me. The necessary fiction Weinberg concocted to persuade him to see me was that I was a criminal lawyer, looking for grounds on which to reopen the appeal of his conviction— preposterous, of course, and I felt guilty about it. Perhaps I mumbled something or other about constitutional reversible errors and racial selection of jurors, etc. He was sitting down behind a glass partition when we arrived, so that I couldn't see his lower body. His shirt, long-sleeved, hung loosely on him, but his pectoral muscles had a more powerful presence than I remembered.

I interrupted him. "Are you saying that you're innocent?" I asked. "I have to know," I added quickly, like a television lawyer.

"I fucked him, but I didn't rape him." He was blunt. I caught the faint whiff of musk in the slot at the bottom of the glass.

"Lotta people, lotta guys, get real nervous when I say that shit. But I fucked him. I was curious. Lotta guys are curious but don't say nothin'. You, too, probably."

He spoke as if in challenge to a duel. I said nothing. I felt heat, though it wasn't hot.

"You, too," he said again. He hadn't recognized me, it seemed. "But I did what other guys've done. I'm not worried about it. I'm not a faggot." This cheerfully enough, but with a force that made the teeth in his smile look feral. "It wouldna mattered if he'd been black, that's what I'm trying to say. It doesn't matter! But he's a white boy and a general's son and was goin' to college, so some shit had to happen behind it. He asked for it. And if he'd been black, who cares? Nobody gives a shit about a black faggot."

He paused while I nodded in grave assent. He looked at me more closely. "So what else do you need to know? I went and read that jury selection case. I don't think it can help me."

I groped for a lie. "Well, there's a Ninth Circuit decision with some language about how a federal statute about rape doesn't extend to violations of the anatomy of the sort suffered by a male victim," I burbled. It was all rather comic, as I look back on it now. The room was intolerably, stiflingly hot, I remember that. Rivulets of sweat ran down from my underarms along my stomach, which, incongruously, made me shiver. "But you say—he asked for it?" (You will note again the devolution of my language as well as my capacity for subtlety: he asked for *it*, I said.)

His eyes flickered upward, toward Weinberg, who stood many feet back, behind me. I was suddenly struck by his eyes— their size and roundness, the soft brown color like a child's eyes. His lashes were long and curved.

"I know you," he said.

I introduced myself then, crafting a smile of some kind, and jokingly invoked the memory of Mrs. Astorbrook. His eyes widened. "We were friends," he said, with, perhaps, a measure of incredulity.

"We were," I replied. And then, of course, I pounced. "And I'll need to know everything in order to help you. From you, not Jeff. As a friend," I said, and swallowed, because I had become thirsty beyond reason. "But ... I have to go now." It made no sense even to me. But I had to leave. It was an imperative. It had to be different from this, I thought. The setting had to be different, and it couldn't happen now, so quickly.

"We'll schedule it," he said, official but gruff.

He stood then. Eric stood, and Danielle. I've said that I would take you through this by steps, but this moment was not a step; it cannot be imagined or understood as part of a path *to*, as a paving stone in the grass of a park winding toward a garden. It *was*, Danielle. He rose: I watched and felt his torso, the dark valley between his legs, rise, slowly, above the horizon of the table, and, to employ the metaphor of the journey, I was *there*. I didn't have to go anywhere, I was there, *it* was there, and *it* was me. Did it puzzle you when I began to describe our conversation, that my story lacked a moment of recognition, a catch in the throat when I first beheld him again, a misty-eyed locking of gazes, a surge of excitement and fear? Perhaps not; this is, of course, not a romance. It is perversion, pure—unspeakably pure—and simple. In the vacuum created by that lack, by the absence of an acknowledged or acknowledgeable link, romantic or otherwise (this was a meeting of shames, after all: his shameful deed to my shameful desire for him—shame deflects; it does not bond)—in this vacuum I sat at the partition without actually sitting there. I looked through the glass without seeing him, listened without listening. But when he rose.

I beheld him. And he was firm, and full, and strong.

Outside the prison, Weinberg asked me what he had said. He was uneasy with the idea of another attorney talking to his client. I thought of Eric's eyes, and asked Weinberg whether Eric was separated from his fellow prisoners. "He wasn't segregated at first," Weinberg said, seeming to catch my meaning. "But he is now." He said no more, choosing for the first time to be mysterious.

In the convertible, I said that I would be returning to speak to Eric again, and wondered aloud whether there might be some way to see him next time without the glass partition.

That night was the first night I didn't call you. I looked at your number in my address book, because I was unable to remember it, but I didn't call. I sat on the bed instead, held there without will to move. To explain why, or how I felt, I have to tell another story, one that took place twelve years ago, the summer after I graduated from high school. It may not do the trick, but the memory of it moved through my mind that night, and it seems appropriate to tell it now: Two fellow track team members and I had planned to drive up to Chicago for a few days—ostensibly for some concert or another where Stevie Wonder headlined a string of performers like Sister Sledge and Ashford and Simpson. I had dreamt of this trip as others dream of a weekend in Paris. I relished the anticipation of laughing in the car with my teammates, of hearing about their scandalous sexual escapades with girls, of—so I hoped—picking up women under their tutelage (or perhaps the same woman, a fantasy towards which my thoughts often tilted in those days, for reasons that now seem more clear). But one of them, the younger one, Kelvin, who was still a junior, backed out at the last moment. Kelvin was a small, svelte boy, but abundantly hairy, with sideburns and five-o'clock shadow and a mass of fine, curly black hair on his trim, chestnut-brown chest. I waited all afternoon by the phone in my mother's house for him to call and tell me whether his parents would let him go on the trip.

A slight and paltry memory, this: But it was with precisely that unnameable longing and unbearable fear that I sat up that night, held upon the bed, poised to make a phone call I never made, until at last I collapsed and slept.

I saw Eric again, two days later. It was relatively easy then, and most times afterward, to be granted an audience, since Eric—quite without my asking—had informed the prison officials that I and Weinberg both were his attorneys.

Each time I visit him I walk through four gates: The first is not a physical construct but an imagined one. The prison building's doors stand atop a wide white stairway that travels up from an innocuous parking lot and a capacious green lawn seemingly open to all. The appearance is almost suburban, as of a great grand house across the street from mother, apple pie and the two-car garage, though I cannot shake the feeling— prisons being prisons, or what we *think* prisons are—of being within a tale more gothic than fifties sitcom. Behind the doors is a rotunda hall with polished floors and large, grim paintings; from that reception I am ushered through the first of several metal detectors into a carpeted rectangle that has the ominous air of an interrogation chamber, complete with an impossibly high desk shielded by bulletproof plastic, and stark gray walls bearing a lone square placard that details do's and don'ts in red letters (DO follow the instructions of the corrections officers/DON'T smoke); and from there past another gate into a long, empty hallway with a low ceiling (no paintings or placards, just glowing EXIT signs pointing the opposite direction); then finally outside the building and into a gravelly courtyard, and through a final gate to a row of dilapidated barracks. At the door to the especially forlorn one where I usually meet Eric one might expect to read *Abandon hope*—or, perhaps, *Arbeit macht frei*. On the other hand—to balance fantasized horror with absurdity—I feel like Don Adams at the beginning of *Get Smart*.

The second or third time I saw him he was waiting for me,

sitting with his hands quietly clasped on a bare table. Always when I first see him there is a moment of disjunction. He is not towering or imposing or *meaty* there as in my fantasies, but a slight, human figure in gray coveralls—grainy almost, colorless like a figure in a videotaped seventies TV movie. It is when he speaks that he ascends to his full power.

That day I sat at the opposite end of the table, and laid a brief-case between us. The guard left us alone, without explanation.

"I'll tell ya something else," Eric said. "Todd was always hinting. At first he was subtle, right, like asking me shit about my girlfriends. Stupid shit you don't really ask like I bet you and her have a good time, tell me the dirty details an' shit. And then laugh like it was a joke. I wouldn't answer. But he'd always find a way to bring it up: I saw Angel today and she was walking funny, so I knew you'd busted her stuff good last night an' shit. Right? After a while I just started waiting, you know, waiting to see how he'd do it. And I thought maybe, you know, he's inexperienced and he's two years younger and he wants to live vicariously 'cause he doesn't get any an' shit. But something didn't feel right. I mean he didn't *touch* me or look at me weird, but I knew something even though I didn't think about it. Maybe it was the way *I* felt around him when he asked that shit. *My* body felt different. And it had to be *him*. You understand that, am I making sense?"

"Yes," I said.

"And that feeling, Jules—you *know* this feeling, man—it got to be *exciting* and shit, right? Yeah." He paused, looked down. I remember clearly, because we both had time to readjust our breathing. "Yeah sometimes that summer I was so bored I looked *forward* to him coming by. I looked forward to him ask-ing, right, and feelin' what was happening when he asked it. I think—well, yeah, that was when I first let him come down to my room."

Something in me wanted to prolong it. "How did you ever start hanging out with Todd?" I asked. "I didn't even know you knew him in school."

Eric laughed, which he doesn't often do. His mouth was enormous. "He was fuckin' *weird*, man!" he shouted. His de-meanor seemed to me outrageous, distorted and lurid like eerie reflections in an amusement park house of mirrors. I twitched again, but by then, sad to say, that had become a frequent occurrence.

"He was *strange!* I mean, an officer's kid an' shit, a *general's* kid, lookin' for jobs doing menial shit off post, in town? He was lookin' for trouble, I think. Nobody even knew who he was. He came up to our house in some Japanese truck and asked my dad if he wanted somebody to mow the grass every week, and Dad said what the hell, I was workin' in Western Sizzlin' full-time, my brother was too lazy. Dad said he'd get a kick out of having a white boy mow his grass, so. Then he started cuttin', started showin' up more than once a week to do the hedges and pull weeds an' shit, for free, he said, but Dad paid him anyway. They got to start talkin' a lot, and I was there, and so we talked, about school at first, and how he wanted to go out for the wrestling team next year and shit. I guess he was about to be a senior then. We *talked*, like I said. I got used to havin' him around, like rich white folks get used to havin' the maid around, right?" He stopped and looked at me suspiciously, as if he expected me to think this a lie.

"So you took him down to your room?" I asked.

Eric smirked—wild again, outrageous. "I had a bench and some weights down there. We went down and lifted. He kept askin' questions that I didn't really answer. I tried to ask him some shit about his girlfriends—I didn't care, but I just wanted to see what he would say. He just smiled, real stupid, and made some bullshit noise about some girl he liked and he was gonna ask her out and he was a one-woman man. Just shit like that. Pretty soon we'd work out together every other day. He liked comin' by, he was always cheerful." He spread his hands on the table and shrugged.

I fumbled, looking at his dark eyes. "But you—did anything unusual happen? You said he *asked* . . ." I couldn't complete the sentence.

He didn't smirk this time, as I expected he might, but he leaned forward. His words and manner, his voice and hands (despite a certain studied dispassion which was his version of the requisite masculine cool), were always intense, taut the way a prisoner needing to do whatever, say whatever, in order to achieve freedom likely must be. But below the neck, other than the hands—I rarely saw him below the waist, you recall—his body was generally relaxed, at indolent rest. He leaned forward then and changed that. I confess I very much wished, suddenly, that the guard had not left us.

"One time," he said in a lower voice, his gaze focused away from my face, "he fucked up and put too much weight on the barbell. He was too weak and couldn't handle it. I'd already warned him, but he was too busy tryin' to be like me an' shit. So the barbell got unbalanced when he was doin' a press and one whole side of it crashed down on the floor. I got real pissed. My dad was right upstairs in the living room tryin' to sleep, and here he was making all this noise, right? I was pissed. I got up in his face. What the fuck, mothafuck, I told your skinny ass not to do that shit. Shit like that. He got scared. White boys like him get scared when you go off on 'em. So you know this little son of a bitch started to *cry*? Not hollerin' and shit, but his eyes got wet, and he was holdin' his stomach in like he wasn't gon' breathe. I was about to just throw his ass outta my house. But somethin'—I mean it was a turning point. Curiosity took over me, like I told you. He had his back to me and I grabbed up under his arms like I was doin' a nelson on him, and just started wrestling him. At first he was scared, saying don't hurt me and whiney shit, but then he figured it out and started wrestling back. I played cat and mouse with him till I got tired—'cause he couldn't even *think* about whippin' *my* ass—but then finally I pinned him down. On the floor. We were both real funky. I held him down on his back, both shoulders down, you know, for a pin, and my face was right over his. He just laid there, pantin' hard an' shit. He looked up at me, right? It was like—when you wrestle, and you pin somebody, they don't look at you like that, most people don't *look* at you, period. He looked, and it was like, like *total fuckin' submission*. Which is a fuckin' weird feelin', man."

He looked sharply at me. "But he liked that shit."

I was by this time insatiable, Danielle, insatiable.

"So you took this to be—an invitation?" Laughable, but I actually said it, and with a straight face. I often found myself, in conversations with Eric, saying such things, playing an odd and utterly fallacious part: my detachment to his passion, my subtlety to his melodrama, psychiatrist to patient, lawyer to criminal. It was, as you can see, quite a farce.

Eric, as he occasionally did, usually at precisely such moments, put on the air of one entirely unimpressed—of someone with power. "What's all this got to do with that Ninth Circuit decision—which I looked up and read?"

"I need to know everything, every detail," I snapped, slipping easily into the television lawyer role.

He stared for a moment, grim, then rose and walked to the door. I looked straight ahead as he passed out of my peripheral vision. My flesh felt horrifyingly—but titillatingly, Danielle—exposed. There was a knock, and the guard entered.

"See you in a couple of days?" he said, turning his head back over his shoulder as I turned mine. He smiled.

Back in the hotel room I cried, and then masturbated until my sweat spread out in a dark pool on the white, pressed sheets.

Later I remembered Todd. I remembered the thick, pale blond hair on top of his head. I remembered this because sometimes he rode the school bus from post with me, and he always looked down, reading, maybe, so that you would see the top of his head if you sat in front of him and looked back. I hated him then—a casual hate, without fire, as one hates the fat kid in third grade who smells like spoiled milk. No one paid attention to Todd, which seemed to me quite proper, since no one paid much attention to me, either. But occasionally when some of the others were laughing and clowning and I, aloof and excluded, was watching them, I saw Todd watching them, too. The expression on his pasty, plain freckled face was ingenuous, and dumb with terrible, terrible need.

I tormented myself, Danielle, as I now no doubt torment you. You know this in me—the compulsion to hold satisfaction at bay, to dangle it out of reach, and suffer trials to reach the place where I myself have set the prize. I visited Eric, many times. The depositions that I had originally been sent to conduct were concluded. You phoned, and I left oblique messages on your machine when I knew you would be out. Weinberg grew testy, but could do nothing. Eric insisted that he would continue to see me. Whether he knows my purpose, my passion, he has not said. But he must. I daresay he may know better than I.

What follows, then, is the climax, as it were, the journey's end. That is for you. For me there is no climax, no end. Perhaps I do not seek one. My obsession is in the details, in the slow, exquisite nursing and labor of this birth which has already occurred, and will never be complete. Eric understands this. But he has given you, Danielle, something as well: an explanation. I do not subscribe to it, but neither do I deny its power.

"It's about power, man," Eric said. He turned his head and blew smoke from his mouth. I brought him, with official permission, a package of cigarettes. We sat at a table again, but two guards stood in the room's far corners. "I thought a lot about this. Read some of that New Wave, New Age shit. Everybody's got power. Everybody. Some got more, some got less, but they got it. And some—*most*, prob'ly—are afraid of it, see what I'm sayin.' They want somebody else to do it for them. Nothin' new about that, right? I mean that's like Nietzsche an' shit—oh yeah, I read some of that, I read some of everything. It's just plain psychology. Passive-aggressive, puttin' themselves someplace where somebody else can accomplish for 'em what they want. It can be extreme, or not extreme. Todd, he was extreme. Little white soldier boy—he was in ROTC, did I say that? He wanted authority in his life. Liked to bend over, right. That day—I don't remember what day, you have to look it up— somethin' made me think about him. I meditated on him. I don't remember exactly—but about his little body, little weak ass, half-flabby body, and that goofy golly-gee-you-my-big-brother shit. And then he called me at work. Right when I thought about it. And he said come over, I got a new weight set. And I got mad, man. He was so fuckin' *goofy*, just thinking about him *wantin'* me, you know, but he couldn't say it because he was so *weak*. So I said yeah I'll be over. I had some rope in the car, so I could move a bookshelf and tie down the hatch. And when I got to his house I'd brought the rope up from the back to the front seat."

He stopped and calmly tapped cigarette ashes into a tray. This was the kind of detail which, evidently, I had somehow communicated to him that I wished to hear. Patiently he allowed me to contemplate the movement of the twine, while he tranquilly blew smoke into the air above our heads.

"And then?" I said thickly.

He nodded, satisfied. "Todd answered the door and looked real proud of himself. Because he got the weight set, I guess. Which made me a little more mad, kinda. I grabbed him from behind after he shut the door, in a full nelson, as he was walkin' up the stairs, and he laughed an' shit, said let's wait until we get upstairs, we'll fuck up my mom's shit. I said yeah we'll go upstairs, all right, and dragged him up, hard, right, with his face down, over the steps. The steps weren't carpeted, they were just bare wood. He was gigglin', though, like a little kid. He kept laughin' and jokin' around an' shit till I tied one of his wrists up. He started squirming then. Which I have to admit was kinda nice. I was gettin' into it. Made me even more curious. But mad, too, a good kind of mad. That energy, that power, right. He still didn't know what was up. All right, that's enough, let's stop, he said. I tied up his last ankle and he said, stop, Eric! Which was funny. That was his moment of power. Stop! Like he was a general. I ripped his pants down to his spread-out ankles and his breath caught. I heard it. He didn't say anything, which was *very* nice. I got hard, man, real hard. You ever feel a boner like that and you'll know how it makes you feel. I pulled it out and it never felt bigger. He said he was gon' scream, so I slapped him and said if you do, I'll kill you. Which he should've known was a lie! But he shut up! Abandoned his power, just like that. He coulda stopped it then, but he wanted it, Jules. He wanted it bad. I dipped my dick in his mouth to get it wet. He slurped it good when I pushed his head down on it. Then I went around and porked him. You ever see that movie *Deliverance*? I almost laughed when I remembered that. Blood got all over his ass and I had him lick everything off my dick before I fucked him again. I did it as hard or as soft as it felt good, but I tried to do it hard mostly, because that's what he wanted.

"You know that whole time he breathed hard and whim-

pered an' shit, but he didn't cry out? What a little wimp. I bent
over close to him and held his shoulders down while I screwed
him, because I wanted to keep my face right in front of his and
look at him, eye to eye. He couldn't hold it, though. After a
while he looked away. He closed his eyes. I felt sorry for him.
I guess it'd started to hurt by then. And see, he didn't expect
that."

He grinned, with frightening and hypnotic charm.

I slumped in my hard chair. I must say—and this will be
the last of these perversities—that my bottom felt tinglingly raw
as it slid forward in the smooth depression of the chair. And I
had gone quite beyond twitching. I couldn't bring myself to
speak.

Finally, Eric did.

I could do it to you, too. Would you like that?

They grabbed him then—I suppose they had heard him—a
veined, straining hand laid hold of his arm just below the shoulder and pulled at him, like the crook of a cane from offstage
at a burlesque show. He rose from the chair without resistance.
He must have known, as he was pulled away backwards, that
I would follow his eyes.

I did. They were gentle.

I have been told that he is in "isolation," and that I won't
be able to see him for some time.

I am sitting now, at a little round table, writing in dim light.
The view from the window of my hotel room is of a dirty,
empty street, parking meters unattended except by a few lone,
dusty cars. It is early evening in August, twilight.

I wish that I had an ending for you. I've been writing for
hours. At the very least, it seems, I should leave you with some
image—something metaphoric, something haunting, if possible.
Something poignant or lyrical, some fantasy construct by which
we—we, as in you and I, separately—might assimilate changes,
by which we might pretend to conclude one way of living or
thinking or loving for another, or reverence that we have known
as if it had truly passed, when, in truth, everything continues
even as everything disintegrates. The obvious symbols of descent and ascent and gates, of heaven and hell, of prisons both

physical and psychological; the unrelenting frenzy and insatiable appetite of desire deferred—these, perhaps, will have occurred to you. They have, no doubt, inspired images of your own, stronger and more true for you than any I might devise.

But you will ignore such considerations. You will want an image. To have communicated the matter to you as a story, with plot and quotes, demands it.

A note, then:

The Leavenworth streets at night are caliginous passageways, as dark as a backwoods country road. Barely illuminated by feeble streetlamps, they meander away into the distance under droopy tree branches to become tunnels of gloom, a habitat for skulkers and prowlers, for ghosts, perhaps, and presences.

I have begun to drive these dark ways, with the windows up and the radio off. So far I've seen only potbellied white men in baseball caps, staggering over rocky driveways towards their trucks. But a thrill, fierce and expectant, returns me to the streets, night after night . . .

I will disclaim this image, whether adequate for your purposes or not. I have no need of images or metaphor, having lived, in this instance, what they purport to represent. But if I chose an image for myself, it would be starker. Like, perhaps, the card I hold in my hand now. I purchased it along with the magazines. On its face is a white man—I could not find many cards of this variety that boast black men, which is both an outrage and a blessing (the latter because I frankly think I would be a bit undone if I encountered a menagerie of Erics, parading themselves in row upon row of pornographic splendor on card shelves).

But the card: The model is white, rather slight and not particularly well built, moderately hairy, with large hands. His undistinguished morphology serves to accentuate a single feature: He has no face, you see; the picture cuts off above his bare shoulders. What he does have, what he *sports*, is a thick and prominent erection, clad—if that is the word—in damp white bikini briefs. At a rightward lean, it laughably resembles a Coke bottle with a ballooned cap, nestled in a man's crotch.

I say *laughable*. I'm not laughing at it. I fear—I know; I don't fear—that this is the image that adorns the altar at which I shall be worshipping for some time.

That is, if one needs images—or stories, for that matter.

Yours,
Julius

Uncle Eugene

Robert E. Penn

I have to listen to adults and follow all their orders. People never listen to me. They say I'm too young. I should be seen and not heard. But I have lots of ideas. They laugh at them. They say I'm a born storyteller. Mother says I'm not. She says I just escape in my dreams and day dreams. Daddy says I'm going to be a garbage collector when I grow up.

I get up early in the morning to read the dictionary. I need to know lots of words in order to tell stories. It also helps me understand grown-ups. But I can only do it for a few minutes before getting dressed. Even in summer, if I'm late for breakfast, they will punish me. I don't want them to know how many words I know.

The only bad part about being in the room upstairs is that I can hear my father gargling in the bathroom. He gargles every morning after shaving. I can hear almost anything going on in the bathroom because my little linen closet is next to it. (One time when no one was looking, I peeped through the bathroom keyhole when I knew Daddy was in there and saw his "thing." I hope mine turns out like that when I'm grown. His looked really good: big and strong.)

Sometimes I can hear if my sister is sick or my mother is constipated. They make such funny noises. I hope no one hears me poot when I'm in there.

Someone moved my socks. I can't find them. This is the top

drawer of my dresser. They should be here. I want the thick
pair Granddaddy gave me for my birthday. Wait a minute, I
think I put them somewhere safe. I really hid them this time.
Here! Got them. Under the bed is the best place: Mrs. Green,
our housekeeper, says she never knows what she'll find there,
so she won't sweep or vacuum under there anymore.

Daddy's probably wearing his new silk robe now, but in a
few minutes he'll be ready for the day in a dark suit, one of
his starched white shirts that Mother sends to the laundry and
a dark tie. He wears one each day for work and on Sunday for
church. Daddy even wears a suit on Saturday when he doesn't
have to work unless he has a special appointment. And he
wears old suits with old ties and shirts that Mother no longer
sends to the laundry when we're on vacation. But they are
suits anyway.

I asked him if he had to wear them all the time. He argued
that businessmen have to dress. "Would you spend a few thousand or even a few hundred hard-earned dollars on a car if the
salesman looked like the janitor?"

If only he had more free time. I wish he would wear a
lumberjack shirt sometime. I think those forest rangers and log-
gers have a lot more time for their children. Sometimes he'll
take off his tie and make me play a little ball with him. I don't
like sports. More time to play with me doing what I like, with
my crayons, my basket weaving, my storybooks or telling each
other stories. Even a cardigan like "Father Knows Best" on TV
would be all right.

He's leaving the bathroom now, walking down the hall in
his velvet slippers. That's the last I'll see, I mean hear, of him
until dinner. He'll probably finish breakfast before I even get
dressed.

Our summer vacation to Missouri was okay. Sometimes it
was hard to find a vacant motel room. I'm home, but Sister is
away visiting Grandmama and Granddaddy for a month. Then
she'll stay with Aunt Cloris for a month. I want to see Grandmama and Granddaddy, but I want to play with my friends,
too. There are no boys my age in their neighborhood. Only girls
and they all hang around my sister, play with dolls and yack.
I don't want to stay with Aunt Cloris. More girls. And only

women in the house, too. In a few weeks, I'll go to summer camp.

I can't wait to get to camp this year. I get to share a tent with Willie. He's great. He's good at sports and pretty smart, too. Daddy likes him a lot. Says I should learn sports from him. Daddy played football in college. He says that's the best way to get a scholarship. Daddy was a math teacher until he started selling cars full-time. He makes more money selling cars now. I don't even know if I want to go to college. Sounds pretty boring to me. And college graduates have to wear suits all the time. All the men, anyway. They don't have any fun.

"Baby."

I hate it when Mother calls me that. I told her I'm too old for it. She makes it sound like it's got three syllables instead of just two. She says that's a good way to send it to the top of the stairs. Make the word sing, she says. It sounds like a snobby scream to me. These socks smell pretty bad. I'll put them on anyway because I like the smell.

"Coming."

"Ba-a-by!"

Guess she didn't hear me answer. Better open the door. "I'm coming. I'm not late."

"Your 'Uncle Gene' is here for a visit. He's going to spend all day with you."

"I'll be right down." I don't even know him very well. He looks just like Daddy except older. Last time I saw him was at Aunt Esther's funeral. He smelled like rotting fruit when he exhaled. Pee-uuu! He gave me this toy last Christmas, it's a kind of puppet, but it doesn't move around a stage. A wooden man flips on a string when I squeeze the handles. It's neat. I wiggle into last winter's dungarees. They're too short now, but perfect for doing nothing.

"Hi, chief." Daddy is still sitting at the head of the dining room table. He's wearing a dark suit and tie and gleaming white shirt, just like I thought. "Remember your uncle, Eugene?"

Uncle Gene is all the way at the other end. Wonder why guests always get to sit at the foot of the table. My uncle is wearing dark green trousers, sort of like the one's Mr. Carpenter wore when he built our garage. Uncle Gene's shirt is pale blue and made like a cowboy's. His jacket is from somebody's old plaid suit. It doesn't match. His smile is different from Daddy's.

"Yes, sir. Thank you for the tightrope puppet. I like it very much." I extend my hand, just like Mother taught me, to shake with my uncle, but I don't get too close.

"I made that just for you." He shakes.

"You made it?"

He smiles. His teeth gleam with Crest. My uncle is cool. He made that puppet. He dresses casual like a television father. I want to know more, "Did you go to college?"

"Nope, son, I didn't. Baby brother is the brains of the family."

I look at Uncle Gene, then at Daddy. I can't believe my uncle said that. Daddy never made me anything. That takes brains. I mean, he does buy me nice things. The train set is fun. And every year he adds some new hill or locomotive or building. We've got it set up year-round on a four-by-eight piece of plywood connected by ropes to pulleys so that we can raise it to the basement ceiling where it's out of anybody's way and safe from my sister and her girlfriends.

"You're going to college someday. That's for sure." Uncle Gene opens his arms for me. "But today you get to play with me."

I just look at his outstretched arms. I don't get hugs anymore. Doesn't he know I'm too old?

"Go to your uncle, baby."

"Yes, ma'am." I move closer to my uncle. He is taller than me even though he is still sitting. Uncle Gene takes me by the shoulder and kisses my forehead. I don't smell stale fruit. "Hi."

"Hi." He points to the large black trunk and big leather shoulder bag beside his chair. "You want to learn how to take photographs?"

I step back, wide-eyed with glee and disbelief because Daddy never lets me touch his Agfa. I look to Daddy, who nods as he straightens his tie. "You're not teasing me?" Uncle Gene picks up the camera bag and hands it to me. "Great!" The bag brushes my knee as I lift it over my shoulder. I look around the room. "We have to photograph the big sofa, and

Poopsey, our dog, and let's go to the park by my school. There's
a bird's nest there to photograph and the kids at the swimming
pool and—"

Daddy interrupts, "Don't wear your uncle out. He's just
come back from a long rest and he's not used to being around
children." Daddy joins Uncle Gene and me at the table's foot.
Uncle Gene stands up. He's afraid of my father. Daddy shakes
hands with his brother. "Take good care of him. He's the only
one I have. Watch out for him outside. You remember how kids
are, they forget to look for traffic sometimes."

I always look both ways.

Uncle Gene yields a smile. Isn't he older than my father?
Why does he shrink beside Daddy? "And you." Daddy turns
to me. "Don't try to do everything in one day. I got Uncle Gene
a job starting next month, so you'll be seeing a lot of him." He
shakes on it with me.

"Yes, Daddy." I wait for Daddy to kiss Mother goodbye
and leave. Mother starts clearing off the table, and I turn to
Uncle Gene, beaming. "I'll show you all the best things to photograph. Are you ready?"

Since Uncle Gene first arrived, we've spent every day together. We photographed all the places I wanted him to see
and then other ones we discovered together: a baseball game,
sailboats on the lake, even a car accident. Daddy opened a
charge account at the Kodak store so we can buy supplies.
Yesterday we bought chemicals and made films. We dried them
overnight. Now we're making photographs.

I can't see a thing. Uncle Gene made the bathroom in the
basement totally dark and set up a machine. It's a darkroom
now. Uncle Gene brought the machine with him in the trunk.
It's got a lightbulb inside a globe on a pole that goes up and
down. The light flashes through the film to make photos. He
told me that he learned about photography almost five years
ago when he was away resting the first time. He also brought
some black cylinders. We used them yesterday to make films.
Films first, photographs second.

Uncle Gene's hand is huge. It completely covers mine as he
guides my fingers. I'm holding wooden tongs and waving a

piece of thick paper in a mix of powder and water that Uncle Gene called "developer."

"Oh. Uncle Gene, look at that!" I forget to stir the paper. But Uncle Gene's warm touch moves my hand and the tongs back and forth, gently agitating the photo paper. "Look! That's the bird's nest. It looks so close! Wow."

"That's your first photograph, boy. Remember the long lens we used? I told you it would make things closer."

"Wow! Except for the black and white, it looks so real."

"Put it in the fixer for five minutes," Uncle Gene instructs me clearly but not lecturing like most grown-ups. "I'll print up that car accident negative. Then we can take a break." He sets the timer to five minutes for me.

Uncle Gene strips down to his sleeveless undershirt. He lights a cigarette, the same brand as Daddy's, in the basement laundry room near Poopsey's bowl across from the darkroom door. "When I have a group of good prints together, I'll be able to show my work to newspaper editors and art directors at advertising agencies. Then I'll be able to get an interesting job taking photographs for money." Uncle Gene inhales the cigarette smoke very slowly between his words. "I'm not really interested in photographing weddings or babies." He exhales a cloud of yellow-grey smoke toward the ceiling. I guess he enjoys smoking.

"I think any kind of photography work would be interesting. You don't need a college degree to do that. Do you?"

"No, boy." Uncle Gene draws on his cigarette. "You don't. All you need is an eye for news and beauty."

"Car accidents are not beautiful, Uncle Gene."

"It all depends how you look at it. A straight-on shot could be boring. But shoot it from the ground up and the cars loom large, the blood flows off the frame, and *voilà!* The tragic event becomes a monument to human error that gets your attention. You could say that's beautiful."

"You don't sound like Daddy at all. Are you two really brothers?"

I think Uncle Gene is choking until he slaps his leg. "Yes, we're brothers. Your daddy has schooling, a credit to our race. I finished sixth grade; that's why I talk funny."

"You don't talk funny. You sound easy, relaxed. Daddy always sounds like he is being watched—putting on a show."

"Occupational hazard."

"What does that mean?"

"It just means that sometimes men and women make some compromises with their personal life in order to achieve success at work. Me, I live poor because I have to buy good photography equipment and because photography doesn't pay much. But I like the work and hope I'll get recognition someday. Your Daddy, on the other hand, has to look good in order to be a good salesman. He has to look like a success so that people trust him. He looks like somebody who will get customers the most for their money. He always has to look like he's ready to close a deal: occupational hazard."

I understand his grown-up talk. "I just wish Daddy would wear play clothes on Saturday. That's all."

"And he just wishes I would get a day job while striving to be recognized as a talented photographer."

"What does that have to do with what I said?"

"You'll understand someday." Uncle Gene talks like he knows something about Daddy that would help me.

I want to know. "Tell me! Uncle Gene, please explain it!" And I wrap my arms around his wide neck, begging for the answer. "Tell me, please."

"No. Not now." Uncle Gene squashes his cigarette under his work boot. "Let's print up a few more photographs so we have something to show your parents."

"Okay, but only if you promise that you'll tell me what you mean."

"I'll tell you in two weeks when you get back from camp, if you haven't already figured it out by then."

The old yellow church bus that's doubling as camp transport this summer is on its last wheels. It inches along the old dirt road and then on the highway heading toward town like a worm. Every car, old and new, Buick, Oldsmobile, Ford, Dodge, Chrysler; every model, 88, Eldorado, Fairlane and Galaxie, speeds by. A Model T would leave this bus behind.

Now that it finally pulls up in front of our house, I grab

my duffel bag and get up. I turn to Willie, who reminds me of our neighbor's pet boxer—stocky and friendly—and punch the air just in front of his chest. Willie grins as he punches back at the air just to the right of my chin. I don't flinch. We're playing. "Camp was good, huh?" Willie smiles. "I'll see you at Sunday School." We shake on it and I rush out, saying goodbyes to all the other boys along the way.

Inside now, I rush to my room, rip open the duffel bag, remove the dirty clothes and two rolls of exposed Kodak film and race downstairs to the basement where I expect to find Uncle Gene working on his portfolio. Instead, I find Mrs. Green running sheets through the wringer on the back of the washing machine. It whines over a clump of cotton and I have to ask her loudly in order to be heard, "Have you see my uncle Gene?"

"Not for a week now. Or maybe ten days." She answers without looking up from her work.

Mrs. Green is working hard as usual in her apron that goes from her neck and all the way down to her knees. It wraps completely around her old but clean cotton dress.

"Where is he?"

"I don't know." She looks at the dainty Bulova that Mother gave her last Christmas, "Your mother should be home about now. She will know, young man."

"Thank you, Mrs. Green." I turn as I speak so that my words have to bounce off the far wall in order to reach back to her. I'm already running upstairs, so I don't really hear her reply, "You're welcome." I just sense that she does because she, like everyone else in our house, church and neighborhood, is always polite.

It seems like I've been lying on my bed forever when Mother knocks. I have already put my one clean shirt away (it's so ugly, but she likes it); stowed my duffel bag in the attic; returned my Kodak Brownie to its shelf; displayed my leather, clay, Popsicle stick and basketry crafts on the top of the dresser and read the latest Superman comic book by the time she opens my door. "Baby"—with only two syllables—"are you all right?" She enters. "How was camp?"

"All right, I guess." I mutter into the pillows, "Where is Uncle Gene?"

"He went away."

"Where? He promised to tell me something."

"It was unexpected, honey."

I sit up now. "Did he leave a note?"

"I don't think so. Daddy didn't mention it."

I sit up so she can see my tearstained face, "Why not? We're always supposed to leave notes if we can't say goodbye in person. Right?"

"Yes, honey. And I'm sure Uncle Gene meant to."

"So why didn't he?"

"I really don't know. Maybe he's sending you a letter when he gets there."

"Where?"

"He didn't tell me."

I guess I will have to pout to get any more information out of her. So I whine, "Does Daddy know?" and collapse onto the bed and stare hurtlike at the ceiling.

"Daddy will be here at his usual time. You can ask him then." She's on to my tricks.

"Can I call him?"

"No, baby. I just saw him with Uncle Timothy at Smolinski's car lot. They were having an important meeting. Daddy may go to work for Mr. Smolinski. It would be a better job. He'll be home in a little while." She goes to the dresser and picks up a clay dog. "Did you make this in camp?"

"Yes." She's just not going to tell me what I want, so I decide I might as well talk to her. "Yes I did. But I like basket weaving better." Lonnie and I threw rolls of toilet paper on Lesley's tent. Lesley looked so angry when he saw it: He put his hand on his hips and tapped his foot just like Sister does. He never figured out who did it. It was a lot of fun. "And Willie and I went swimming every day. I'm getting stronger. I pulled him all the way across the pool in lifesaving class." I snuck extra brownies from the mess hall three times without getting caught once. "Maybe I'll be as strong as Willie by next year, in time for camp."

"I got you a fresh box of vanilla wafers. Let's have a snack."

She knows that I can't resist those cookies. Grown-ups are always in control. "Okay."

At the dinner table, I eat patiently while my parents complete their adult talk. They discuss every old or sick person in the church and every couple having problems, usually with their children—using code names instead of their real names so I won't know who they mean. They think. Now they're finishing up with births, deaths and the details about this year's annual Labor Day church picnic: since church membership has reached nearly fifteen hundred, it'll be held in the park by the Waukegan River; Mrs. Jordan is chair of the food committee and Sister will be back in time to go.

Daddy's tie is still neatly knotted beneath his still-fresh-looking starched shirt collar. His suit coat airs on the empty chair to his right where my sister usually sits when she's home. He notices me playing with the not-so-well-mashed potatoes and catches my eye just as I risk a fleeting glance at him beyond my mother sitting between us. "So, chief, how was camp?"

"Same as last year, Daddy. Lots of things to do. I learned about some new trees: sumac and another type of elm. I don't think they were there last year. At least I don't remember them. I shared a tent with Willie. We got an award for the best-organized tent. And I learned to swim the backstroke."

"That's great, son, excellent. Maybe this year there will be a weekend camping trip during the fall. Would you like that?"

"Yes, Daddy. As long as Willie and my other friends can go."

"It will be the same group, chief. Just as usual." Daddy smiles approvingly, then looks at Mother.

Now I intentionally eat the last of the mashed potatoes because I know he won't listen to me, seriously anyway, if there is still food on my plate, and place my fork where Mother taught me. "Daddy?"

"Yes, son."

"Daddy. Where is Uncle Gene?" ·

He looks away toward the telephone within his reach. People always call to ask about cars or to discuss something to do with church business when we're eating dinner. Daddy's an important deacon. Everyone in town knows they can reach Daddy between 5:10 and 6:30 P.M. at home with his family. But the phone is not ringing.

Daddy looks back at me. His left eye is now pointing out left, like he's trying to see what is behind him. Is that cross-eyed? No. There's another word. But I'm not going to ask him now because he looks different from how I've always seen him. "Daddy, did I do anything wrong?" I blurt without realizing I want to know something other than Uncle Gene's whereabouts. "Are you all right?"

"Yes, chief. I'm fine. No, you didn't do anything wrong." He wipes the corner of his mouth with his napkin. "But your uncle. Well, your uncle ran into a little trouble." Daddy is speaking so slowly like he does sometimes at church when he's reading Scripture or making an announcement about a really serious subject like Korea or praying for the families of lynched men down South.

I can't wait. "Is he dead?"

"No, son. He's not dead. He's, uh, well." Daddy's left eye returns to the front.

"Daddy. Please, tell me. I have a right to know. You always say that. We have a right to know." I remember the word: cockeyed.

Mother raises her hand to her mouth and I can see that she's trying not to laugh. I scowl as mean as I can at her. My question is not a joke.

Daddy looks at the congealing pork chop gravy on his plate. "When Uncle Gene came to town, we agreed on some conditions. He broke one of them the day after you went to camp, and I don't want him around you or around this house until he corrects the situation."

"What do you mean? What did he do? Did he take something? Wouldn't you give it to him if he needed it?"

"No, he didn't steal anything or break any other commandment, exactly."

Mother silently gets up and takes her plate into the kitchen.

"What did he do? When will he be back?"

"What he did, I can't explain to you right now. Maybe in a couple of years you'll be old enough to understand."

He always says that and I have to listen. Uncle Gene must have learned it from him. Mother returns with the coffeepot and pours Daddy a cup before sitting back down.

"And, chief, I don't know when he'll be back or when I'll let him back. He knows what he has to do. It's up to him."

I don't get it. But I can tell from his tone of voice that he's not going to tell me anything else, so I guess I'll make them feel bad for keeping this secret from me. "May I be excused, please?"

They exchange surprised glances. Then Mother answers, "Yes, de-ar."

I get up and push my chair back to the table. "May I look at *Ebony*?"

"Yes. Just don't take it out of the living room."

"Thank you." My voice falls to the floor like a burst balloon and I slink to the magazine rack and grab *Ebony* and *Jet*. I sprawl on the living room floor where Daddy can see me.

Mother reports to Daddy what Grandmama, Aunt Cloris and Sister wrote in their weekly letters to her.

Good, afternoon light streams through the blinds of the picture window that looks out over our front porch, walkway and lawn. I flip through the pictures, thinking Uncle Gene could take more interesting photographs, until I doze off.

My nap is ruined when I hear Daddy shout something to me. I'm still lying down and drowsy, but I look toward his voice. I shake my head awake. I squint and can see his glistening shoes and well-creased pants legs, but the table is in the way of his face. I can't read his lips. He shouts again.

There is a knock at the door. Maybe he told me to answer the door. From Daddy's seat at the head of the table he can see guests arriving up the front walkway. Except for door-to-door salesmen whom Daddy calls carpetbaggers, we usually open the door just as the person reaches the porch. We are punctual.

"Don't answer the door."

I shake my head, force myself up from the floor and stumble to the door. I think he said, "Go answer the door."

"Don't answer the door." His voice is so much louder.

Mother never lets me scream in the house. "I am, Daddy." I heard him the first time. "I am." I'm still sleepy, but I'm moving fast. Is he angry with me? Must be someone important. I unlock the top lock, remove the chain.

Loud, fast footsteps start from the dining room and get

closer. Before I know it, Daddy is towering over me, glaring at me, his left eye checking his back. He pushes me away from the door and blares, "I told you, 'Don't answer the door'!" He is still looking at me with his right eye as he leans against the door, blocking our visitor's entry.

I am shocked, lose my balance and fall down hard. "I thought you said, 'Go answer the door,' Daddy." I hold back the tears, "You always do when there is someone coming to visit."

His left eye relaxes and looks at me, too. "Okay. You're right." Daddy moves from the door to help me up, but someone pushes it in and he has to block the door again. "I have to talk to Uncle Gene."

My heart leaps when he says "Uncle Gene" and I get up to join my father outside, but he closes the door before I can take one step. I have no choice but to watch through the window.

I hear Daddy tell Uncle Gene to leave. He just stares blankly at Daddy. He is silent. He doesn't move: planted to a spot on the porch, wobbling like a baby tree in the breeze.

Daddy grabs Uncle Gene by the collar of another second-hand windbreaker and forces him off the porch. He walks with bent knees like the scarecrow in *The Wizard of Oz*. I notice that his pants legs are torn with saw teeth almost like that movie character.

At the end of our walkway by the curb, Daddy shakes Uncle Gene by the collar as he says something to him. When Daddy releases Uncle Gene, he falls. Daddy lifts Uncle Gene's face up from the concrete, cradling it in his palms.

"Mama, Uncle Gene fell down."

Daddy tries to get Uncle Gene to his feet but can't and leans him against one of our young trees instead. Mother watches from the table. "Yes, he did. Your father will know what to do."

But instead, Daddy leaves Uncle Gene there and walks to the side of the house. Mother gets Daddy's coat, "You stay there," and goes out the back door to join him.

"I didn't do anything," I tell the picture window.

Uncle Gene lies motionless like a lump of straw.

Daddy backs his car around the corner, gets out, lifts Uncle

Gene and carries him to the car. Mother joins Daddy at the car and opens the back door for him. Daddy struggles to get Uncle Gene in the back of the car. He says something to Mother and drives off.

I sit down on the sofa, careful not to put my feet on the upholstery, and flip through *Jet*. Mother returns through the front door, which she locks and chains behind her. "Daddy and I are sorry that you had to see Uncle Gene like that, baby. When Daddy gets back from the hospital, he wants to talk with you." She passes me on her way to the dining room.

"But I didn't do anything. I thought he told me to open the door."

Like clockwork, Poopsey wags into the living room and nudges against my hand.

Mother is clearing the table. "I know, honey."

I leave Poopsey whimpering for affection and drag myself upstairs to my room.

"So does Daddy," Mother promises me.

Even so, I am petrified when Daddy knocks softly on my bedroom door two hours later. "Chief, may I come in?"

I nervously reach for Uncle Gene's puppet and squeeze the handles so tight that the tumbler does a double back flip. "Yes, Daddy."

He must have left his suit coat downstairs or in his room. His shirt is messed up now. He walks straight up to me, sort of smiling, but not like a soldier as usual. He's not angry. I have never seen Daddy like this before today. At least both eyes are forward looking at me. He seems calm. But he did push me. So hard that I fell onto the floor. He never did anything like that before. Never!

Daddy runs his fingers around his curling collar to make some room between it and his neck. Then he loosens his tie and unbuttons the top shirt button. "Son, I owe you an apology."

"What for?"

"I'm sorry I pushed you that way. There was no excuse for it. All I can say in the way of explanation is that I was so concerned that Uncle Gene not come around here in his condition that I forgot to take care of you. I'm sorry."

"What condition, Daddy?"

"Your uncle drinks too much."

"If you drink a lot, you urinate a lot."

"Yes. But if you drink alcohol, like the eggnog Mrs. Jordan gives your mother and me at Christmas, you lose control."

"You and Mommy don't." You are always in control. In charge, wearing your suit.

"Because we only have a small glass of eggnog while we're watching the nine-o'clock news. It takes us all twelve days of Christmas to finish that quart bottle. And we don't have any more until the next Christmas. Your mother never finishes her nightly glass. She throws it out the next morning."

"And Uncle Gene keeps going?"

"He doesn't know when to stop. That's why he has to go for another rest. Maybe he'll lose interest in drinking."

"Oh."

"Do you forgive me?"

"Yes."

"Let's shake on it."

And I shake hands with Daddy, who hugs me, too. He hasn't hugged me since I started elementary school, I think. I am really glad he is hugging me because he is strong and I feel safe in his arms.

"I have to make some arrangements for your uncle. I'll come back and tuck you in later."

"Excuse me, Daddy. Uncle Gene said you want him to work a regular job. Why do you want Uncle Gene to do some work besides photography? That's what he likes."

"Well, chief, he has to pay his bills: apartment rent, food, tithing at church, like every other adult."

I am not convinced, but it's not important. "Daddy, do you know how to work in a darkroom?"

"No, I don't, son."

"It's a real job. Uncle Gene can teach you when he comes back. And you don't have to wear a suit to do it."

"That's a good idea. The three of us can develop photos together." He looks at me. I think he knows I am not finished.

"Daddy, is drinking an occupational hazard for Uncle Gene?"

Daddy is surprised that I know this word. "I don't think so. Photographers don't have to drink in order to do their job."

"Good. Then Uncle Gene will come back and you can borrow one of his cowboy shirts and wear that in the darkroom."

"Good idea, Junior."

I smile like a baby because he only uses that nickname on special occasions. "Thanks, Daddy." I collapse back onto my bed before Daddy can close my door. I am glad Daddy came to talk to me, especially since he held me tight, but I'm still worried about Uncle Gene and angry that I can't have a darkroom lesson, not until he gets better anyway.

I am wearing a new black suit. It is the first summer one Mother got me with long legs. I am glad to have long legs. I am too old to wear short pants like children do. I don't want to look like a kid at a time like this.

Sister and I are walking slowly down the aisle with Mother. Uncle Gene's camera bounces lightly against my hip with each step. Aunt Faith, Daddy's sister, is right in front of us with more of Daddy's relatives. It is like a wedding procession, but everyone is in black. Daddy is sitting up in the pulpit with Reverend Minister looking down on the shining brass trunk. I can just see Uncle Gene's nose sticking out of the box.

Aunt Faith stops in front of Uncle Gene's body. She cries out loud, "Gene. Gene. My favorite brother. I raised you while Mama cleaned houses and took in laundry to buy us food. God will take care of you now. Please, God, forgive him. His heart was always good." Then she falls to her knees and mutters something I can't understand. I start to help Aunt Faith up, but Mother holds me back. I look up at her, curious, but she looks serious, so I obey.

Mother and I sit in the third pew right behind all of Uncle Gene's sisters, brothers, cousins, nieces and nephews who could make it. I see Mrs. Green nearby. She nods at me and sort of smiles. I clutch Uncle Gene's camera. While the organ music continues, I dare whisper, "Mother, why did Aunt Faith fall down?"

"They are sanctified in her church. This kind of 'display' is part of the way they worship."

"Why wouldn't you let me help her up?"

"Because Daddy and I don't want to encourage that kind of show. So we ignore it."

The music stops just as I am about to begin my next question. Mother turns away and looks at the pulpit and the funeral. I want to know why she and Daddy don't approve of being out of control, crying and feeling bad and calling to God for help. But then I hear Daddy talking about his brother. His deep voice attracts my attention. It is so calming. I'll give him credit for this: his tone is sweet and he looks good when he's being a deacon. I laugh to myself when I imagine how he would look doing church business in a lumberjack shirt, cowboy shirt or even a cardigan. I bet he would still do a good job.

Mother elbows me and I stand up as Uncle Gene's box leaves the church.

Everyone walks quietly out.

Daddy and Mother don't talk as we drive to the graveyard. I don't remember a word of the service. Not one. I do know that Uncle Gene saw a lot of beauty in many things. I see a lot of things. It hurts me when I can't show them to Mother, Sister and Daddy. Maybe Uncle Gene saw too much. Maybe that's why he drank too much. He couldn't take seeing all that beauty all the time, all by himself, surrounded by people so tight that they couldn't see. Or maybe he took pictures because he had been watched too long, performed enough and wanted to relax a little.

We follow the box to the grave.

Four men slip a wooden one out of the brass trunk and place it next to the grave hole.

The church matrons cover it with bouquets.

Daddy speaks of Uncle Gene again and all of his family burst into tears. Aunt Faith throws herself on the ground beside the casket. This time I don't try to help her, but I look knowingly at Mother. It's just an act Aunt Faith does. She could control it if she tried, if she were better educated. It's not for me.

The coffin sinks into the ground with the help of some pulleys and ropes. Daddy pours a shovel of dirt on it and the Minister recites a biblical quote about dust and ashes. Most of the people, even Aunt Faith, file away before three graveyard men toss more and more dirt on Uncle Gene's box. Even Sister walks to our car. Mother starts to leave but stops when she sees that Daddy and I are just standing under the awning in silence.

I watch and wonder how much camera and darkroom equipment could fit into a box that size. "Daddy, may I take a picture?"

He hesitates, then turns to me. "Of what?"

"I don't know exactly. I just want to. Uncle Gene would take a picture."

Mother wipes tears from her eyes and digs her face into my father's shoulder.

"Yes. You may. We'll get out of the way."

"No. Please don't. Please stay there. I want you in the picture, too."

I walk some distance away from them, my back to the sun just like Uncle Gene taught me. The fresh brown soil reminds me of hoeing the soil for our garden. Fresh-cut grass scents the wet air. Mother holds on to Daddy's arm as if she is afraid of falling into a grave. His face wrinkles with sorrow. He is thinking about Uncle Gene.

I capture this moment and, in spite of the sadness, make it beautiful: Daddy and Mother stand tall above the clumps of freshly dug dirt on top of Uncle Gene's box. Their feet are hidden by the unpacked mound as if they are stuck in the ground. *Voilà*, a photographic monument to life and death.

I follow each instruction to the letter. I mix the developer and fixer. I turn off the lights. I load the film into the black tube. I dry the negatives overnight. I focus the image onto the base. In the darkened room, I light a red safety bulb. I place the photographic paper on the base. I set the timer. I turn on the projector. I turn off the projector. I slowly jiggle the paper in the developer. I turn it over. I turn it over again.

I watch my mother and father materialize on the paper. He is very strong: strong enough to go play a game of football this afternoon. (He had a football scholarship to college.) She is very bright: her refined face surrounded by the black shawl. (She knows etiquette and teaches music.) They are standing by the mound that Uncle Gene built. He is very sad. She misses Gene.

They are in pain, ashamed. They regret that Uncle Gene didn't live long enough to stop drinking. And they are proud, determined not to be caught by the traps so many Blacks fall into, to make a mark.

I wish I had a photograph of Uncle Gene. Something more to remember him by. I can't see his smile anymore. It was different from Daddy's. Daddy's is wide and winning. He influences people. Uncle Gene's was more personal as if he were living more for himself than anyone else. Except for me, since I was a little nosey and asked him about his photography. It was easy.

I am very sorry that Uncle Gene couldn't stop drinking even though he knew it was hurting his liver. He couldn't stop. I wonder why he couldn't stop. I'm glad Daddy doesn't drink. He's pretty okay except he has most things all figured out and set in stone. I love him and need him around even though he is too busy most of the time.

If I begin saving my money now, maybe I will have enough by Christmas to buy Daddy that lumberjack shirt. Maybe Sister will chip in, too. Then we can both convince him to forget his occupation for a week and to hazard wearing casual clothes while we're on vacation.

Tom and Brock

Charles Wright

In the humiliating heat of a late summer afternoon, Tom and Brock sat on a pebbled ledge in the Chinese zone of Roosevelt Park. A tenement backdrop and a stately line of ancient trees sheltered them. The babbling blur of voices and pitched staccato sound of traffic lumbering off Manhattan Bridge and the surrounding streets completed the litany. This was their open-air home away from home. Even when the weather verged on inclemency, more than likely one or the two of them occupied the ledge. The tryst began in the splendid bicentennial year of 1976. Of course, there were long arid periods of separation. Brock, reclusive, homebound in Park Slope. Tom, gigging as an assistant golf pro in Westchester County. Plus neither man was remotely addicted to the telephone. They preferred the park's Oriental ambience to the Bowery bars, so determinedly hip and artistic. Wedded by Vietnam, sports and drink, the middle-aged friends were basically solitary. A profound sense of decency cemented their relationship. Frequently Tom and Brock discussed the fickle nature of people, as if lobbying for a purple heart.

And now, moored to their ledge, they were silent and comfortable, and sipped lukewarm beer. There was absolutely no breeze; the air was surprisingly odorless except when they inhaled deeply and caught the pungent smell of urine. The purgatorial sky offered no dividends. Cloudless, stationary—it was just there. Another facet of life on the lower East Side.

Thirty feet away, below ground level, was a large basketball court. The Chinese youth played with ferocious determination and skill, repeatedly missing shots as if trying to fix the game.

"What do you think," Tom asked, "1999?"

"Yeah," Brock agreed. "A lot of promise down there, and they're getting taller."

"Yeah, the Mongolians are really shooting up."

Brock flashed his perennial teenage grin. "The Chinatown All-Stars of 1999. Can't wait."

Just then, a myopic, voluptuous Chinese girl walked by with vogue henna streaks in her long dark hair, wearing a black and white mini.

"Lordy, Lordy," Tom exclaimed, "look at that ass. My tongue is salivating. Jailbait."

Tall and lean, burnt ginger by the sun, Tom had perfectly coiffed blond dredloks and gloried in affected black street talk. Brock had mocked him and angrily walked away more than once. Sometimes Tom trailed him, defending his love of black slang.

"Look, man," Tom said, "we go a long ways back. Plus, you're supposed to be a saint of compassion," Tom would whine sarcastically in these moments when Brock spurned him.

"Look," Brock would answer quietly, visibly trembling, his voice rising, "can't you mothers see that I'm tired now? Oh, sure, I can keep fox-trotting. But I can't make the world a better place. Sorry."

Brock remembered this. He said nothing now as they sat side by side on the ledge of the Chinese zone of Roosevelt Park.

"Man. This beer is given me the trots," Tom said. "Wanna split a pint?"

"Too early in this fucking heat."

"I sure could use some pussy."

Brock sighed, "What else is new?"

Careful technician of emotions, Brock usually controlled his urges for sex. Love had always been elusive. Brock kept to his little routine of drinking, smoking dope, and pill popping. Serene and stoned, he diligently prayed that others would find sex and love. Hadn't he abstained from life? If your emotions were not involved, oh, you could offer a mountain of damaged charm.

"Easy for you to talk," Tom told him. "If I had your thlong, I'd charge admission."

Brock grimaced. Clichés were so incestuous as far as Brock was concerned. Sexual discussions with white men usually depressed or angered him. Of course, Brock regretted that he was not the first son of Long Dong Silver. Nevertheless, Brock was extremely pleased with his sculptured penis. And he often wondered if, among the twenty-third-century minorities, Anglo-Saxon men would continue the myth of black sexual prowess.

Brock grimaced again. He turned his mind back to sports. Remembering he was five years older than Tom and shorter, but still had a boxer's physique. Occasionally the veteran friends sparred.

"Man. You'd still be a hell of a contender for The Golden Gloves."

Brock would laugh happily. "Yeah 'cause I got these fucking smart reflexes."

"Yes," Tom would agree, caressing Brock's stomach, "but you're gettin' a little gut."

"I'm solid, you flabby mother. At least I don't look pregnant like you."

That elusive breeze ran past their faces again. Tom finished his beer and looked down at the Chinese youths drinking trendy bottles of Poland Spring Water, wiping their faces with their tee shirts.

Brock turned to Tom to express an idle thought. "These days I'm celibate and basically happy. As my houseboy in Nam always said, "Why go to Momma-san and spend two dollars when you've got five fingers?"

"Man. It ain't the same. I need some loving."

"Can't you get a whore?" Brock asked.

Tom stood up. "Fuck you, buddy." He began walking away.

Brock watched him move toward Grand Street with his combat soldier's exhausted pace, looking left and right. Brock obeyed military code and watched his back.

Brock moaned audibly and closed his eyes. When he opened them again he thought, "Well, what is it? Emotional puke, self-pity or just the usual unlucky collection of misery?" He stood up with the ringing of loud voices and traffic still in his ears and began talk-singing a Marvin Gaye classic. "I'm coming apart, baby ... moving on down the line." He carefully surveyed the park, bolted towards a tree, urinated, rezipped his jeans and walked towards Grand Street, musing that unlike Tom he moved like a soldier on parade.

It was almost five in the afternoon and the heat wasn't breaking. That terrible blue sky hadn't moved. It would be hours before the blessed darkness. He didn't want to return to his tiny studio in Loisado with the tall window overlooking the vacant lot, where men repaired cars and laughed good-naturedly, lulled by sweet salsa music and female voices from The Pentecostal All Saints and Sinners Redeemer Church. He believed his options were limited, and so they were.

On Grand Street he turned west, on Allen he turned north. Its island of young trees, garbage and solid wooden benches was occupied by men and women whom Brock thought lobotomized by the past. Still he pressed forward to his destination. These strangers were part of his world of drugs and alcohol. He understood them, listened to them, offered advice, spare cigarettes and change, but kept his distance. He would keep his own misery private, thank you—a simple act of self-protection.

Brock was grinning now, one more block and he would see a familiar smiling face. The gold-toothed Chinese liquor store owner was always gentlemanly. "Small or large today?" he would ask politely. Brock would answer, "Large, thank you very much." After all, it was his heart, and he knew better than to try extracting compassion from a stone.

Dusk had evaporated, but the tormented sky remained. Brock, uplifted by inexpensive scotch and feeling absolutely no pain, returned to the Chinese zone of Roosevelt Park.

"Why not a fucking Hallmark sky?" he said aloud.

The benches surrounding the basketball court were crowded. A loud group of methadonians, addicts nurtured by methadone, sat on a ledge fronting the playground.

Fronting the Sanitation Department's Palladian-style build-ing, hard-drinking Bowery men occupied their regular elegant stone tables.

So Brock walked up the wide steps adjoining the Sanitation Building which gave on to a rubberized field for baseball and soccer. Tiers of stone benches surrounded the field. On the west, a line of beautiful trees blanketed sweatshops, a defunct brothel and the Grace Faith Church. The monolithic Confucius Plaza Projects loomed in the background.

There were only several Roller Bladers. Brock, grateful to be alone, wearily sat down on a bench. He took a long drink of scotch and almost gagged. For the time being, he thought, my misery, anger and loneliness are in a safe-deposit vault, thank you. I will be serene until morning. Brock leaned against an upper bench and crossed his legs and looked towards the Sanitation Building and moaned. Tom was veering towards him with the confidence of a policeman. His left hand secured an orange Chinatown plastic bag.

"Ole buddy." Tom grinned. "Planning to sleep out?"

"I don't know what the hell I'm going to do."

Tom placed the plastic bag near Brock. "I know you like the Aussies' Foster. So here's a beer."

"Thanks," Brock replied. He opened the beer and took a delicious drink.

"We'll get it together," Tom told him, "sooner or later."

"Hope so." Brock clutched the cold beer and looked up at Tom. "I love you like a brother. That's all."

"That's all? What do you mean, you stoned bastard?"

Brock shook his head and yawned, exhausted. "Literally speaking," he said, "that's all."

Zazoo

Larry Duplechan

I can still remember the smells of that summer. More than anything else about it, the scents of that years-ago summer cling
to my soft inner tissues like the cold I am nursing today. I recall
the smells of wetness, the perpetual, all pervading, endless Louisiana wet, that suffocatingly hot wet that fell as warm rain,
only to dissipate into steam just above the ground. The scent
of the damp grasses that grew thigh-high to my father around
the muddy little lake where we went crawfishing once—my
father, my brother Dalton, my cousin Curtis, and me—using
bits of pork rind on a string. The dark semisweet scent of the
mud, mud that seemed nearly as omnipresent as the wetness
and the heat, clay-red and seemingly alive in its power to suck
your shoes under.

I remember the sickening sweet-sweet smell of the Off insect
repellent that Duchess liked to say was like whiskey to the
mosquitoes that relentlessly bit our arms and necks and faces,
no matter how slick and shiny and smelly with bug spray. I
remember the odor of Curtis's teenage sweat, sharp and pungent, an odor that no amount of Right Guard deodorant could
entirely mask.

Even now, as L.A. rains one of its all too infrequent spring
rains, making the backyard muddy and soft (at least I assume
it's soft—I haven't been out today), making it smell as much
like the Louisiana bayou country as it ever does; as I sit up in

bed with the new Vidal in my lap and an ugly head cold pressing against the backs of my eyes, the smell of the rain-soaked Bermuda grass takes me all the way back to the summer of 1968. It was the summer before I turned eleven, the summer Great-Grandma Eudora died, the summer my cousin Curtis showed me. Showed me how.

It was the summer Mom and Dad finally allowed me to go hunting with Curtis. Mom insisted I was still too young to go hunting, as if Curtis felled great brown bears with double-barreled shotguns, instead of picking off wild birds and small game with a BB gun. My father hesitated only on the grounds that Great-Grandma Eudora's funeral had been less than twenty-four hours earlier, wondering whether it might not be disrepectful of the recently dead for any of us to go hunting so soon after the burial of Duchess's mother, my mother's beloved grandmother. Unlike our annual Christmas visits, this was not, after all, a pleasure trip.

Still, I begged and pleaded and whined—I didn't resort to whining often, but when I did I was expert at it—and not only did my parents finally acquiesce, but they even decided to allow Dalton (a full two and a half years younger than I) to go along. Even though I considered it the height of unfairness that Dalton should reap the benefits of my begging, pleading, and whining, in my joy at the prospect of finally accompanying Curtis into the woods that began just across the muddy dirt road from Duchess's house, I let it slide and ran immediately into the back room (the "extra room," as Duchess always called it) to pull on my high-top tennis shoes—I owned no boots.

The mud smells and moist green smells of the heavy-branched trees (what varieties of tree grew in the little forest I didn't know at the time and, frankly, still wouldn't know) mixed with the stronger scents of wet fur and animal droppings as we walked with some difficulty through the woods. The mud suctioned at my shoes as if it meant to keep them, and the mosquitoes hummed bebop solos in both my ears as I followed behind Dalton (though younger, he was just as tall, much more robust, and a good deal more adventurous than I), who followed Curtis. Curtis and Dalton each carried a BB-shooting air rifle. I had agreed to let Dalton carry the second gun, which made me look like Mr. Nice Guy in front of the folks, when actually I simply hadn't the smallest desire even to hold a gun. I shoved distastefully at mossy low-hanging tree branches that brushed against me as I walked. Although we had not been gone ten minutes, already the steamy heat had rendered my sweatshirt sticky wet and uncomfortable; the insect repellent was doing me no good—indeed, it seemed to lure the mosquitoes—and I was beginning to doubt the wisdom of coming out at all. I had no taste for the hunt itself, anyway. My only desire was to be with Curtis.

I had a crush on my cousin Curtis bigger than the State of Louisiana and a goodly chunk of Texas. Curtis was three years my senior. He had a voice nearly as deep as my father's and a smile that made my toes curl: a smile full of so many teeth that they stacked on top of one another on one side, a smile that deeply dimpled his handsome mahogany-brown cheeks. He also had one of the most beautiful bodies I had ever seen outside of a Hercules movie or a Charles Atlas Dynamic Tension ad in the back of a comic book. Curtis wasn't very tall (only an inch or two taller than I), but he owned an ancient iron barbell set, black and rusted and noisy, and he exercised every day.

I'd seize every opportunity to sit on Curtis's bed, my back against the whitewashed plaster wall, and watch him, shirtless and barefoot, pressing the barbell up from his chest (exhaling with an audible *pshoop*), and then lowering the bar back (inhaling slowly, *sssssssp*); up and down, again and again, Curtis's face a mask of concentration, the veins in his big arms distended, one blood vessel throbbing rhythmically in the center of his forehead, his muscles seemingly capable of bursting his glossy brown skin. I'd sit, watching him as if he were my favorite TV show, my legs pulled up and crossed tightly around my hard penis. I often got hard watching Curtis; but then, I often got hard sitting in math class, or at the dinner table, or just sitting. Dalton often sat with me, but I'd ignore him as completely as I could, pretending to be alone with Curtis, that Curtis was performing for me, only me.

After he finished lifting, Curtis would stand in front of the slightly warped full-length mirror bolted to the bathroom door, flexing his muscles and studying the imperfect reflection of his perfect body. Then he'd turn to me, smile (each of his cheeks indented with a long, deep dimple), and say, "Boy, ah'm built, yeah!" Usually, I could only smile—he was so beautiful I could hardly speak.

Before we had gone deep enough into the woods to lose sight of the house, I looked down to find that the mud had lapped over the tops of both my shoes, ruining them—the stubborn red clay would never wash out. A huge, long-limbed mosquito swooped at my face, just missing my right eye, and I stopped and swatted wildly at the winged nuisance with both hands, and cried out a high-pitched little "Ah!" Dalton turned, quickly sizing up my predicament, rolled his eyes, and made a little tapping sound with his tongue. And I knew I'd done a sissy thing. Whenever I did a sissy thing—made a wild, futilely short throw of a softball, or hid my eyes during a scary movie, or cried when angry—Dalton would give me one of those looks, and I'd know he was wondering to himself what he could possibly have done to deserve such a big brother.

I hoped Curtis hadn't noticed what I'd done. Curtis seemed to like me—possibly (I thought) even more than he liked Dalton—and it was of the utmost importance to me that his affection and respect for me not be diminished by some inadvertent sissified action on my part. I looked toward Curtis and was relieved to find he was not looking at me but had run on ahead, obviously having heard some significant sound deeper into the woods.

"C'mon, y'all," he called over his shoulder.

I don't really remember what hit me first, but it was probably the smells: wet fur and blood, fear and pain.

"Lookadat!" Curtis gestured toward the ground with the barrel of his gun. There on the wet mossy ground, a large brown rabbit was caught by the hind foot in one of the traps Curtis kept set for raccoons, muskrats, and other rodents, whose hides he expertly removed from the carcasses and sold, and whose stringy flesh Duchess often stewed with canned tomatoes for supper. (Oh, how my L.A. stomach spasmed at the scent of simmering coon. While my family's lips collectively smacked over the oily meat, I preferred a supper of Rice Krispies and milk.) The rabbit's eyes were big and shiny as brown marbles. The fur of its trapped foot was matted with blood; I could see the startling white of bare bone where the animal had obviously gnawed through its own flesh in a wild attempt to free itself. Its other three limbs scraped furiously at the ground as if on a treadmill gone beserk, its instinct for escape far outweighing its power.

The rabbit's mouth was open far wider than I would have imagined possible. And it was screaming. An impossible sound, at once high-pitched and guttural. I had never before heard a rabbit make any sound at all—I had no idea one could scream.

I could feel my morning meal (pancakes and Duchess's homemade pork sausage) rising toward my throat. I turned and ran blindly, only managing to go a few feet before colliding with the trunk of a tree, at the roots of which my stomach unquestionably offered up my breakfast. The pounding of my head nearly obscured the sound, the clean, hard *phttt* of the BB gun shooting the rabbit dead. I assumed at first the gun had been Curtis's; then I heard Dalton's voice calling, "I *shot* it! I *shot* it!"

I leaned against the tree, crying and puking, until I felt Curtis's hand touch me (with surprising gentleness) on my back.

"Hey, Zazoo, you all right?" Curtis often called me Zazoo. To this day, I don't know why. No one else called me that, no one ever had. Maybe there was something in my often nervous, jittery, hands-aflying manner that reminded Curtis of Zazu Pitts (who was still very much in evidence through daily reruns of *My Little Margie*). Maybe I just looked Zazoo to him. At any rate, it gave me such a feeling of specialness that Curtis had this strange little name for me—he always called Dalton Dalton—that I never questioned it.

"I—I—" I stammered through hiccuping sobs. Who knows what I might have been trying to say? I stood against that tree, mud and vomit splattered across the tops of my sneakers, my face streaked with tears and snot, while, in my tear-blurred peripheral vision, I could just see Dalton, shaking his head in utter disgust, his right hand clutching the rabbit's carcass—limp and bloody and minus a hind foot—by its long ears. I wiped at my running nose with the side of my arm. My degradation seemed complete. I had shown myself for the sniveling sissy crybaby I truly was, and I had done so in grand style.

"Aw, c'mon, Zazoo," Curtis crooned on one note, his hand making little downward stroking motions between my shoulder blades. He reached into his back jeans pocket, retrieved a wrinkled wad of a red bandanna, and offered it to me. I brought the cloth to my face (it was full of Curtis's smells), wiped at my mouth, blew my nose, and pocketed the bandanna.

"You all right, Zazoo?"

I sniffed snot and said Yes (sniff), thank you, still looking down at the puddle I had left at the base of the tree, not daring to look at Curtis's face, noticing how my vomit seemed to blend into the colors of the fungus-covered ground.

"Zazoo," I heard Dalton repeat in a mocking stage whisper. "Heck!" I turned quickly toward Dalton, filled with temporary fraternal hatred, but turned back just as quickly at the sight of the bloody animal clutched in Dalton's fist.

"We better get on back," Curtis said. "Have Duchess give you some'm fuh yuh stomach."

"But we just *got* here," Dalton protested.

"We come back another time," Curtis said.

"But we're *leaving* tomorrow! Shoot!"

"C'mon." Curtis ignored Dalton, put his arm around my shoulders, and we started back.

"Shoot!" Dalton shouted from behind us. "You big baby. You always ruin *everything*. Big baby!" I could hear the loud wet slaps of Dalton's stomping steps behind us. And I didn't care. Curtis kept his arm around me all the way back to the house, and that was well worth Dalton's wrath. It was even worth throwing up for.

"Duchess," Curtis called as the screen door slapped shut behind us, "Zazoo got sick to his stomach."

"Big baby," Dalton grumbled, "ruin everything. Duchess, can I have a tea cake?"

Mom, Dad, and Duchess were seated at the kitchen table having strong black coffee and Duchess's tea cakes.

"What's the matter, baby?" Duchess said, putting down her cup.

"Now," Mom said, "I knew you shouldn't o' gone out there. You always had a weak stomach."

"Dalton, don't be callin' yuh gran'ma Duchess," Dad said. "Call her Gran'ma."

"But, Daddy," Dalton said, grabbing three big tea cakes from the plate on the table, "Curtis calls her Duchess and she's his gramma, too."

"I'll fix you some chamomile tea," Duchess said, taking the big old black kettle off the stove to fill.

"I didn't *say* Curtis," Dad said. "I say *you*."

"You best go wash your face, Zazoo," Curtis said, patting me on the small of the back.

"Thass all right if he call me Duchess—everybody do." And almost everybody did. According to my mother, Grandpa Sherman had given her that name, and it was all I had ever heard him call his wife to the day he died, though no one (not even Grandma) could seem to remember when he began calling her Duchess, or why.

"Naw, iss *not* all right, Miz Mary," I heard Dad saying as I shut the bathroom door behind me.

The boy in the mirror smiled at me. His face was stained with tears and snot, but he was smiling. I had shown my true self—sissy, crybaby, the works—and Curtis had not forsaken me.

My heart threatened to explode with love.

I spent the rest of the afternoon in the spare room, with the big old Philco console radio on, rereading *Tom Sawyer* (I had found a tattered copy in Curtis's room), my embarrassment wrapped around me like a big old sweater. I wondered at my own reaction to the sight of the trapped rabbit. I had cried less at Great-Grandma Eudora's funeral, and even that had been more a reaction to my mother, sobbing loudly from beneath Dad's big, comforting arm, and Duchess, her tear-beaded eyes closed, rocking herself and moaning My Lord, my Lord, than any real sense of loss at the death of Eudora, whose large, warm, kitchen-smelly presence I knew relatively little. In fact, upon viewing Eudora's remains, it had occurred to me that I had never before seen my great-grandmother's hair (now at last revealed as short as my own and entirely white); she had worn a checkered kerchief around her head Aunt-Jemina-style on every other occasion I could remember having seen her.

I was amazed that the rabbit's death, loud and bloody and right before my eyes, was so much more real to me than Eudora's: a silent, painless expiration in her sleep nearly a week before, while I too had slept, nearly half the country away.

As I pondered this, staring toward if not exactly at the opposite wall, fingers tucked between the pages of *Tom Sawyer*, Curtis burst into the room, wearing only his baggy once-white boxer shorts, dancing a silly head-down, hip-shaking dance across the hardwood floor, singing out of tune with Otis Redding on the radio, "HOLD huh, SQUEEZE huh, nevah LEAVE huh!" And I laughed, as uncontrollably as I had cried before.

Curtis stopped dancing and stood, fists on hips, screwing his face into a parody of anger, looking beautiful and ridiculous.

"You laughin' at me, boy?" he said, lowering his voice a gruff octave. I shook my head no, convulsed with laughter.

Curtis fell to the floor, tickling me in the ribs and belly, making me laugh until I nearly peed my pants. Then he did a quick tippy-toe from the room, leaving me in a spasming heap, tears in my eyes and giggles leaking from between my lips, my penis stiff as a Popsicle stick.

The afternoon had about exhausted me. Shortly following a supper of Duchess's okra gumbo (during which Dalton made an obvious point of not speaking to me), I crawled into bed early without being asked to. I shared Curtis's bed on our visits, a turn of events which I considered a privilege far surpassing Dalton's having a bed to himself. Most nights I purposely kept myself awake, feigning sleep until I was sure Curtis was sleeping. Then I would slowly reach out my hand and touch Curtis's humid back. Or lean toward him and smell the grassy scent of his hair. Or, if I was feeling particularly adventurous, I would tickle the sole of his foot with my toes, just enough to make him grunt in his sleep and kick out at the sheets.

That evening, I remember, Curtis had gone out to visit some friends of his from school, so I slid over to the far side of the old spring-twangy bed, pressed my back against the cool wall, and allowed the ever-present swamp cooler to hum me quickly to sleep. I dreamed of Curtis and me sitting in the corner of the spare room, both of us with our shirts off, Curtis's arm around me, both of us smiling and laughing. The feeling was sweet and warm, and it was still with me when I suddenly awoke, hot and covered with sweat, my penis so hard it hurt. It was pitch dark, and I had no idea how long I had been asleep. Curtis had not yet come to bed, but I could hear Dalton's snoring from the opposite side of the room, over the sound of the swamp cooler.

My pajama bottoms were twisted and bunched around my thighs, lodged securely up the cleft of my behind: I shinnied them down past my knees. I continued the movement of my hips even after pulling down my p.j.s, enjoying the feeling of the slightly damp sheets against my skin. It was something I'd been doing quite often for a year or so, this rubbing-against-the-sheets thing. Not every single night, but often. Suddenly, an image of Curtis pressing his barbell up from his chest popped into my mind uninvited; I welcomed it in, and it added to my enjoyment.

I didn't hear Curtis come in. When I felt the weight of him on the bed, I stopped suddenly, breathlessly, embarrassed at being caught in my private pleasure. I lay completely still for a long moment, not knowing what, if anything, to say. Curtis was silent for several breaths, long enough for my eyes to become accustomed to the darkness, so that I could just make out his form, dark against dark, his shorts looking so white they seemed to glow. Curtis finally whispered, "I know why you're doing that."

"What?" I was genuinely surprised. Did this mean Curtis did it too? I had assumed I'd invented it, or at least discovered it.

"I know what you're doing," Curtis rephrased, a bit louder.

"I just," I stammered, raising myself up on my elbows, not easily accomplished with my pajama bottoms wadded around my calves. "It just feels—I dunno, it's—"

"You don't even know, do you?" Curtis said. "I bet you don't even know."

"Know what?"

"Know how."

"How?" I said.

"Shoot," Curtis said. I could see his smile in the dark. "You don't even know."

"What do you mean?" I said. I kicked free of my pajamas and sat up, pulling the sheet up around my waist.

"Here," he said, pulling his legs up onto the bed. "I'll show you, if you want. I'll show you how."

And to my amazement, Curtis reached into the long opening of his boxer shorts and fished out his penis. I could almost feel my pupils dilate. I was not, I hasten to mention, one of those boys with a long history of playing Doctor with the neighborhood girls, or touching wienies with little boyhood chums around somebody's swimming pool while Mom and Dad are out playing Pinochle. I had, in fact, never engaged in any sort of sexual play with another child, not even with Dalton. This was a first. And I was fascinated.

I watched in rapt attention as Curtis's penis stirred, then grew beneath his fingers; its head, purple-brown like his gums when he smiled, peeked out like a turtle from a collar of skin my own organ did not have. His penis seemed impossibly large; my own seemed small and babyish by comparison.

I wanted to touch it. I leaned forward slightly, toward it. Curtis whispered, "Go ahead." He'd probably meant it as a direction to mimic his slow stroking motion on myself, but instead I reached out (my heart pounding loud enough to deafen me) and stroked up the underside of Curtis's big thing with trembling fingers. It was startlingly hot, and it moved at my touch like some strange little animal.

"Do yours," Curtis said, pushing my hand gently away.

I moved my hand from him reluctantly, and began to mirror Curtis's hand motion as best I could, finding the sensation neither more nor less pleasurable than my usual sheet dance. Watching Curtis, though, was wonderful. I gazed enraptured (is that too strong a word, I wonder—no, I think not), as Curtis's head finally fell back against the wall, his eyes closing as if falling asleep. And then his penis was spewing long white ribbons that fell in bright contrasting stripes against his dark brown thighs and belly and fingers; and he was humming low in his throat. My first climax was much less dramatic, merely a long head-to-heels shudder, like a sudden chill, and a drop of clear liquid (it looked like Karo syrup) that dripped slowly from my penis and down the back of my hand.

This moment, this thing that Curtis had somehow chosen to share with me on this night, was like nothing I'd ever before experienced—wonderful, frightening, mysterious. I could not have felt closer to my cousin if we had shared our darkest secrets or mingled our blood. I loved Curtis at that moment like never before, with a terrible aching love the likes of which I have yet to recapture in any or all of the loves that have followed (and there have been two or three).

When he had finished, Curtis opened his eyes, looked at me through the dark, smiling what seemed to be a secret sort of smile, and said, "See?" Then he tiptoed the three or four steps to the bathroom. I heard the water running for a bit, and then Curtis came out, wiping his hands on a towel, which he then handed to me. I wiped myself off, pulling up my pajamas, and lay back, my heart racing as if I'd been running for blocks, feeling somehow different, wondering if I might look different now. I fell asleep almost instantly.

When I awoke, it crossed my mind that I might have dreamed it. But I knew better. Curtis was gone; he had set off hunting on his own. "Before day in the morning," Duchess said. He had not returned by the time we were ready to leave for the train station, and I didn't get to say good-bye to him. It felt terribly important that I see Curtis before we left, though for what reason I couldn't say. Maybe I expected some sign— a look, another secret smile, some reconfirmation of my sense that Curtis and I had in the night become special to one another, joined somehow.

I craned my neck toward the woods in search of Curtis even as we lit out, Dad behind the wheel of Duchess's huge old '60 Chevy; the weight of it, us, and our luggage digging twin trenches in the muddy road before finally taking off. As the car lurched away, I squirmed completely around in the car seat—"Hey, cut it out!" said Dalton, his first words to me in nearly twenty-four hours—hoping to see Curtis running from the woods, having forgotten the time, wanting as much as I wanted to say good-bye. Or at least to catch a glimpse of him walking that big-stepping walk with some carcass or other slung over his wide shoulder. But no. I turned forward in the seat ("Cut it *out!*" whined Dalton), my fists clenched with all my strength.

"Bless yo' li'l heart," Duchess said when she noticed the tears coming down my face. "You gon' miss yo' gran'ma, yeah."

"Big baby," Dalton mumbled.

I didn't see much of Curtis after that summer. We all got the Hong Kong flu that December and did not return until the following July. By that time, I found the three years that separated Curtis and me had become a wider, deeper valley than it had ever seemed before. Curtis was dating and had little time to spend with younger cousins, and (it seemed) little desire to spend it. I wondered at first if he felt ashamed for what we had done together the summer before, but it became obvious to me (by then twelve years old and fancying myself reasonably sophisticated) that Curtis was becoming a man, while I was still very much a boy. In any case, we never again did the thing together. But no matter. I had adopted it as my own, and enjoyed it often.

Shortly after he turned eighteen, Curtis got a girl pregnant (no one ever told me this—I overheard it); and some months following the birth of their child (a boy they named Curtis), he married the girl and they moved to Oklahoma, where Curtis when to work in the oil fields. And I never saw him again.

By the time Dalton called to tell me Curtis had died of colon cancer somewhere in Tennessee at the age of thirty-four, I hadn't even spoken to Curtis in over fifteen years. When I heard Dalton's voice on the telephone, I knew it was death—since we had grown up and grown apart, Dalton seldom called me for anything less.

"I got some bad news," he said, and took in a deep, audible breath. "Cousin Curtis passed." The short sentence seemed to take the whole breath.

Tears fell as he told me the when and where of the funeral, but I wasn't listening. I knew I wouldn't go; I have never understood the practice of viewing remains. It reminds me of the animals Curtis used to carry back from the woods—hides, carcasses.

"Remember that name he used to call you?" Dalton said. "Zazzy or something."

"Zazoo," I said.

"Yeah, right. Zazoo. Where'd that come from, anyway?"

"I never asked."

I thanked Dalton for the call; said, Yes, I'll see you at the funeral—Dalton went to them all. I hung up the telephone and immediately poured myself a brandy.

Strange. I'd been thinking of Curtis that very day. You see, it was raining.

Heathcliff, Ivan and Me

Greg Henry

You see me first.

I am on the couch, laid out tastefully, next to a bowl of plums, selected for their rich color; a leather bag from someone's trip to Mexico; a black leather jacket, two sizes too small.

Past the hall that leads to the bedroom, a Chagall hangs. Trace your hand along the wall and follow the rug—more art pieces hang here. One is a black painting. There is nothing on the canvas but black paint, impeccably shaded. The bedroom is next. Heathcliff stands near to the entrance, careful not to touch the wall, though it seems like he must be leaning against something. He is looking at you.

Go past him quickly and enter the bedroom. Ivan smiles down at you from the ceiling. There is where I've hidden him.

Heathcliff comes and goes through this house. It is his, after all, and almost nowhere is safe from him. His fingerprints are all over my diary. I noticed this about three weeks ago, and now I am forced to lie in it daily, to keep him from getting angry. He knows everything. And yet he never looks up at the ceiling. This is why Ivan is safe—because Heathcliff is known for always looking straight ahead. He is known for being very straightforward. He is known for heading the corporation.

Mostly, I am known for being young.

Ivan is known for twists and turns, for bench presses, and for dancing onstage with very little clothing on. Once, five years

178

ago, he posed nude for *Blueboy,* a job for which he was paid
$250 and then given a turkey sandwich after everything was
over. The photographer was rude to him, called him "scenery,"
and Ivan couldn't bring himself to eat the sandwich. When they
put his picture in the magazine, they did it so that the staple
would go over his left eye, making it look like he had been in
a bad fight.

But, despite all this, the picture still looks as though he is
the only person in the world who is good for anything.

You may wonder: how could Heathcliff sleep in the bed
with me all night, get up in the morning, get out of bed, and
still not see the picture that hangs above him every night? How
could he not see it during the evening, when he is home from
the office?

I am not sure, but I think the answer has something to do
with humility. Heathcliff has none. He cannot imagine me desiring Ivan, desiring anyone but himself, so he does not see him.
This, and the fact that the cleaning woman comes twice a week
now, and he doesn't have to look for dust anymore. All he has
to do is work.

As you know, Heathcliff is the Heathcliff of Heathcliff &
Heathcliff, Inc. But there is no other Heathcliff—he just thought
it sounded better that way, with two names, so that was that.
I'm not sure what he does all day while I stay at home, trying
to write a book and longing for Ivan, and I'm not sure I want
to know. I know he deals with a lot of the money, that we
know. I know he is involved with oil. He wants to obliterate
Channel 13.

Sometimes he tries to involve me in his work. Sometimes
he tells me that it is good that I am young, that I am between
the ages of eighteen and forty-nine, that I am smart and funny,
and that my opinions could mean something important to him.
On these days he walks through the door with sheafs and sheafs
of paper containing endless questions that he asks me over
supper.

Like: "What," he says, "would you think of flavored
sugar?"

"What do you mean?" I say, my mouth partly full. "Do
you mean like Kool-Aid?"

He puts his hand over my mouth. "No."

I tell him I will sleep on it. But I don't sleep. In his sleep, Heathcliff kisses me very, very deeply. His lips are touching the back of my throat, and it feels like he is trying to feed a pillow down my mouth, like a pill. Then his throat makes a noise and he begins using his teeth. When he is done, there is blood in my mouth. In the morning, I tell him that I think flavored sugar is brilliant, is great, who thought of it? He beams and buys me a bathrobe.

You could say that we have come to an understanding.

What must poor Ivan think of all this? Six years ago, in 1983, when I met him backstage after one of his shows, he was impressed by my poetry. He said I would go far. He protected me from the jeers of his fellow dancers. He was surprised that I was just fifteen. He gave me his number and told me his real name.

"Troy," he whispered into my ear fervently, pressing a piece of paper into my palm, getting baby oil on my sleeve. "Troy Davis."

I thought for sure that I had touched the face of God. I went home. I waited one day to be sure. I waited two days, I waited three. Then I called his number.

Of course, it had been disconnected.

The next night, when I went back to the club where he had danced, one of the other dancers told me he had moved to Michigan, that he had given up "the business." Then this other dancer tried to give me his beeper number, so that I could call him later that night.

"I'm only fifteen!" I said.

He seemed surprised, but also not surprised.

As for me, I went mad, I think. I ran into a church and asked a priest for forgiveness. What can I do? I sobbed, thinking I would get ten Hail Mary's and one Our Father. Instead, the priest told me to grow older. I did. Just barely. Just barely. Now I am twenty-one.

Now I have Heathcliff. We met when I was twenty. We have, I think, a good life. Sometimes he has an odd energy to him, but he is fine mostly. Sometimes, after a whole day of his sneering, he will fall asleep next to me, and his finger will start tugging piteously at the top button of my pajama top, unable to work it open. It is then that I know that he loves me, that he would do anything for me. All he wants is to know that I am his.

Am I? I *think* so, but still there is this . . .

After Ivan left for Michigan, I phoned directory information and got his number, which I wrote down on a corner of his picture. I told myself I would never use the number, that it was there just in case. And I tried to live in the moment with Heathcliff, really. That's the best thing about Heathcliff—living in the moment. It's killing me. When I want to write my novel, he takes me to the south of France. When I want to attend a seminar, he sulks until I relent and watch TV with him in bed all day and then fix him his orange juice and a piece of toast with salt. Whenever I think that, because I am still young, there is still time for me to develop genius, he finds some way to kill even more time. I think he wants me in stasis. If he sees me taking off my pajamas after a day in bed with him, he will kiss me and kiss me for hours at a time, with me half in, half out of a pajama leg, no good to anybody.

I got mad and ask him:

"When will it be time for *my* work!"

He writes down a figure on a piece of paper and hands it to me. I am appalled. "So soon?" Then he goes off to work. One hour later, his secretary calls me and asks me where I would like to live, if ever I am separated from Heathcliff. She says she is taking a survey for a night class she is taking. But I don't think she would have time for a night class. Look at her now—it is 9 P.M. and she is still in the office, in case Heathcliff needs her.

"Um," I say, "Alburquerque?"

"Oh!" she says. I think I hear her rustling some papers near the area of her lap. Then I also hear Heathcliff in the background, murmuring something for her to tell me.

I hang up. Frantic, I call up Ivan in Michigan, to ask him if I can come and live with him forever. He answers the phone groggy. I look at my watch. It is 9:15 P.M.

"Ivan. It's me," I say.

"Who?"

Oh. I forgot. I try to explain who I am. I draw a scene for him of a summer afternoon at an all-male strip club in Manhattan, where we met in 1983. I tell him what he was wearing and what I was wearing. (I was wearing a black leather jacket that fit me perfectly; he was wearing a loincloth). I recite a poem that I told him. I ask him if he remembers giving me his home phone number and telling me his real name.

"Troy," I say, tentatively. "Troy Davis?"

He considers this. "Don't," he says finally, "ever call me again."

He puts down the phone.

I keep holding it, hopeful that he will pick up his end again, even just to phone for the weather or a pizza, and that it will still be me on the other end, waiting for him. I look at his picture, which I have taken down from the ceiling, and I listen to the tone of the phone. All around me, there are sounds from this house. The bed creaks. Heathcliff comes home and is walking around somewhere within these walls. I cannot hear these things. The phone is my life right now.

Which is why Heathcliff is able to surprise me. This is the position in which he finds me. This is what he does. First, he wrests Ivan from me and tosses him onto a burner of the stove, lighting it with his other hand. Ivan twists and turns one last time, then curls up like a fist and dies. Then Heathcliff walks back into the bedroom where I am shivering on the mattress and breaks my arm. My head lolls up. What happens after this, I am unsure of. Just that, when I come to, he is crying and holding me and I cannot move. He is stroking the hair on my arms.

". . . so awfully young," he is saying, while moving his hand over my stomach. Moving his hand over my legs, my face, my shoulders. "So terribly, terribly young."

I think for a moment, in wonder, that I am even younger than ever. That I have even been reduced to a fetal position.

"Don't you worry, my darling!" he is saying. "We're going to get you fixed up all better after this! I promise. Oh God, I'm so sorry!"

And "This is what they made me do!"

Then he sees that my eyes have opened a crack, and notices

my trembling, and his eye closes down on me. He cups my cheek. "You should not have been doing that, should you, darling?"

No.

"You are mine, I am yours, isn't that so, darling?"

Yes.

"These things—these things of the flesh should not concern you, am I right?"

Yes.

"You are twenty-one."

No. He is wrong. I am twenty-two.

I am twenty-three. I am twenty-four. I am twenty-five.

At twenty-six I grow old, and at that point, none of this matters anymore.

My Son, My Heart, My Life

John R. Keene, Jr.

Sandalwood, Jaime whispers to himself, recalling the vendor who had sold Tony and him the three little vials of the scented oil and the five foil packets of incense from his makeshift stall outside the bus terminal in Dudley Square. Wearing an elaborately embroidered red and black tarboosh and an immaculately white T-shirt, on which had been silk-screened in exquisite calligraphics the simple phrase "Life is the finest art," he was probably in his early twenties and handsome, Jaime now recalls, though hard living had so weathered his face and hands, his gestures, that he looked much older. His thin, dark fingertips, sallowed by the oils, the incense, cigarettes, perhaps even the plate of curried goat that sat at the edge of the display table, fanned slowly over the array of offerings, patchouli, lavender, musk, rose of Sharon, anise, something called "Love," something else called "Power," which Jaime had not noticed before. Which one *you* like?" *Sandalwood*, Tony had snapped without deliberation: It was the only scent Tony had ever worn.

—What*ever* you do, baby, don't forget your algebra notebook! Jaime's mother's call rings from the kitchen, where she is preparing breakfast for his two younger sisters, Tatiana and Tasha. Having awoken early as always with his older sister Teresita, Jaime has already wolfed down a banana and a piece of white bread with strawberry jelly for breakfast, before his mother and the girls rise, to stay out of their way. Sometimes

184

he will drink a cup of coffee and chat with Teresita—whose position as an assistant to the first-shift foreman at the nearby springs-manufacturing plant occasions *her* early mornings—but not this morning. He has spent the entire time since he woke, ate and showered in reading over his poem—*his poem!* which his teacher and classmates, everyone, including perhaps even his mother, will all be talking about for weeks to come—and checking his equations. Usually Teresita begins her morning with a cigarette or two, or on Saturdays, if she is not working and their mother is out, with a blunt; while she lit up her second smoke this morning, he struggled over an unsolvable "xy" and came up with the only answer that allowed the equation to work: this, he tells himself, calls for a celebration, a *game*.

—*Sí*, Mami, I promised you I wasn't gonna forget it again. That stupid notebook, Jaime grumbles, why can't he forget it altogether! He sits up on his bed, which he has just prepared to his mother's former specifications (since Antonio's death, she no longer has to scold him every morning, he now makes it instinctively), and opens the palm-size, amber-colored vial, one of the few personal effects of Tony's that neither his mother nor Tony's girlfriend has taken to hoard as her own. As he had observed Tony do every morning for the last few years, he places his index finger over the opening, upends it, then daubs the sweet, masculine fragrance under both ears; again, then lightly across his collarbone; one last time, a straight line from the point where his Adam's apple has begun to appear to the soft point of his chin.

This fragrance, Jaime realizes, still lingers upon the surface of everything in the apartment—the matted wool comforter on which he sits; the corners of the particleboard dresser that he and Tony had shared; this and every room's doors' tin-alloy hinges, their water-rotted sashes, their spiderwebby moldings; upon even the mildewed plaster antislip stars plastering the bottom of the bathtub, all redolent as though permanently coated—as if to ensure that Tony will not be forgotten.

Done, he shakes his head aggressively, as Tony would, then hides the vial under the stack of underpants in the top drawer of the dresser that has become his alone. He feels like a black-board from which everything has been erased, on which anything can be written. How long, he wonders, before Tatiana's or Tasha's lingerie turns up in there? Nothing in this family remains in anyone's sole possession for long.

Silent now, thinking of nothing, he can hear beneath the floorboards his uncle, Narciso, rearranging the merchandise on the shelves of the bodega he and his wife, Jaime's aunt, Marisol, own and operate. Above him, their apartment slumbers. Jaime is glad he does not have to help out this morning. Mostly he aids in moving big pieces of meat around the cold locker and shelving newly arrived canned and boxed goods when his uncle asks him to, but often his mother will send him downstairs to seek something to do after she has awakened the girls and begun to get them ready and before his bus arrives. Undoubtedly there is some bubble-gum box to be refilled, some soup cans to be shifted around or transformed into a stable pyramid, some moldy bread to be turned over so that the nearby loaves will mask it. This morning, however, her mind has latched completely on to that notebook.

Outside this room, music, laughter, the cacophony of glass against metal, voices and the television against the hour's stillness.

Tony, Jaime reminds himself, had never helped out. He had gone simply from fifth grade to the streets and a crew of similarly minded boys and couriering, which meant that Uncle Narciso and Aunt Marisol never wanted him around; his presence, at least in their eyes, and that of his associates usually spelt trouble. It was an easy out to which Jamie had no recourse: *Send Jaime down to help me out,* Uncle Narciso was always saying now, *so I can make a man out of him, keep him out of trouble.* Jaime's mother only too eagerly assented.

Hoisting his backpack onto the bed, Jaime pulls out his Spanish poem, which jogs his memory: Why aren't they writing essays yet? Because of the "turdles," as he and Vinh, his classmate and best and only friend, have often laughed to themselves at lunch, though neither would dare call the mass of their classmates, even the girls, this nickname face-to-face. Besides the occasional poem or paragraph, they are mainly doing multiple-choice quizzes, nothing more advanced, even though this class is supposedly accelerated. As usual Mrs. Donovan gave them nine regular words and a bonus word, and this time, as before, they were supposed to create a poem of at least one hundred words from these. *Too simple*, Vinh had cracked under his breath, to the general groans of the class; Jaime agreed. Now he is even surer his will merit an A, just like Vinh's, and Shonelle Watkins's and Gloria Velez's. Most of the other kids, even those whose first language is Spanish, will end up with Bs or Cs, whether they hand in homework or not, since Mrs. Donovan is unwilling to embarrass anyone, even the most slow-dropping of the "turdles," with anything lower. At any rate, they will *never* get to essays, Jaime sighs.

The words read, in this order:

hijo (son)	*parar* (to stop)
pedir (to ask for)	*cada* (each)
corazón (heart)	*broma* (joke)
hallar (to come across)	*sangre* (blood)
anochecer (nightfall)	*fugaz* (brief)* BONUS WORD

Such words! Vinh had said after fourth period that Mrs. Donovan had torn up a Spanish dictionary and picked the entries one by one out of a hat, but Jaime is convinced that she pulls some of them out of something she has been reading, some novel, some book of poetry, because there are always strange or unusual words, like *fugaz*, that are nowhere to be found in their Spanish book. He has never heard anyone, not his mother, nor Uncle Narciso nor Aunt Marisol, nor any of the Spanish speakers in the neighborhood or at church, nor even his grandmother, uncle, aunts or cousins in Puerto Rico, ever use this bonus word *fugaz* even once in conversation—he and his sisters speak only English regularly [as did Tony]—which for him is the giveaway. *This* word, he thinks, she has selected just for me.

As a result, he wrote (with the translation beside it):

Cada día al anochecer	Every day at nighttime
voy esa cama y pienso	I see that bed and I think
sobre mi hermano muerto,	about my dead brother,
Antonio José Barrett.	Antonio José Barrett.
Fue mi hermano solo	He was my only brother

y tuvo quince años y medio.	and was fifteen and a half years old.
Yo halle la sangre y su cuerpo	I found the blood and his body
que estaba acostada sobre la acera como un G.I. Joe.	lying on the sidewalk like a G.I. Joe.
Durante el funeral mi Mami preguntó al Dios,	During the funeral my mother asked God,
"¿Por qué, God, por qué	"How come, God, how come
mi hijo, mi corazón, mi vida, mi Tony	my son, my heart, my life, my Tony
por qué my baby ahora?"	why my baby now?"
Mi tío Narciso dijo toda la iglesia,	My Uncle Narciso said to the whole church,
"¿O Dios, mi amigos, quando la muerte va parar?"	"Oh God, my friends, when is the dying going to end?"
Nadie le respondió.	No one answered him.
Desde entonce hay una cosa que yo sé:	Since there is one thing I know:
en mi barrio vivir es muy fugaz y el futuro estará una broma grande.	in my neighborhood living is too brief and the future is a great big joke.

One hundred and eleven words he counts, and he has used the past tense correctly every time; he has verified this twice against his Spanish book. No misspellings that he can spot, and even some words they have not yet learned, but which he has gathered from regular conversations or his own reading: Mrs. Donovan will *have to* give him an A! When he recites it, she will comment on the rhymes in Spanish, on the flow, on the feeling: in her eyes there is *nothing* he can do wrong.

Pausing before his own piece, Jaime asks himself, what did Vinh write about? Probably not Vietnam, since he never writes about Vietnam, or Thailand, or New York or Washington, D.C., any of the other places where he and his family have lived; his poem is probably about comic-book superheroes, or American history, or something that happened in Boston a hundred years ago. In fact, Jaime muses, Vinh's poem is probably perfect, exactly one hundred words, dope rhymes, rolling off the page like a song or an ad or something you would find in a poetry book. Jaime looks at his poem again, wonders if he should change or add anything, then remembers the assessment he had spied on one of Vinh's personal evaluations: *his work, while generally excellent, lacks life.* Jaime decides not to alter a thing.

What else was there for today? For social studies he has his notes for his presentation on a country in west Africa; he had elected to report on Senegal, where he imagined some of his father's (and mother's, maybe) ancestors had come from, instead of Cape Verde, his other option—Vinh had gotten Colombia or Norway!—where Federico Nunes, his classmate, whose family owns the bodega across the street, was born. Federico had not even known where Cape Verde was on the map: When asked to point it out, he had placed his finger on Madagascar! Well, Mr. Wooten had said to the class's several rounds of laughter and Federico's embarrassed nod, at least he knows it's an *island* country! Jaime had written "turdlinho" on a sheet of paper, which he immediately passed on to Vinh; both had laughed without uttering a sound.

Federico, like most of the Cape Verdean kids Jaime knows, says he is Portuguese, but he didn't even know where Portugal lay on the map either, when Mr. Wooten had asked him. Finally Mr. Wooten left him alone. It did not matter, however; Federico had pulled out his beeper and fat roll of bills once Mr. Wooten's back was turned, to the silent oohs and aahs of most of the rest of the class, and grinned: he does not need any geography for what he is doing. Vinh whispered. He is *getting paid.*

Jaime, who knows all about Cape Verde, Portugal, and any other country you can name, rarely says *he* is Spanish, though this is what some of his family call themselves, what other kids have labeled him. He had even done a report on Spain, for which he had received an A-; he had not said enough about all that country's regions for Mr. Wooten's taste, and had played too much "the fool" during the question-and-answer session. Then as now he does not say he's anything at all—because what *is* he? Spanish? Puerto Rican? Black? he used to ask his mother, to no response, neither affirmative nor negative—but he does know where his father's family is from, both in Boston and in North Carolina, just as he knows where the city of Mayagüez on the island of Puerto Rico lies on any map.

He shuffles his notecards in order: there are seven. He makes sure they are all there, then stores them in his backpack on top of his Spanish notebook. He has no homework (when do they ever have homework?) for Language Arts, no homework for Health Sciences, no homework for Introduction to General Sciences, and no homework for physical education, but what sort of homework could you have for physical education, he muses: sit-ups? push-ups? dribbling a basketball? He would certainly fail to do any of them. And then there is the algebra homework, cleanly printed on the required loose-leaf, on which he spent two hours last night, and one this morning. . . .

His sisters are clamoring in the kitchen; his mother never tells them to shut up anymore, or even slaps Tasha when she talks back as she had always done before. Jaime never talked back in the first place, though she would still sometimes slap him for whatever reason (because he would not clean his room, because he sulked all through dinner, because he was switching and batting his eyes, because he reminded her too much *of the man who had left her*), but now she is always asking him what he is doing before she gets home, how he is progressing in school, what he is *feeling*. My son. He always lies and tells her nothing beyond the barest outline of what happens to him each day, because he is convinced she would not understand anyway, or care; she has never understood a thing about him before in the previous thirteen-and-a-half years of his life, nor cared, and understood even less about Tony, whose name was always on her lips. *Antonio*. My heart. Nor about Teresita, who usually spends most of her time with her boyfriend Erick when she is not hogging the television in the apartment or hanging out with her friends; nor even Tita, who is twenty-three, has three daughters herself, lives with her boyfriend in the South End projects, and who, like Tony, was never subject to any of the rules his mother laid down for the rest of them. My life. Tatiana, the *true* baby, seems to gain her care and concern, though how long will *this* last? Jaime wonders.

Why is it so quiet downstairs? He descends the stairwell

quietly and crosses the narrow, unlighted hallway, through the double-hinged door into the store. Quiet, empty. His uncle Narciso has obviously gone into the storeroom down in the cellar, or perhaps out into the small cold locker in back, and Aunt Marisol has not yet come down. The shade on the front door is still drawn, and the triple-bolts have not been unlocked, nor the gratings raised and furled.

Jaime leans back against the wall of candy racks behind the cash register and brushes curly, raven bangs back from his forehead. In the mirror of Plexiglass surrounding the register area before him, he chances upon his reflection: facially the spit-and-image of his father, whose actual face he has not seen in two years, he finds himself *almost* handsome, though not like Tony was. He, Jaime, is still too plump, "muy gordo." Though no calls him "Porcelito" anymore, since he has lost some weight, his first cousin Niño, who had been a year ahead of him at school until he flunked out and was placed in Catholic school, has not stopped calling him "Gordon" every chance he can. At least he no longer has to hear that nickname at school, or Niño's other gem, "Chunky and Chinky," for when he and Vinh were together. Being "gordo," however, no one has ever expected him to be cool or popular or have a girlfriend or have *juice.* Those expectations fell upon Tony, who satisfied them amply, which allowed Jaime thus to be the inverse, his reverse: the "smart," "quiet," "artistic" one, the fat little former asthmatic who spends hours in his room, drawing, reading, writing, devising imaginary scenarios and games by and for himself . . .

Since Tony's death, however, not even Niño or his mother calls him those *other* names that had lacerated Jaime in their truth and viciousness, though no one, not even his mother, had dared say them in Tony's presence. Now, Jaime is her *only* son, since Tony failed to father a little boy, thereby transforming Jaime automatically into *the only man* in his mother's life. . . . The thought sometimes makes him shudder, as now.

Beyond the diaphanous barrier, the meticulously stocked rows of shelves.

Alone, he empties into his mouth an already-opened box of Lemon-Heads which was sitting under the register and probably belonged to Narciso, Jr., or Aunt Marisol, who is always munching on something sweet. At his feet he notices about six chewing-gum wrappers, which meant that Narciso, Jr., worked the closing shift: Uncle Narciso would never tolerate trash lying anywhere on this floor, so he has not yet been back behind here. Jaime gathers them up and, as he is tossing them in the wastebasket, notices the Browning Hi-Power 9mm semiautomatic, clipless, poking out from the lower shelf. Why did Narciso, Jr., leave this thing out? Catching no light, the barrel does not flash as it normally would; Jaime's thoughts recoil from the cold metal. He is uninterested in guns, though, and anyway he has held this handgun before; with his toe he pushes it back onto the shelf so that it is no longer visible.

Before his uncle returns, he pulls the shade to peep out the front door. A small throng of people is collecting at the bus stop several feet down from the front of the store. This group of about seven, all of them neighbors, mostly work downtown or in Cambridge, and there is a woman Jaime recognizes as one of the teacher's aides in the special education program now housed at the back of his school. Hardly anyone is milling around, as usual, so frozen are they to their spots, even at this time of year. Within seconds the bus, already half-full, screeches up. These commuters, as is customary, are pushing and shoving each other out of the way to board. Jaime's mother always says that the Orientals push hardest because they have to claim seats first or they will never be able to muscle their way into them, that the Portuguese will give up their seats if you look tired enough because they are a sad people, that the Irish usually smell like whiskey or beer so you will want to give them your seat, that the West Indians do not care how tired you look if you do not look West Indian, and that black men never give up their seats for an older woman, unless it's their mother. But Jamie knows these kernels of maternal wisdom do not hold; he was once knocked out of his seat by another Puerto Rican, and Tony always gave up his seat for an older or a pregnant woman, if she was black or Puerto Rican or Cape Verdean. Truth is, everyone, as Jaime knows, can be rude, mercenary, self-interested.

—¿Ai, Sándalito, qué tal? Jaime feels the thick, strong fingers softly digging into his shoulders, the protuberant stomach pressing against his slope of his shoulder blades. It is his uncle Narciso. He relaxes. His uncle's breath, warm and somewhat stale, wets the hairs on the back of his neck, as his hand slips like a scarf around Jaime's neckbone.

—*Nada, Tío.* Jaime turns around to face his sloe-eyed uncle, a virtual mirror-image of his mother, in male form. Like his sister, Uncle Narciso is of medium height—Jaime has never been able to guess heights on sight, but Narciso is taller than Tony, who was five feet eight inches—and wiry, except for the belly, with a low forehead, a broad nose, thin lips and skin golden-brown enough to be *trigueño*. His hair, straight but bristly as Jamie's mother's, he wears in a closely trimmed Afro; his mustache is as thick as a small hairbrush. Uncles Eduardo, who lives in New Haven, and Rubén, who lives in New York, are both older than Uncle Narciso and Jaime's mother, and are lighter-skinned, but have the same thick black hair and slender builds. Only his aunt Adelina, Niño's mother, is overweight, but she has a movie star's face, Aunt Marisol always says, so pale and with such high cheekbones that she could be from Spain itself, and hair so black, straight and long that it cascades off her head like a fountain of oil. She did make a good marriage on top of it, to Jaime's uncle Nelson, who owns his own chain of gas stations, whereas Jaime's mother, Aunt Adelina liked to say, could not keep a man *if her children's lives depended upon it.*

—You didn't come down this morning. I was waiting on you. His uncle grins, exposing teeth like kernels of Indian corn.

—I was working on my algebra. I'm failing, you know. His uncle is not listening, as usual.

—*Tío* was *waiting* on you. I had a lot for you to do this morning, didn't your mother let you know? He approaches Jaime, both his hands squirming beneath his bloody apron like small, trapped birds.

—I was just checking to make sure the bus was on schedule. Jaime rolls his eyes, darting out of his uncle's path, towards an aisle. I'm gonna be late if I don't hurry up.

—You don't got any time left to help *Tío* this morning! I was *waiting* on you. Jaime cants his head around the corner to read the clock: he has only fifteen or twenty minutes before his bus arrives. His uncle sweeps a lock off Jaime's forehead, reaches down and tightly embraces him. Like always, he is mouthing something onto Jaime's earlobe, his neck, but Jaime has long since stopped paying any attention; he just goes slack and waits for his uncle to let go. In the back of the room, beyond the door to both the apartments and the cold locker, he can now hear someone, probably his aunt Marisol, heading to the storeroom in the cellar. Abruptly his uncle releases him, picks up the cash box at his feet, and closes behind him the door that forms a clear, though somewhat rickety, protective partition around the register.

—I'll help you tomorrow morning, *Tío*, I promise, Jaime yells out, before bounding out of the store and upstairs so as not to be late. When he reaches the top of the stairs, he hears his mother saying:

—And I told Mr. Morris to call me if you was skipping class or not doing your homework, Jaime, because I don't want you failing math again. Had she heard him come upstairs or had she just automatically launched into this? he asks himself. His mother, splendid in her nurse's aide's whites, emerges from her bedroom, and now stands before him in the narrow strait of hallway between the rooms. She is frowning, blankly.

—Did you *hear* me?

—Yeah, Mami, I heard you. I'm not gonna skip algebra anymore, and I *did* my homework, just like Mr. Morris wants. Do you want to *see* it? As though by default she shakes her head no; she seldom looks at any of his homework, though she will sometimes check to make sure that he has at least packed the notebook in with the rest of his school materials, and she never looks at his other things, his other notebooks, full of his writings and drawings, which he now keeps hidden behind his bed in a small bag that had belonged to Tony. Most of these he has shown to no one except Vinh, who draws pictures of his own, keeps similar notebooks. Vinh's consist mostly of action figures like the X-Men or the Fantastic Four, which he copies from the comic books he collects (Jaime collected them too at one point but stopped when his mother got laid off the last time), but he always changes all the eyes and hair so that they become Vietnamese and usually much more muscular than they appeared originally. Jaime's, all drawn from his storehouse of memories and fantasy, usually consist of people he has seen on the bus or on the street or in the bodega, or at Downtown Crossing or in Central Square when he slips there on Saturdays or sometimes after school, and occasionally he even draws pictures of Tony, and rarely his father, though never any of the other members of his family. Other renderings, completely from his imagination and of a different, vivid and more explicit nature, he reveals to no one. So much no one knows about him, he realizes, now that Tony is gone.

As they stand there wordlessly, Jaime places one hand on his hips and licks the palm of his free hand, flips back his bangs coquettishly, bats his eyes: this always used to provoke a reproach from his mother, but no longer. Before she can attach a comment to her obvious look of disapproval, his youngest sister, Tatiana, just barely five, materializes, her jumper misbuttoned and her socks mismatched, her ponytails uncoiling from beneath her barrettes. She drops in loud sobs to the floor at his mother's feet. Jaime flees into his bedroom.

A glance at the Teenage Mutant Ninja Turtle clock—had he really been *so* into them?—alerts him that he has only about five minutes to spare. He checks his backpack to ensure everything is there, including that stupid algebra notebook. He even makes sure that he has the loose-leaf copy of his algebra homework tucked into the front inside cover of the notebook; Mr. Morris likes to receive the homework this way, so that he can verify the answers on the loose-leaf by the preparatory work in the notebook. Only for such a *white turdle,* Jaime notes, does everything have to be so complicated. On top of this, Mr. Morris is always pushing Jaime to do better, cornering him after class, stopping him in the hallways, calling his mother *at home!—he could easily be an A student, Ms. Barrett*—but all those variable and commutative laws tend to drive Jaime to distraction; he likes Spanish and Language Arts and social studies much better, since they afford him the freedom to order things—words, worlds, his life—to his satisfaction. Still, he has to admit that there is no reason he should *fail* algebra, because if he does, it will probably spell the death of his chances of getting into the

Latin Academy, where he, with Vinh, has vowed to be, come ninth grade . . .

Below the clock's green-diode glimmer, Jaime gathers up the change off the small desk he had shared with Tony, and funnels it into his pockets. Maybe he will buy a pack of dough-nuts from Uncle Narciso to eat on the way, or maybe he will save the coins for a tonic after school. *Tony.* It is so quiet these mornings, and evenings too, now that Tony is no longer around, and yet he no longer has to keep quiet when he wakes for fear of awaking Tony, who would be lightly snoring by now, having come in just around dawn from a long night out, probably dealing. This last year and a half Jaime would occasionally find a few dollar bills, mostly ones but occasionally a five or ten, lying in his house shoes when, still half-asleep, he climbed out of bed to go the bathroom in the morning, and he did not even have to look across the room to realize these signified Tony was home and in bed. Although nothing save the general narra-tive of their lives had presaged Tony's demise, Jaime had been saving these small gifts, which totaled about fifty-six dollars (after a few withdrawals), and now kept them tied up in a sock in the back of his drawer, for a future emergency. He had told no one about this, not even Vinh.

Mi hijo, mi corazón, mi vida.

As though it were a talisman he fingers his sock-bank, re-stashing it carefully, then slips on a green plastic wristband that he had won at the West Indian Festival last summer, before zipping up his backpack and heading downstairs.

His mother had said nothing about his yellow T-shirt, his baggy red shorts, or his matching red high-top sneakers when she saw him earlier. Teresita would surely say he looked like a clown, but she had left for work already. No one would even notice the wristband, he bets, or what the colors together repre-sent. His keys: he pats the three of them, which hang from an extralong shoelace beneath his shirt down into his briefs.

—Mami, I'm going. Where is she?

—Jaime, honey? In the kitchen. He pokes his head in the doorway.

—You be good and be careful, okay?

—I will. She has Tasha in one hand and Tatiana in the

other. The two girls are dressed like twins, even though Tasha is three years older. His mother is obviously on her way out as well.

—Jaime, you got your algebra notebook? He nods yes, tapping his backpack where he thinks it is tucked away—*because I just want you to do well, to not end up like your brother, to get out of all of this*—then gives her a quick kiss on the cheek.

As he runs down the stairs, he can hear the *I love you* trailing his steps.

Through the bodega, where his aunt Marisol is now planted behind the register, chewing on a stick of gum, past his uncle Narciso, who is lifting the last of the outside grates and larks out a good-bye in Spanish and English, onto the already hot, uneven, tar-gummed pavement: the bus has not yet arrived. Jaime crosses the street to his bus stop.

Only one other person is waiting for this bus: a young man, Corey Fuentes, who had once been dating Jaime's sister Teresita, though at the time he was as old as Narciso, Jr. As Jaime looks up and smiles, Corey sneers in reply, then lights up his Newport. Corey is out of work, has been for about a year, Jaime has heard, but this morning he is wearing alligator loafers, nice pressed gray slacks, an ironed white shirt, and holds what appears to be a brand-new clip-on tie in his free hand, which leads Jaime to suppose that he is going in for a job interview (very unlikely), traveling somewhere to meet his parole officer or some new criminal associate (more likely but still unlikely), or heading downtown to make a court date (most likely). Jaime does not dare inquire.

The spring heat has not yet fired the streets, and a breeze, almost gauzy in texture, carries pieces of trash and some seedlings airborne down the street towards the horizon. The other bodega, owned by the Cape Verdeans, stands behind and cater-corner from them, somewhat dilapidated on the outside, with its warped grates, yellowed newspapered curtains and its faded beer signs, unopened. To their right across the street in the distance, down near the wrought-iron fence that garters the Social Services building, a corpulent straw-haired white man, whom Jaime recognizes as Father Peter O'Hanlon, is chatting with a woman employee, unknown. So what if Fr. Pete was

removed as assistant pastor of St. Stephen Protomartyr's for
spending so much time with the gangs? Tony, Jaime remembers
him saying, *is not a lost cause.* He will surely be in the bodega
gossiping with Aunt Marisol and sipping a Coke, laced with
rum, in about twenty minutes.

—Where *is* that fucking bus? Corey hisses, checking his
wrist graced not by a watch, but by an ornate gold bracelet.

He leans uncomfortably against the bus-stop sign-pole. He
is staring off into the distance, envisioning what? Jaime wonders. What sort of plea bargain his attorney will arrange?
Whether his new girlfriend will show up to escort him back
home, on his own recognizance? What the penalty will be for
"uttering checks and credit cards" for the third time within one
calendar year? Jaime is familiar with quite a few of the court
careers of other people, such as Tony, and Narciso, Jr., and
Teresita's boyfriend Eric, and her ex-boyfriend Antray, so that
it is not too difficult for him to extrapolate what this small-time
booster, as Tony had labeled him, might be facing.

As he ponders Corey's fate, his eyes trace an invisible
line from the slicked, raven crown of hair to the full, pink
lips to the satiny brown neckbone, which a white undershirt
almost completely conceals from view. He has dreamt about
Corey before. Jaime's eyes linger on that downward slope
and the cloven pectorals below, imagining them supple beneath his grasping fingers like the earth beneath the saplings
that his Earth Science class spent all last month planting. Corey's skinny arms pale, in Jaime's estimation, to Tony's knot-
tier, longer arms, and especially to the more bulky extremities
and the ample chest of the guy who sometimes drives Jaime's
bus route—Jerome—whose name he has inscribed on the inside back cover of the notebook he remembered to bring with
him today. For a while Jaime feared his mother might see his
name and interrogate him about it, but then he realized she
would not touch anything of his, save perhaps that algebra
notebook, under any circumstances, unless perhaps he were
dead.

Turning and catching Jaime in his spell of appreciation,
Corey glowers, murmuring, "You li'l *freak.*" As Jaime looks
away, unembarrassed, Fr. Pete lumbers his way up the street.

*   *   *

Another breeze is bearing up a fresh offering of debris as their bus scuds up to the curb. Corey boards first, tamping out his cigarette and tossing it over his shoulder so that it bounces off Jaime's arm. Jaime says nothing, and hops aboard after him, perfunctorily flashing his pass as he passes into the aisle. The bus is mostly vacant, but before he can grab a seat, the bus driver has pulled sharply away into the street, stomping down on the accelerator, thus hurtling Jaime headfirst towards the back. Obviously this bus driver is *not* Jerome, who has a velvet touch on the pedal—Jaime visually verifies this: No! Oh well— but instead Randall, who from time to time works this morning route but more often drives the Columbia Road evening route, which Jaime has taken on those occasions when he had to drop off something at Tita's job.

For a moment he debates whether he should sit up near Randall, whom he has never really paid much attention to, or sit in the back of the bus and write in his notebook: *¿Qué va hacer?* He decides to perch himself on the last forward-facing seat on the right side of the bus, near no one; Corey is sitting near most of the other passengers in the forward-facing seats near the front, an unlit cigarette poling from his lips.

Randall's driving this morning is certainly a lot more jerky than Jerome's. Extracting his writing notebook and a pencil, he sketches Randall's face, and then Jerome's face and torso, which he can summon from memory as sharply as if he were staring right at it, before writing beneath both pictures:

AM: RANDALL—Almost turdle of the bus drivers—iron foot. No Jerome this morning. Randall instead ... will have to settle for second best ... not the best start, but J will make do!! Fugaz. What is the game for today? Tony.

The bus slithers along its usual path, people board, Jaime looks up periodically to see if any of them catch his eye: a few girls who were once classmates of Teresita's or Tony's and who are now cradling babies in their arms or in strollers; a few teenagers his age, none at his middle school, boisterous, listening to hip-hop or dance-hall blaring from headset speakers,

their backpacks rattling with drug paraphernalia, perhaps, or
forties; an old woman, dressed in a filthy white blouse and
yellow shorts, a pink hairnet framing a face drooping like melting brown wax; another older woman, white and in an appli-
quéed blue frock, yammering excitedly to herself; an older man,
maybe forty-five, somewhere near Uncle Narciso's age, in a red
and white striped polo shirt, brown polyester beltless pants and
matching brown buckled loafers. He slides into the row of seats
across from Jaime and smiles. Jaime acknowledges him, almost absently.

Light is now flooding the bus. May sun. The fragrances of
sandalwood, a cologne that must be Brut and newsprint com-
mingle in Jaime's consciousness: he turns slowly towards the
man who has a full head of graying wavy hair and an almost
lacquered black mustache. The man pulls out the sports section
and starts reading the back-page write-up of last night's big
boxing match, which Teresita and Eric and his mother had been
watching on Pay-Per-View. My hurt. Jaime had been printing
out his index cards, and had telephoned Vinh with a question
about one of the languages in Senegal, which Vinh, of course,
knew about. They had spoken for about twenty minutes; Vinh
told Jaime that his mother was doing her usual nothing but
watching television when she was not attending his three
smaller sisters and brothers or his grandmother, her mother,
while his stepfather (Vinh's real father having never gotten out
of Vietnam, his mother remarried shortly after arriving in the
United States) was still at the small bonding agency he operates
and never leaves in Field's Corner. My love. Vinh was in the
midst of doing what he spends all of his free time doing, like
Jaime: reading or drawing.

Jaime examines the man more carefully. He must be still in
his forties, because although gray salts his hair, his face does
not look *that* old. Skinny almost, he has a complexion not unlike
Jaime's own, the color of an unshelled almond; and thick lips,
like Jaime's father, like Corey. Through the small triangle created by the placket of his shirt Jaime can almost see the hairless
chest. It looks like it may be toned; the man cranes slightly
forward, obscuring Jaimie's view. Jaime watches him study the
scores, and draws a picture of him. What does he do all day,

who is he, where is he going? Jaime writes these questions down, in order. The bus stops, people board and get off.

When Jaime looks out of the bus window for a change, he sees a forteen-year-old girl he knows, named Mercedes, whom they call Dita, in front of the liquor store, stepping out of a fire-engine-red Samurai with two boys from a gang that hangs out at Four Corners. He bows his head so that he can watch her unobserved, though it is unlikely she even notices the bus's presence. She had wanted to have Tony's baby so badly, just a year ago, but since Tony's death, he hardly saw her. One of the men wraps his arm around Dita's waist, eases his hand down the side of her leg, slides it over onto her behind . . .

Jaime turns back to the man, who has been staring at him.

The man gets up and slides in next to Jaime, who pushes his knapsack against the window. *What does he do all day, where is he going?*

—Hhhiiih . . . Jaime says, his voice breathy and tremulous, like a vibrating reed.

—Hey, the man replies. How you doing this morning? His voice is pure ice.

—Fine.

—Tha's good, the man says, baring his straight, yellowing smile. Jaime spots the wedding ring on his left ring finger, which, like all the others, is long, unwrinkled and spoonlike. Maybe he is younger than Uncle Narciso. Setting the paper in his lap, the man slowly examines the riders on the bus, his head angling and turning as if it were a movie camera. Jaime searches the bus for anyone who might call him out. Corey is still up front, but he is now conversing intensely with one of the young mothers. The man appears to mime placing his hand on Jaime's knee, but does not. He simply looks down at Jaime and smiles. The teeth gleam like butter-covered knives. Jaime can feel his underarms beginning to moisten. *My son.*

—Where you headed? the man asks.

—What's your name?" Jaime answers.

—I like that, "what's your name?" . . . My name is Vernon, what's yours? He lays a hand on the seatback next to Jaime's shoulders. Jaime licks his palms and sweeps back his curls; this man's name cannot *really* be Vernon, Jaime tells himself; he must be playing a game as well. He looks out into the traffic alongside the bus: cars snake past on their way to wherever.

—Tony.

—Tony ... Where you headed, Tony?

—Cuffe Middle School ... Where you headed?

—Nowhere, I got the day off ...

Vernon purses his lips, then asks—Tony, why don't we get off at the next stop? I'll walk you partway there. He smiles again, as the fingers, like the petals of some exquisite brown flower, flutter out to an alluring pattern on the seatback. Jaime inhales deeply, his mind flooded with questions, of which the main one is: is he going to miss *algebra?* because Mr. Morris will surely telephone his mother and admonish him in front of the class. The bus halts at the stop, and they both slip out through the back door. As the bus pulls away, Jaime reminds himself that although he has never taken a game this far, Vernon seems decent enough, and he has on a wedding ring, so there must be someone he is going home to ...

The sidewalks have become grills. Sun glints off of every metal surface in dazzling spars, forcing Jaime to put on the pair of sunglasses he keeps in the front pocket of his backpack. Vernon dons a pair too; where had he stored them? At the green light, they cross the street together, walking quickly, almost in tandem, then walk several blocks up before turning in to a side street, where they pause, Jaime's hands, like Vernon's, are pocketed. He scans the main street to see if anyone he knows is passing by. Not a soul.

Pointing in the direction of the projects, to their left, Vernon tells Jaime—Now, if I'm correct, Cuffe is about six blocks that way. Jaime wrinkles his lips several times, then nods in agreement.

Running his hand over the lip of his pants, Vernon continues—Cuffe School, Cuffe School ... I remember when the Cuffe School first became the Cuffe School ... Used to be Wendell Phillips School when my kids went there, then they decided to change the name. Always do. Can't leave well enough alone. Can't say I actually know who Cuffe is, you know ... or Wendell Phillips for that matter ... I guess you kids don't care who it's named after, though, hunh?

All this talk annoys Jaime, who says nervously—No, no, nobody cares. He brushes the hair back from his forehead: Vernon is plumper than Jaime thought, or perhaps it is just that he has a gut like Uncle Narciso; he begins to wonder if he should not just run off . . . What time is it anyway? he wonders.

—Turn around so I can see how *handsome* you are. You are so *handsome*, you know? Jaime follows the instructions, revolving in a gradual circle. Vernon now looks older than he did at first, on the bus; the sunlight colors in the slight sagging of his chin, the almost slack quality of the skin on his arms, like a sheet of crumpled brown plastic.

—How old are you, Tony?

—How old are *you*, Vernon?

—There you go again, answering my question with another question. My age doesn't matter, Tony, but I'm forty-nine. Now, how old are you?

Jaime throws his head back, closes his eyes, says casually— I'm fifteen . . . I got kept back a few times and I look young for my age . . .

Beginning to laugh, Vernon inspects Jaime up and down— Now, Tony, I ain't no *fool* . . . I don't think you're even thirteen, at least. Either way, this could turn into a crime in the state of Massachusetts, you know that? Jaime remains silent, fiddling anxiously with his Day-Glo wristband, which is now primed with sweat. *My heart.*

—Look, if you're gonna call me a liar, I can just leave. Vernon flashes those teeth again in a furious grin.

—Who said anything like that, about you being a liar?

—Anyways, if I did leave, where would that leave *you*? Jaime bats his eyes, turning his back to Vernon.

Vernon moves closer to Jaime and rests his hand on the boy's shoulder—Why don't we take a walk behind that old filling station there. I knew the man who owned it, you know, Vernon whispers, his voice trailing off. Jaime reminds himself just because they go back there, nothing really *has to* occur. It's a game; he's *Tony*, this man is playing along, nothing will happen. He also thinks, if Tony were alive and he knew about this, he would put his gun to this man's temple right now and pull the trigger until the clip was completely emptied so that the

eyes and snot mixed into the ground like spilled soup and then
stomp on the head until the face was unrecognizable. So unrecognizable that no one could figure out who he was, but Jaime
had known instantly, just by that scent; instead that very thing
happened to Tony and now he is lying six feet under a head-
stone in a cemetery in Jamaica Plain, his face shattered into a
hundred pieces like a porcelain doll, his body so twisted that
they could barely fit the suit on him, and no one is here to stop
this game stop it at all save Jaime from anything from *himself*
no one cares not his mother not his father not his aunts or
uncles or sisters not Teresita not Tita not even his *abuela* no one
the only one who ever cared and showed it is silent and silenced for posterity so why not see what is going to happen
this morning—

They head down a oil-slick gravel driveway toward the rear
of the abandoned gas station, which abuts a narrow alley, bor-
dered on three sides by a brick wall, covered by ivy and other
climbing vines. This seems secluded enough: Jaime has passed
by this site before, though he has never actually ventured back
in here.

Vernon leans against the back wall of the station. He un-
buckles his pants, then opens his zipper. Jaime faces him, his
eyes now alighting everywhere but on Vernon, who has begun
to expose himself, urging the boy to approach him. Is this part
of the game? Jaime asks without rendering the words audible,
fixed to his spot, his eyes still wandering, his mind leaping
alternately from Tony's veined brown hands gripping that
9mm—that's what it was wasn't it a 9mm a Tech Nine pulling
the trigger again again again him finding the body back behind
the Dumpster behind the store like garbage dumped in the middle of the night his mother not able to say anything at all for
days her lying on the floor beside the pew convulsing in tears
at the funeral him under his comforter shivering in the over-
heated room working himself into a frenzy at the sight of that
body that horrible corpse that face mangled beyond recognition
beyond even hideousness as the bed across from him lies empty
empty empty—

—Com'ere, Tony, Vernon clucks, his eyes closed and his
body arched back against the wall. Jaime stands in front of him,

stone-still. Come on, boy, come *on*, shit, we don't have all *day*. Jaime just stands there, his eyes now fixed on Vernon's hairless and pocked torso, paler than his arms or face, like the flesh of a plucked chicken, which he has revealed by raising his polo shirt. Come on *now*, Tony! Tony! Vernon is hunching over, breathing heavily. Turn around for me again, Tony! Tony?

Jaime feels himself slowly losing his sense of balance distance time letting everything go why can't he concentrate? why can't he end this game? end it now? get closer to Vernon? run? why is this happening like this why is this happening he begins to find the headcrumpled like a toy doll fall shoot convulsed in tears on the floor of the pew my god porque when he hears

—Oh, Tony . . . Tony, *oh* . . .

He opens his eyes suddenly. What time *is* it? Vernon's left hand is groping for Jaime's shoulder, his right hand . . . he feels his chest collapsing. He glimpses Vernon's watch on his right hand . . . he's late for his algebra class! he is going to *miss* it! Jaime leaps up, stumbles backwards, knocking over his knapsack, spilling the contents upon the stones.

—Wha? Hunh? Vernon murmurs, writhing against the wall like a felled fowl struggling to alight, riven with bliss, unaware of the boy's actions. Panicking, Jaime snatches his knapsack, stuffs everything back in it, hoists in onto his left shoulder, hesitates. *My life,* he feels rising on the top of his tongue: No one is going to save him from anything, ever, *not a soul.*

—Wha's the matter, Tony? *Tony?* Jaime, refusing to look in Vernon's direction, runs off madly down the driveway, his backpack now half-open and dangling from his back. In about five seconds he is onto the street that leads through the projects and into the front door of the Cuffe Middle School, past the hall monitor who is yelling out his name *Jaime Barrett Jaime Barrett Jaime?* up onto the third floor, into a seat in the back of the class as Mr. Morris is chalking a series of dizzyingly elaborate equations upon the black slate that is as flat as the voice that is explaining the marks made with hand and chalk, and Jaime, in the back row, is fumbling around madly in his bag, his hands searching furiously for that algebra notebook—where *is* it? he *knows* he packed it, he remembers having placed it in there this morning—which is *nowhere* to be found.

Then he sees it, he sees it as keenly as if it all were unreeling right before him, *here:* As Vernon gets ready to depart, he spots a notebook, lying several inches in front of him. A black and white wire-bound gridded notebook that has ALGEBRA I—MR. MORRIS, FIRST PERIOD etched across its front. Picking up the notebook, he flips through it, seeing all the red marks and the heavily annotated margins of the pages, which, like an old scratch-and-sniff sample held close to the nose, emit a faint but perceptible scent: sandalwood. He casts the notebook to the ground, beside the discarded newspaper, laughs at the folly of it all, at this boy who cannot even keep up his role in their game, walks off down the driveway towards Dudley and the rest of his life—

His bangs now plastered like a veil to his forehead, his breathing so labored as to drown out even his own thoughts, he looks up, to the puzzled expressions of Mr. Morris, of Vinh, of Shonelle Watkins and Gloria Velez, of every student in his algebra class: Their faces are screens of bemusement, showing only the recognition of his strange and novel presence before them; their eyes are fixed upon him as if he were the last boy on earth, as if they had never seen such a pitiful and enigmatic creature in their entire lives.

The Initiation

Severo Sarduy

He had wandered along the street of show windows—among purple cushions, on lynx skins, cuddled in vast wicker chairs whose backs formed a circle of Moorish stars around their heads, whores lay naked—sipping anise in old bars, beside flower-belled gramophones.

Not daring to enter, he had passed near the little door, beneath the wrought-iron insignia—a coach.

Drugstore

He saw himself in a mirror, surrounded by a drawerful of disheveled scarves, a plastic sphere filled with water—in the back, bubbles, several watches—ties with golden branches and another mirror, where he appeared backwards. It caught the image of his hand among the fabrics—attentive to the saleslady's movements—opening the buttons of his jacket, stuffing the black scarf inside, against this chest. He leafed through a magazine. He was sweating. He turned around, absentmindedly, leisurely. He smoothed his hair, with his knuckles he caressed his beard, he adjusted his belt, dusted the chamois leather of his boots. Little by little he pulled out the wool band. He ripped off the price tag. He tied the scarf around his neck. A black sash girded his chest, the other fell from his shoulder to his waist: the saint of a Ravennese mosaic, phylactery of black stones.

He bought a newspaper. He unfolded it, leaning against a column which open hands engulfing celluloid globes joined to the ceiling. Oval shields with eyes and lips for coats-of-arms hung from the walls; on curved-legged tables silver muses danced: the trains of their gowns were flower vases, and their heads, decorated with butterflies, lamp fixtures.

copenhagen   *brussels*   *amsterdam**

Outside, beneath palms of an acrylic green, a mulatto woman dances. Over the sand, orange light; kites over the black bands of sidewalk.

appel   *aleschinsky*   *corneille*   *jorn**

He put the newspaper, folded, on a pile of magazines. He picked it up again, taking one.

Undulating corridor of mirrors.

*poisonous snake of India**

Plexiglas flowers open. The same record in English begins again. Vinyl circles overlap. Hum of Japanese movie cameras. Double images. Reflection of symmetry. Multiplication of reflection. Repeated photographs, overexposed. On the whiteness of a book cover, a porcelain head covered with black ideograms. Volumes of Bakelite. Intersection of edges. He knew he was going to find them.

*he receives his wages in the paymaster's office.**

Empty sequences.

In the Bar

Now he moved along the corridor, over a black carpet which hid a net of tigers and white letters. Almost without realizing,

---

*Anagrams and synonyms (or hypographs for COBRA: 1) COpenhagen BRussels Amsterdam; 2) appel aleschinsky, etc., a school of artists centered in these three cities, known as the COBRA group; 3) poisonous snake of India = Cobra; 4) he receives his wages in the paymaster's office = the verb *cobrar* and thus cobra, third person singular conjugation of this verb. Cobra is also the name of a singer who died in a plane crash over Fujiyama, and the name of a motorcycle gang that frequented St. Germain des Près. (Translator's Note.)

he had opened the little wooden door. He felt his own breathing, his footsteps, the arches of his feet light upon the tapestry, heel to toe. Near the animals, smearing the white of the letters, the traces of his steps were caught for a moment, in the tangles.

At the end of the corridor, in a corner which received the diagonal precision of the bar, in front of a black chalk drawing projected upon the back wall, TUNDRA appeared. As he moved, black lines fled across his face, across the edges of his body. *A–13470, Los Angeles, Calif. USA. Good-looking man of 33, height 5'10" (photo and particulars available); interested in meeting a good-looking, well-built, education-minded, dominant male, possible motorcycle-type leather fan. Photo and sincerity appreciated (and if in L.A. area, a phone number).* Cracked black leather. His dirty, straight hair fell in tangles to his shoulders. *A–13486, New York, N.Y. USA. Handsome male of 30, docile nature, well-built, wishes to meet or correspond with boot-wearing men interested in the subject of discipline, Levi's, boots, belts, leather clothing, uniforms of all types: would like to meet and correspond by letter or tape with dominant men interested in these subjects.* At his waist, welded to a chain of forged links, a tin rosette. *A–13495, Vancouver, B.C. Gentleman of 40, of dominant nature, very sincere and understanding, with varied interests, would like to meet slim man between 20 and 45, not over 5'8" tall, of docile nature and interested in the subject of discipline. Also would like to hear from "Foot Adorer" in issue of November 25th.*

"We were waiting for you."—And he turned around. He wore his name on his back, tattooed in the leather, dull black upon the shiny black of the hide.

In the drawing projected on the wall two men were fighting. Or not. The blanks formed other figures: the same men jumped toward each other, but to embrace, naked.

"It's a good thing you came. Today's the day. Because to be a leader you have to pass through submission, to gain power you have to lose it, to command you have to first lower yourself as far as we want: to the point of nausea."

SCORPION wore around his neck a funeral amulet: in its middle circle, protected by two pieces of cut glass, surrounded by amber beads, little porous bones with filed edges were heaped—baby teeth, bird cartilage—bound by a silk hatband, lettered in black ink and Gothic capitals with German names. On his wrists, eagles with blue dots. His boots, untied.

/Bleeding skeletons stick to caryatids. Burning bodies. Ashes. White mausoleum. Shrouded in brocades and coarse jewels, toward the towers they escort the dead infant.

From TOTEM's coat dangled little bronze cymbals, bells with broken clappers, dented cowbells, Mexican jingles. His straight eyebrows were joined, his high cheekbones, yellow. Torn pants, mended with patches; in the pockets penknives and glass; from a sweater tied to his waist, sleeves hung down to his knees. A rattling of junk, the rusty creaking which announces a row between Chinese shadows, the apparition of a devil in the Indonesian theater, the tumble of a monkey acrobat, measured his gestures.

/Sudanese soldier. Abyssinian water carrier. Horse rider from Ethiopia. Pitch-black body, smooth and shiny, grape-colored pupils. He drinks from an ox horn and pours over his genitals an opaque and acidulated mead. Face down, he rubs his tense frenum—*masenko* fiddle string—his bulbous, purple glans against a buckskin stained by cum. He turns around. Starchy puddle on his belly. Laughter. A little twangy song. Eating sorghum bread. In the corners of his mouth, and of his eyelids, the sign of monsters.

Behind shelves of bottles, opaque screens, and the curves of Turkish tools, a light filtered by algae emerges from the bottom of the aquarium which occupies an entire wall of the bar; slow shadows—vibrations of tiny wings—blur that neon daylight submerged among stones and white polystyrene coral, beneath motionless seahorses of fluorescent glass and lily-white rustproof flowers, always open.

In front of the light which gushes from the water, where the shadows of fish are black butterflies, TIGER dances, smokes, hits himself, inhales again, impelled by the kif he jumps, bursting Tibetan necklaces, diagonally into midair. Now he runs cir-

cles around me, looking at me. Underwater transparency.
Looking at me. Hothouse light. I revolve too. Glass on the floor.
Looking at each other. He bangs on the glass of the fish tank
with open hands. Slow, flat, lanceolated animals, open symmetrical leaves with tenuous nerves, hurry back and forth. Streaked
with mercury. Mayan faces. Their glowing orange flagelli follow, entangle them.

I am smoking. The weed is blowing through my ears. I am
running circles around them. Looking at them. They are revolving too. A glass breaks.

   /Behind the bar three naked women appear, gilded.
   The fish have clouded it all.
   Behind the wall zebras are fleeing.

TUNDRA: "We will assign you an animal. You will repeat his
name. La boca obra."

SCORPION: "So that you'll see that I am not me, that one's body
is not one's own, that the things that make us and the forces
which put them together are passing fancies"—and he cuts the
palm of his hand with glass, then rubs it against his face; he
sucks his blood (laughing.)

/The burning bodies, blue corpses burnt to ashes, brimstone
feet and eyes shrouded with mushrooms, fall into the white, still
river. Into the river, somersaulting in the air; into the still water
the cremated, the leprous fall. Among gurus who pray, gods who
give out rotten oranges, and children who beg, bones in flames
fly over the astrologer's choir loft, into the water that doesn't
move, and also rotting genitals, corroded faces, slashed hands:
blood clots. Along the banks, flames, the cries of gongs, the night.

TOTEM paints on his chest, over his heart, a heart. He dances
and smears himself with scarlet. A snake shines phosphores-
cently on him, curled around his phallus. Its soft head sticks on
to the glans. Sharp, dripping cum, the little tongue penetrates.

TIGER: "In a dream I saw myself walking past a tent crowded
with boots, shoes, mountings and buckled straps, but those ob-

jects were not made like ours, and their material, instead of leather, seemed like dry and sticky blood. I told it to the Instructor: 'A total absurdity,' he said to me. Later, when I saw them, I understood that they were objects that westerners use."

And he bangs on the fish tank again. And to the puzzled bartender: "What's the matter? Don't you like it? Do you want me to say a word, a syllable and turn you into a bird? Do you want me to conjure up five thousand minor demons right this minute, to prick you, to poison your precious body fluids? Make me a gin and tonic."

/Behind the aquarium—black stripes ripple when the water moves, through the white, fish glide—zebras continue rushing. Chessboard loins. Viera de Silva loins. Parallel bands spread behind the glass, skulls, necks which cross, tails, manes which open in slow motion, lips discharge strings of silvery drool which dash against the glass; parallel bands which shrink, seen in a concave mirror. The galloping sound, muffled by sand, by water, mixes with the percussion of the orchestra; its rhythm is the banging on the fish bowl. The zebras leap in files, at regular intervals, a file of black zebras striped white, a file of white zebras striped black; they reach the top—the height of the water—they fall, front legs bent, they rise and flee in disorder while another file behind the glass rises, flies.

On another wall in the bar, in black and yellow dots, a blonde cries—her tears are enormous—; in a bubble, gushing from her lips, the words *"That's the way it should have begun! but it's hopeless!"*

We went out.

Everything had changed.

The corridor was white.

On the floor, skull-goblets, femur-flutes, striped scepters, swastikas, wheels, were arranged in an indecipherable order among cubes of a rainbow-hued glass.

The street door opened automatically.

We could barely stand the night's glare, the noises reverberated in our heads. The motorcycles were lying on the sidewalk. It was raining. In the square one could hear the guitar-strumming of the inns, far-off. At the subway entrance a frightened woman appeared. She was wearing a red hat; its ribbons, falling from the brim to her black cape, hid the gold flowers on her face. Her makeup was violent, her mouth painted with branches. Her orbs were black and aluminum-plated, narrow beneath the eyebrows and then elongated by other whorls, powdered paint and metal, to her temples, to the eyes, but in richer, kaleido-scope colors; instead of eyebrows, fringes of tiny precious stones hung from the rims of her eyelids. Up to her neck she was a woman; above, her body became a kind of heraldic animal with a baroque snout.

We're moving now—in the suburban silence the rumble of motors; over yellow bands, black flashes—on our motorcycles, at full speed. No hands, we shut our eyes, we pass—an alarm bell—under the barriers. Zigzag between crossing locomotives: from open train windows handkerchiefs come out, straw hats pulled by wind, a girl shouting. Our wheels don't touch the ground; on the asphalt arrows pass, in enlarged letters, names of cities, numbers.

TUNDRA repeats a formula, flings a bottle which breaks against the pavement: green spot; SCORPION accelerates, takes off his helmet: "the skull is a casket: let my brains spill over the road!"; TOTEM hugs him by the waist, braces his head against his back, TIGER opens a hand and in the air a strip of sulphurous powder remains, spreading, unfolding; orange strata, fluores-cent cumulus clouds: chemical twilight. We take off, yeah, we rise, higher, higher: we are flying!

Sounding sirens, in pursuers with ultraviolet headlights, with poisoned arrows and crossbrows, bottles of bacteria and ballistas, the greenish agents of the orgy patrol follow us—mon-strous syringes—waving night-sticks of war, miniature lasers in each cavity, macromolecules in their ears.

> *We turn at every corner,*
> *we blow up the bridges behind us,*
> *we turn traffic signs around,*
> *we spray nails and blazing phosphorus,*

we make traffic lights red.
Thrice do we paint the raging sea.
With the triptych we close off the street.

To urge them to turn back, TUNDRA delivers a speech to the pursuers. He translates it into every language alive and dead: when he's going through Sanskrit they respond with a tactical atom bomb; the BOOM makes the earth quake.

SCORPION blocks their way with pyramids of skeletons which stir and creak like crabs; he shows them, on a magnificent neck chain, their heads spitting coins.

TOTEM writes on a kite: FATE L'AMORE NELLA GUERRA and flies it high; from the tail condoms and bells fall.

"Stop!"—TIGER shouts—"or I'll stamp my foot three times and make an army of gigantic cats rise up and charge against you!"

And he stamps his foot three times: out of season and place, flowers sprout everywhere: sandalwoods and white lilies bud on the enemy motorcycles; gardenias on the handlebars, white orchids on the exhaust pipes and big sunflowers which paralyze them by becoming entangled in the wheels. The foliage covers the cops, remains of petrified pursuers; the weapons have been caught in creeping ivy, taken, hooked in the green tangles. The vice squad, in its frozenness, is already a snapshot, a photostat copy of the primitive squad, a wax museum, a gathering of cardboard demons, the abandoned props of a cheap circus which are disappearing among the weeds, in the dust, into the ground, which no one remembers and are only visible by the darkest green of their shadows, in certain aerial shots, taken at twilight and after the snow.

The Ruins

The archaeologists studied them by deciphering the shadows, believing they were from a Roman theater.

Others suggested an Indian observatory with its hourglasses, sundials, telescopes, celestial charts, and astronomers viewing Orion, draped in a tapestry of fossil shells—proof that the sea had once invaded it and that in another era it had been embalmed in a river of lava.

They dug them up.

With the weapons they founded an arms museum.

They filmed them in Cinerama.

Planeta devoted an issue to them.

Coco Chanel engaged them for her winter fashion show.

From everywhere tourist caravans stream.

Straddling the sergeant's head, a little boy eats a strawberry ice cream cone.

Praise and Glory to the Victors

TO TUNDRA

Your locks are golden and around your body an orange halo glows; you sleep upon the tree of Rhetoric: your voice is the unit of all sound, your body, which rocks the leafy treetop, is the standard of human form: your height is exactly eight times your head, your eyes are perfect ovals and around your navel a circle defines the curve of your hips, the Gothic arch of your thorax, and the implantation of hairs in the hollow of your pubis;
at your footstep one hears music of the five-tone scale, the trees bend to give you shade;
you walk leisurely.
By the way you moved your right foot I knew you were a god.

TO SCORPION

To the gems, pastries, and toys with which we have filled your barge, we add new offerings. To favor your voyage, close to your body, which the damp adorns with tiny flowers and which is cloaked, from your feet up, by lichen veils, we place an ibis, a pineapple, several coins and a chart of the river, a stone fallen from the moon, another which will make your dream, and another, yellow like lynx urine, which will be clear or cloudy depending on whether you are happy or sad.
We know you will return.
We shall wait for you in the murmur of the night that precedes the river's flow.

Our emblem shall be the bird you become.
You are the jaguar that springs toward the summer sky and
turns into a constellation.
We lick the pus, the wax from your feet.

TO TOTEM

Your phallus is the largest and on it, as upon the leaves of a
sacred tree of Tibet, all of the Buddhist precepts are written.
Without having been ciphered by anyone, starting in spiral for-
mation from the orifice, the signs of every possible science are
inscribed around the head. Your buttocks are two perfect halves
of a sphere; we come to trace purple and gold concentric circles
upon them, and to pour ointments over your hands.
Look at us.
We have covered your bed with striped orchids,
the chamber with Persian tapestries, pillboxes, fruits, and astro-
labes. So that you come to inhabit them with your laughter.

TO TIGER

Your mother bore you beneath a tree: from her belly you leapt to
the ground; where you fell a giant lotus flower, of every color,
burst forth.
You pronounced a name:
on your left and on your right two cascades spouted, one of cold
water and one of hot; four gods descended to shower you.
Your name, recorded on an aerolite.
You enter the water without wetting yourself, the fire without
burning yourself; you walk over clouds and mist.
At the passing of your horse the forest opens.
Sacred monkeys, elephants, and disciples follow you in caravan.
If you command
a rain of stars will fall at once over the earth.

The Park

Over the tiles of a poplar grove the motorcycles glide, between
gazebos cracked by dog-chewed mint sticks, dry roots.
(Through the crevices white lizards slip away.) We accelerate,
we brake suddenly: skid, capsize, rapid hoops of mud. Bell-

flowers close, the dark green tangles around broken capitals, unfinished marble heads, upside down on the ground, tremble. Armadillos curl up beside the whorls; frightened hares flee through stone ducts. From left to right. From right to left. We circle a dry fountain until we're dizzy. We urinate in the mouths of dolphins: the porous stone drinks the yellow stream they vomit, foaming drivel.

> We strip a small wood of willow trees.
> We rain pebbles upon a ridge.
> The park: a burning embankment, beneath the humus.
> Pollen in flames. Black grass.
> Ashes consume the last branches.
> Plain razed by night beasts to sea level, cyclone, napalm.
> Over the white even surface, fossil flowers.

We continue toward the outskirts. Identical avenues. On either side unfinished Gothic castles of reinforced concrete pass, a second before collapsing—in the oval windows, ladies of stone—churchless towers whose electric bells toll the Angelus, gas stations, lamp stores, parallel lines of blinking yellow lights, smoked glass crematories. Under the silver-plated signs of Esso and dripping oil tanks, sitting on the ground among wax mannikins, families spread flowered blankets over the mustard grass. "A nice day!"—they comment with their walkie-talkies—they open Coca-Colas and cans of herring.

Naves lie at ground level, the neon brilliance of hothouses.

A dam.

An antelope crosses the highway.

We are going into a forest.

We have left the motorcycles and are walking along a narrow path, sheltered by dry branches. In the distance, the hum of the highway. On the ground, among black feathers and snake scales, mixed with pebbles, perforated, drooling eggs break against the palisaded sides as we pass; biting the rushes, bathing them with their thick saliva—blurred pupils—iguanas, fierce chameleons watch us; in the brush, snakes battle: we hear panting, overturnings in the hay, torn membrances, creaking cartilage, splitting fangs; we hear cooings, seeds rupturing, cottony flowers opening, sap rising, buds sprouting. We hear our breathing, the murmur of the night, the wind.

I am afraid.

We come to a clearing.

Silence. Laughter. A bird passes.

TUNDRA: "Now you pass over to the other side: Look."—And he opened a box in front of his face.

A drooling animal jumped on me, with cold paws, his toes stuck to my cheeks, like suction cups.

The jack-in-the-box jumped on him, sounding its toy croaker. Out of the box came springs, a stream of water, a little key from one of the frog's legs. SCORPION wound it up again. TOTEM wet his lips with beer, helped him undress. With open arms and an unraveling skein of hemp rope placed on his right arm like a bracelet, TIGER started to run around him.

Tied to a tree.

Triangles of bindings on his chest.

Two bloodied furrows swelled his knees and fists, cut into his ankles.

They stepped back to look at him.

"Not bad"—said TUNDRA. "Set the camera."

Flash: icon lacerated by infidels // white fang mask against the white fungi of the tree // ashen actor who bends under the weight of his ornaments and falls over a drum // plaster death mask; conjurings in green ink.

SCORPION: "On your guts, on your rotting liver enormous pale butterflies will come to rest."

TOTEM: "You will drink of my blood"—and he poured a bottle of ketchup over him—; "of my cum"—and he opened a container of yogurt over his head.

TIGER: "I am going to blind you"—a flash, in his eyes.

It wasn't Indian music. It was the Beatles.

It was Ravi Shankar. The tabla served as background for a

Shell commerical. TUNDRA repeated, yawning, "You have gone through submission, you have lost power," etc. Another raga followed the pause that refreshes.

SCORPION: "Now what, do we kill him?"

TOTEM: "He has to be fucked."

TIGER: "No. Let him loose. He's to get dressed now."

TUNDRA: "He needs a name."

SCORPION untied him, pulling the bindings to break them, cutting them with a knife against the skin. TOTEM took his hand and put it on his penis. He wet his index finger with saliva and caressed his lips. He blew into his ear. TIGER stirred a mill of noon prayers.

TUNDRA dipped the paintbrushes.

SCORPION sketched on the back of his jacket a vertical arch which opened in the hide, dripping, soaked in by the plush, writhing like a mangled snake.

TOTEM, who slept among the stones—drunken god upon a miniature landscape—jumped up: with a single stroke, expert penman with an angular style, he drew the circle of Divination, twisted over itself and edgeless, the perfect hoop. With a stone seal TIGER stamped beside the circle a square mark: BR. TUNDRA branded into his shoulder an A.

SCORPION: "Cobra?"

TOTEM: "Cobra: so that he will poison. So that he will strangle. So that he will curl around his victims and suffocate them. So that his breath will hypnotize and his eyes will shine in the night, monstrous, golden."

TIGER: "So that he will ooze and blend with the stones. And bite ankles. And with a whack of his sharp scales, strike."

COBRA: "What now?"

TUNDRA: "Nothing."

We took the road back.

The scenery had changed. Through the fog one could see pines, cypresses, and winter plum trees. We went along a ravine. One of the walls fell vertically, carved, neat like a screen; strains of different sands crossed it—still waves—so polished and shiny that we were reflected in them. The stone corridor echoed our voices, our footsteps on the wet grass, deformed and opaque like the images on the wall.

The opposite slope was not as steep; from its crevices wild olive trees sprouted—*ilex pedunculosa*—whose branches descended to the ground, arborescent peony flowers, lianas and ferns. Among the pebbles dwarf fig trees grew—*ficus pumila*. On the ridge, frost covered a forest of willow trees whose threads, along with those of the frozen water, fell from the summits, cascade of fibers. Among colorless and dry rushes cranes perched; the fluttering of their wings shielded our path. As we advanced the murmur of the water grew louder.

From the highest clefts, skimming the rocks, hemp ropes with baskets tied to their tips were lowered. In those crevices, marked in the cliff by palisades of hay, Buddhist monks lived, naked and alone, mute examiners of the void. The birds knew them and made their nests nearby; hovering around and chirping, they guided the few pilgrims, who brought tea and barley meal, to the hampers below the hermits' refuge.

In a corner of the wall *there were several peasant boys who were looking for mushrooms in the grass. They laughed at us, as if surprised at seeing so many strangers in that place.*

We went along a frozen river the hermits always crossed on a blue buffalo when retiring from the world.

Following its winding and ever wider course, covered by white stones, angular and smooth like the vertebrae of prehistoric reptiles, we came upon a meager grotto where the water stopped, crystal-clear; in the white sand at the bottom a dark red glass grew.

The ravine came out onto a misty landscape, of white planes evaporating toward the horizon, where a band of moisture floated over a lake. Milky trunks. Long silvery leaves. Further on, a frail bridge, a small boat. White on white, a bamboo forest. The towers of a monastery.

As we went into the mist we discovered forms, colors appeared. In their burrows—velvety spheres, peaches—startled, ready to roll into a ball, armadillos hid. Among nearby branches, unable to keep their balance, pheasants flew before us, burdened with ornaments, slow in the thickness of the air. Noise among the rushes: it was a fleeing tiger, orange-striped and covered with black marks.

Making our way among the stalks which surrounded us by the thousands, road to the towers, we came upon a stone wall whose junctures were split by bramble-bush. We followed it until we found an opening: a winding road, passing over a bridge in the form of an arch, led to the door of the monastery crowned by a vignette of sealing wax with the inscription "Salut les copains!"

As we opened the door, the face of Buddha appeared before our eyes. His gold colors combined their reflections with those of the green clusters which gave him shade. The steps of a stone staircase and the base of pillars were covered with a moss smooth like cloth. From the back of the great room another staircase began, vertical like a wall, protected by a stone balustrade. This led to a terrace, facing the west: from here we saw an enormous rock more than twenty feet high, in the shape of a loaf of bread. A thin belt of bamboo decorated the base. Continuing to the west and then turning toward the north, we went up a slanting corridor leading to the reception room, which consisted of three transoms and faced directly onto the great rock. At the foot of the rock was a fountain in the shape of a half-moon covered by thick bunches of a kind of watercress and fed by water from a spring. The sanctuary, properly speaking, was to the east of the reception room. It was dark and in ruins. A dark green coating, which at certain intervals thickened into yellowish, granular islands with white borders, shrouded the floor. A grey fuzz covered the stone of three of the walls; from the corners, filled with goiters of dark pulp, minute, purple flowers proliferated. Rust signs which seemed sketched in saffron striped the ceiling; drops hanging from these spots lingered a while, and finally fell to the green mold with a dry sound. In the center of the room were the ruins of the altar. The bas-relief of the foundation—a god dancing within a hoop of fire, upon a dwarfish devil; with one of his right hands (a cobra curled around the wrist) the dancer shook a tambourine, with one of his left he raised a torch—it was a nest of mollusks. On the crown mushrooms grew.

A large window sealed by great leaves in the shape of broken circles, like water lilies, filtered a whitish light; beside the window, along the wall, there lay a pond dug into the floor, also carpeted with moss. Swollen white roots were fixed to the bottom, with bony, shiny nodes injected with wine-colored veins.

Joining hands—we could barely walk on the slippery floor—we managed to draw near to the pond. The water was muddy, and in the shadow of the roots, duplicated by the reflection, ivory though deformed symmetries, lethargic and bulbous like the roots, slow fish traveled in a vegetal slumber, wrapped in jelly-like veils, in a tangle of fibers. They let themselves be touched. They did not flee.

We were leaving when TIGER slipped headlong into the pond. He banged the bottom with open hands. Slow, flat, lanceolated animals, open symmetrical leaves with tenuous nerves, hurry back and forth. Streaked with mercury. Mayan faces. Their glowing orange flagelli followed, entangled them.

We helped him up.

It was then that at the door, as if popped by a spring, a monk of the red hat sect appeared: "Do you want me to say a word, a syllable"—he threatened, with clenched fists, frowning—"and turn you into a bird? Do you want me to conjure up five thousand minor demons right this minute, to prick you, to poison your precious body fluids?"

"Make me a gin and tonic"—TIGER answered.

Red Leaves

Melvin Dixon

It wasn't just me," I told the police. Red leaves are tiny mouths
falling through the sky. They dry on the ground and talk back
in a scratchy, girlish voice. They say things like, "You ain't
never had a chance. You ain't never had a chance." And they
dirty my sneaks saying, "My boy. My boy, Christ Jesus!" Shit.
You have to step on them to shut them up. You got to keep on
stepping sometimes until they come off the ground and come
off your shoes with a sigh. Leaves leaving. Ain't that a bitch?
And then they brush back, leaving the chalk outline of a guy
you want to fuck. But leaves leaving in November say, "No.
No. No." And you talk back to those lips crackling underfoot,
saying, "Shit man. I make my own chances. I make them myself." And they lay there scattered like blood in the street,
shocked, brittle, open, and hard, like pulled teeth that won't
shut up. And I get to asking myself why Moms had to be there
cackling at me like that. I told her once how things happened
the way they did. I told everybody and signed my name in
ink where they told me to sign. Even the doctor promised me
clean sneaks.

Now the leaves talk very little, or I just don't hear them as
much as before. Soon they'll all go away and I can walk on
lighter feet. See some sky. Never hear them voices again. Never.
I'll shut them up like the guys tried to shut me up. They didn't
want me to say nothing. And even Metro didn't know nothing

until it was too late. I didn't realize it either until the voices
came back with bodies when they locked me up to wait for
trial. The bodies and the voices attacked me this time, and I
had no room to hide in or get away to. No fucking where to go.

"It wasn't just me," I said when the doctor wanted me to
come clean. "It wasn't just me." And I must have talked out of
my head because the next thing I knew Cuddles, Max, and Lou
was filing into the precinct with their sweatshirts pulled over
their heads and hiding their faces from photographers. Then
before the TV cameras they showed themselves off proud. Camera lights blared everywhere, and you'd think that the tiles and
linoleum floors had lights on them too. Blinding lights. The
officer said he was Detective Stone. I told him my name—all of
it. He said it was first-degree murder and bail would be pretty
high. Then they brought Moms in and she wailed up and down
the halls like I was her precious somebody who ain't never
been in trouble before. Which was really a lie, 'cause when the
judge set the bail that high she said I'd be better off in jail
anyway than home with her or out in the streets, where I'd be,
mostly. The others came later and even they couldn't pay bail.
Not Cuddles, Max, or Lou. But they never signed their names
like I did, which started all this shit. Which had started for me
when the leaves was talking, and what was I gonna do but talk
back. Tell them everything. The others said they wasn't guilty.
That I'd done it by myself. But when some doctor said there
was too many stab wounds on Metro to come from one person
and that even though he was drugged up with Valium and
Librium and shit to calm him down, he died of the stab wounds
from different knives. You know, knives of different lengths.
Not the clean knife I dropped running out of there. So it wasn't
just me, I said. In fact, I don't remember it being me at all.

It was just a blow job. Just a crazy running in the streets.
My knife was clean. They must know that. It was clean. My
fingerprints, if there was any, was on his head, holding it, and
in his thick hair when it got to feeling good and I couldn't stop
myself. Then his voice made the air thick. He was screaming.
But I couldn't breathe and I couldn't stop hearing him crying
or touching the red coming out of him bent up with Max and

Lou at his back. Then I was alone with him. Metro. I found my feet and used them. Shit. I made room for myself. I got the hell out of there.

But it didn't end with running or dropping the goddamn knife that was clean. I went back to him. Maybe just to touch him, but he wasn't there. Only a chalk outline of his body bent like a leaf. Round and scraggly. The police found me and brought me here to face the others. And when we was left alone, like there was a goddamn signal I didn't read, they was all on me, doing an Irish jig on my head. Shit. Just 'cause I signed for myself and told what had happened. Just 'cause my knife dropped clean to the ground, just 'cause I heard them leaves falling and they sounded like lips calling my name, saying, "Lonny, Lonny," and saying, "I never touched you, man. Never." And when I told the doctor about it, he said they'd stop talking like that. And them leaves did stop talking like that for the split second before Maxie's fist found my jaw and Cuddles squeezed at my throat. Moms in night court was squeezing, too. And Moms in the visitors' gallery was yelling all out of her head and mine in the same scratchy voice, "He ain't never had a chance, Christ Jesus." Which was a lie. I had my chance. Better than that, I took my chance, Moms, and I'm gonna tell everybody about it. You all hear me out there? "Shit. I took my chance. I'm self-employed."

The one who ain't had a chance wasn't me at all. It was Metro. That's something I knew about all along. Which probably explains how I got to jail in the first place and why I even went back where they stabbed him. I wanted to tell him he never had a chance. I did, and I took my chance. And if Cuddles didn't have his knife on me, or if Maxie and Lou was really friends like I thought they was and not the crumbs they turned out to be, I'd have stopped them then and let Metro go. We was just gonna fuck him up a little bit, you know? But I didn't stop them. I couldn't. Don't ask me no more how it happened. Don't ask me no more about who he was to me, 'cause all I know is what he was and what I hate. Telling me his real name didn't change nothing. Not like he wanted things to change. Get to know me maybe. Talk shit and get high. Chase cock, not pussy. So why was I even watching Cuddles fuck that whore

up near Columbus or hiding my face in his denim jacket? I was
really hiding in it, you see. Cuddles ain't nothing to me. He
proved that when he made his steel talk in my face. Not stain-
less this time cause it could have been my blood on the blade.
Or my ass open like that for all the craziness Maxie and Lou
had stored up inside them. It could have been me. Which is
what I told myself when I was alone in the cell and nobody
was looking and I could rub smooth the bruises Cuddles left
on me. Not just the prick of steel. They didn't allow that in
there. But the hammer of his hands and backhand jabs hard to
my stomach and head. And the guards? Shit. They just pretended I wasn't even there. Your ass ain't worth shit around
there. 'Specially if people are holding crap against you. And
when you find out the hard way that your friends ain't your
friends, you take your own chances 'cause you're the only one
you rely on from then on. You go solo.

"Only thing worse than a faggot is a stool," Cuddles says.

"A stool faggot," goes Maxie.

"So you told them, huh? You probably told them about the
herb, too. You must have told them everything," says Lou.

"I signed, goddammit! I signed my fucking name. Yeah, I
told them. You guys never saw that guy Metro. You never
looked back. You never heard the sound of leaves falling red
or curling up dry on the goddamn ground. Don''t give me none
of that stale shit."

"You yellow, Lonny."

"But who was fucking him, Max? Who was fucking him?''

"Shit."

"Yeah, a great, big, stool faggot."

"If I'm a stool then what are you? All of you?"

But they wouldn't let up. They got in close. I called the
guard over and he acted like he didn't hear me. He didn't move
from the door. The rooms was close and hot and they was
crowding in on me. The guard watching away from us, watching the outside. Cuddles's fist came first. I swung back. Caught
Lou and swung again. But Maxie had me then. He had me from
behind. Fists dancing on me. I couldn't feel my teeth anymore.

"You ain't gonna fuck with me!" I yelled.

The guard finally came over. "Cut that shit out," he said. "Cut it out."

But Maxie held tighter. The guard looked away. I couldn't move my hands. Cuddles and Lou at my face again until my eyes closed on red and my throat got tight with spit and acid coming up from my belly. I tasted blood. I ate it. And it was mine. Mine.

I couldn't open my eyes for two days. I could hardly eat. They had me go to the infirmary for a few hours. Then sent me back the day I had a visitor. Someone I wasn't planning on seeing ever again. Moms. She was there with my sister Patty. I didn't want to see them. Not the way I was looking. I could barely walk to my place behind the glass booth when, suddenly, she saw me and wouldn't keep her mouth shut from screaming. Her screams were metal, metal on metal, knives on knives. I held my head. I couldn't say nothing 'cause my mouth was still purple and fat and would let only air come through, and even that hurt. But she kept yelling at me, making my head hurt worse. "Look, Moms," I said to myself and to her silently through a swollen mouth, hoping she could hear me somehow, even if the words never came. *I'm doing it. I'm taking my chance.*

"My boy! Christ Jesus. Look what they done to my boy."

My knife was clean. I never stabbed Metro. I was caught in it as much as he was. I never stabbed him, really. Really. But that's what Maxie is saying, and Lou and Cuddles too. Maybe they'll believe me 'cause I'm youngest. The public defender didn't listen to me. "They got your confession," he said. "You might as well come clean." Come clean, come clean. Shit. Everybody wants you to come clean like you nothing but shit anyway. My knife dropped on the ground. I went back to see him. I went back to touch him, like he wanted to be touched. I was there, wasn't I? Inside his shape? I was inside the print of his hands and feet and head. I was lying inside all of him. And the cold in that chalk shape was mine.

After they beat me I got put in a separate cell. The cops told me that I was going to a juvenile home upstate until the trial date. I don't know what's going to happen to the others. I don't give a fuck. Cuddles wanted it big. Let him have it big.

I only signed because they said it would be easier if I went along with the cops and told what happened, told what I did and what they did, which is all I said. What I didn't expect was to see it all typed out on a page all neat and clean like a government paper for somebody's file. Mine. And I didn't expect to be locked up this long either, just 'cause we couldn't pay bail. The doctor who talked to me said they'd transfer me upstate, but there wasn't no room there just yet, no openings. I'd have to stay put for a little longer until something could be done. Something arranged. We're in separate cells. I don't know nothing about the others. We met together only once after they beat me. The guard was watching them differently that time.

What did I expect out of those bums, anyway? What did I expect out of the cops and guards? Wasn't I looking on when they stabbed Metro? Didn't I know it was going to end up like it did? How the hell could I blame anyone? I had red on myself now. Red eyes. Swollen red lips. A head that wouldn't stop pounding at the slightest footsteps. And all you could hear is feet dragging on metal. My feet dragged too. But inside the metal catwalk the floor is concrete. Walls are cinder blocks stacked high and glazed with gray paint. Each one measures twelve inches by six inches. And there are thirty blocks on the wall below the metal bars and window. One window. I've seen some cells that are just metal and air. Then some with walled metal slats for ventilation. Space for names and fingers, maybe. Nothing else. And one square lock to remind you how far the space goes out, how far you can walk forward without coming back, then walk back again. One five-step run from locked bars to back window. Then an iron-pole bed, an open toilet, and me. Five steps this way, five steps that way. *Step-touch, step-touch, step-touch back.* And the pacing, the pacing back and forth, back and forth inside my head.

Take the "A" Train

James Earl Hardy

"Oh shit!"

The alarm clock was doing that low hum, which meant that it had been ringing for some time. I reached up and slammed down the off button, squinting to see the time: 7:45!

"Damn!"

I rolled out of my futon, banging my right knee on its hard wood base. Instead of clutching my knee and wallowing in the pain (which was rather intense), I just smacked it, grunted "mother-fredrick," and hopped my way to the bathroom. Forgetting that the bathroom door was closed so that the cool air stayed in my one-room studio, I ran right into the door. I flung it open and flicked on the light. Ripping off my yellow boxer shorts, I almost tore the shower handle out, trying to turn it on. The water was a little too hot, but there was no time to adjust it. I just soaped up, rinsed down, and was out in three minutes. While drip-drying, I scrubbed my teeth, gargled for a second, and sprayed my arms with Brut.

I briskly walked back into the outer room to the corner opposite the futon, where two black folding chairs (i.e., my living room furniture) sat. On one of them was my outfit—white briefs, black Spandex, and a white tank. I slipped it on, as well as the white socks and black Nikes. I jogged back into the bathroom to check myself in the mirror, cleaning my glasses and putting them on. I then turned off the air conditioner, grabbed my wallet and keys off my desk, tossed them in the black leather tote bag (which was hanging on my work chair), scooped up the two subway tokens on top of the television set, threw my black BROOKLYN cap on top of my bald head, and flew out the door.

The train station was just a block away from my brownstone, but according to the very cheap Timex on my left arm, my train would be pulling out in exactly forty-five seconds. Uh-huh, my feet started kicking up that dirt. But my marathon run up the block wasn't fast enough: a stream of folks coming out of the station met me at the stairwell. Damn, that bastard was early. I kicked the pavement.

"Don't worry, brother, another train's gonna come," chuckled one of those exiting, a fella with small brown eyes, a neatly styled short fro, and flawless ebony skin. He was a few inches shorter than me (I'm five eight) and had a muscular build. He wore a grey muscle tee and it was tucked inside a pair of blue jeans that were so tight I couldn't imagine how he got them on and over that ass, which stood up at attention. Hmmmm ... just my type. Dark, lovely, and he's got boo-*tay*.

I smiled. He, too, smiled, but he shouldn't have. His two front teeth were missing. He saluted me and went on his way.

Yeah, I missed the train, but there would be another one, right? So motherfuckin' *what*. Who the fuck asked him to comment? I made the trip down the stairs defeated. I dusted past one of the homeless stragglers, a woman, probably in her fifties with a shopping cart, ignoring her "Good morning." I dropped one token in my bag and the other in the silver turnstyle, going through it with such force that it stopped at a half-staff position. I sucked my teeth and breathed through my mouth, letting the air out through my clenched teeth. It was the dead of August and it was hot—ninety degrees above ground, more than likely over a hundred below—but I knew my temperature topped them both.

But I got even hotter and my frown changed into a smirk when I got to the platform and saw the real reason for my mad rush.

He was in his favorite spot. I know it's his favorite spot because, since our first "meeting" a month ago, he's always there. His very round, very high rump was parked on the far left side of a six-seater wooden bench. His giant feet—they appeared to be twice my size-nines—were planted firmly on the ground, two feet in front of him. I swear, he has the longest legs I've ever seen on a man; they just stretch and stretch and stretch. He's at least a foot taller than me and weighs much, much more than my measly 175 pounds. He's a big man—stocky and solid—but not muscular. When he stands, he towers and it makes me shiver. Naturally, he has to duck when he gets on and off the train. For some reason, I find it sexy.

His head was where it always is: buried in the *New York Times*. With his body hunched forward and his elbows leaning on his thighs, he holds it with both hands. I love the way he handles the paper: it's folded in quarters, no doubt so he can read it more easily (it's so classy). But I'm sure he also does it like that so he doesn't inconvenience anyone turning those big pages. He always starts with sports, breezes through the Metro section, and by the time his stop comes (59th Street/Columbus Circle), he's on A-1. Most folks read the paper on the train with a stone face, but his head will often shake and his dark brown eyes will dart if he comes across something that has struck a nerve.

As I approached him, I could see he was dressed in a short-sleeved light brown shirt, unbuttoned at the top, a tan pin-stripe tie which sat an inch below his opened collar, tan dress pants, and mahogany brown dress shoes that matched his skin. This is his usual ensemble, and there's one thing that has always puzzled yet intrigued me: he never wears socks. God knows that it *is* too hot for them. And from what I can tell, he didn't carry around a pair so he can put them on at work. But it does leave me wondering exactly what he does for a living. I've been tempted to ask about this—not to mention what his name is, how old he is, where he lives, what his phone number is and if he's "married" (there's no wedding band, engagement ring, or "bonding bracelet," but that don't mean a damn thing). But since I find myself tongue-tied around him (something that has *never* happened to me before when a man was at stake), I haven't.

Instead, I did what I always do: take a seat on the opposite end of the bench. This is where the gazing game begins. I pretend that I'm looking straight ahead when in fact I'm staring at him through the corner of my left eye. He acknowledges me by grinning (I can tell he is because the dimple appears in his right cheek) and nodding. Then he takes me in, from head to toe, at which point I have to hold on to my knees because they start knocking due to my nerves. I clear my throat and lean forward to see if the train is coming. When I look in his direction, he returns to his paper. It is then my turn to look—and I do. He now checks me out through the corner of his right eye.

Someone usually sits between us by this time. There were several people coming down the stairwells on either side of us, but none joined us; it was almost as if they knew not to, that I didn't want them blocking my view. Then I realized the reason why; the buzzer had sounded, which meant that the train was coming. I turned to him; he was already up, rolling up his paper and moving toward the edge of the platform. He stopped, placed the paper under his left arm, and leaned against a pole with his left shoulder. He played it off like he was watching the train pull into the station when he was in fact watching me. As I rose off the bench, I noticed that my shoelace was untied. What a coincidence! As the train whizzed past us, I took two steps forward and bent down to tie it. His eyes widened; he gasped. He rubbed his clean-shaven chin and that attractive square jaw. As the train stopped and the doors opened, he boarded it with a silly grin. He loved the view. Mission accomplished.

There was no room to board the train where I was standing, so I quickly walked over to the door he entered and managed to squeeze in, making my way toward a pole and reaching over a white woman so I could hold on. I looked over the crowd but couldn't find him. Damn, where did he go? He *had* to be here, I told myself; you couldn't walk between the cars since the doors were locked. And it ain't like he can just fit in a neat little corner out of view.

For the next ten minutes I scanned the space, trying to locate his oval-shaped head, his shirt, his pants, even his feet among those sitting down, mindful that every stop we came to brought us closer to his. I decided not to leave where I stood: I was in the middle of the car, so he couldn't escape without my seeing him. Of course, the folks around me made my search hard: the pushing, the shoving, the cursing and carrying on. At one point two women got into a very nasty shouting match: one accused the other of having grown up in a cave since she didn't have any manners. I wanted to tell them both to shut the fuck up, as well as demand that the teenager to the right of me pump down the volume on his Walkman and the little girl to the left of me stop stepping on my foot, because they were all disturbing my concentration.

Finally his stop was next and I was not the least bit thrilled. I know that panic and worry were all over my face. As folks prepared to get off on either side of me, jockeying for position, my head was going in a million directions. It's bad enough that I didn't have the chance to sneak a peak every now and then as he'd stand against one of the doors reading. My day just wouldn't be the same without at least seeing him walk off the train and out of my life . . . at least until tomorrow morning.

The train stopped, the doors opened, folks began filing in and out, and I felt like screaming. I also felt like knocking the shit out of some of these people, particularly those who, like that frustrated woman had declared, never heard of the phrase "Excuse me." Just then someone brushed against me just a little too close and I was ready to draw blood.

I turned to light them up, but my mouth dropped to the floor and my body started to quake as I came face-to-face with my target. Where the hell did *he* come from? We were eye to eye, and I'm sure my eyes looked like they were about to pop out. This is the closest we had ever been and I knew I was about to faint. I was in shock; I couldn't speak.

But he could. He smiled, said "Sorry" with lips so thick they could swallow you whole and a voice so warm it could melt butter, and slipped a piece of paper under the left strap of my tank, allowing his fingertips to lightly caress my chest. I began to tremble. As he removed his hand, his thumb lightly brushed my left nipple. My body tensed. He winked. I watched his long body bend and step off the train as the doors were closing.

My eyes darted from person to person, hoping that no one

saw the exchange. It didn't seem like it; nobody was paying me any mind. As the train pulled off, I snatched the note from inside the strap, touching my nipple. I had to catch myself. I wanted to moan—I *needed* to moan—because it was so hard, just ripe to be plucked and sucked. I hissed and grunted instead.

I unfolded the paper, which was really an index card. Its message was written in pencil:

> *YOU WERE LATE 2-DAY.*
> *DON'T B 2-NITE.*
> *8 O'CLOCK.*
> *MY SPOT.*
>
> *J.R.*

I had a serious grin on my face the rest of the day.

The View from Here

Brian Keith Jackson

"White folks always love l'il colored babies," says my Momma
to my Poppa when she decided to tell him she was carrying
me. "Miss Janie won't mind if I bring her to work with me.
She loves colored chil'ren. She's always saying how clean and
well behaved colored chil'ren are; 'none more mannered than
a colored child,' she says. It won't be no problem. No problem
at all. You remember how she was with Junior? When he was
coming up? Sweet as she could be. Treated him just as good as
if he was one of her own. Remember? She would give us old
books and toys that her chil'ren had outgrown. Remember?"

Momma was saying all this to convince herself. She had
had this conversation, with the walls that framed our house, on
many occasion, until the words were placed as neatly as the
seams of the paper that covered them. But all that seemed fruit-
less now. She knew Poppa wasn't entertaining the conversation.
She had been putting off telling him for as long as she could,
constantly reminding herself of his saying he didn't want "no
more chil'ren"; it had been seven years since Momma was last
pregnant. She had an idea as to how Poppa was likely to take
the news of me, but through it all, remained hopeful. He had
said time and time again that he already had "too many mouths
to feed." I would make number six.

Momma was well into her fifth month with me, and hiding
it was no longer possible. The winter months, if you want to

call them that, though never severe, were over, stripping her of her layers. She could no longer blame it on putting on a few pounds here and there to fight off the cold that, from hearing of it, was always "goin' round." She was showing and there was nothing else to do but to tell Poppa, hope, and pray for the best.

"It's not going to be no trouble, J.T." My Momma always calls Poppa "J.T." when she's trying to get on his good side. It makes things seem more personal-like. Poppa's full name is Joseph Henry Thomas. People who know him, including those that work at the lumber mill, just call him Joe.

"I can get baby clothes from Miss Janie. Being her two chil'-ren grown now, J.T. She wouldn't a bit mind me using the clothes she's got stored away up in her attic. They just sitting up there in boxes collecting cobwebs. She's got no use for them now. I'm almost sure she wouldn't mind. J.T.? Well, anyhows, I'll talk to her when I go in to work on Monday. How's that sound? J.T.?"

Poppa didn't say a word. He just kept eating, adding more to the place that held his answer before what was already there could be swallowed. Momma had been in the kitchen all day preparing his favorites—catfish, collard greens and fatback, hot-water bread, and the purple-hull peas she had bought from the farmer's market a whiles back and thawed out today to cook just for this occasion. For dessert, blackberry cobbler with sugar sprinkled on top of the crust, "just like you like it, J.T."

Momma had been antsy and riled all day. She cooked and talked to me, saying not to worry, everything was going to be all right and Poppa would come round. It would just take some doing and that I'd see. I'd see, everything was going to be just fine.

She had to sit down every now and again. The heat from the stove would make her dizzy. Mississippi's springs may be filled with rain, but when it isn't raining the temperature has never been nothing to play with lightly. Many a day you can see the heat dancing in the distance, blurring the view.

After Poppa ate, she filled his Mason jar with ice tea and three wedges of lemons, "just like you like it, J.T.," and he went out on the porch to read the *Free Press*, the colored newspaper.

Poppa never drank a drop with the meal, always after, to wash his food down. Though the sun had called it a night, it was still hot and humid out, and the jar began to sweat, each drop finding its way to the next, making a clean but crooked trail down to the porch where it left a ring, joining those that had stained the wood from years past.

He sat in his rocker. It was his rocker and no one dared sit in it or even joke about doing so. It was like he could tell if someone else's behind had been there. He once said he could tell if someone had been in his chair due to an "ol' war injury." But Momma said Poppa was just poking fun. That he's never been in no war; no war to speak of. But even if company came over, which was rare, Momma would offer her chair, but never his. It was his property to do with as he pleased. As was Momma, and for the time being, as was I.

"How was your meal, J.T.? Everything sit right with you? I made it special for you. Spent the whole day. Me and l'il Lisa," says Momma, coming out on the porch.

Lisa. That's my name. I've been called that since the first day of sickness. Some folks may have thought it was a cold or that she had eaten something spoilt that made Momma sick. Never would they have conjured up the notion of a child. Not now. Maybe had there been other women around, they would have known. But Momma was the only one; and after five chil'-ren, you don't need no doctor, or midwife to tell you you're expecting.

"Was work all right?" she asked. "I heard tell that things are picking up all over and people are ordering more. Sounds like good news. Doesn't it?"

Poppa remained silent. His huge hands gripped the *Free Press* at each side. He had the kind of hands that were like iron. More like what you would expect to see on a statue in the town square instead of on a living, breathing man. The wedding band on his third finger seemed small compared to the knuckle that many years of labor had invited. Poppa's been working at the mill lifting and moving lumber for the last twenty some odd years. His body is naturally built by a day-to-day routine that the mill controls.

Momma kept on talking. Her voice was filled with promise.

Poppa never flinched. He just continued staring at the paper, or at least looking at the pictures that centered each page. Momma began to cry. She knew not to do so too loudly or in his presence, but all the same the tears fell, silently, as tears so often do.

She went back in the house and sat near the door to watch his every move. My brothers knew when my father was this way they best just sit down in the house and be as quiet as possible, whereabouts they don't cause no distractions. Even the slightest wince from the pine floors could prove to be the lightning that set off a clap of thunder. As I said, Poppa was heavy handed, and no one wanted to get in the way of those heavy hands. Through experience, they knew any l'il thing could set him off. Today I was that l'il thing.

Momma kept sitting, watching him. She was watching him so close I could feel her breaths become his. Breathing out, then in, as he did. His lungs seemed to be the keyhole to the future.

"You can have the chile," says Poppa, not even looking away from the paper, as if the words were written on that very page and he was just reading them.

Momma's breaths became her own, ours, again as she swung open the screen door, running out to his side, "Thank you, J.T. Thank you."

"But you cain't keep it. We cain't risk it. It might be two again. My back is breakin' awready and I don't need another screaming chile runnin' round keeping up racket. Clariece can't have no chil'ren and she need some help round they place. If they be willin', we'll give it to them to raise so James' name can go on. I'll go round pay a visit on Sunday. Talk to them about it."

After that, Poppa said no more. He had spoken and nothing more need be said. Momma knew this. There was no need in questioning something that she knew had been settled. As fast as swatting away an anxious fly, happiness fell from her face to the splintering planks on the porch floor where the rings of water waited for company.

Taking the same steps as she did a moment before, she walked back through the screen door, being careful to catch it before it slammed, not wanting to disturb Poppa. She didn't want to make matters worse. It was hard to believe that things could get much worse, but Momma didn't want to chance it. Many thoughts ran through her body, never forming a complete one. Thinking seemed useless now, for reality, had cancelled what, at least until this day, was a possibility waiting to spring forth. For five months she had waited for an answer. Now she had one.

Clariece is Poppa's older sister. She's the only living kin he knows of. She married James, a preacher, some time ago but wasn't able to provide a living child. Three had made their way through her, but all had died before they ever took their first gasp. It didn't seem as if Clariece'd be able to provide James with a name child. Poppa was hoping I would be such said, and it was that he would speak to them about this coming Sunday.

After washing up the supper dishes on Saturday evening, Momma pulled out the ten-pound iron, putting it on the stove. After testing it with a spit-moistened finger, when it was good and hot, she took out the ironing board and pressed everybody's Sunday clothes. Everybody's but Poppa's. Poppa never went to church. Didn't believe in it. But he always made my brothers go and represent the family. He didn't want Momma going by herself. The eyes of the Lord may have been good enough for everyone else, but he wanted only his eyes peering down on Momma.

Since Poppa had made his decision as to what would become of me, Momma has been dreading this evening. She knew the day after, Sunday, tomorrow, would determine my fate. Poppa would talk to James and all would be decided. Decided without her voice.

After she pressed the clothes, she hung them up so in the morning my brothers could get ready without too much of a fuss. Any kind of uproar tomorrow easily would prove to be too much for her. Too much for us.

Momma and I were always the last ones to go to bed. It was our quiet time. If Poppa and his friends were out at the Rusty Nail, the local juke joint, we would always wait up just in case somebody wanted something to eat so the liquor would

have something to stick to in the night, relieving a foggy head
from entering a new clear morning.

"Now, I know you're worried, but everthing's going to be
just fine," says Momma, rubbing her stomach and nibbling on
the shiny top of the last piece of corn bread from tonight's
dinner. "We've still got time on our side. Time and the Lord.
Between the two, you've got nothing to worry about."

"Who you talkin to?" says Poppa, opening the screen door.
His voice silenced the crickets that always filled the night's air.

"J.T., I didn't hear you come up. How long you been standing there?"

"Long 'nuf. I heard you talkin'. Who you talkin' to? I don't
see nobody here. You talkin' to yaself? Only crazy folk talk
to theyself."

"No, Joe. I'm just passing the time with l'il Lisa till you
come home."

"Don't be callin' that chile no names. That ain't yourn to
be doin'. That's for James and Clariece to do. Bad luck to be
callin' it a bitch name anyhows. James don't need no more
womens round. So don't be jinxin' this here baby. You hear?
You hear?!"

"Yes, Joe. I hear you. No need in making no ruckus, you'll
wake the boys."

"They mine to wake, ain't they?"

Momma doesn't answer, but with a smile she asks, "You
want me to warm you up something, J.T.?"

"Nah. I'm goin' to bed. I got to gets up fo' day. It's gonna
take a good spell to get over to James' place. I'll have to try
and hitch a ride."

Poppa went on to bed. Momma and I stayed up awhile
longer, cleaning an already dirt-free kitchen. Sometimes a clean
spot can look dirty if you stare at it long enough. Momma kept
walking around on light foot, looking for old things, seen for
the first time. Anything to pass the time, only to reach what
would seem like forever. There wasn't no use in trying to
sleep—not tonight.

"Your poppa doesn't mean no harm. I know at times it may
sound like it, but he doesn't mean no harm." Momma says this
to me without opening her mouth, fearing Poppa might over-

hear, waking a concern that for the time being needed to sleep. That was the kind of relationship we had. Momma and me. Momma wasn't so much afraid of Poppa, but she knew him better than he knew himself, and sometimes in that comes the hurt, and the understanding.

After sitting at that old wooden kitchen table until there was absolutely nothing else to do, Momma lowered the oil lamp and we, with held breath, went and slid in bed beside Poppa. The cool sheets pacified us, embracing a body warmed by the woes of the day.

Just as we were getting comfortable and about to relax into rest, Poppa rolled over and placed his hand on Momma's shoulder. She knew the night wasn't over for us. Not just yet.

From what I'm told and what I've heard, Poppa wasn't always this way. It's said he was kind and charming. I'm sure in some way that's true. Momma and Poppa had met many moons ago at the Mt. Olive Church picnic when they were just "younguns." Of course, Poppa wasn't a member of the congregation, but he would show up for the social functions. Even the finest of Christian wouldn't be evil enough to kick someone out of a church function. Besides, young boys could always get away with such devilment and it be tolerated, even attractive. Boys will be boys, and girls will giggle at them, with closed mouth.

The place for all this socializing was always at a church function. All the best courting took place at these functions because this was where all the young people knew all the other young people would be, whereabouts they could see one another without sneaking around at night, risking getting a couple of rounds of buckshot shot at them for trespassing on somebody's property.

These functions were a guarantee that clothes would be pressed and baskets filled with the results of the best recipes each kitchen had to offer, each aiming to outtaste the rest. Young folks didn't have much opportunity to meet in social places with that of the other sex, so these picnics were the place, where, in the name of God, sinning was permitted.

I was told that first day, the day the courting began, was a beautiful one. The honeysuckle vines, wrapped around the church's white picket fence, let off a fine smell that yelled spring. The tempera-

ture was pleasant and the sermon, "praise the Lawd," wasn't too
long. The choir sung and the mothers on the Women's Auxiliary
shouted on cue as if the choir director had conducted it as such. It
was a great day for a function and for courting.

"Did you see Sista Campbell hollering and carrying on like that?"
said Momma. "The Spirit really moved her today."

"You can say that again. The Spirit moved her right up and
down the church. And when you thought she was finish, back again,"
said Ida Mae. "It took all three of her sons and the entire usherboard
to calm her down. I know Barbara was shame, having her momma
screamin' and carryin' on like that."

"Barbara told me that her momma and Sister Dawson take turns
trying to outshout each other. That if one of them shouts the first
Sunday and cleared an entire pew, then you could rest assured the
second Sunday the other would shout, not quitting until she had
cleared two."

"Who you tellin'? Sittin' by either of'm is just askin' for a bruis-
in'. When you see that hand start to goin' up in the air and wavin'
round, you know it's just a matter of time 'fore the dancin' begins.
You'd think she'd been down to the Rusty Nail the way she carries
on."

"Ida Mae, stop it! Somebody's gonna hear you."

"I'm speakin' the truth, and the truth shall set you free," said
Ida Mae, waving her hand through the air and throwing her head
back as if the Spirit had hit her.

Ida Mae had been Momma's best friend since they were l'il girls
playing beauty shop. And like in that place where women are being
pampered, there was nothing they wouldn't tell each other. Momma
kept Ida Mae tame and Ida Mae made Momma feel as if she wasn't.
People seem to enjoy when you play on the edge. They keep all eyes
focused upon you, in hopes of witnessing the moment of your fall.
Eyes were forever upon Ida Mae, for she was as near to the edge as
they came. If it could be done, Ida Mae had done it, was in the process
of doing it, or was thinking about how she could do it without getting
caught. But Momma could rest assured that as soon as the deed was
done, she would be the first—or the second as the case might be—to
hear about it, and that's the way it had been for years.

"Ol' Clayton Jamison was just a-hummin' round my honey jar
last night at the Nail," said Ida Mae, while biting into the drumstick

she had in her basket. "I told him if he had half a tooth in his mouth, I might just let him, but since he don't, to buzz on 'way from me."

"Ida Mae, why you so mean?" said Momma, teasingly. "That boy has been chasing you for as long as he's been able to stand on two legs and you've always been mean to him."

"Anna, as long we been friends, you still don't know nothin' 'bout no menfolk, do you? In all this time, I guess I ain't taught you nothin'. You gots to be mean to'm if you want'm to keep your taste in they mouth. It's like a challenge for'm, see. You know they out there tellin' all they business to they no-'count l'il friends. Once they done that, then they gotta keep after you 'cause if they don't get you, then they friends don't ever let'm live it down 'cause that's how menfolk is. The meaner you are to'm, the more they think it's worth it when they finally get you."

"You mean you gonna let Clayton Jamison . . . ?"

"Hell, nah! I wouldn't let him within a whiff's distance of a cowpatty. But he don't know that, and that's what keeps him after me. And that's what keeps my glass full at the Nail. Speaking of which, you wanna l'il drank?"

"No, thanks. I got some lemonade that Momma made and—"

"Anna. What am I gonna do witchu?" said Ida Mae, pulling out a bottle of gin. "I mean a drank, honey. A real drank, not no Goddamn lemonade. And definitely not that grape juice that they passin' off for wine in that there church house."

"You gonna get us both in trouble, Ida Mae. Put that bottle away. If my momma sees you with that she's gonna skin our hides, then you know she's gonna call your people and you gonna get torn up again."

"I might get it, but if I do, I wanna have a l'il fun meanwhiles. Here's to you, precious." Ida Mae raised the bottle to her lips and took a hearty swig. Her face soured for a minute and then slowly returned to normal. "Ain't bad. Ain't bad at all. Come on, Anna, have a taste. Just a little one. It's Sunday. One Spirit deserves another."

Momma took the bottle and poured a peach pit full into her jar of lemonade, looking around to make sure nobody was watching. She shook the jar to mix it and then took a swig. Ida Mae and Momma sat there under that old oak tree near the creek that breezy Sunday afternoon, long ago, talking. Ida Mae telling tales that Momma never could decide if they were true or not, but would always listen, gladly.

Momma would live the life of each of Ida Mae's stories to the fullest, if nothing more than in her mind, and as far as Momma was concerned, that was plenty.

As the day went on, the lemonade disappeared and Momma was getting friendly, even from her peach pit full of gin.

"That's really nice," said Momma taking the last sip from the jar.

"My cousin Lester, in Detroit, I think you met Lester one time when he was last down here, well, he says gin is the 'preferred' drink up north."

"No, Ida Mae. I don't mean the gin, though it is nice. I mean Joseph Thomas over there. Don't look. OK. Now. Look."

"Girrrl, I know you must be drunk."

"Maybe I am. Maybe I'm not."

Poppa had been walking back and forth along the creek, and Momma had been watching him while Ida Mae's tales carried the storyline. Of course, at the time she wasn't Momma and she certainly didn't know he would be Poppa. It was just a crush, is what I've heard. A church function crush.

"Don't you think he looks handsome, with those bowlegs and all?" Momma said, smiling and swaying on that blanket like she could hear her favorite hymn playing in the distance from the now empty church.

"Hell, nah! He's trouble. Trouble, I tell you. Don't eva trust no boy with no bowlegs. They get round more than a wheel on a wagon, and that's too much for my taste," said Ida Mae, finishing off her bottle of gin and pulling out yet another from what seemed to be an endless supply. "Now, if you wanna be happy, stay 'way from bowlegged mens. And anyhow, you know yo momma would have a conniption fit if that boy came a-callin' on you. He ain't nothin' but a heathen. Always been a heathen. Ain't gonna be nothin' but a heathen."

"No such a thing. He's sweet."

"Precious. Melons are sweet. Bowlegged mens ain't."

"But look at him over there. I think he'd suit me just fine. He's got a job down at the mill and making good money. A girl could do worse for herself. And anyway, who you to talk? You sure ain't no candidate for the Women's Auxiliary."

Momma took a swig from the new bottle of gin, and just as she was bringing it from her lips:

"Anna! Anna! Lorda be! You put that devil water down this instant, young lady." It was Gram, standing, rooted next to the oak tree that only moments ago served as shade. But no amount of leaves could shield Momma from the heat of Gram's stare. Momma knew she was in for it. Every time Gram called her "young lady," she knew she had it coming.

"But, Momma, I—"

" 'Momma, I'? Momma, I nothing. It's too late to be 'Momma I'-ing. You should have thought of 'Momma I' before you let that filth pass your lips. Now, that's what you should of done. But being you didn't, you gonna get it when you get home, young lady. Now, come on with me," said Gram, pulling Momma up by the sleeve of her dress. *"And I know this is your doing, Ida Mae Ramsey, and don't think I'm not gonna tell Correne when I see her."*

"But, Mrs. Anderson—"

"Don't say another word. Not another single word, Ida Mae, or I'll have the mind to take a branch from this tree and tan those big old legs of yours right here and now. The good Lord knows a switch couldn't do nothing to them. Now, come on, Anna.

Gram and Ida Mae had had many rounds of this sort. Ida Mae knew it was hopeless so she didn't say another word. Not another word.

Momma didn't get a hiding that day; just sent to her room, "to think about what she'd done." Ida Mae did, but she was used to it. Getting put on "restriction, young lady" hurt Momma, but not as much as her knowing Joseph Thomas, Poppa, saw her being pulled away by her own momma, Gram.

Gram was a gracious lady, "refined," it's been said, but she didn't mind shaming you in front of people if you happened to get out of line. To her it wasn't about shaming you, but "setting you straight." I've heard good stories about Gram. Early on, Momma used to say how she wished Gram was around now because if she was, she would know what to do. She would know how to handle Poppa, and that she would make everything all right for me. But Gram ain't around now. It's just Momma and me. Just us.

We were up and about early this Sunday morning. Never got to sleep, really. After Poppa had finished doing his do, he just rolled back over and was asleep before Momma could even mumble the words "Have a good night's rest?" She just lay there with the quilt pulled up enough so that I was covered and warm. Every time Poppa moved or rolled from his left to right side she would hold her breath, hoping he wouldn't wake up. Praying he would stay asleep until it would be an appropriate time for her to get out of bed and begin her day. At long last, that time had come.

It was still before day and Momma knew Poppa would be getting up soon to go talk to James about he and Clariece raising me. Me and Momma started out in the yard; March mist covered the Johnson grass, making the surroundings heavenly, though things seemed far from it.

"It's gonna be a fine day today. It's God's day, l'il Lisa, and nothing bad is coming on God's day."

We picked up the kindling for the stove and went back inside, careful not to let the screen door slam behind. Momma lit the stove, and the early morning chill that visited our house in the night was soon replaced by warmth. A warmth that, from here, I'm used to. Even though my fate was to be decided today, in a matter of hours, Momma always kept me warm, protected; no kindling was needed for that.

"You want to help me make some biscuits? You know biscuits are your favorite," says Momma. "You move like the dickens ever' time we have biscuits." This time she said it through a soothing hum so as no words could wake the morning from its sleep. "I know you enjoy them smothered with butter and hot maple syrup. Why don't we fix them up like you like them. Today is your day."

Yes. Nothing is more soothing than a mother's hum.

Momma kept the big tin of flour near the stove. Every time she bent down to get a cupful, I could feel myself moving nearer to her heart. She would get as many cups as necessary to feed the seven mouths she had to feed and the eighth one that Poppa wanted Clariece to feed. After she sifted all the flour she needed, she sprinkled two handfuls along the kitchen table so the dough wouldn't stick.

She kneaded.

She did all this with a gentle ease, care going into each movement, dough taking shape under her hands, between her fingers. Yes, she kneaded. The head of the Mason jar shaped the biscuits to a perfect size, and from one came many, all by the same hands, each receiving no more or less. She took the leftover scraps of dough and rolled it, making one biscuit for herself. It wasn't as pretty as the others, but would taste just the same.

When Momma was cooking there was always a dishrag nearby. It served as a close friend just when needed. The dishrag was kept in arm's reach, never really being used for much, just something to fill those moments when the next instant was forming but hadn't quite been built. A touch here, a dab there, a moment to breathe. Wipe the sweat from her brow. Like a writer from the *Free Press* might use a comma, Momma used that dishrag. It took her to the next step; the time between thought and creation. Being the only woman around, she needed a friend, something to hold on to, when being held seemed so far from reach.

As Momma put the biscuits in the stove a noise came from her and Poppa's bedroom. It didn't startle her. She was used to it.

"You hear that, l'il Lisa," she says, smiling like a young girl meeting a young boy for the first time—after it had just been decided that it was all right to like boys. "That's your Poppa in there snoring up a breeze. I'm surprised he doesn't snore his nose off. He must have rolled over on his back. His mouth tends to fall open when he sleeps on his back. Now, I know it's loud as can be, but you'll get used to it in time where it won't even bother you so. He's just sleeping real good, that's all. He needs his rest. Rest'll do him good. The smell of these biscuits oughta fill up that nose of his in a minute."

As Momma took out the first batch of biscuits, and put them in the lined wicker basket that when not in use hung on the kitchen wall, the ol' house rooster, perched on the barbed-wire fence post in the yard, crowed and she knew our private time together was nearing an end. Poppa's voice, too, would soon be heard.

"Junior?" Screams Poppa from the bedroom. "Boy, you up? Junior? Junior, get up and watch the house. You gonna have to be in charge a thangs round here today."

"J.T., why don't you let the boy sleep. He works hard all week long and it ain't really nothing for him to do till it's time for Sunday school," says Momma as Poppa comes into the kitchen. She piles biscuits on a plate, placing it at his place at the table, hoping the smell of the butter melting and the maple syrup tempting his taste buds would moisten his mouth, soften his words.

"He ain't the only one who works hard round here," says Poppa, taking the butter and syrup from Momma and putting more on his plate. "If I'm up, then he needs to be up too. I'm gonna be gone for most of the day, and somebody needs to be round here to look after things. Junior?! Junior, are you up, boy? Don't let me have to call up in there again."

"Yessir! I'm up."

"Then why don't I hear no movin' round up in there then? Get the molasses out your ass, boy, and get on in here. Hear?"

"J.T., please. It's Sunday. Don't wake the rest of them. He's up. Give him a minute," says Momma, grabbing hold to the dishrag and walking over to the sink. She had her back to him when she said it. She didn't want to see what he was thinking and she didn't want to upset him. Not today. She knew too much was depending on it.

Junior came out of the bedroom and sat down across from Poppa.

Junior is my oldest brother, and being her firstborn makes him almost as close to Momma as I am. He, too, worked at the lumber mill. He was mostly quiet, keeping to himself as much as possible. He knew what it was like to go out to the chicken coop and be gentle when it came to taking the eggs from the nest. He knew the best way because he had been around the longest. Junior didn't rightly understand why he had to get up, but he wasn't about to question it. For him, sleep was always light anyhow.

"I wants you to watch the place today, you hear? See that your brothers mind ya Momma and gets off to church. I needs you to stay round the house." Poppa says this without looking at Junior or without missing the rhythm in which he sops up the syrup with his biscuits.

"But, Poppa—" Before Junior can continue his thought,

Momma gently, but firmly, places one hand on his shoulder and with the other puts a plate of biscuits in front of him. "Thank you," he says.

"You're welcome," says Momma, again walking to the sink, grabbing the dishrag that always waited on her.

Junior enjoyed church. It was the one place he felt as if he wasn't being watched. For six days of the week, whether at work or home, he felt eyes were always on top of him, waiting for an opportunity for their stares to be translated into words or actions; even when they blinked, a sun-cast image of Junior was burned into that instant of darkness. There was no rest for him, for once those eyes opened again they only stared harder to make sure the image was the same as before and nothing was missed.

"I wasn't plannin' on takin' this trip," says Poppa, almost as if spitting the words at Momma, "and it's gonna throw me off for the rest of the week. 'Sides, you almost too old to be runnin' off to some church ever' Sunday. You a man now, and God can't do nothin' for you you can't do for ya own self."

Poppa pushes away from the table, throwing his napkin on the empty plate. Momma picked up his plate, taking his napkin and wiping the beads of sweat strung just above her lip.

"Something to drink, J.T.?" says Momma, to Poppa's stiff, uninterested back.

"Nah."

Junior sat, watching, picking at his biscuits. Flake by flake. Layer by layer. It was like a routine that everyone knew, but not necessarily enjoyed.

"I'll be back 'fore dark," says Poppa, walking out the screen door, again it slamming behind him. This wakes my brother, Leselle, who starts screaming.

"I'll try and get him back to sleep," Junior says, picking up his half-eaten plate of biscuits and putting it by the sink.

"Thank you," says Momma, as she nibbles from his plate, more for my sake than for her own.

"Ida Mae," said Poppa, tipping his hat.

"I don't know why you sayin' no 'Ida Mae' to me, Joseph Thomas. You know it's Anna you wants to talk to."

"Ida Mae, stop it," said Momma in a whisper, escaping her teeth, trying to keep a straight face.

"I'm just tryin' to be polite, is all," he says, and then turning to Momma, "You lookin' right nice today, Anna. That dress sho nuff suits you."

"Why, thank you. I—"

"She look nice ever' day. Who you think you foolin', fool? 'Be polite.' Joseph Thomas, I'd like to know where you got that notion? You haven't been polite a day in your natural born life, and now, now you 'spect us to carry the notion that you tryin' to 'be polite,' Nigra, please!"

"Ida Mae!" said Momma, pinching Ida Mae.

"Ow! Girl! Why you do that? . . ."

"Well, I see you fine ladies are busy. I'll just be moseying on 'long."

"You do that. And you! Don't be pinchin' me like that. You know I hate that. It 'minds me of yo momma. She's always pinchin' me. You turnin' more and more like her ever' day."

While Ida Mae was going on about the pinching, Poppa was walking away and Momma's eyes marked every step as close as if she were following them wherever they would lead. She couldn't even hear Ida Mae anymore. All she could think about was Joseph Thomas and missing her chance at him once again.

"You see that? You see that? You made him uneasy and shooed him away," said Momma, pulling her feet out of Riley's Creek.

"So what? He ain't no kind of catch. He must of followed us out here. Ol' bowlegged rascal. Don't nobody come out to this here creek but us. Don't you think it's a bit strange that he just happened upon us out here? Use your head for more than a hat rack." Ida Mae said all this in one breath, yet never taking her legs out of the water. Her already ample calves appeared double in size under the water, and she liked the way they looked and the way the water wrapped around them like the finest of stockings from up north. "If you ask me, he followed us out here hopin' to get a sneak peek."

"No!" said Momma, hoping the answer was . . .

"Yes."

"No!"

"Yes. Two nice-lookin' girls like ourselves, out here by our lone-

some. I bet he thought he could see a little somethin' to go back and tell his triflin' hangout buddies about."

"Why he need to come here to do that, when you show it around at the junk joint anyhow?"

"Anna!" Ida Mae pulled her legs up out of the water and started running towards Momma. Momma took off running, laughing and screaming, "No," all the way. Ida Mae hiked up her dress and let her calves do their thing. Before long Ida Mae caught Momma and they fell to the ground giggling and rolling around in the clovers, wishes waiting to be claimed.

Breathing heavily, Ida Mae said, "He didn't come out here to see me, Anna. He came to see you."

"No such a thing. Joseph Thomas could have any girl in Welty County, and any neighboring one if he had a mind to it. Why would he want to look at me?"

"Ain't no need in tryin' to question the truth. All I have to say is watch yourself. I ain't gonna be there all the time to keep the wicked away. Speaking of, it's near 'bout dark. You'd better get on home 'fore Missus Anderson come lookin' for you."

Grabbing an old dandelion, Momma said, "Ida Mae? You think you ever gonna get married?"

"I don't know. I 'spect so. To tell the truth, I guess I haven't put much thought to it. I don't rightly see myself with nobody. No one somebody. But I s'pose anythang is possible. Why?"

"Just asking."

"You?"

"Yeah. I think I'd like to," said Momma, closing her eyes and blowing into the dandelion. The wind took each of the seeds and they vanished, floating with baited breath into the beginning of night.

Momma had been nervous all day. We spent most of it back and forth between the bathroom. It's near night and Poppa ain't back yet from talking to Uncle James.

We went to church and Momma just rocked back and forth in the pew, but the choir wasn't even singing. She just rocked. She rubbed me as she did, telling me over and over again that I had nothing to worry about.

"Everything is gonna be fine, l'il Lisa. You needn't worry one bit about that." And though she was saying it to me, the congregation could be heard saying, "yes" and "well" and "say that," verifying the truth in what had been said. Were it only that easy. She kept right on telling me it was going to be fine. And she was right, I needn't worry about a thing. For as she sat in that third pew rocking, as if trying to put a baby to rest, I knew she was worrying enough for the both of us.

After church the walk home was tiring. Junior usually was the one who ran the train, making the boys stay in line. But as Poppa had told him, he had stayed at home, leaving Momma with her hands full.

"Momma. I think Stanley's momma was sad."

"Why's that, Leselle?"

" 'Cause she was cryin' and all those men had to come and take her outside."

"That's 'cause she was shouting, fool."

"Edward James Joseph!" Momma shouted. "What did I tell you about callin' people a fool? Now, tell your brother you didn't mean it."

"But I did mean it, Momma. Any fool can tell you when a woman shouts she feelin' the Spirit."

"I ain't no fool, either," screamed Leselle. He and Edward had to share a bed, keeping them constantly at each other's throat and keeping Momma on guard. Today she just didn't have it in her to keep up with them. Her mind was elsewhere. But being Momma, she tried to explain.

"No, Leselle, you're not a fool. You see Stanley's momma. Well, you see, she had what we call the Spirit. She was happy. I know sometimes it can look like they're sad because they're crying, but it's a good thing, what they're feeling. It's hard to understand at first, but you'll soon come to realize it's a good thing.

"The first time I was old enough to remember going to church with your Gram, we sat up on the front pew. It was an Easter Sunday, so ever'body was dressed to the nines in their new clothes, trying to show out for ever'body else and passing judgement along the way.

"The choir sang and the voices were as clear as an autumn sky, making sounds like that of angels. And me and your gram were sitting there. She was clapping in time and ever'thing seemed fine. Then a whiles later I looked up and your Gram started crying; slowly at first. But as the singing continued it soon became something more than tears. Whenever they would get to the end of the song, the pastor, because he could see the congregation was feeling it, would get up and tell the soloist and the choir to keep on singing. So the piano player would start up playing again and the choir would join in singing on time, getting louder with each refrain. Gram would get worse, and before long it got wheres they had to take her out.

"I sat there by myself and I got scared and the preacher kept making the choir sing more, and I started crying. The people on our pew scooted next to me, putting their arms around me because they thought I was feeling the Spirit too. But I was just afraid, and mad at that mean ol' preacher for doing this to Gram. I wasn't feeling the Spirit at all. I was just scared, like you were."

"I wasn't afraid," said Leselle in defense of himself.

"No, Leselle. I'm sure you weren't. Big boys like you don't get afraid."

"But if Gram was happy and feelin' the Spirit, why did they take her out? Why didn't they let her stay in and be happy?"

"That's a good question, Leselle. I wish I knew the answer. Maybe you can get too much of it so they have to take you out, so . . . I don't know, Leselle. I don't know. It seems like if it was truly a good thing, they wouldn't take you out, would they?"

"Do you sometimes feel the Spirit now, Momma?"

"Yes, Leselle. Sometimes I do. But there's nothing for you to be afraid of. It's just the Spirit. They're happy. The Spirit won't hurt you."

"Why don't I ever see mens gettin' the Spirit?"

"Well, I'm sure men feel it too. It's just they show it in a different way."

"See, Edward. I told you I weren't no fool," says Leselle, plucking Edward's ear and running off down the road towards home. Leon and Leo didn't say a word the whole time. They each walked on Momma's side holding her hand, while I walked with her in the middle.

When we got back home, Momma began to prepare supper.

She always did most of it the night before or in the morning before she went to church. That way when she got home she could try and relax, if just for a moment.

"You need some help, Momma?"

"No, thank you, Junior. There's not that much left to do." Momma stopped for a moment and looked at Junior. "You know your poppa doesn't mean no harm, don't you? You just the next one in line and he's proud of you. He wants you to grow up to be a good man, that's all."

"I know, Momma. I know," he said, leaving the kitchen and going out on the porch. Momma looked at him through the kitchen window. He sat on the step below where Poppa's rocker sat. With his hand he rocked it back and forth, every now and then taking his hand and placing it under the chair's curved leg, stopping it in midflow.

As darkness settled around our house, Momma knew Poppa should be back at any time. She kept finding reasons to walk by the door or go outside. The night is silent except for the locusts playing tag in the cornfield. How happy they sounded. Momma had turned off the lights and lit candles. When Poppa arrived she didn't want him to see anything, good or bad, in her face. As she was standing in the door she was startled by a scream.

"Momma! Edward called me a fool again!"

"Tattletale! Tallletale, hang yo britches on a rusty nail."

"I ain't."

"Yes, you are."

"Ain't neither."

"Both of you just stop it," Junior screamed in from the porch where he was reading his Bible. Leselle and Edward became silent. Junior, too, was waiting to be taken off duty. Waiting for that figure to come walking through the gate, yet having no idea what to expect from it once it did.

The twins, Leo and Leon, were always quiet. They had themselves and never really needed for much more. Poppa would sometimes scream at them just because I think they scared him as much as he scared them. He didn't like that. They stayed out of the way most of the time. Momma never had to worry about them, for they had each other. They were the last born and are probably the reason Poppa is turned off of me. He wasn't expecting two, and when they came he blamed Momma. It was then that he decided she couldn't have no more chil'ren. In some odd way it was as if Leo and Leon knew this, and for that reason they were pleased to have each other; unlike Edward and Leselle, who were more than two years apart and acted like they couldn't stand the breath that made each of them live.

Edward and Leselle would often fight the twins, but were no match for this duo. In their silence was strength. You never knew what they were thinking; I suppose that is why Poppa rarely says anything to them.

They say Momma was really big when she was carrying the twins. So much so that Gram had to come and stay, which really kept Poppa on his heels. They say Gram was the only one who could actually keep him in check, which is nice to hear, but it doesn't change what's going on now, as we waited for Poppa to return from speaking to Uncle James and Auntie Clariece.

"Ida Mae, I'm so nervous. Momma'll be here any minute and you know how she and Joe are."

"I know exactly how they are. Just like two porcupines tryin' to make love. One is busy tryin' to stick but gettin' stuck at the same time," said Ida Mae, taking a chug from her bottle.

"Ida Mae, you are a fool," said Momma, wobbling over to a chair at the kitchen table.

"You better not let Missus Anderson hear you usin' that word, she'll give you a hidin', pregnant or not."

"You know Momma too well."

At just that moment a knock came at the door. It was Gram. Usually a knock precedes an entrance, but with Gram a knock and entrace proved to be one.

"Hello! Is anybody gonna come help an old woman or do I have to carry these bags another ten miles?"

"Momma, you're early," said Momma, trying to get up from her chair. Momma was still months away from giving birth but was "big beyond belief."

"Well, what you want me to do, turn around, go back, stand on the trail a l'il while, then come back later when it's more convenient for you?"

"No, ma'am. Junior! No, ma'am, now is fine. Junior?! Your gram is here. Come fetch her bags, please. No, ma'am, see, I was gonna have Junior meet you at the cross section, but I didn't expect you so soon."

"Well, sooner or later, I'm here now, so there's no need in carrying on and fretting about that subject one moment more. Now, Junior, be careful with that bag," said Gram, almost screaming, "because I have a present in there for you and I don't want it to get messed up." Gram pinched Junior's cheek and handed him a five folded in fours. She always gave Junior large sums of money as if that could make up for other things that she couldn't rightly control; money for time served. Junior knew Gram Anderson always sounded as if she were in a bad mood, but never was. She had no reason to be. She was her own woman and answered to no one. She did as she pleased when she pleased, and what pleased her now was to be with her daughter. Even the best mothers need to know they're still needed.

"I just saw you two Sundays ago and it looks like you've gotten three times bigger," said Gram, walking around Momma like she was a prize sow at the Mississippi State Fair.

"Ain't she big, Missus Anderson? Big as the house she standin' in, and I tell you—"

"Who asked you, Ida Mae?"

"Nobody. But—"

"Right. Nobody. Then mind your beeswax and keep your opinions to your own self. If I want to know what you're thinking, I'll tell you. 'Big as the house she standin' in.' Now, what kind of sense does that make, Ida Mae? 'Big as the house she standin' in,' huh. Now, come on over here, baby, and let Momma feel that stomach." Gram ran her hands along Momma's stomach and then put her ear on her belly as if it might speak. "Lorda be. The way it's sitting and the sound of it, I think it's twins."

"I told you! I told you, Anna. I told you it was gonna be twins. Sure as I'm standing here, I said it," shouted Ida Mae, slapping her hands together. Gram gave her a look, blinding Ida Mae's huge grin. "But I did tell her."

"Well, Ida Mae. It seems, for once—thank God for small favors—

*you're right. It's definitely twins. Junior! Stop snooping in that bag
now. I'll give you the present when I'm good and ready, and not a
moment before. Until then, stop snooping. Curiosity killed the cat,
and what he found couldn't bring him back."*

"Yes'm," screamed a guilty Junior from the bedroom.

"Momma, now how did you know he was in your bag?"

*"A mother knows thing. And one thing I know is that you car-
rying twins, so . . ." And with the swiftest of transitions Gram looked
down at Momma's ankles, raising Momma's dress a notch. "Lorda
be, look at those tree trunks. I've seen trees with years of rings thinner
than this. That no-good, trifling husband of yourn has been working
you to death. Figures. Well, not to worry, Momma is here now, so
just sit yourself down and rest these stumps.*

*"If Ida Mae was of any account, she would be doing something
to help out around here. But it's evident to me she doesn't see fit to
do so." Gram took Momma's apron from around Leo and Leon and
began cleaning up. "Junior! come from out of there. I told you I'd
give it to you later. Now, where is Edward and Leselle? Those little
mannish devils. Hiding, huh? I guess Gram is going to have to steal
some sugar if she wants some. Well, I guess we'll just see how that
is when I start pulling out presents . . ."*

*Leselle and Edward came running out the room to the sounds
of that. Gram had taken over. Ida Mae and Momma just watched
in amazement.*

*That was how Momma knew Leo and Leon would be twins, and
from then on, never doubted it for a minute. She was glad Gram was
there because it would be easier to tell Poppa the news. Ida Mae
wasn't allowed around the house when Poppa was around, so she
wasn't going to be able to help. But Gram, Gram knew how to handle
Poppa, and usually it only took one glance.*

*The secret present Gram brought for Junior was a Bible. It be-
longed to her mother and her mother before. Its cover was still hard,
sturdy; but the pages were fragile to the touch. It seemed only right
it should come from Gram. Junior would spend many a day reading
that Bible. Gram left many fond memories in our home, but the Bible
was something that could be held, something that wasn't Poppa's
property.*

*That gift would be the last gift from Gram. She passed away
shortly after that visit. There's no such thing as sudden death, but*

*that's how it looked back then. Gram would never know if her predic-
tion of twins was right, though time would prove it true. Even death
bears a life of its own.*

*Momma took the news as any child would after being cut off
from their lifeline, when that didn't seem possible.*

"It's nice out," says Momma, joining Junior out on the
porch.

"Yeah, since those two shut up in there, things seem right
peaceful, for a change."

"Sometimes I enjoy hearing them fight. It makes me know
they're alive."

"I guess. But then I guess it depends on what they're fighting about," says Junior, looking back down at his Bible.

"Can you see out here?"

"I can see awright."

"Yes. I'm sure you can." Momma gets up and goes back in
the house. She peeks in on the boys. Leselle and Edward are
asleep. Leo and Leon are pretending to be, but as soon as
Momma opened the door, they looked up at her.

"You boys aren't sleep yet?" she said in half voice.

"No, ma'am," says Leon. One always speaks and the other
is silent, as if they know when and which answer was theirs to
claim. "We're not sleepy just yet."

"All right. But don't stay up too late now. You boys need
your rest."

"Yes, ma'am," says Leo. Momma starts to walk away.
"Momma?"

"Yes, Leo?"

"We love you," he says in such a truthful and youthful way
that I feel a knot pass my body, sitting for a second near Momma's heart before making its way up and lodging, for a gentle
rest, in her throat.

"I love you, too. The both of you," said the knot, as she
turned and walked out the door. As the first tear began to
roll down her cheek, there was Poppa standing at the screen
door. "Joe?"

"It's done," he says.

There was no remorse or pleasure in his statement. No sign

of anything. He gave her nothing more than that. "It's done."
He said it and then went to the kitchen and sat in his place at
the table, waiting for Momma to follow behind to fix his plate.
Junior stood there in stillness looking at Momma, and I felt that
single tear fall, bringing an echo around me, certain to last
generations to come.

Wash Me

Randall Kenan

. . . You must go on, I can't go on, I'll go on.

—Samuel Beckett

How Gideon Stone wished it would rain. He remembered a song by that same title, "Oh, how I wish, I wish it would raaaaiiiiinnnn," and it played over and over and over in his head. Oh, how I wish, I wish it would rain.

At two o'clock the temperature hovered in the nineties, almost a hundred. The sun, that great ball of fire, seemed to mock—regal, disdainful, distant, but oh so near. *Work!* said the sun. *Damn you,* said Gideon. He despised this hateful work. The tobacco field lay massive before him, stalk after stalk of green tobacco for yards and yards—maybe even a mile, until the rows reached the edge of the woods or a field of soybeans or corn. As far as Gideon was concerned, he and the other four men were all prisoners of the sun—isolated, pitiful, wretched in this vast, open-air dungeon of eternal and damnable green.

Why won't it rain?

His cousin, Joe Henry Williams, an agricultural extension agent for the county and farmer and deacon of the church, had asked if he would help put in tobacco. Gideon actually liked his pipe-smoking, thin-as-a-rail, fifty-nine-year-old cousin, who was less a hypocrite in Gideon's eyes than his fellow deacons—an all around decent man. Each time he saw him, Gideon remembered, oddly, the time shortly after Joe Henry's wife died, when Gideon was in kindergarten, him taking young Gideon fishing down at the creek, and inexplicably sobbing. Neither of them had said a word, but at five Gideon felt he had witnessed something sad and tender in a grown man, something he would never forget.

Gideon's Morehead summer internship at a Northern newspaper had ended; he would be back at Chapel Hill to commence his junior year in two weeks, and he had wanted desperately to say no to Joe Henry. But his mother stood right there. Joe Henry was in powerful need of an extra hand, and Gideon would look like a lazy so-and-so if he said no; or worse, look as if putting in tobacco was beneath him, a college boy, and Viola Honeyblue Stone's son was not *above* nobody. No sir, no ma'am, no way.

So that morning he had risen at four, and joined the men in the barn, in the dark, using flashlights to empty the barn of the cured tobacco, hung there the week before. All week the leaves had been slowly cooked, the barn itself a humongous oven, heated by the propane gas burners that covered its sandy dirt floor like a miniature space craft; the once luscious, plump, lime green leaves now transformed into sweet-smelling, parchment-brown and parchment-thin sheets, their black stems the thickness of toothpicks. With sand and dust blowing everywhere, two men climbed into the tiers of the barn to hand down two sticks at a time. Gideon stood beneath them, sand falling into his hair and mouth, while he passed the sticks out the door to Joe Henry, who stacked them on a trailer to be taken to a pack house. When they finished around six, he went home to eat breakfast, cursing the day Columbus stumbled upon the damn plant in Honduras and took it back to Italy or Spain or wherever it was, so that Sir Walter Raleigh could go and make it into a fad that would never go away, or however the story went.

Now he was filthy again, along with the others, six men cropping tobacco. This was the first day; "lugs" they called it. Lug days were the most backbreaking, for you had to bend deep down to snap the first leaves from the stalks. Gideon lagged behind everyone else, with an armful of leaves. Sweat rolled stinging into his eyes, his hands black from gum and dirt. He stood downwind of the tractor Joe Henry drove, pulling the trailer full of the cropped leaves of tobacco. The tractor fumes and the hot air and the dust from the leaves and the sharp, biting smell of the tobacco filled Gideon's nostrils, and his skin, like highly polished wood, glistened with sweat. In the small of his back the muscles throbbed from stooping and bending, stooping and bending; his arms ached from carrying the heavy bundles of leaves, and his legs were so tired that he stumbled over the uneven ground. All he could think about was a cool drink of water fore he died and a nice air-conditioned bathroom with a huge, steaming tub. Or *Please, God, just a little rain.*

"But I tell you, man, that is one fine bitch. Did you see that ass on her?" Ray Simpson, with the too-bushy sideburns and the acne-ridden face said to Benjy. They were dumping their loads at the same time as his cousin Noah Earl.

"Heard she puts out, too." Benjy cut his eyes toward Gideon, who guiltily, involuntarily, glanced at Benjy's big arms, covered with dirt and tar.

"Shit, she couldn't handle me."

"You? You mean she can't handle this." Benjy patted that place between his legs and winked.

"Shit."

To Gideon the snapping of the leaves in the field and their flapping in the air created a sound like what he imagined raiders tearing through a forest would sound like. Spanish conquistadors marching through the Amazon jungle. The large leaves, browning at the tips, drooped into the dirt, their green stems covered with a fine hair-like fiber. Small grass sprigs and weeds the herbicides did not kill grew between the plants that rose as tall as a man. As Joe Henry made the tractor lurch forward it clanked and sputtered with a belch of black smoke and a goatish *baaa*ing sound.

As he watched Joe Henry atop the old Farmall, a brief twinge of nostalgia intruded into his daydreams, and he remembered a time when he, as a boy too young to crop, drove the tractor up and down the many rows, looking back at the big men at work, hearing their banter and their laughter, wishing powerfully hard to be in their midst—one of the men. Now he could not help but shake his head and chuckle to himself, *What happened to that dream deferred?*

A gnat buzzed in Gideon's ear, tickling the entire side of his face. He slammed the side of his head against his shoulder, his arm full of tobacco, his throat dry as cotton. He went to dump his load in the flat trailer—the "truck" they called it— stepping over the slightly raised rows and into the furrows, his feet getting heavier and heavier. No rain in sight.

"Well, Gideon, you getting much pussy up there in school?" Benjy, in his mid-twenties, was Joe Henry's son. His younger brother, Sam, now in the Navy, had been Gideon's very best friend all through school. Benjy's teeth were strong and white and his skin, somewhat darker than his father's burnt orange complexion, seemed to glow with wetness. He smiled a devil's grin at Gideon, and Gideon liked to think that Benjy was taunting him on purpose—all the while knowing better, but enjoying the fantasy.

"No, man, working too hard."

Benjy had been IT all during Gideon's growing up. Gideon and Sam did everything to match Benjy. They walked like Benjy. They talked like Benjy. They cursed like Benjy. Benjy had driven a bus when he was in high school, and he let Sammy and Gideon do anything they wanted, he sitting back, smoking, laughing at their silly stories, and telling them about sex and dirty jokes. He could do no wrong. Gideon had never wanted to disappoint him. In truth, Benjy figured largely into Gideon's first wet dreams. To think of them even now aroused Gideon plenty.

"I bet you working ... working 'tween them legs." Benjy slapped Gideon's shoulder and winked.

"Shit. He ain't had no pussy since pussy had him." Ray grinned. "Come on, Gideon. Ain't you had none of them fine white bitches? Talk like they got some fine white ass up there where you is." Gideon could not look him in the eye. He could only watch the nape of Benjy's neck, the flesh smooth and taut.

"No, man, don't mess with 'em." Gideon's voice cracked on the last word.

"Whatsamatter? Scared?" Ray said as he spread his tobacco out in the truck. "Bet he's scared to death of 'em. Is you scared, Gideon? You want your mama to come up there and scare you up some pussy, boy? Hhhmmmm? You want Miss Viola to come up there and scare you up some pussy?"

"Go to hell, Ray." Gideon wiped sweat from his forehead, his hand trembling slightly, and he gave a weak giggle. Just like with his own hard and scramble brothers, who worshipped at the temple of the vulva, he had to spar and mislead, defend, duck, and hide among these men. What would they think? . . .

Benjy winked again. "Well, is you getting it or not?"

"Now, ya'll hush all that talk," Joe Henry said from the tractor. "Looks like a cloud's 'bout to come up. Don't want to be out here in the rain this afternoon."

Thank the Lord Jesus! Gideon thought. *YESSSS! Rain!*

Everyone went back to work, though Gideon's cousin Noah Earl had not stopped. He stooped and cropped way ahead of the rest of them, serious and intent upon his work. No foolishness. No small talk. Noah Earl stood almost six feet five, in his forties, fast approaching fifty, with nine children—all girls—and a wife who was never satisfied, and no steady job. Gideon remembered him as hardworking, always doing something outdoors, sweating, dirty. He had to work at odd jobs, when he could find them, and in the fields. Beneath his nylon bibbed cap, his short cropped hair was mixed with gray, and a scar hooked down from the left side of the corner of his lip, halfway down to his chin. His breath often had a hint of alcohol.

Gideon remembered a time when Noah Earl had broken his leg and his wife had thrown him out, so he had to stay with his mother. Uncle Jeremiah had taken Gideon along to visit him there, and Gideon had been surprised to see this big mahogany-colored man in a soft bed, in a bright room, dressed in clean white pajamas, the smell of liniment mixing with the spring air. At five it had never occurred to Gideon that a man so hard, so like steel, could actually be broken.

On the table by the bed that day sat a large bowl of oranges, their perfume ripening the air, tempting the little boy's nose. "Can I have one of those?" Gideon had asked, partially afraid, yet overwhelmed by the glowing sight of the bright fruit.

Noah Earl had burst out in laughter. "One of THOSE? Well, I reckon you can have ... one of THOSE." He reached over, still laughing, and threw one to Gideon.

"Thank you." Gideon had no idea what was so funny; yet Noah Earl's warm grin caused him to laugh as well, merrily transfixed by Noah Earl's scar as it made funny shapes.

Afterward Noah Earl would always tease Gideon. "Hey, boy. 'Can I have one of THOSE?' " Always breaking into laughter. As Gideon grew older Noah Earl stopped teasing him so much, stopped smiling. Gideon never had any idea what Noah Earl had found so hilarious.

On into the day they worked. By three o'clock the temperature dropped a few degrees but Gideon felt so tired it didn't help—he had been on his feet lugging since seven-thirty. He looked ahead at Noah Earl, who had to do such work to survive, and at his cousin Joe Henry sitting on the tractor, who knew no other way of life, and felt a brief twinge of sadness. What if I don't get into medical school? What if I can't find any other kind of work? What if I wind up right back here cropping tobacco? Could I do this for the rest of my life? But he knew he would and he knew he could and knew he wouldn't and knew he wouldn't have to, and oddly this made him all the sadder.

Clouds gathered from the south, a mass of black warriors set upon attacking the sun, gliding across the sky. Gideon's back was on fire. His arms were heavy weights. Even his neck felt thick and tired. Itchy. Grimy. Heavy.

Please, please, please, rain, rain, rain.

"Shit!" Ray jumped over two rows, dropping his tobacco, knocking over several stalks. He stumbled, tripped, and rolled down between a row into a clump of grass.

"Look at that sucker! Look at it!" Everybody stumbled over the tobacco rows, shoes breaking into the dry dirt, making the dust fly. The cottonmouth, its white mouth wide, hissed and raised its head high, curling its head back onto its neck in a movement so liquid it made Gideon shiver as if ice water had been poured down his shirt. Confused, the snake was ready to strike at anything, wanting to escape, swaying back and forth, from side to side. Slowly. At one moment it was still, a liquid statue; then it would move in an ungodly way, making Gideon's skin crawl. The snake's eyes, which Gideon knew could not focus, seemed to focus—angry, deadly, two dots of black poison. It's tongue flicked and flicked from its scaly mouth.

Noah Earl grabbed a tobacco stalk and yanked it from the earth before Joe Henry could say, Hold on, now, and quickly, stripping off the leaves, jumped in front of the snake, whose head darted at his leg as fast as a black arrow. Noah Earl stepped aside and brought the stalk down on its head. A quick strong movement. Again and again. Again. Again. Again.

The snake quivered and shook. In death's throes it rolled in the sand and dirt and grass, flailing its body, twisting, twitching. Gideon winced.

"Looka there. Looka there."

"He got him. Man, you got him. Look. Look."

Soon the snake's movements slowed. Its head, a bloody mass of pulp, was still, while its body made gentle flowing movements. Thunder began to roll in the distance.

"Damn moccasin." Noah Earl looked down at the creature wiggling in the sand near the toe of his brogans and threw the stalk over the other rows of tobacco into a ditch.

"Looka here." Ray was again on his feet. "Let's hide the snake in the truck. I bet them women'll love that."

"Now, ya'll . . ." Joe Henry was climbing back onto the tractor.

"Aw, Paw." Benjy had an evil look. "It ain't gone hurt 'em. Let's do it." He turned to Ray and then began to put the snake in the middle of the truck of tobacco. Noah Earl went back to cropping.

"Benjy." Joe Henry had said the name as though clearing his throat. He looked annoyed; his tone was as if to a child. "Don't put the snake in the truck, son. Okay?"

"Okay, okay." Benjy sighed and rolled his eyes. "We won't do it." With a quick movement he snatched the snake from the truck. "Satisfied?"

Joe Henry looked at the boy, made a sharp sucking sound through his teeth and sat back down on the tractor. He shook his head, but when he turned his back, Ray flipped the snake back into the truck and covered it quickly with leaves. Benjy looked at Gideon and winked.

Snakes. Now Gideon had to think about snakes, too. They had already been slithering in the back of his mind, their ripe and deadly possibility, but now that he had seen one, how could he not imagine grabbing one unawares. He just wanted to go home, go to bed. The heat felt like a thick wool blanket wrapped around every inch of his body. He was sure he would suffocate. His entire body ached; he felt each muscle, sore to the bone. He felt so dirty that in the back of his mind a demon whispered to him, *You'll never get clean, you'll never get clean, and you'll have to go to school, go to church and everywhere with dirty hair, gummy black hands, and dusty gray feet, smelling like tobacco juice and sweat. Always thirsty. Dry.* Gideon looked to the sky, and the fat clouds. *Let it rain, Lord, please.*

The clouds that had been gathering at last, finally, mercifully burst like plump gray sacks of wine. Water from the leaves splashed into Gideon's face as he flapped them under his arms. He could barely see. Water rolled into his eyes. The leaves getting heavier, soaked in rain. As the ground became sticky mud, walking became more and more difficult. Gideon had gotten his rain, but the work had simply gotten harder.

When the men came to the end of the row, they headed toward the barn, wind blowing, rain falling in torrents, the tractor bobbing as it puttered down the field path. Standing on the back of the tractor, Gideon wondered what Alex would be doing at this very moment. Alexander Anastassopoulos, a sophomore back at school, the first boy he had had sex with in college, with his curly black hair and exceptionally hairy forearms, was probably in Greece on his uncle's yacht. What would he think of Gideon if he saw him now? Dirty, rain-pelted, tired? And all the other boys back in his North Campus dorm?—none of them, to a one, surely, ever having worked or ever to work in a field. At this moment. What would they say? What would they think about their young Morehead scholar on tobacco row? Something like shame, something like hate, something like self-pity, something like fear welled up within Gideon. He could not remember ever wanting to be elsewhere so intensely, ever wanting so much distance from where he was. When he thought of home, his home—his brothers rude, his mother crude, his father drunk—he felt nothing but revulsion. And then wrong for feeling it. And then pitiful for it all, for himself. He felt homeless. He was alone. He was a work in progress. Would the work ever be completed? *You made it rain, Lord. Now take me elsewhere.*

At the barn, under a tin roof that sloped from the main building on all sides, the women were set about the business of tying the leaves. They stood on either side of the truck and picked up three or four leaves of tobacco, which they patted two or three times against the heels of their palms, and backhanded to the woman standing behind them at the tie-horse; and the woman took the leaves and looped the bundle once, twice, in twine, with a twine sound, and she would bring it up snug against another, left, right, left, right, creating a flurry of looping and sliding and slipping and twining, until the stick on the tie-horse became festooned with hanging leaves. This was the rhythm of the tobacco barn, the work and the rhythm that Gideon had known since birth, so familiar, so dreaded. A good tobacco tier made her tie-horse buzz with a constant high-pitched twerping and twirping as string zipped against the firm stems, turgid with the tart juices, a sound that tickled the ear and haunted the brain. *Twerp, twirp. Twerp, twirp.* A gnawing sound. A young sound. Firm. Fresh. Wet.

The sky grew dark and the wind blew in strong sudden gusts and lightning, blindingly white, struck somewhere in the distance and in a few seconds thunder answered with a mighty clap. The earth seemed to tremble as the rain made a brassy racket on the tin roof. The women's gossip chimed in with the sounds all about them.

"Child, he told her head a mess."

"No, he didn't?"

"Yes, he did. Told her if she ever thought about seeing that man again, that he'd kill 'em both."

"Now who does he think he is?"

"Marie, did you see *Days of Our Lives* yesterday? Talk like Roman is in trouble, child."

The men went to get water and Gideon followed. The older men stood around the plastic watercooler discussing old Miss

Peter's funeral, while Benjy and a few others joined the women, picking at them, taunting the younger girls, flirting with the cute ones. One boy put a tobacco worm on a girl's shoulder, right up to her cheek. She screamed a high-pitched scream and swung at the boy, socking him in the eye.

Miss Ruella Thomas, almost seventy, famous for her piety and her church shouting, turned to Gideon. "So how you liking school? You know, everybody was so proud of you getting that fancy scholarship and everything. We 'specting great things from you, Gideon. How is it up there?" Everyone became quiet and watched Gideon, while continuing to work.

Gideon looked at Miss Ruella, a feeling of dread waxing in his belly. Several moles were scattered about her face, her head wrapped in a red rag. Her smile, so genuine, so sweet, so well-intentioned, made Gideon smile instantly, and he simply had no idea what to say. What could he say?

The silence, the expectant eyes and expectant ears, made time seem to stop for Gideon. And though it would have been silly, he wanted to weep, to take the older woman in his arms and put his mouth close to her ear and whisper, "It's awful"; to tell her how he was surrounded by white boys he could think circles around, but whose touch he craved hourly, and whose acceptance, and whose money, and whose background he coveted; to tell her how, though he knew better, he was daily made to feel inferior; that he was an imposter, a fraud, an outsider; to tell her how he felt that he belonged neither in this world of tobacco and labor, here with you Miss Ruella Thomas, you sweet woman, who I hate and love impossibly, and can't live without, can't imagine a world without, with the snuff on your chin and the smell of your hair; nor in that world of privilege and power, of preppies and fraternities, and white folk who ask me to bring them drinks at parties; to tell her how the anxiety, the expectation, the longing made him seriously, seriously want to end it all, and to end it quickly; to tell her how he thought about it, but in the end, was too damn spiteful, too damn mean, too damn smart, at base, too damn eager to prove himself, to cut his own throat and give anyone the satisfaction of saying that Gideon Stone didn't have what it takes—

"I like it fine, Mrs. Thomas. Just fine." She nodded as

though some preacher had read her favorite bible verse. Everyone turned back to what they were doing.

Gideon drank cup after cup of cold water. He could not get enough. He could not remember feeling anything so fully. The wetness was almost shocking, taking his breath away. So tasteless it was sweet. So crisp, so wet. With the cool water sliding down his gullet, he thought, *Yeah, as somebody once said, "I will not only endure, but I will prevail."*

The back of his neck bristled cold from the wind, and the smell of the mellow cured tobacco—long gone from the inside of the barn—and the bitter smell of green tobacco met in his nose, and even though he was tired, Gideon was beginning to feel a little bit better.

Benjy sat over by the high pile of tobacco, listening to the *twerp, twirp, twerp,* snickering to Ray. His teeth seemed to glow in the dim light, with a crisp, wet sweetness, like the water's taste. The ridge of his nose was perfect, straight, and covered in grimy sweat. Presently, Gideon realized that he had been staring, and in this moment of soul refreshment—as if the water and the weather were making him new—he saw Benjy as if for the first time, after all these years: an overgrown child. As beautiful as he was, he would never understand Gideon and—

"Eeeekkkkkkk!" Myrtle Phelps flew from under the shelter out into the rain.

"I'll kill you sons of bitches! Which bastard put this thing in here?" Myrtle had grabbed a hunk of snake instead of a handful of tobacco. She, a big, blue-black woman, whose nostrils now flared bull-like, was not a woman to mess with. The other women stood back, eyeing the snake, but Myrtle glared at Benjy and the others, who were rolling in the dirt under the shelter, laughing and laughing. Benjy clutched his stomach, his laughter high-pitched like a nickelodeon.

"I know you niggers did it. I ought to strangle you with it!" Lightning struck something in the woods, making a loud and electric crack. The snake still moved, just a bit. "Now you get it out of there. Get it out!"

Myrtle grabbed a tobacco stick and swung it dangerously close to Benjy's head, who ducked just in time. He scampered to his feet and ran, still laughing, and Myrtle gave chase.

"Nigger, I'll kill your black ass!"

"Stop, Myrtle! Myyyrrrttttlllee! It was just a joke. Come on. *A Joke!*" Benjy could hardly talk for laughing and running around and around the barn. Everyone joined in the raucous laughter, but Gideon felt a little removed, as if watching this all from a great distance, so far from Tims Creek, so far from this humanity, these people, his own people, so far from his own confusion and pain.

"Now, ya'll ..." Joe Henry looked annoyed, but still in a trivial way, as though a child had called him a bad name. "I told you fools not to put that snake in there. You want every soul I got here to quit on me, you knuckleheads? Benjy, get it out of there, please, sir. Okay?"

"Yes, SIR!"

Benjy took a stick and lifted the snake out of the truck. "Ain't gone hurt nobody. It's dead. See ..." He shoved it in front of three girls who shrieked in unison and grabbed the sides of their faces.

"Benjy!" Joe Henry hollered, his impatience with his son apparent and glaring. "Goddamn it! Quit!"

"Yes, sir," Benjy said, a bit cowed, a bit deflated, surely feeling a fool, a grown man being chastised by his father. Gideon watched him carry the snake out into the rain, thunder crashing overhead, to the edge of the woods, and fling it into the trees, the lust in Gideon's heart sorely tempered by the shame he now felt for Benjy.

Noah Earl watched all this comedy with manly disinterest, sitting alone in the doorway of the barn. Gideon remembered him in that bed so many years ago and the sound of his laughter. *Can I have one of THOSE?* Those not them. At five, Gideon had marked himself apart, and Noah Earl had seen it, knew it, knew that Gideon would come out at the world striking, like a cottonmouth—fast, brilliant, correct, deadly and forever in danger—a little black boy willing himself into a better world, yet a world bent on his destruction, a future he himself, Noah Earl, could never have. Knew that like THOSE instead of them, he was one of THOSE and not one of them. That if Gideon won or lost, in the end, it was all quite funny. Win or lose. So why not laugh?

Gideon caught Noah Earl's eye and the older man winked at him, a wink and a smile which Gideon took as a benediction. With a feeling of calm Gideon thought, *I shall never work in tobacco again.*

Noah Earl lit a cigarette and took a drag, squinting, smoke in his eyes, the scar by his lip curling and uncurling, not watching anything, anyone, staring out into the grayness of the storm. The smoke drifted up over his head, where it briefly hung as though a halo, until a strong gust of wind lifted it off, like a stray thought, never to be seen again.

All, Nothing

Bruce Morrow

It's a nice spring day, not the first good day of weather to come with the changing of the seasons, but the first day the scent of flowering trees has overwhelmed the smell of car exhaust in the city. Traffic on Central Park West at its normal bustle for a Saturday, a stop-and-go rush of mostly taxis filled with tourists heading downtown to Broadway matinees or a movie at the Ziegfield or shopping at the new Barney's uptown. As Paul Canfield crosses the street to enter the park, he stops and yawns, long and hard; the air, fresh and sweet for city air, has made him light-headed, dizzy, and he can't stop himself from yawning and stretching his entire body from his curled-up toes to his long thin fingertips. He stands on tiptoe and extends one hand up to the sky as if to pick a delicate pink cherry blossom from overhead or toss a hat in the air like Mary Tyler Moore. Each disk in his spine realigns, each striated muscle in his body extends to its fullest length. It feels so satisfying to yawn, to not hold back. But then he feels heat rising from a yellow dented car and he realizes that he's standing in the middle of the street, the light has changed, and all of this horn honking going on is directed at him.

Scared more for his life than embarrassed by his absent-mindedness (he'll be embarrassed later), he blindly runs to the crowded sidewalk on the park side of the street. He swiftly slips into the line of an ice cream stand, hides and tries to catch his breath. There are five people queued up in front of him and he decides he might as well stick it out and have his first Dove Bar of the season. A middle-aged couple, about forty-five or fifty, Paul guesses, dressed in matching warm-up suits, mint green nylon with purple accents patterned like splattered paint, argue in front of him.

"Let's just get one and split it," says the man. It takes only one look for Paul to decide that they're from out of town: over bridge or under tunnel, spending a day in the city shopping and exercising—or exercise shopping; hence the warm-up suits and the weighted bags in each hand.

"No, you get your own and I'll get mine," the woman says, putting her Bloomingdale's and Lord & Taylor bags in one hand.

"But it's too rich. It's just too much."

"Then throw it away if you don't want it. Steve, just give it to one of these beggars around here if you can't finish it."

"Irene, I don't think they want to share an ice cream with me."

"Okay. Okay. Why can't we find that store that just opened, the one with the funny cartoon ads? Let's ask someone? Ask him," she says, pointing to Paul. "It's got to be cheaper than that Bendel's—they didn't have my size in anything. I think I want a whole one, Steve, and I want chocolate-chocolate. You don't like chocolate-chocolate, so you can get your own."

Steve presses his thin lips together and looks back at Paul, embarrassed—or for compassion, or out of habit when disagreeing with his wife, Paul doesn't know, isn't sure and he stares back at them blankly, as if he's totally unaware of them. But actually he's been repeating everything they say in his mind; memorizing it; or remembering it as some argument his parents had years ago. "Meatballs, not meat sauce," his father would say. "You know I hate ground-up meat in the sauce, honey."

Paul's face now begins to warm with embarrassment—because of his yawn in the street and because of his compulsive eavesdropping, which he thinks has deep psychological implications. When he was growing up he listened in on his parents' conversations all the time. Now he does it whenever he's around couples of his parents' age, people who dress and act like his parents. Except his parents' would have never noticed he was standing in line behind them, wanting an ice cream, too. His parents, like lovers still on their honeymoon at Niagara Falls, the Canadian side, would have bought two ice creams and walked away comparing chocolate-chocolate to vanilla-chocolate without even looking back.

"Didn't you just love it when the helicopter landed on-stage?" Irene says. "I can't stop thinking about it. It's like one might land right here. It was so real, like Epcot Center."

Paul can't take listening anymore. He decides to skip the ice cream after all and save the money; $2.50's way too much anyway. He jumps out of line when the next group of street crossers is deposited on the sidewalk and he follows one of the curving paths into the park. He wants to find the right spot to sit and read and not watch the other people who're getting their fill of spring trees and wet grass today. An empty bench will do. Or maybe he can find a rock large enough and flat enough and out of the way enough so he won't get distracted from the two books he's brought along; he just started *Madame Bovary* and he's been carrying around the *Collected Poems of Pablo Neruda* for weeks.

That's just like Paul. He likes to read two or three books at the same time. A little fiction here, a little nonfiction there, some poetry along the way.

Walking beside him, at the same exact pace, Paul sees a dark-haired young man, Latino, shorter than himself, wearing an oversized bright orange backpack that makes him slouch forward and stick his chin out. Is he walking beside me on purpose? Paul thinks; but can't get a really good look at the young man to tell. He can't stop thinking about him either even though he wants to be distracted, even though this is the reason he left his apartment in the first place: so he could stop thinking about how much he doesn't want to go to work next week, how much he wants to quit his laboratory technician job. Now he's getting lost in desire and he doesn't want to be lost in that kind of desire; he wants to simply follow the curving path into the park, find the right spot to sit and read and not think about anything at all.

He sees it, his dream spot, an empty park bench under a

flowering dogwood tree. Dark delicate branches holding clusters of small white blossoms. Why's it called a dogwood? he
wonders as he hurries his pace. He sits. And as soon as he
does, the young man with the orange backpack sits down on
the bench next to him. Wouldn't you know it? Paul thinks,
trying to dismiss any possibility of a possibility.

See, Paul has resigned himself, at the age of twenty-five, to
a life of aloneness. But he doesn't mind. He's used to it, being
alone, doing things by himself. That's how he grew up, in
Shaker Heights, the child of parents so in love with themselves
they forgot their only child most of the time, left him to his
own devices, at home, without a baby-sitter at the age of twelve
while they went off to the opera, to basketball games, dinner
parties, Baskin-Robbins. Paul stayed home all alone many a
night, reading Samuel R. Delany stories after Margaret Atwood
novels, watching reruns of "Knot's Landing" or "Nature" or
"Adam Smith's Money World." He didn't care.

In the summer he would set up his bedroom on the
screened-in porch off the upstairs bathroom. He would drag in
a mattress and portable black-and-white television set and
watch horror movies on the "Big Chuck and Little John Show"
all night. It was the best, he remembers, not the cheap teenage
slasher movies, but the sudden breezes on the screened-in
porch, being suspended above everything and seeing, over the
hedge, the house behind his; the lights in different rooms turning on and off, in the kitchen, the bathroom, bedroom, and
finally going completely dark and still, allowing him to glimpse
pieces of a silver moon between branches heavy with shiny
green leaves. This was where Paul grew up, alone, in a dormant
house, on a quiet, Valium-induced suburban street.

Now it doesn't matter to Paul if he gets his parents' attention or not. They disapprove of him, of what he does and where
he lives. If he didn't live in New York, his mother told him, he
would be a doctor by now instead of just a lab technician. If
he didn't live in New York, he could afford to pay his rent
instead of supplementing his income by slowly selling pieces
from his grandfather's collection of Fugio cents—club rays, extremely fine. Paul's father vows never to leave the state of Florida now that he's retired—taken the exit ramp from "the road

to success," as his father always describes his now-ended career in plastics. Paul's mother always chimes in with "That's why we're so happy" even though she was only allowed to be successful in bridge and canasta and "Jeopardy!"

Paul calls and talks to his parents regularly, briefly, once a month, and that's enough. He always runs out of things to say. And there are always these long pauses, silences filled with ghostlike conversations from other phone lines. Leaking. Bleeding. Faint, incoherent chatter. Dull, senseless laughter.

It's the things he doesn't talk about with his parents—about his aloneness, his lovelessness, his life—that always make his calls so brief, so fractured, so empty.

He's been by himself his whole life. He hasn't had a boyfriend (or sex, for that matter) in more than two years. His is a life in pursuit of more than an occasional one-night stand— not that he's ever had one. He surprises people often with the fact that he's never picked someone up, or been picked up in a bar. He met his last boyfriend at a small party given by old college friends. Jeffery Solanges was tall and handsome, an artist bohemian who liked to wear Birkenstock sandals with socks. Paul was a pale city boy, a lab tech, who always dressed in black. Jeff's idea of a good time was running five miles a day (around a lake in the country if he could), camping out, and whitewater rafting. Paul liked to eat out, see lots of movies or watch TV, or sit in an armchair and read a good book. And Paul smoked. (He still does.) Jeff never found out, but Paul would make excuses and not see Jeff for days so that he could have the pleasure of smoking after meals, while reading, before going to bed.

Like many young men in the city, Paul has been voluntarily celibate ever since Jeff; he proudly tells people such; he counts the days (746), marks anniversaries (2 years this past March), boasts of the freedoms (from frivolity, from fashion, from flesh): he thinks he doesn't need to get tested ever again. He's studied biology. He knows what a retrovirus is. He's safe, suspended above it all.

Paul has been watching the young man sitting on the park bench next to him. The young man, or boy—Paul can't decide on his age: over or under twenty-one?—has taken out of his

Day-Glo orange backpack a pair of fluorescent orange roller skates and is putting them on carefully, slowly, as if he knows the skates will turn him into a Mighty Morphin once on his feet. Paul watches out of the corner of his eyes; he doesn't want to scare the poor boy or give him the wrong idea.

Not at all, too young, Paul thinks, assuring himself that the young man sitting next to him isn't gay.

Then, quite unexpectedly, he hears this:

"Do you have any tips for a first-timer?"

"Excuse me?"

"Any tips for a first-time skater?" The young man has a slight accent, Spanish–New York, and an unexpected low voice, calming to Paul in his excited state.

"Well, I haven't skated since I was a kid," Paul says, then hesitantly adds, "but I do remember that you have to make sure your ankles are supported. Make sure you're laced up tight."

"Thanks, my friend."

"Don't you know how to skate?" Paul asks, feeling the words slip out of his mouth like the white petals from the dogwood blossoms falling all around him.

"Nope. This time is my first. I'm going to teach myself and by the summer I'll be whizzing around everywhere." The young man smiles, then slowly attempts to stand. His eyes light up, his limbs stiffen: a Sleestack caught in bright light. Paul watches him walking on tiptoe; the orange rubber stops worked well. Onto the grass, over the curb, to the roadway. The young man stands with both arms out from his sides, shifting his head back and forth, moving inches with each step. He stays close to the curb, out of the heavy traffic of weekend recreation experts.

Paul can't decide, can't figure it out. The kid's definitely gutsy. Cute. Not beautiful like some of the other Latino kids that live in his neighborhood in northern Manhattan, with their trendy clothes and precision haircuts, throwing attitude at anyone who notices; but cute. Definitely handsome.

"Should I?" he thinks. "Should I give up my books and solitude and help that boy?" He does. He stuffs his books into his pockets and quickly walks up to the young man with the orange backpack just in time to grab his arm and avert the first fall.

"I thought you might need some assistance," Paul says as he gets the young man vertical again.

"*Gracias*—thanks. But I'm sure I'll fall sooner than later." The young man's eyes flash only momentarily in Paul's direction.

"Don't try to walk. Skating's not like walking." Paul continues to hold on to the arm. He looks down at the bright orange, old-fashioned skates. They're the same kind of skates Paul had years ago, the same kind you used to be able to rent at roller rinks, with wheels attached to ankle-high boots. "Let your feet push out and bend the other knee," Paul says. "Then switch from side to side. Don't try to pick your feet up . . . That's it. Side to side."

Paul doesn't want to take his hand from the young man's arm: he can feel warmth underneath the jacket sleeves, can imagine the skin, tan and smooth like the skin on the young man's face (angular with high cheekbones and slanted eyes), the muscles of the young man's arm, chest, glowing in this soft early spring sun.

"OK?" Paul asks.

The young man answers yes and Paul lets his arm go.

He wants to clap and jump with excitement, but he keeps himself in check. He's not comfortable coming on to someone, letting himself go. No, that's not Paul. He prefers to maintain an even keel, a nonchalance that confines his emotions to his mind—as if his mind's a box, a small cube, where he can keep enthusiasm, glee, depression. It's better that way, he's often thought, staying in check, avoiding any chance of disappointment, nailing the lid shut.

When he first moved to New York Paul thought Central Park was definitely overrated, not a park at all, but a shabbily manicured backyard open to the public. Today, though, it's the patch of green it was designed to be, a new spring green of tender baby leaves, soft on the eye, distracting Paul from his old opinions. The young man with the orange backpack's helping, too. They're not talking much. The young man's skating a few feet in front of Paul, fighting that inevitable fall. And Paul's watching. He wants to run and hold on to that strong warm

arm each time he sees the young man's feet moving out from underneath him; but he doesn't. He can't seem too protective, overbearing, attached already.

They make their way to the skating circle where loud disco music plays all day. Paul takes a seat on the sidelines and watches the young man with his arms held out from his sides, his eyes shifting from the ground blurring under his feet to the other skaters whizzing by, doing cross-over turns and scoops to the steady, nonstop bass beat. To be fearless, Paul thinks, fearless of the new, with no fear of failing. Although he hasn't gotten far in his reading, Paul already knows the story of *Madame Bovary:* she marries an earnest doctor, then quickly grows bored; she becomes aware of a social standing other than her own and daydreams of extraordinariness; then she lives carefree in the arms of a gentleman, then a man much younger than herself. Madame Bovary rides fearlessly through the streets of Paris in a carriage with the shades half-drawn.

Paul's seldom felt bold, fearless, but he'll reveal it next week, next Saturday when the young man with the orange backpack dines at Paul's apartment, a thoughtful meal of linguine in a red sauce with vegetables and capers, a tossed green salad with tomato and basil dressing, warm garlic bread and many many full glasses of red wine. After dinner they'll listen to Paul's Brazilian music collection while Paul inches his way closer and closer to the young man's arms. The young man will hold Paul tentatively, then return Paul's kisses and let himself be taken in Paul's mouth, let the now fearless Paul climb on top of him and let himself be squeezed inside of Paul. Fearless Paul, with his head thrown back, will already be imagining himself and his new lover staying that way for days, weeks. But it won't end that way. The young man will quickly get dressed, mumble goodbye and run away like a rabbit narrowly escaping a trap—baited with a carrot. Paul will be left alone, panting, then still, completely still and wanting.

It's while sitting in the grass in the park, watching the young man with the orange backpack make his way around the skating ring, that Paul allows that little black box in his mind to crack open, its hinges creaking, its contents at first shrinking from the soft green light, then rumbling with anticipation. He imagines over and over a night that will never be.

They exchange phone numbers when it's time for the young man to go to work—he's a night doorman in a Midtown apartment tower. From the exchange of the numbers they discover that they live within blocks of each other.

"What part of Washington Heights do you live in?" Paul asks.

"One Hundred Seventy-first between St. Nicholas and Broadway."

"Oh. I'm on One Hundred Seventieth and Haven. Why haven't we seen each other before?"

But as soon as Paul asked he knew the answer: Although they live in the same neighborhood, they live in different worlds. José Valasquez lives in the world of the Dominican immigrants who are the dominant presence in Washington Heights; Paul lives by Columbia Presbyterian, the economic center of all of northern Manhattan. The two worlds meet only in the crowded emergency rooms of the hospital and every once in a while when an adventurous employee, like Paul, decides he prefers saving money, living in a cheap apartment, and walking to work than spending all of his money on a tiny studio with a kitchenette and noisy neighbors downtown.

They exchange smiles after they exchange phone numbers, shake hands, talk a little about literature and the books Paul likes to read. They walk a short way together after José has taken off his skates and can walk without hesitation beside Paul.

It's without a doubt a mutual liking, Paul thinks as he waves 'bye and the young man turns and walks out of the park and down the street without looking back.

The window next to Paul's desk at work has years and years worth of soot on it, but he still spends many hours looking out of it. Over the black tar pitched roof of the Armory, also the largest homeless shelter in New York. Past the steeple of a church decorated with primary-colored Contact paper that looks almost like stained glass from a distance. A view of the George Washington Bridge wedged between the three poured concrete and brick residential towers of Columbia University.

Even farther, on top of an elementary school, the American flag waving, forever flapping, in a milk-blue sky clouded by black incinerator smoke.

Paul watches the sky slowly change to sunset colors on this late Friday evening; the oranges and reds settle out of the dark blues and purples of sky like sediment at the bottom of a river. He sits and thinks about work, although he wants to think about his dinner with José tomorrow—he's going to make some kind of pasta, but he won't decide until he gets to Fairway and buys everything, fresh. He doesn't like thinking about the monotony of his lab job, numbering test tubes from one to ninety-nine, adding microliters of this and that to the tubes, incubating them for ten minutes, isolating the radioactive-labeled end product, then counting the radiation levels and tabulating the data—all to characterize hormone receptors. He tries not to think of work and listens to the radio, classical music, instead, reads the paper when he has the chance or stares out the window.

Earlier that week he had made the mistake of thinking about what he was doing and it had made him ill, unnoticeable to his co-workers, but sick inside. He'd gone to the eighteenth floor, to the Animal Institute—to the Necropsy Room. The same radio station he listened to in his laboratory played in the halls of the Animal Institute. Piped-in Chopin. He hummed as he worked. But after sacrificing fourteen of fifteen albino male rats; after collecting blood from fourteen anesthetized (still living) animals; after excising each rat's heart and preserving them in a chilled isotonic solution, he realized he'd forgotten to add heparin to the blood he'd collected: the contents of the beaker had already solidified and looked like a cup of black cherry Jell-O. His work had been destroyed. Fourteen rats were already dead. Fourteen rat hearts were worthless without the blood.

After a pause—he doesn't remember if it was long or short, but now it seems like his moment of hesitation was no longer than a blink of the eye—he started working again. With a new-found curiosity, he bled the fifteenth rat. He watched the red liquid slide down the side of the 250-milliliter beaker and pool on top of at least one hundred milliliters of blood clot. He felt the rat, warm, soft, helpless in his hand, losing its life, gasping for air, jerking to get away; life, desperately fighting, then reluctantly giving up, dissipating, then quickly evaporating—out of the rat, out of his hands, a whisper. He cut the rat's heart out and placed it in the appropriate beaker—a tumbler of martinis with fifteen maraschino cherries.

Now, even though it's already past six, Friday evening, the beginning of the weekend, and the heavy sun had drifted downstream and out to sea, Paul sits at his desk lost in thought. He could use a good stiff drink. He can't do this anymore. He can't do that again: order fifteen more rats, prepare to kill fifteen more rats, murder fifteen more rats—watch life spill out of fifteen more beings. He's done nothing but procrastinate since Tuesday, made himself look busy during the day, cleaning, organizing his desk, the refrigerator, the minus-eighty-degree Celsius freezer. He ordered fresh heparin and fifteen more young male albino rats. He wrote protocols and procedures, tabulated old data, took long lunches by himself and sat and read. One word after another. One day—two pages. He doesn't like M. Bovary at all; he wishes he could grab her by the shoulders and tell her that life and love can never be the way they are in a story, a novel, a movie, a magazine.

The day after they have dinner José calls Paul and apologizes for leaving so abruptly but he had to get home to help his mother with some things around the apartment. He says he wants to be friends with Paul, but he's too busy to hang out. "In fact, my friend, my wife called last night. She still lives in Santo Domingo. She's coming to live with me as soon as we save enough money."

Paul thinks this an elaborate and interesting lie, but he doesn't say so. All he wants to do is be with José as much as possible, hang out with José, go for walks with him in the park. In Paul's mind he's already taken his first Spanish lesson from José, walked through Central Park renaming trees and grass, boats and lakes—"*Esto es un arbol . . . La yerba es verde . . . Mira el lago.*" He wants to go bike riding with José and his friends and just hang out. Paul has taken in all of the stories José told him over dinner and placed himself in them right beside José. They'll go riding down Riverside Drive or through Fort Tryon

Park at night. They'll jump the fence at a public pool and go skinny-dipping. They'll see four movies in one night in Times Square and play pinball afterwards, walk all the way home, laugh and joke and eat mangos on the way. They'll translate the poems of Neruda themselves and make copies to give away in the library. They'll eat fresh fruit and yogurt every day. And rice and beans. And mofongo.

Never thinking that people in places like the Dominican Republic would be interested in macrobiotic diets and yoga, Paul wants to completely change his life. He's even quit smoking.

"Why don't we go riding today? Go to Central Park?" he asks every time he calls José. And José always says he can't and makes the same excuses: "I have to go shopping with my mother and then go to work. Maybe next weekend, okay? I have to go. Thanks for calling. See you."

"Okay. Another time, José. Oh, José." Paul likes repeating José's name. "Have you been skating?"

"No, but I want to. I really have to go, my friend. See you."

Paul likes to keep the receiver to his ear until he hears the dial tone return.

He feels he's making a fool of himself, chasing after a nineteen-year-old boy. Old and silly. He hasn't told anyone about José, but he wants to. He's looked through his phone book—the same black Filofax he's had since college, since Jeffrey, his first boyfriend—more than a few times to find just the right person to tell, but there's no one. No one, he thinks, will understand.

He runs into José once on the subway, on a Saturday afternoon when he just had to get out of his apartment, and he sees José again one morning at the grocery story on Broadway before going to work. José acts surprised and very formal at these chance meetings, shaking Paul's hand, and immediately making excuses that he's late for work or yoga class.

Paul starts riding his bike around the neighborhood at different hours of the day hoping to run into José, but he doesn't, not until the summer's almost over and the only time it's cool enough to ride a bike is after midnight.

He's not scared to ride late at night, a lone white boy in

Washington Heights. He's practiced his Spanish with cassettes, picked up some slang words on the street and cut his hair short the way the kids in the neighborhood wear theirs. *"¡Dios mio!"* *"Miro degracio."* "Fuck you, buddy." *"¡Oh coño!* Watch it." He keeps a red Swiss Army knife in his front jeans pocket.

Without providing any real reason for leaving (he didn't tell them he was tired of killing for science), he gives two weeks notice at his job and tells everyone he's moving to Florida—at least for the winter. No one will see him in the neighborhood, he hopes.

He calls José and tells him everything, about quitting his job, about not ordering rats for two months and getting ridiculously behind in his research. José tells him his philosophy:

"We don't kill, my friend. Yes, most of the people in the Dominican do slaughter pigs, chop the necks of chickens. But it is a necessity of food for those who live off the land. But when we move here, we don't kill. There is no need for it. The food, we can buy in the grocery stores here. And we can't afford good meats, anyway. And I'd rather not eat it. No, we don't kill. The ones that believe, believe in the gods from home, don't even kill roaches. They are welcome, the roaches, to whatever they can find. The lady downstairs puts spells and curses when someone sprays in our building. She says it hurts her more than the roaches. It kills her. And if the roaches can't live in this horribly dirty place we live in, then she can't either. This is what I believe, too: if they die, I will die, my family will die."

Paul listens to what José says. He always listens to José's words for hours and hours after hanging up the phone, calling upon the distant sound of José's voice and the now faded—but enhanced image—of José wearing his fluorescent orange backpack and orange skates in Central Park, José paying no attention to the deep bass disco beat, only fighting his inevitable fall.

When Paul moves to another apartment in the same building—he saves a hundred dollars a month by moving into an efficiency but still has to sell pieces from his grandfather's colonial coin collection to subsidize his unemployment check—he asks José to help, but José never shows up, never returns his call.

His new apartment is darker than the last one: there's no direct sunlight, and all the windows face the windows of another apartment. Separated by a ten-foot-wide alley, Paul can see most of the activities of his neighbors, an extremely large extended family. There's a young-looking mother with dyed auburn hair, a lumbering father who usually wears a white tank top and blue work pants, two daughters, one a soon-to-be teenager, the other in her late teens, a son who looks about the same age as Paul, and three other miscellaneous persons who could be uncles or older cousins or very close live-in friends. Paul constantly watches the family across the alley. Prime time begins at sunset.

The youngest daughter leans out the window and yells at the boys playing in the alley below; her mother yells for her to get out of the window and finish her homework; but the young girl, shiny black hair in two long ponytails, gets carried away, shouting taunts and commands at the boys below; and the mother suddenly yanks the girl out of the window and tells her to finish her homework, now. The daughter and mother exchange words in lightning-fast Spanish, and Paul's left knowing only that the mother got the last word in. The father crosses the living room many times during the night, commenting on what's on the TV and asking the oldest daughter to translate to Spanish what's happening to Bart now. All of the family's activities revolve around the living room, which is also the son's study and bedroom. Paul thinks the son looks like an older José with a thin mustache and goatee. The son sits at his desk, a folding card table, reading and occasionally glancing at the TV. The son usually takes off his shirt and closes the white eyelet lace curtains around eleven; he turns off the living room lights and stands in the blue light of the TV rubbing his stomach, scratching his head; he moves things around, opens the convertible couch, leaves the room (Paul thinks to brush his teeth), returns, then turns off the TV. Everything goes black, but Paul, stooping by his window, smoking a cigarette in the dark, waits anyway, a few minutes, a half hour, for some activity, for the boy with the mustache and muscular chest and flat stomach, all covered in a honey-colored skin, to return.

After waiting for a few minutes, a half hour, every night, for the guy to show himself, Paul calls José at work, and either no one answers and the phone rings fifty times or another doorman says that José isn't working tonight.

Paul rides his bike around the city every night after the lights go out across the alley and José doesn't answer the phone. Up through Fort Tryon Park, around the Cloisters, up to Inwood, through Baker Field, around the northern tip of Manhattan to Highbridge Park. At night the air's cooler than in the day but still warm. His skin radiates in the streetlights. His muscles grow taut with the nightly exercise and he becomes more interested in his health even though he's back to smoking his pack of cigarettes a day.

Tired from his nightly ride this late Thursday night in August, Paul stops for a smoke at Highbridge Park. Endorphins and nicotine: double your pleasure, double your fun. He hears noises coming from inside the fenced-in pool. Throaty laughs, ripping splashes of water, screaming male voices shouting in rapid-fire Spanglish. Does he recognize one of the voices? He climbs over the fence and advances slowly to the edge of the pool where a group of four boys are fooling around, diving into the pool, climbing out quickly and jumping back in.

"José, *cómo estás*? It's me, Paul. José?"

"Paul, man. You've come for a swim, my friend? The water's great." José sits on the edge of the pool splashing the water with his feet. His hair is cut closer to the scalp since the last time Paul had seen him. He smiles openmouthed as Paul approaches him. José and his three friends had stripped down to their underwear, brightly colored bikini briefs. "Long time no see," José says, and disappears under the water, chasing one of his friends to the other side of the pool.

Paul doesn't get too close to the edge of the pool; he watches instead, standing more than an arm's length away from the pool's edge. They're so beautiful, Paul thinks, José and his three friends playing, fooling around, with each other, slapping each other on the backs, pushing each other into the water, jumping and chasing each other without a care in the world.

"Come on, Paul. What are you, chicken?" Paul doesn't answer. "Paul, get in," José says with a slight edge to his voice. "No one's going to catch us. Get in. These are my friends."

"I can't. My bike's over there." He looks back and sees that his bike is indeed still there.

"I said get in. Take your clothes off. Come on, man. You only live once."

Paul reluctantly tugs at the bottom of his shirt, takes it off. He sits down and unties his shoes, pulls them off. His socks, his shorts . . .

He hadn't noticed José getting closer to him with each successive dive, or José's friends getting out of the pool. José grabs him from behind and José's friends take his legs. Paul tells them to let him go, but José starts laughing, singing out, "Get soaking wet."

Paul jerks and yanks, tries to free his body. He yells some more. "Come on, José. No. Guys, let me go. Okay? Come on." His side hurts each time he tries to yank himself free. "Guys. *Amigos. Sueltame.*"

He sees José laughing above him, José's white teeth, the roundness of José's head dark against the yellow night sky. He tastes chlorine, feels the sting of water in his nose, his eyes. Blue, swirling blue, white foamy blue. It's the place where the river water mixes with the salty sea. He can't get his legs to kick. He thinks someone's still holding his legs as he tries to get his head above water. He wants to surrender, to give it all up and sink to the bottom of the pool, but his arms keep moving, flapping to keep his head out of the water, to keep the water out of his lungs.

It's his shorts tangled around his ankles that keeps his legs immobile, but he doesn't realize this until he pulls his shorts back up for some reason. He's started swallowing water to get it out of the way. He can't see. He flaps his arms until his hand hits something hard, the edge of the pool, he hopes. He can't stop coughing, can't stop his shaking, the tears. For a while he can't find the energy to pull himself up out of the water. Half swimming, half pushing himself with his hands along the edge of the pool, he finds a ladder and climbs out.

"Come on, Paul, man," he hears as he crawls far enough

away from the pool to think. And then they're gone. He tries to spit out as much chlorinated water, salty, as possible. He finds his T-shirt and sneakers and puts them on. Before climbing over the fence, he takes a deep breath. His bike is gone.

On his way back to his apartment, he starts crying again. He hadn't given up. In the pool a voice had told him to give up, but he hadn't. He couldn't give up yet. The voice hadn't been loud enough; it was more a whisper or like the tiny voices you hear leaking in from another phone line. But it had been there, trying to force the life out of his body. His hands shake uncontrollably each time he remembers the sound of the voice. That night. Almost every night. The voice said, *Vena tu hogar,* come home.

When Dogs Bark

Charles Harvey

New York's got two bad bad habits—she'll trip your ass up and she's one long stinking fart. I've been here three days and this place never stops belching and farting—buses, sirens, taxis, trucks, subways, jackhammers, mouths yelling "fuck yoooou!" New York sounds like it's been eating beans all its life.

I'm here with Eartha Pearl visiting one of her relatives, the cousin with the buck teeth. She wants to be an actress. But between me, you, and the woods I think she's only cut out for playing Bullwinkle's sidekick Rocky. I mean that girl can stand toe-to-toe with any beaver who decides some damn forest is in its way.

Eartha and this cousin get on my nerves after a few days of sitting in this tiny apartment—they doing that girl talk about men and me in particular—dishing up men's shortcomings. Stuff like, "I don't know which is uglier, a naked man or a baboon turned inside out."

EARTHA PEARL: Some days I think I married a baboon . . .

COUSIN: One man can outstink a whole herd of goats . . .

EARTHA PEARL: I know one who can outstink two herds . . .

COUSIN: And, honey, not a brain in their heads . . .

EARTHA PEARL: Lord, the biggest muscle *some* folks got is in their heads . . .

290

I growl softly at Eartha. She looks at me and hushes. Her cousin keeps jabbering away—those big teeth sawing the air as if it's wood. I begin barking.

"Oh, Diane, I picked up a cute Butterick pattern for a pant-suit. It's virgin leather or something. I wish I could sew," says Eartha Pearl to change the subject. Eartha's cousin looks at me like I'm queer.

"It's just his nerves when he gets cross," Eartha says, smiling as if she's explaining a puppy's bad habit. I get up and put on my shoes to go out. Eartha Pearl tries to establish her ownership rights to me.

"Who you know here? Where are you going?"

I say, "I got eight million friends here and ain't a damn one in this room!" I slam the door behind me.

Now by the time I get from the eleventh floor to the first, my mind kicks in. It must have been the blood on the wall on the fifth floor. My mind says, "Now, Jethro, this is a crazy city. All of these eight million people ain't your friends. One of them will kill you if you let him. Go back!"

Naw. I ain't going back. Eartha Pearl and her cousin will just laugh at me. And I'd have to kill them to prove I was a man. I peep out the door and it looks innocent enough outside. Men and women passing by. Trash blowing in a circle. The sky looking like faded blue drawers. So I go out and sit on the stoop. I look east and I look west. Then I look west and I look east.

I say, "Now wait a minute, Jethro, you ain't gonna have no cultural experiences stuck scared here on this stoop. Suppose Columbus had just sat on a stoop all his life. Just suppose. Shit. A man must take action!" While I sit debating, this big white dude in chains and leather walks toward me. Now these chains ain't dainty little things you get from Spiegel's catalog. These chains come from the navy yard. I mean these chains can lift submarines. He wears three around his neck, five on each wrist, and two on each ankle. Now the chains do not bother me. The fact that he has on funky raw uncured leather does not bother me. Even the glass eye—I hope it's glass—dangling from his left earlobe on a chain does not bother me. What bothers me is when he turns in my direction and grabs his grapefruit-sized

crotch and smiles—that's what bothers ol' Jethro here. I say,
"Uh-oh Jethro, somebody wants you to swing a certain way.
And I don't swing that way." I wonder why he pick on me. So
what if I do have on these black high-top sneakers, shorts with
Texas bluebonnets all over them, and a pink T-shirt that says,
I BRAKE FOR MOONERS—that don't mean I'm gay. Shit. I'm just a
colorful dude. Well, okay if you want to count that time when
I was in the eighth grade and me and Johnny Scardino grabbed
each other's rods behind the gym bleachers. I wouldn't have
gone back there with him, but he told me he had *two* and he
would show me if I showed him mine. Okay it tickled and I
got a hard-one when he grabbed me and I grabbed him out of
reflexes, but I haven't *seen* Johnny since the eighth grade. I
dreamed about him once, since I been married to Eartha Pearl.
But I woke up and made love to Eartha real quick.

So anyway I hang my head and growl softly at the man in
leather. He must think I'm calling him to dinner 'cause he
moves a little closer. When I see him step, I bark louder. And
not yap like a poodle either. I'm Doberman and Great Dane
combined. I rattle nearby windows. New York people stare at
me as they walk by. And they tell me you're doing something
when you can get a New Yorker to stare at you eye-level on the
street. The dude slinks away like he's carrying a tail between his
legs.

I say to myself, "Damn, Jethro, my barking stuff is right on
time. Damn if I'll ever let a head doctor take it from me. Fuck
Eartha Pearl's suggestion." I get off the stoop and walk down
the street barking my ass off. Nobody messes with me. Not
even that gang on the corner with bones sewed to their leather
jackets. I'm free as a pigeon. Do *I* stand up on the subway?
Hell no! I have a whole car of seats to myself.

Eartha Pearl and her man-hating cousin never want to go
nowhere. When it's daytime, they say it's too hot. When it's
evening, they say they don't want to get caught out at night.
And when it's night, Eartha and her cousin share the bed and
give me a rug on the floor with my feet in the bathroom and
my head in the kitchen. So I spend most of my time riding the
subways and checking out the humanity that rides with me:

Brothers singing opera or preaching Malcolm X; cripples on crutches hustling dollars—throw a dime right back at your ass; folks changing clothes—stripping down to their Swiss cheese drawers and looking indignant at you for looking at them.

The most excitement for Eartha Pearl was the suicide that jumped out the window of her cousin's building. Of course, that was something to see. We hear this screaming in broad open daylight and look out the window. There's something spread out like a bloody chicken on a car's roof. Downstairs in the middle of a circle of people, a young white boy lies naked on the roof of a black Cadillac with cow horns on the hood. His legs are spread as if he's relaxing on a bed instead of frying in his own hot blood. The car's owner stands with his arms folded across his chest. Every now and then he kicks a tire or fender and yells, "Goddamn!" In a window above us, an old woman waves and screams like a hawk.

"Goddamn! What she want me to do? Throw him back up to her? Who's gonna pay for my car?" the car owner asks as he kicks a fender. Eartha Pearl has to have two Valiums and a bottle of beer to make her eyes stop bugging out and her hands stop shaking. So maybe that's enough for her. But I have to have something else. Something to make the blood rush through my heart like fire.

One day I'm sitting on the subway barking softly, but loud enough for people ten feet away to hear. I look up and see this sweet white chick in a pink leather miniskirt so high up her thighs she has to cross her muscular legs three times to keep out any drafts. So I stop barking and growl softly at her. I had heard all you have to do to get a New York girl is to say, "Hello, I'm straight and AIDS-free." I growl at her again. She looks at me. I see her glance down at my legs and look off, slightly cutting her eyes at me. She plays with a lock of blood hair that's curled behind her ear. I look down at my legs and have to admire them myself. I mean I'm no freak who stands in the mirror looking at my buck naked self and saying, "Oh daddy-o what a sweet daddy you are." But these legs always catch women. (They caught Eartha Pearl, who when she isn't mad at me, and when we're in the bed, runs her hand up and

down my smooth brown thighs caling me "doll legs.") I ask
the chick what time was it. "Tony," she says in a husky voice.

"Tony?" I ask.

"T-o-n-i," she spells out slowly.

"Well, hey, forget about the time. All I got is time. I'm
Jethro from Houston."

"I went to Texas once. Nothing was happening. Everything
was flat and brown as a mud cake."

"Well you see, you hadn't met me ...".

"I've met every man, Mister Dogman."

My brain searches for something clever to say, but my eyes
stay on her smooth white legs twisted around each other—two
long loaves of sweetness. I can see my legs twisted with hers—
locked like a pair of brown and white fingers, soft, warm, and
sensual. "What part of Texas was a chick like you roosting?" I
ask her.

"Dalhart."

"Dalhart? Where in the hell is that?"

"You're from Texas. You ought to know, Mister Dogman."
She flutters her lashes.

"What were you doing in Dalhart?"

"I was stationed there in the army."

"Baby, you don't look like any kind of army girl I ever
seen."

"I'm not." Her answer is sour as a lemon. Something tells
me I have parted my lips before I listened to my brain. Damn,
Jethro, be yourself cool, man. You don't want the pussy to turn
cold before you even get to the front door. What could C.C.
say? Shit, he even gave you some of his glow-in-the-dark rub-
bers that he uses for special occasions like birthdays and Christ-
mases. Can't let C.C. down.

"You look like a nice man." Toni's voice brings our eyes
together.

There's a flutter in her lashes as if she's lying or has specks
in her eyes. Her teeth are too big and her chin is too square for
a woman's, I think.

"Ohh, so this is what's going down. You can dig this,
Jethro," a voice says to me. "Don't look a gift horse in his big
mouth. Guy or girl, a mouth is a mouth is a mouth." "Close

your eyes and you'll like it better," Johnny Scardino told me once as he tugged my pants down in his warm oily garage.

"Well, I think I am. I mean I am nice. God knows I'm nice," I say. The sweat of my thighs glues me to the subway seat.

A young woman the color of ebony sitting in front of us glares at me. She has been reading a book, but the nervousness in my voice makes her look up. Her gold earrings shaped like Africa tremble. She looks at Toni and goes back to her reading. Suddenly she slams her book shut and folds her arms across her chest. When she gets off the train I see her look into the window at us and shake her head like we are to be pitied. She makes an ugly sign at me with her forefinger. Before I can make one back the crowd swallows her.

"Don't you scare off my cat, Mister Dogman," Toni says as she opens the door to her apartment. She led me to her place—inviting me to smoke some herb and have a little drink.

I step into a pink zoo. Pink stuffed animals are all over the couch and chairs—elephants, turtles, bears, lions. Two pink alligators perch on her bed, mouths open waiting to bite my buck naked ass when I drop my pants and Toni gets down to business, I think.

"You sure have lots of animals, baby," I say, stroking her for-real white cat with pink ears.

"I like all kinds of animals."

"I see," I say, looking at myself in the huge gold-framed mirror on the ceiling above the bed.

"Pull your shoes off and relax. I'll get us a little smoke."

"I'm cool as a cat," I say, clearing my throat. For a moment I think I see Eartha Pearl staring at me from the ceiling. I bend over to pull off my shoes and my eyes fall on a small photograph in a gold frame. A square-faced white boy in an army suit smiles a toothy grin at me. My head starts to spin. I'm shaking all over as if an ice storm just blew into Toni's window. I stand up, but my feet are stuck to the floor.

Toni comes back and hands me a bubble-shaped glass of amber liquid.

"Sit, Mister Dogman," Toni says calmly. "Nobody's going to take you on a trip that you haven't made a reservation for."

She sits a flattened-beetle ashtray on the table and lights the twisted end of a cigarette. She puffs, holds her breath, and hands the cigarette to me. While I'm hitting it, she gets up and puts a Jimmy Smith CD on the box. "This baby knows what's happening," I think to myself. A white girl in Houston had tried to entice C.C. with some country music guy singing "Them Ol' High Alabama Trees." C.C. said he couldn't make nothing happen.

Toni takes a hit from the cigarette. She smiles and asks me to dance. I take her hand and put my other one around her waist. Her back feels tight and muscled, not fleshy like Eartha's. We rock back and forth like a pair of old people. Jimmy Smith's "Midnight Special" and Toni's weed put me in a traveling mood. We start to glide all over the room. The organ's rhythm pulsates through me and moves down my thighs. Toni puts her face next to my cheek and cries softly.

"My whole family is gone away. I'm all alone, Jethro. What can a nice man like you do for a lonely one like me? Can you hold me? Can you squeeze the loneliness out of me?"

"Yes, baby, I can hold you," I say quietly.

We sit down and she sits on my lap. She feels heavy. Her wrists are thick, not thin and feathery like a woman's. Her lips are rough as work gloves. The whiskey and the weed soon lighten and smooth all of Toni's rough edges. Her skirt and legs have the same velvety tickle. She brushes my hand away from her crotch. I pull down Toni's bra and caress her small breasts.

"I'm so lonely. Are you a nice man?"

"Yes, baby, yes. Let me show you how nice I am. I'll take you to Kilimanjaro and we'll smoothly ride down the Nile. Just let me get on the train, baby. Just let me ride." That Nile and Kilimanjaro works with Eartha Pearl, unless she's in her hurry-up-and-get-it-over mood.

Toni reaches up and pulls a cord. The lights go out. "Can you put on a condom in the dark?" she asks.

"Baby, better than the queen can put on her gloves. I got my own." In the dark, my rod glows like a bright yellow banana. Toni's deep laughter fills the room. I curse C.C. under my breath. The cat's bright green eyes move side to side as he follows my swaying rod. Toni and I bray like mules. Then I smother Toni's laughter with kisses. I take another hit off the weed and the wheels of the train start to turn. I'm Casey Jones and I make train noises in Toni's ear. She throws her arms around my neck and kisses me. "Just drive your train, Daddy. Just drive it. Just drive, Daddy. Ooh Daddy, just drive. Lord have mercy. Drive me, sweet Daddy," Toni screams in my ear.

When I wake up, Toni stands over me with a bunch of cherries taped above each of his nipples. The cherries dangle juicy and red from their stems. He straddles my body. I pucker my lips around one of the cherries and pull it. Toni giggles like a young girl.

"Oh, you're so much fun, baby. You're so much fun." I pull another cherry off Toni and eat it. I spit the pit toward the ceiling. It clatters to the floor.

"Ooh, you animal," Toni softly scolds me. I pull a handful of cherries from Toni and stuff them in my mouth. "Ooh, you big bad baby," Toni croons to me. "Give me the pits." Toni holds his hand under my mouth. I grab his fingers and put them in my mouth. Toni squeals and I pull him down next to me. We kiss.

"What do you want to eat?" Toni asks, slipping into his short silk kimono.

"Pancakes and eggs," I answer.

"Again?"

"I like the way you lick the syrup off my chest."

"I like the way you like me to." Toni giggles and bounces off to the kitchen.

I look up at the ceiling at me staring at myself in the mirror. You don't look like no punk, I say to myself. You don't wear lipstick and false eyelashes like Eartha's "Aunt Don"—that fat sissy with his big feet jammed in pink high-heeled slippers. I spread my legs and look at the outline of my sex under the covers. Shit, I'm a man, am a man, am a man! I fuck. I like the Celtics. I work my ass off. I made a baby once. So what if Eartha Pearl lost it in an aisle of plastic flowers in the middle of Woolworth's? I still made it. She the one who couldn't keep him. Toni Toni Boboni! Why didn't I knock the hell out of you? Got a rod bigger than mine. And I can't leave. Why can't I leave? I'm not a punk. I don't walk funny. Johnny Scardino walked funny. Johnny Scardino kissed my thigh after he blew me. I just stood there. Just stood there like a statue. I'm not a punk. Lots of men take a side trip now and then. I can leave. Just get up and toss Toni a dollar or two and say later alligator ...

"Sweet, sweet honeydew," Toni sings from the kitchen. "I can't get over this pageboy haircut you gave me. Are you sure you're not a hairdresser? The girls at the ball tonight are gonna flip when they see me dressed like a man."

"I don't know about that bullshit," I answer.

"Are you still sore about the leash I wanted you to wear? I told you it wasn't racial."

"Always a nigguh got to have a chain around his neck," I answer.

"I wasn't thinking anything racial at all. I was thinking of your barking dog routine. We could really work those girls' nerves!"

"Well, you're not putting a chain around my neck. You don't have to remind me I'm a nigguh."

"Oh, Jethro, for the last time! That's not what I meant! If you hadn't given me such a hairdo, I'd shoot you!" I can see Toni staring at his hair in the reflection of his coffeepot. I look at the nightstand littered with marijuana roaches and condoms. I look at the gray tube of K-Y jelly squeezed violently by my own hands. I hate Toni and I want to beat him lifeless.

Toni brings the breakfast tray to bed. The fat pancakes are as smooth and brown as Eartha Pearl. "I can't wait to go shopping for our tuxes," he says. "Imagine me buying a tux! Me in pants. Girl, my friends ..." I spit a mouthful of pancakes at Toni.

"I told you not to call me that." I grab Toni's arm and twist his wrist.

"Oww, baby! I'm sorry. I just forgot."

"Just don't forget again." Toni wipes the pancake from his cheek. He tries to kiss me.

"Let me eat."

"But you've got syrup all over you."

"And you've got shit all over you. So beat it!"

Toni burst into tears. "Oh, Jethro! Jethro, don't be so mean to me."

"Shut up acting like a sissy!" I shout at him. Toni stops crying. A tear rolls down his cheek. He sits with his cat in his lap. They both stare at me as I eat—Toni as if I'm a god. The cat looks at me as if I'm a piece of shit. "Sit with your legs apart!" I bark at Toni. "Men sit with their legs apart!" Toni parts his knees as if I've tossed hot coals between his legs. The cat falls to the floor, clawing Toni's thigh as he tries to hang on. It looks up at Toni and hisses before walking away. Toni shivers in the chair with his knees apart. I brush past him on my way to the kitchen. I stand for a moment at the sink and listen to him whimper and sniffle. A wave of sorrow washes over me. I want to hold him. (I'm the same with Eartha Pearl. When I hurt her and make her cry, love and remorse come up from the pit of my stomach. I get on my knees and beg her to forgive me. I kiss her thighs and hands until she rubs the back of my neck softly.) I walk over to Toni and put my hand on his shoulder. He stiffens his body at my touch. I gently soothe him.

"I'm sorry, baby," I say. "I'm so sorry." I wipe away the blood from his thigh with my fingers. He leans his head on my shoulder. His tears flow down my arm. I kiss him and coax him back to bed.

"Jethro, you've got to hurry! Will you come on! It's four o'clock and the stores close at five!" Toni races ahead of me wearing a pair of red platform shoes. His bell-bottomed pants hug his ass and dangle like loose pajamas around his ankles. His shirt with red and pink roses squeezes his body like a sausage casing. His steps are short and prissy as if he's stepping on spit. People raise their eyesbrows at us. I try to walk far behind Toni, but he turns around and pulls me next to him. My head swims. All I see are flowers and eyes circling me— frowning eyes, arched judging eyes, eyes burning us like hot coals.

"C'mon, Jethro, c'mon," Toni sings to me over his shoulder. Three young men dressed in gold chains and baseball caps pass me and Toni. I hear them snicker like mice. "C'mon, Jethro, c'mon," one mimics Toni's singsong voice. I look around at them. The darkest one tugs at his crotch. I start toward him. Toni grabs my arm. "No, baby, you'll get us killed!" Toni pulls me away. "Ignore them, baby. Ignore them . . ."

I snatch my arm from Toni. "Stop walking so womanish and don't lean on me! Don't even talk to me." We walk on. Toni's shoulders are bowed. I've hurt him again. But all of this shame I feel. I'm hurting too. All of these eyes on me. "I'm hurting too, bitch," I shout at Toni. "Look what you're doing to me—dragging me through your fucking gutter! I don't want to go to some punks' ball. I don't want to bark my ass off for a bunch of queers. I want to go home, watch the Celtics, and play with my wife. She's got real knockers. She can't have a baby, but she's got real knockers!" I can see Toni shuddering like it's zero degrees. I feel a sharp pain in my tailbone. I grab my back.

"Hey, faggot, that's how my ten-inch dick will feel up your ass!" I look around and a hurricane of bottles and rocks blow toward me and Toni. We turn and run. I feel the needle pricks of glass pierce my legs. I run fast and hard until I feel I'm reaching the edge of the world. It's not the bottles I'm running from. I hear a voice screeching like a wounded animal. "Pleeease stop, Jethro! Don't leave me, baby! Pleease! Pleeease!"

Honking horns drown the voice and I stop running. My legs feel as if they're wrapped in thorns. Every building is the same—tall, gray, and ugly. I imagine there are spirits flying out the windows and bumping into me on the sidewalk. I walk in circles and zigzags until I see the horned Cadillac. I look up into the faces of Eartha Pearl and her cousin looking down at me—mouths open like two screaming cats.

"And you just walk in from nowhere and don't say a word about where you've been. Just walk in like King Jethro and don't have to give nobody an explanation. Ha! We owes *you* an explanation about why we standing there with our mouths open. Lord have mercy," Eartha Pearl yelled at me all the way to the airport in the taxicab. "Legs all bloody. And then insulting my cousin the way you did. Lord have mercy. I know it'll rain ice cubes in hell before she invites us up here again. 'Did you screw my wife while I was gone?' What kind of question was that to ask my cousin?"

"All of y'all know she's a dyke," I say smugly.

"It's nobody's business what she is. And how dare a fool like you call her names. She was the one on the phone all day and into the night calling hospitals, morgues, city police, transit police in every county in New York."

"Boroughs. New York has boroughs."

"Bastard, don't you dare correct me! Girl crying herself to fits being put on hold, hung up on, and screaming into that damn phone and here a son of a bitch like you call her a dyke and try to talk back to *me*! If I had half the guts of Momma's Aunt Carrie, I'd gut you like a pig. Just like she did that husband of hers. Cut his roots off too! That's what a nigguh like you needs!"

The cabdriver laughs. I know what he's laughing at. Some vision of me running down the street without my "roots," blood running from a hole beneath my belly. I try to kiss Eartha Pearl. But she's on fire with anger.

"How can you kiss me after what you've done to me and my cousin? When I let you kiss me again you'll be so old and senile, you'll think I'm a man," she says with a sharp jab in my ribs.

Back in Houston a few months and the dust has settled, almost. I've gone back to work. The pain from the rocks and broken glass is gone out of my back and legs. Eartha Pearl has let me make love to her once. I've worn out my tongue telling C.C. about the hot chick I met on the subway, how she made me buck like a wild horse, and her fairy brother.

"Yeah, man, her brother wanted to give me a blow job—but I drew the line there."

"Shit, nigguh, uh-huh, I bet you did," C.C. says back to me. "I'da took him on and I know I ain't no punk, but turn down a blow job? Shit . . ."

Yeah I'm almost back to normal. If C.C. had said those words to me a month ago, I would have barked at him. But those words don't trouble me now. It's just, it's just that damn piece of paper that troubles me. I wish C.C. had thrown it in the trash instead of hollering out, "Well, looky who's got them a letter from New York! Mister Jethro Green, Manager, Exxon, Baytown, Texas, United States of America—Lord have mercy! Manager? Nigguh, what you tell them folks in New York you a manager of? You manages that shovel all right, though!"

I snatched the letter from C.C. The first word I saw on the envelope was TONY. I jammed it in my back pocket. "It's just that chick's nutty brother," I said to all the laughing faces around me.

"Ha! I knowed you was lying about that blow job," C.C. bellowed.

That damn pice of paper—I crumbled and toss it in the trash, then sneak into the kitchen late at night and wipe the coffee grounds from it. I place it next to my heart.

Dear Jethro:

Please, baby, Jethro, please call me. I love you. Here is some of my hair that you asked me to cut. Remember? I made it into a little bracelet for you. Don't that prove I love you? I thought you were going to be my life. You mean so much to me. Can you see the red tearstains on the letter? My heart is so broken my tears are red. I thought you were going to be my life. You loved me and made me love myself. Why did you run away? Please, please call me. 718-622-2169.

Love,
Toni
your love

Some nights after I read that letter, I go out on the back porch and I bark and bark until the far-off sky turns red like Toni's tear-filled eyes. And Johnny Scardino's phone number rumbles through my head—all sevens and a zero.

Citre et Trans

Samuel R. Delany

One

... all that we have been saying is as much a natural sport of the silence of these nether regions as the fantasy of some rhetorician of the other world who has used us as puppets!

—PAUL VALÉRY, *Eupalinos, or The Architect*

"All Greek men are barbarians!" Heidi jerked the leash.

Pharaoh's claws dragged the concrete.

I laughed, and Pharaoh looked around and up, eyes like little phonograph records.

"Heidi," I said, "you just can't talk about an entire population that way."

It was too bright to look at the sky directly—even away from the sun. The harbor was blue, not green. And if I stared into the air anyway, it was as though I were watching the water reflected in some dazzling metal, brighter than, but equally liquid as, the sea.

"*Half* a population," Heidi said. "I like the women. They don't have any style. But I like them." She wore her black and white poncho—which, only after I'd been living with her in her Mnisicleou Street room two weeks, I realized was because she thought she was fat.

"Barbarians—*hoi barbaroi*—"I pronounced it the way my

303

classics professor back at City College would have, rather than with what had been the surprising (for me) Italianate endings, despite spelling, of modern Greek: "It's already a Greek word— the Greeks gave it to us—for people who aren't Greek, who spoke some other language—*ba-ba-ba-ba-ba!*—like you and me ... Germans, Americans—"

"They also wrote Greek tragedies." The green ferry sign's painted wood was bolted to the two-tiered dock rail. "From the way they behave today, though, *I* don't think they still have it." HYDRA, SPETZA, and AEGINA were painted in white Roman capitals. Below, the same names were printed in smaller upper-/lowercase Greek. Heidi shrugged her broad shoulders as we strolled by.

Once, when I'd commented on how strong she was, Heidi told me that six years before, when she was nineteen, she'd been women's swimming champion of Bavaria. She also told me she'd recently graduated from Munich University with a degree in philosophy and a minor in contemporary Hebrew literature: she'd arranged to study for the year in Tel Aviv, with special papers and letters of introduction. But because she was German Protestant, in Israel they wouldn't let her off the boat. She'd ended up in Athens. Then, when we'd had some odd argument, tearfully she'd explained—while I showered in the pink tiled stall in the room's corner—that she suffered from a fatal blood disease, not leukemia, but like it, that left no sign on her muscular, tanned torso, arms, or legs. But that was why she'd left the American artist she'd been living with in Florence to come to Athens in the first place: likely it would kill her within three years.

That last one kind of threw me. At first. And I wrote my wife about it—who wrote about it in a poem I read later.

At various times I believed all of Heidi's assertions. But not all three at once.

"I don't know whether to kiss David or never to speak to him again for getting me this job—baby-sitting for the children of rich Greeks is just not that wonderful."

"The parents want them to learn German. And French."

"And *English!*" she declared. "Believe me, *that's* the important one for them. Are you still mad at John"—who was this

English electrical engineer—"for taking that job away from you
at the Language Institute?" Heidi's French, Italian, and English
were about perfect; her Greek was better than mine. And one
evening I'd sat with her through an hour conversation in Arabic
with the students we met at one in the morning in the coffee
shop in Omoinoia.

"I was never mad at him," I told her. "He thought it was
as silly as I did. His Cockney twang is thick enough to drown
in, and he can't say an 'h' to save himself. But they wanted 'a
native English speaker'; as far as they were concerned, I was
just another American who says, 'Ya'll come' or 'Toidy-toid
Street.' John would be the first one to tell you I speak English
better than he does."

"And you've written all those beautiful books in it, too. He
said he'd read one."

"Did he? English John? He never told me." We were halfway along the pier.

"I really don't know which is worse. Rich Greek children,
or that museum stuff I was doing . . ." Suddenly she closed
her eyes, stopped, and shuddered. Pharaoh sat and looked up,
slathering. "Yes I do. I hate German tourists. I hate them more
than anything in the world—with their awful, awful guide-
books. All they do is look at the books. Never at the paintings.
I used to be so thankful for the Americans. 'Well, that's reeeal
perty, Maggie!' " Heidi's attempted drawl on top of the Ger-
manic feathering of her consonants produced an accent that, I
knew she knew, belonged to no geography at all. But we both
laughed. "Even if they didn't know what they were looking at,
they looked at the paintings. The Germans never did. If I'd been
there another week, I was going to play a trick—I swear it. I
was going to take my dutiful Germans to the wrong paintings,
and give them my little talk about an entirely different picture—
just to see if any of them noticed. You know: in front of a
fifteenth-century Spanish Assumption of the Virgin, I'd begin,
with a perfectly straight face: "And here we have a 1930 indus-
trial landscape painted in the socialist realism style that grew
up in reaction to Italian Futurismo . . .' " She started walking
again, as though the humor of her own joke had rather run out.
"Rich Greek children it will be."

"Heidi," I said, "I think I've spotted a German national trait: you Germans always talk about everybody, even yourselves, in terms of 'national characteristics.' Well, it got you in trouble in that war we had with you when you and I were kids. I wouldn't be surprised if it ended up getting you in trouble again."

Heidi took my arm. "It isn't a German trait, dear. It's a European trait—and you Americans, who are always fighting so hard against generalizing about anyone, look terriby naive to the rest of us because of it. I'd think you American Negroes especially, with your history of oppression from white people, ought to realize, of all Americans, just how suicidally—no, genocidally, there's the nasty word—naive that is. If you pretend you can't know anything about a group, how can you protect yourself from that group—when they're coming to burn crosses in your yard; or to put you in the boxcars." She seemed suddenly very unhappy—as if that were just not what she wanted to talk about.

"Well, I like the Greeks, myself. There's a generalization. Is that okay for you? Did I ever tell you that story about David and me, when I first got back from the islands? You know how David is, every time he spots a new international: coming over to say hello and have a glass of tea. Then, somehow, he was going to show me where something was, and the two of us ended up walking together down Stadiou Street, him in his jeans and t-shirt, and that blond beard of his. And me, right next to him with my beard."

"A cute little beard it is, too." Heidi leaned over to ruffle my chin fuzz with her knuckles.

With one arm, I hugged her shoulders. "Cut it out, now. Anyway, I didn't know how the Greeks felt about beards back then—that the only people who wore them—here—were the Greek orthodox priests—"

"Yes, I know," Heidi said. "David's told me—they all think that bearded foreigners are making fun of their priests, which is why they get so hostile. Frankly I don't believe it for a minute. Greece is only two days by car away from the rest of the civilized world. And there've been foreigners coming through here—with beards—for the last hundred years. If you'd have cut yours off just for that, I'd have been very angry at you. Remember, dear: David is English—and the English love to make up explanations about people they think of as foreigners that are much too simple; and you Americans eat them up. The Greeks are just angry at foreigners, beards or no. And a good deal of that anger is rational—while much of the rest of it isn't. I'd think you were a lot cleverer if you believed that, rather than some silly over-complicated English anthropological explanation!"

"Well, that's why I was going to tell you this story," I said. "About the Greeks. We were walking down Stadiou Street, see—David and me—when I noticed this Greek couple more or less walking beside us. He was a middle-aged man, in a suit and tie. She was a proper, middle-aged Greek wife, all in black, walking with him. And she was saying to him, in Greek (I could just about follow it), all the while glancing over at us: "Look at those dirty foreigners—with their dirty beards. They mess up the city, them with their filthy beards. Somebody should take them to the barber, and make them shave. It's disgusting the way they come here, with their dirty beards, dirtying up our city! Well, even though I knew what she was saying, there was nothing I could do. But suddenly David—who's been here forever and speaks Greek like a native—looked over and yelled out, *'Ya, Kyria—ehete to idio, alla ligo pio kato!'* Hey, lady—you have one too, only a little further down! Well, I thought I was going to melt into the sidewalk. Or have a fight. But the man turned to us, with the most astonished look on his face: *'Ah!'* he cried. *'Alla milete helenika!'* Ah! But you speak Greek! The next thing I knew, he had his arms around David's and my shoulder, and they took us off to a cafe and bought us brandy till I didn't think we could stand up, both of them asking us questions, about where we were from and what we were doing here, and how did we like their country. You know 'barbarian' isn't the only word the Greeks gave us. So is 'hospitality.' "

"No," Heidi said. "You never did tell me that story. But I've heard you tell it at at least two parties, when you didn't think I was listening—for fear I'd be offended. It's a rather dreadful story, I think. But it's what I mean—about the Greek women having no style. If someone had yelled that to *me* in the street, I would have cursed him out till—how might you say it?—his balls hoisted up inside his belly to cower like frightened puppies." She bent down to rub Pharaoh's head and under his chin. "Then"—she stood again—"*maybe* I'd have asked him to go for a brandy. Ah, my poor Pharaoh."

Heidi pronounced "Pharaoh" as three syllables—Pha-ra-oh—so that, for the next twenty-five years, I really didn't know what his name was, even after I saw her write it out in a letter to me, only then, one day (twenty-five years on), looking at the written word for the Egyptian archon, suddenly I realized what she'd meant to call him. But because we were in Greece, and because in general her faintly accented English was so good, I always thought "Pha-ra-oh" was some declension I didn't quite catch of *pharos*—lighthouse.

"Here in Greece," she said, "you really do lead a dog's life—don't you, dog?" She pulled the black leather leash up short again. The collar buckle was gleaming chrome—from some belt she'd found in the Monasteraiki flea market; she'd put it together herself on the black leather line. It was unusual looking and quite handsome. Under the poncho she wore black tights and black shoes, with single white buttons on the front. "I take him for a walk in the city—they run up on the street and kick him! You've seen them. Don't say you haven't. And he's so beautiful—" She grinned down at him, slipping into a kind of baby talk—"with his beautiful eyes. It was your beautiful eyes, Pharaoh, that made me take you in in the first place, when you were a puppy and I found you limping about and so sick in the back of that old lot. Ah," she crooned down at him, "you really are so beautiful!"

"The Greeks just don't keep pets here, Heidi. At least not house pets."

"I know," she said. "Costas told me: you have a dog on a rope in the city. They think you're probably taking him off somewhere to kill him. They run up and kick him, they throw a stone or a bottle at him—and think it's great fun! They give him meat they've spent twenty minutes carefully sticking full of broken glass! I take him on the subway, and the police say I have to put a muzzle on him!" She made a disgusted sound.

"You see somebody with a dog on a leash like this—you would have to be stupid not to realize it's a pet! They don't like foreigners; they don't like dogs. It's just their way of getting back at both. And even so, on the underground out here this morning, you saw how everyone cowered back from him—they think my little dog is a terrible and vicious beast! I had to put that awful muzzle on him. And he was so good about it. Well, you don't have it on now—my darling Pharaoh!"

Pharaoh wasn't a big dog. But he wasn't a little one either. He was a broad-chested coffee-colored mutt with some white patches, as though a house painter had picked him up and maybe shaken one of his forepaws before washing his hands. Heidi'd had him about six months—which was twice as long as she'd known me. One of his ears and the half-mask around his left eye were black.

"They're just not used to dogs, and he makes them uncomfortable."

"They're uncomfortable with him because he's a dog. They're uncomfortable with you because you're a Negro—"

"They're uncomfortable with you because you're German."

She smiled at that. "Well, *that's* barbaric! When I go to David's silly baby-sitting job, are you going to be all right?"

"I told you, DeLys said I could stay at her place up in Anaphiotika, while she's away. I'll be off to England the day after tomorrow. And then back home to New York."

"That odd old Englishman, John, from Turkey, is staying at DeLys's too, isn't he?"

"He's not that odd. When I was in Istanbul, DeLys gave me his address so I could look him up. After Jerry and I hitchhiked there, I hadn't had a shower in a week and was a total mess—he was just as nice to me as he could be. He fed me all one afternoon, till I was so full I could hardly walk. He told me all about places to see in the city, the Dolma Bocce and the Flower Passage. And what Turkish baths to go to."

"Did he feed Jerry too?"

"No. Jerry was scared of him because he knew John liked guys. DeLys had told Jerry about him before we left. So Jerry wouldn't go see him."

"You like guys. You like Jerry, I think."

Which was true. "But Jerry," I said, "and I are the same age. And we were already friends. I told Jerry I thought he was acting silly. But he's a southerner, and he's stubborn."

"That was a lovely letter Jerry wrote you." She quoted: " 'Don't step on any low flying birds.' I always thought he was just another stupid American, too tall, and too awkward, with nothing very interesting to say—even though you liked him. but when you read me his letter, I really began to wish I'd gotten to know him better while he was here. You're very sensitive to people, in ways I know I'm not. But sometimes, I suppose, we just miss out. Because, as you Americans say, of our prejudices.

"But he is odd," she went on, suddenly. "Turkish John, I mean—isn't that a funny name, for an Englishman? Cosima says he gives her the creeps."

"He's a little effeminate—he's a queer," I said. "But so am I, I suppose." Though I didn't really think I was—effeminate, that is.

"I wonder why so many women like you." Pharaoh went around behind her and, when she jerked him, came back between us, drawing black and white felt one way and another across her shoulder. "DeLys, Cosima, me . . . Even Kyria Kokinou likes you." (Kyria Kokinou was the landlady Heidi had decided not to risk angering by having me stay in the room while she was away with her Greek children.) "Do you think there's any particular reason for that?"

"Probably *because* I'm queer," I said. Then: "I wonder why we didn't have more sex, you and I?"

Now she leaned away with an ironic sneer, backed by her big, German smile. "*I* was certainly ready!" Heidi and I had slept in the same bed for two weeks; but we'd only made love twice. "I think you were just trying to prove a point," she said. "That you *were* . . . 'queer,' as you say." Suddenly she straightened. "I'm really not looking forward to this trip. The ferry will have to go out by the paper mill; and it's going to stink. And I won't ever see you again, will I? Look, if you can stop for a day in Munich, you must visit the Deutsches Museum. I used to go there when I was little. It's a science museum. And they have almost an entire real mine in the basement that you can walk around in and watch it work—that was my favorite part, when I was a little girl. And wonderful mechanical toys from the eighteenth century—you can see actually functioning. I know you'll love it. You like science, I know it. From your lovely books—that you write so carefully. I'd love to know I shared that little piece of my childhood with you. So go there— if you possibly can." She looked around at the ferryboat. "Well, you have a wonderful trip home. And write me. You'll go home—you'll see your wife again. And everything will work out between you. I bet that'll be so. It's been an awful lot of fun. I hope you and your wife get back together—or something good happens there, anyway." She leaned forward and gave me a kiss. I gave her a hug back, and she came up blinking. And grinned once more. Then she turned and went up the plank onto the deck, Pharaoh dashing first ahead, then suddenly back as if he'd forgotten something, so that, with a few embarrassed smiles at me, she had to drag him on board.

At the gangplank's top a man in a gray suit and an open-collared shirt, lounging against the rail like a passenger, suddenly stood up, swung about, and became very official, pointing at Heidi, at Pharaoh: an altercation started between them, full of "... *Dthen thello ton skyllon edtho ...!*" (I don't want the dog here) and much arm-waving on his part, with many drawn-out and cajoling "*Pa-ra-ka-looo!*" and "*Kallo to skylaiki!*"'s from Heidi. (Pleeease! and He's a good puppy!) It didn't resolve until she went into her black leather reticule under her poncho to pull out first the John O'Hara paperback she was reading (it ended on the deck, splayed and spine up, by the rail post), some tissues, a pencil, and finally Pharaoh's muzzle, waving the leather straps at the boat official, then stooping to adjust them over patient Pharaoh's mouth and ears—while the other passengers stood close around, curious.

At last she stood up to blow me a kiss.

I waved back and called, "Get your book!"

She looked down and saw the upended, thick black paperback, laughed, and stooped for it.

"*Ciao!*" she called. "Bye!"

"*Ciao!*"

I walked back through the Piraeus market, under the iron

roofs with their dirty glass panes above tomato and sea-urchin stalls, eggplant and octopus counters, through the red-light district (where, for a week, on my first return from the islands, I'd stayed with Ron and Bill and John), past blue and white doors and small wooden porches, to the subway that would return me to Athens.

Two

By all the gloom hung round thy fallen house,
By this last temple, by the golden age,
By great Apollo, thy dear foster child,
And by thyself, forlorn divinity,
The pale Omega of a withered race,
Let me behold, according as thou said'st,
What in thy brain so ferments to and fro.

—JOHN KEATS, *The Fall of Hyperion,* Canto I

"I may be bringing someone home with me," [Turkish] John said. "A man, I mean." John had a long nose. "You won't mind, will you? We'll use the bed in the kitchen; I promise we won't bother you. But ..." John's blond hair was half gray; his skin was faintly wrinkled and very dry—"it probably isn't a good idea to mention it to DeLys."

"I won't," I said. "I promise. By the time she's back, I'll be gone anyway."

"I meant in a letter, or something. But believe me," he said, "I only pick up nice men. Or boys. There won't be any trouble."

And later, on the cot bed in the front room of the tiny two-room Anaphiotika house, set into the mountain behind the Acropolis, I went to sleep.

In 'Stamboul, just off Istiqlal, John had had a sumptuous third-floor apartment, full of copper coffee tables, towering plants, rich rugs and hangings. When I'd been staying at the Youth Hostel, one afternoon he'd fed me a wonderful high tea at his place that had kept me going for two days. A pocketful of the leftovers, in a cloth napkin, had—an hour later—even made dinner for timid, towering Jerry.

I woke to whispered Greek, the lock, and two more Greek voices. One laughed as though he were coughing. *Shhh*ing them,

John herded two sailors, in their whites, through the room. The squat one halted in the door to the kitchen (in which was De-Lys's bed that John used), to paw the hanging back. He had a beer bottle in one hand. He laughed hoarsely once more. Then the tall one, towering him by almost two heads, shoved past, with John right after.

I turned over—then turned back. Frowning, I reached down and pulled my wallet out of the pocket of my jeans where I'd dropped them over the neck of my guitar case sticking from under the bed; it was also my suitcase. I sat, slipped the wallet behind the books on the shelf beside me. Then I lay back down.

John came back through the hanging. All he wore now was a blue shirt with yellow flowers. He squatted beside me, knees jackknifed up, to whisper: "There're two of them, I'm afraid. So if you wanted to entertain one—just to keep him busy, while I did the other one—really, I wouldn't mind. Actually, it would be a sort of favor."

"I'm sorry, John," I said. "Thanks. But I'm awfully tired."

"All right." He patted my forearm, where it was bent under my cheek. He smelled drunk. "But you can't say I didn't ask. And I certainly don't mind sharing—if you change your mind." Then he said: "I haven't spoken Demotiki with anyone in more than a year. I'm surprised I'm doing as well as I am." Chuckling, he was up and back into the kitchen, thin buttocks grinding below blue and yellow shirttails. He disappeared around the hanging, into the lighted kitchen, Greek, and laughter.

I drifted off—despite the noise . . .

Something bumped my arm. I opened my eyes. The little lamp in the corner was on. The squat sailor stood by my bed, leg pressed against my arm. Looking down at me, with one hand he joggled his crotch. Then he said, questioningly, "*Poosty-poosty* . . . ?"

I looked up. "Huh . . . ?"

"*Poosty-poosty!*" He rubbed with broad, Gypsy-dark fingers. A gold ring hugged deep into the middle one's flesh. Pointing at my face with his other hand, he began to thumb open the buttons around his lap-flap. Once he reached over to squeeze my backside. Hard, too.

"Aw, hey . . . !" I pushed up. "No . . . No . . . !" I made

dismissive gestures. "I don't want to. *Dthen thello Phevge! Phe-vge!"* (I don't want to! Go away! Go away!)

"Ne!" Then he repeated, *"Poosty-poosty,"* emphatically.

The flap fell from black groin hair, that, I swear, went half-way up his belly. His penis swung up, two-thirds the length of mine, but half again as thick. His nails were worn short from labor, and you could tell his palms and the insides of his fingers were rock rough.

"Hey, come *on!"* I pulled back and tried to sit up. "Cut it out, will you? *Dthen thello na kanome parea!"* (I don't want to mess around with you!)

But he grabbed the back of my head to pull my face toward his groin—hard enough to hurt my neck. For a moment, I figured maybe I should go along, so he wouldn't hurt me more. I opened my mouth to take him—and he pushed in. I tasted the bitter sharpness of the cologne he'd doused himself with—and cologne on a dick is my least favorite taste in the world. Under it was the sweat of someone who'd been drinking steadily at least two days. While he clawed into the back of my neck, I thought: This is stupid. I tried to pry my head from under his hand and push him out with my tongue. And thought I'd done it; but he'd just moved fast—across the bed, on one knee.

It was a hot night. I hadn't been sleeping with any covers.

He grabbed my underpants and, when I tried to dodge away, ripped them down my legs.

"Hey—!" I squirmed around, trying to pull them back up.

But he pushed me, hard, down on the bed. With a knee on one buttock and leaning full on my shoulders, he shouted into the other room—while I managed to lift myself (and him) up first on one elbow, then on the other.

I was about to try and twist him off, so I didn't see the tall one come through; but suddenly he loomed, to grab my arms and yank both, by my wrists, forward. I went off my elbows and down. The sailor on top began to finger between my buttocks. "Ow!" I said. *"Ow—stop . . . ! Pauete!"* That made the sailor holding my arms laugh—because it was both formal and plural; and it probably struck him as a funny time for me to be asking him formally to stop.

The tall one let go one wrist and made as if to sock me in

the face. He had immense hands. And when he did it, his knuckles looked like they were coming at me hard. I jerked my head aside, squeezed my eyes, and said, *"Ahhh . . . !"*

But nothing connected—it was only a feint. Still, I hit my jaw on the bed's iron rim.

When I opened my eyes, the tall one grinned and said: "Ha-*ha*!"—then shook one finger, in a slow warning. Still holding my wrist with one hand, he moved to the right, grabbed my leg just above the knee, and yanked it aside.

The one on top got himself in, then. Holding both my shoulders, he pushed, mumbling in Greek.

The tall one moved back to take my free wrist again and squatted there, his face very close. He kind of smiled, curious. His breath smelled like Sen-sen. Or chewing gum. He had very black hair (his white cap was still on), hazel eyes, and tawny skin. (By his knee, the other's cap had fallen on the rug.) Cajolingly, he began to say, now in Greek, now in English: "You like . . . ! You like . . . ! *Su aresi . . . !* Good boy . . . ! *Su aresi . . . !* You like . . . !"

I grunted. "I *don't* like. It *hurts*, you asshole . . . !"

This pharmacologist, who'd first fucked me, told me that if I pushed out as if I were taking a shit, it wouldn't sting.

But not this time.

The one on me bit my shoulder and, panting, came. The one kneeling glanced up at him, then sighed too, let go, stood, and grunted down at me, as if to say, "See, it wasn't *that* bad . . . ?"

The one behind got off the bed and stood, pushing himself back into his uniform. Once he said to me, in English: "Good! See? You like!" like the tall one had. He picked up his cap from the floor—and (he'd missed two buttons on his lap) pulled it carefully over his head, then pushed one side back up to get the right angle.

I sucked my teeth at him and tried to look disgusted. Frankly, though, I was scared to death.

In Greek the squat one said: *You want him now? I'll hold him for you—*

The tall one said: *You jerk-off! Let's just get out of here!*

The squat one bent down again, picked up my jeans, and began to finger through the pockets.

Then the tall one drew back his hand with the same feint he'd used on me: *Come on! Forget that, jerk-off! Let's get out of here, I told you!*

The squat one threw my jeans back down, and they went through the kitchen hanging. There was a back door, but I don't remember if I heard it or not.

I lay on the bed a minute, without moving, propped up on one elbow. Then I reached back between my buttocks. When I looked at my fingers, there were little pads of blood on two fingertips. I got up and went to the stall toilet in the corner—

Urine covered the stone floor. On DeLys's blue rug, it had darkened an area three times the size of someone's head. John must have sent one of them in to use the toilet while I was still sleeping—before the first guy woke me.

I reached inside, holding the jamb with one hand, and got some paper from the almost empty roll. Still standing, I wiped myself, but with a blotting motion. It hurt too much to rub. When I looked at the yellow paper, there was a red smear, with some drops running from it, and slime on one side. My rectum stung like hell.

I felt like I had to take a crap in the worst way; but the other thing the pharmacologist had said was to wait at least half an hour before you did that.

When I went back to the bed, I saw the light in the kitchen had been turned out. As I sat down, gingerly, on the edge, on one cheek more than the other, from the dark behind the hanging, John asked: "Are you all right in there?" He sounded plaintive. For a moment I wondered if he was tied up or something.

I called back: "I think so." Then: "Yeah, I'm okay."

A moment later: "Did they take anything from you?"

I pulled my jeans back across the floor toward the bed with my foot. Then I looked at the bookshelf. Between fat volumes by Mann and Michener was a much read Dell paperback of Vonnegut's *Cat's Cradle*, a quarto hardcover of Daisy Ashford's *The Young Visitors*, a chapbook of poems by Joyce Johnson, and Heidi's copy of *L'Ecume de jour*, which every few hours I'd taken out to struggle through another paragraph of Vian's playful French.

"No," I said. "My wallet's safe."

At the very end were the paperbacks of my own few novels—and the typewritten sheaf of my wife's poems, sticking up between two of them. Wherever I stayed, I'd always put them on a shelf so I could see them, to make me feel better. They were the books I'd stuck my wallet behind.

"Good," John said. Twenty seconds later, he said: "I don't think they'll come back." And, a few seconds on: "Goodnight."

After a minute, I got up again, went to the kitchen door, and switched off the lamp. I didn't look behind the hanging. (The big light, still out, you had to stand in the middle of the room to reach up and turn on.) But John wasn't asking for help. So I went back and lay down.

I tried to think of all the reasons I hadn't called out. They might have beat me up, or hurt me more than they had. What would neighbors—or the police—have thought, coming in and finding me like that? Or thought of John? I might have gotten DeLys in trouble with Costas, from whom she rented the house. Or I might have gotten Costas in trouble with the police: he was a nice guy—a Greek law student at Harvard, home for spring break, who probably wasn't supposed to be renting his house out to foreigners anyway. But, lying there, I couldn't really be sure if any of those thoughts had been in my mind while it had been happening.

Again, I pushed out like I was trying to shit.

The stinging was just as painful. Then a muscle in back of my left thigh cramped sharply enough to make me cry out.

Three

Oh, man is a god when he dreams, a beggar when he thinks; and when inspiration is gone, he stands, like a worthless son whom his father has driven out of the house, and stares at the miserable pense that pity has given him for the road.

—FREDRICH HÖLDERLIN, *Hyperion*

At five-thirty, since neither of us was asleep, John got up to make coffee. The sun came sideways through the shutters. Birds chirped. John kept touching a bruise on his cheek with three fingers pressed together. "Now they were not nice boys at all!"

In his light blue robe with the navy piping, he shook out yellow
papers of grounds, of sugar, into the long-handled pot on the
Petrogaz ring. "Why I brought home two, I'll *never* know! You'd
think I hadn't done this before. But when I first met them, they
were both so sweet." He turned on the water in the gray stone
sink. "One of them hit me." He turned it off again. From the
shelf he took down a jar of marmalade, examined the green
and gold label, shook his head, then put it back. Again he
touched his cheek. "Scared me to *death!* Once he hit me, though,
I decided I'd just let the two of them do anything they wanted."
He fingered his bruise again. "He took money from me, too,"
he said, confidingly. "I don't like it when a boy takes money
from me. I don't mind giving a boy a few drachma, a few lira,
especially if he's in the army—or the navy. Nobody could be
expected to live off what they pay you there. That's why the
entire Greek army hustles." He touched the bruise again. "You
know, you really didn't have to clean the piss up off the toilet
floor this morning." The near corner of the bed with its ivory
crocheted cover, the ancient refrigerator with the circular cool-
ing unit on top, and the blue table with the three blue chairs
with flowers decaled on their backs made a kind of crowded
triangle on the red tile. "I would have done it myself if you'd
left it. That was just rudeness. Believe me, they weren't *that*
drunk! You know?" Moving about on bony feet, he pulled out
first one chair, then the other. "I really thought, because you
were colored, they weren't going to bother you and isn't *that*"—
he went on, as though it were the same sentence—"the dumbest
thing I could possibly have said this morning! But that's what
I thought. Come, sit down now. And have some coffee."

I stepped away from the doorway where, just inside the
hanging, I'd been leaning against the jamb. I'd put all my
clothes on, including my shoes. For all the dawn sunlight, the
house was still nippy.

"But when that boy struck me—who'd been just as sweet
as he could be, an hour ago—the chunky one . . . ?" Pouring
little cups of coffee like liquid night from the brass pot, John
took up his apologia again. "A perfectly dreadful child, he
turned out to be. The other, I thought—the tall one—was quite
nice, though. Basically. I don't think he would have done any-

thing, if his friend hadn't put him up to it. But I was as scared as I've ever been before in my life! I'm awfully glad somebody else was here. Not that it did much good."

Four

This vast irregular sheet of water, which rushes by without respite, rolls all colors toward nothingness. See how dim it all is.

—PAUL VALÉRY, *Eupalinos, or The Architect*

I got my ticket for London that morning. When the man behind the brass bars said I'd be taking the Orient Express, it was kind of exciting. There'd be no problem, he explained, my stopping off in Munich.

Back up in Anaphiotika, I came in to find an ecstatic John: "Really, I *don't* carry on like this when I'm at home. But you know, in 'Stamboul, because, I guess, it's part of the culture— every father of a teenaged son is busy negotiating which of his wealthiest friends is going to get his boy's bum—you just don't find it running around in the street, the way you do here. You'd think, after last night, I wouldn't be back in business for at least a fortnight. But it's like getting up on the horse as soon as you fall off: here, it's not even one o'clock in the afternoon, and I've already had three—and three very nice ones, at that!"

I laughed. "Once, about six or seven weeks ago, John, I had three before nine o'clock in the morning."

"With your looks and at your age—? I just bet you've had a bloody dozen since you left here!"

Actually, it had only been two. But I thought I'd better not say anything to John, in case his own conquests were more imaginary than real—to make him feel better about last night. "Are you doing anything this evening?" I asked. "Some friends of mine and I are going to go out."

"Out to do what sort of thing?"

"Go to a concert—sort of."

John shook his head and his hands. "I'm afraid every free moment I have is booked. I've got half a dozen moviehouses to explore. I need to make an official inspection of at least eight public loos. There are parts of several parks, here and uptown,

I haven't come anywhere near examining. No—I'm afraid my social calendar is filled to overflowing. But it was sweet of you to ask."

I laughed, relieved. Five minutes before, I'd decided not to invite him. He was so flamboyant, I could see him causing something of a problem with the others.

I'd agreed to meet Trevor at sunset behind the wire-mesh fence along the top of the Theater of Dionysus—the big outdoor theater on the side of the Acropolis hill. Stravinsky was conducting his farewell concert that night. Lots of students and poor foreigners would gather there. You couldn't see very well, but the famous acoustics of the Greek amphitheater easily lived up to their reputation.

Earlier that month, I'd gone from being twenty-three to twenty-four; which meant Trevor had gone from being a towheaded English guitar player three years younger than I to a towheaded English guitar player four years younger. It seemed to make a difference.

The sky out toward Piraeus was purple, flooded through near the horizon with layered orange. On good days you're supposed to be able to see the sea from the Acropolis's rim. But here, half a dozen yards below it, the waters beyond Piraeus were only a pervading memory.

The white lights down on the stage told me for the first time that the platform there was gray-painted wood. During full daylight, just glancing at it when I'd passed, I'd always assumed it was rock. About ten of the orchestra had come out to take their chairs. Sloping down from the fence, the tiers of stone seats were filling. In silhouette, scattered before me, were hundreds of Athenian heads.

Trevor let go of the hatched wire and glanced back. In its canvas case beside him, his guitar leaned against the metal web. Trevor wore two denim jackets, one over the other—though it was a pleasantly warm evening. In the quarter light, his cornsilk mop made his face look smaller, his gray eyes larger. "Hello," he said. "It's his last concert, tonight. I didn't know that."

"Whose?" I asked. "Stravinsky's?"

"That's right. He's retiring. I knew he was conducting, but I didn't know that this was it."

"I think I read something about it."

"The Swiss Bitch is supposed to come by, too. I hope she gets here before they start. I mean, you either hear him tonight or you don't. It's really quite special."

The Swiss Bitch was Trevor's nickname for Cosima; I never saw anything particularly bitchy about her. I don't think Trevor did either, but something about the euphony had caught him. And the first time he'd referred to her as that, Heidi, who was Cosima's best friend, had burst out laughing at the kafeneon table, so that it almost sounded as if she approved. Trevor had kept it up. "Cosima told me you were staying up at DeLys's with some English poofter."

"John?" I asked. "I don't know anything for sure about his sexual preferences—but he's really quite a nice guy." Although Trevor knew perfectly well I was queer, I liked generating ambiguity about anyone else who came up.

"God," Trevor said, "almost all DeLys's friends are faggots! I can't stand them—most of them"—which I guess was for my benefit—"myself. I wonder why that is, with some women?"

Then, behind me, Cosima said: "Hello, you lot."

We moved aside, and Cosima stepped up between us to gaze through the wire. "I think they're about to start. Is that the whole orchestra?—my, there're a lot of them tonight." Cosima was twenty-six and had black hair. She wore a gray jacket with a black fur collar. And a gray skirt. Now she said: "Well, how have you been, Trevor?"

"All right." He pretended to pay attention to something down on the platform.

A few feet away from us, two Greek boys wore short-sleeved shirts. One, with his fingers hooked in the wire above his head, swung now this way, now that, his shirt wholly open and out of his slacks, blowing back from his stomach.

I had on my once-white wool island jacket—too warm for the evening. But we internationals—like the Paris clochards, in their two and three overcoats even in summer—seemed to wear as much of our clothing as we could tolerate, always ready to be asked over, to stay for a few days, or at least to spend the night. That way, I suppose, we'd have to go back for as few remaining things as possible.

On the other side of us, half a dozen schoolgirls in plaid uniforms kept close together, to giggle and whisper when another arrived.

"This is his last time conducting," Cosima said.

"So I read and so Trevor told me. Robert Craft is conducting the first half of the concert."

"Who's Robert Craft?" Trevor asked.

Cosima shrugged—a large, theatrical shrug. Often that's how she dealt with Trevor.

"He's sort of a Stravinsky person," I said. "He writes a lot about him; and he did a wonderful recording of Anton Webern's complete works—about five or six years back."

"Who's Webern?" Trevor asked.

Cosima laughed. "Have you ever heard him conduct before? Stravinsky, I mean?"

"Yes," I said. "Once, one summer when I was about fourteen—back in the States. It was at a place called Tanglewood. There's a big tent there, and the orchestra plays under it. They did two programs that afternoon. Carl Orff had written some new music for *A Midsummer Night's Dream*—to replace the old Mendelssohn stuff everybody knows, I guess. They did the whole play. And a comedian I used to see on television a lot named Red Buttons played Puck—even though he was getting pretty old. The orchestra did the music, which was all in unison, with lots of gongs and drums. Then they took the whole stage down. A chorus came out. And Stravinsky conducted the premiere of a piece he'd just written, *Cantium Sanctum.* It was very atonal. The audience wasn't very appreciative; when people left the music tent, there was a lot of snickering. But I liked it more than the Orff." I stood on tip-toe because some of the paying audience just entering—about twelve feet in front of us—hadn't sat yet. "Tonight Craft is going to conduct *The Firebird.* Then Stravinsky's going to do *The Rite of Spring.* It's an awfully conservative performance for him to go out on. But . . ." I shrugged. I'd read the whole concert program two days ago. I wasn't sure why I hadn't wanted to tell Trevor.

"*Mmm,*" Cosima said.

Trevor said: "You're going to be leaving in a couple of days. I bet, after you've gone, that English fellow, John, would let me stay up at DeLys's—if I went there and asked him. Nicely, I mean. He's supposed to like boys. And, after all, DeLys is my friend, too."

"I don't know," I said. "I'd stay away from him if I were you, Trevor. What are you going to do if he gets after your bum?"

"I'd beat the shit out of him, if he tried anything!" Trevor pulled himself up, to turn from the fence.

"But why would you go up there if you didn't want him to try?" I asked. "Besides, people will *think* you wanted him to try. If you went up there, knowing the sort of fellow he is, if something happened, no one would ever believe you hadn't egged him on to it. I certainly wouldn't believe it."

A couple of times, when we'd hitched to Istanbul together, Jerry's fear of John and anything else queer (except me) had annoyed me—like the afternoon he'd flatly refused to go to see John for tea in Turkey. But Trevor's "I'll beat you to a pulp if you touch me, but aren't you supposed to like me anyway because I'm cute?" (and often with a "Can you spare a hundred drachma while you're at it?"), and all with perfect Dartington manners when he chose to drag them out, actually made me mad. John had had a tough enough time; I wanted to keep Trevor out of his hair.

I waited for Trevor to say something back. But my own position as a self-confessed queer, married, and with an occasional girlfriend, made Trevor, if not most of my friends, not know what to say to me at all. I liked that.

Cosima said, "Oh! They're starting . . . !"

Applause swelled as, in his black tails, Craft walked out across the platform in front of the orchestra.

The Firebird, The Rite of Spring—they're pieces you've heard so many times you'd think they couldn't be interesting anymore. But precisely that music, when it's done well, is so embarrassingly moving. The Athenians certainly applauded enough.

Listening, however, I remembered when Trevor had gotten a recording of the Ninth Symphony. (Jerry hadn't yet gone back to Kentucky.) Above the orchestral photograph, the Deutsche Grammophon label was brutal yellow. Cardboard on European albums is thinner than on American albums. And Trevor had held this one in both hands, in front of his jeans. Both the knees were torn. The sun made his hair look like some white plastic fiber pushed back from his soap-white forehead, reddened here and there by a pimple. I stood a step below him on Mnisicleou Street, while he said: "The Swiss Bitch told me all of us could come up to her place tonight and hear it. I hope you and Heidi can make it."

"All of us" turned out to be: my recent roommates, John (who was from London) and Ron (who was from New Jersey); and [English] John (the Cockney electrical engineer); and Heidi (we'd locked Pharaoh in her room, but he barked enough while we were going down the stairs that, in her wire-rimmed glasses and green apron, Kyria Kokinou came out and started arguing that the dog was not healthy for the children in the apartment upstairs—which, finally, we just had to walk away from; with Kyria Kokinou, sometimes you had to do that); and the tall redheaded English woman (who had been first Ron's, then John's, girlfriend); and DeLys (who was from New Orleans and whose gold hair was as striking, in its way, as Trevor's); and Gay (the American woman who played Joan Baez and Leonard Cohen songs at the 'O kai 'E); and Jane (Gay's tense, unhappy, mid-Western traveling companion); and Jerry (who, with his slightly stooped shoulders, was about twice as tall as anyone else, and had huge hands and feet like some German shepherd puppy); and sports-jacketed law student Costas (DeLys's landlord, who kept laughing and saying, "Well, we'll squeeze ... I'm sure we can think of something ... there's always a way, now ..."); and me.

"Oh, my God ... !" Cosima said, at the head of the stairs. "I don't think we'll all *fit* ... ?"

In a kind of attic tower, Cosima's single room had a desk and a bed in it, with a couple of travel posters on the walls— one from Israel, one from North Africa. It wasn't any larger, though, than the chicken-coop arrangement I'd left on the roof of Voltetsiou Street; or, indeed, than Heidi's at Kyria Kokinou's, which I'd left it for (though Heidi's room had a shower). I wondered what Trevor had been thinking when he'd invited us. The phonograph was one someone's ten-year-old sister might have gotten for her birthday: a square box with a pink cover that swung up from a yellow base with dirty corners, on which the table turned.

"I'm going to put it out here in the hall," Cosima said, "so as many people can hear as possible."

We sat on the steps, most of us. DeLys, [English] John, and Heidi rested their heads against the gray, unpainted wall-boards. In his black sneakers and white jeans, all scrunched up on the step above Jane, Jerry took his pink-framed glasses off to listen, his eyes closed, his head to the side. (Probably he was taller than the tall sailor.) At the bottom, hands in his jacket pockets, Costas lounged against the newel. The orange light from Cosima's open door fell down among us. A window high in the stairwell wall showed a few raindrops outside on the little panes.

We were very quiet.

Cosima started the record.

The opening intervals of the Ninth dropped through the stairwell—from the scratchy speaker. Where I sat, the step above digging into my hip, my back pressed against the wall, I had one hand on Heidi's knee; she put one hand on mine.

After the second movement, while Cosima turned the record over, DeLys started coughing. Costas pulled out a handkerchief and handed it up to her—but she waved it away.

"Oh, it's clean," Costas said, laughing. "Don't worry."

"I *know* it's clean!" DeLys coughed again, the back of one hand against her mouth, the fingers in a loose fist that grabbed after something with each head-lowering hack. "That's not it at all and you know it . . . !" She coughed some more.

Then Cosima played the adagio.

When the choral opening of the "Ode to Joy" finished and the baritone solo began, Heidi squeezed my hand and I thought of Beethoven, arthritic, deaf, and thinking his work a failure after he'd finished conducting the Ninth's premiere, because he'd heard nothing behind him. Then the soprano stepped down to take him by the arm and turn him to see the standing Viennese, clapping madly—

Without any noise, I started to cry, while, there behind the fence, we listened with a silent avidity—to *The Rite of Spring*.

—but by the end of the Ninth, for our several reasons, all of us had been moved:

Jammed together on Cosima's steps, the physical discomfort and social preposterousness of the situation had made us listen with intense attention. A number of us in that stairway had been wet-eyed.

We'd said, "Goodnight," and "Thank you," and "*Ciao*," to Cosima, quietly. Then, our hands against the narrow stairwell walls, some of us, we'd filed down to the street, now and again glancing back to smile. In the doorway at the stairs' head, holding the album cover, Trevor had stood, raggedy-kneed. Just behind his shoulder, in her long skirt, Cosima had watched us.

Outside, it had rained enough to slick the sidewalk under the corner lamp. Heidi and I had walked back to the bottom of Mnisicleou . . .

Between the standing Athenians, clapping madly, I could see, down on the platform, someone hand Stravinsky another pink and yellow bouquet. In his black tails, with his white tie, bald head, and glasses, he held two in his arms already. Three more lay on the gray wood beside him.

Craft came out again to take Stravinsky's arm and lead him off. Once he shifted the flowers and waved at the audience.

On the other side of Cosima, the Greek boy closed two buttons of his shirt. With his friends, he turned to leave the fence—the school girl beside me, whispering and worried that they were already late, had hurried off as soon as the applause began.

Applause swelled again. I said, softly, in Cosima's ear: "There. Now his career as a conductor is finished. It's over. Like that."

Her face near the wire, black fur moving in the wind that, with the later hour, had started, Cosima nodded.

Five

To construct oneself, to know oneself—are these two distinct acts or not?

—Paul Valéry, *Eupalinos, or The Architect*

A good number of people were on the platform when I got there. I had my guitar case—and a shopping bag. At the bottom of the bag was Heidi's Vian. Then my underwear and my balled-up suit. On the top were my novels. Two had actually been published while I was here—though I'd written them before. My wife had sent me a single copy of each, as they came out. I'd figured to reread the newest one on the train—for more typographical mistakes; or for stylistic changes I might want to make. And maybe reread the typescript of her poems. It was as sunny as it had been on the Piraeus docks when I'd seen Heidi off to Aegina. Shabby-coated lottery vendors ambled about. Ticket streamers tentacled their sticks. A cart rolled by, selling milk-pudding and spinach pie and warm Orangata, big wheels grumbling and squeaking. Sailors and soldiers stood in groups, talking together, among the civilian passengers.

When I saw him—the tall one—with four others in their whites, my heart thudded hard enough to hurt my throat. From the surprise, the back of my neck grew wet. I swallowed a few times—and tried to get my breath back. But—no!—I wasn't going to go up to the other end of the platform. I wasn't going to let the son of a bitch run me all around the train station. I took a deep breath, turned, and looked toward the empty tracks.

But I hoped the train would hurry up.

Not that he could do anything here, with all these people.

The third time I glanced at him, he was looking at me—smiling. He was smiling!

Another surge of fear; but it wasn't as big as the terror at my initial recognition.

Next time I caught him looking, I didn't look away.

So he raised his hand—and waved: that little "go away" gesture that, in Greek, means "come over here."

When I frowned, he broke from his group to lope toward me.

He came up with a burst of Greek: *"Kalimera sas! Ti kanis? Kalla?"* (Hello, you! How you doing? All right?)

"Kalimera," I said, dry as a phrase book.

But with his big (nervous? Probably, but I didn't catch it then) smile, he rattled on. In front of me, the creaseless white of his uniform was as blinding as a tombstone at noon; he towered over me by a head and a half. Now, with a scowl, he explained: *"... Dthen eine philos mou ... Dthen eine kalos, to peidi ..."* He isn't a friend of mine ... he's no good, that fellow ... Where're you going? It's beautiful today ... Yes? (*"Orea simera ... Ne?"*) You all right? He's crazy, that guy. He just gets everybody in trouble. Me, I don't do things like that. I don't like him. I go out with him, I always get in trouble—like with you and your friend, up there, that night. That wasn't any good. You're taking the train today? Where're you going? You're Negro, aren't you? (*"Mavros, esis?"*) You like it here, in Greece? It's a beautiful country, isn't it? You had a good time? How long have you been here?

I didn't want to tell him where I was going; so I mimed ignorance at half his questions, wondering just what part he thought *he'd* played in the night before last.

I was surprised, though I wasn't scared anymore. At all. Or, really, even that angry. Suddenly, for a demonic joke, I began to ask him lots of questions, fast: What was his name? (*"Petros, ego."* Peter, that's me.) Where was he going? (*"Sto 'Saloniki."* To Thessalonika.) Where was he from? (Some little mountain town I'd never heard of before.) Did he like the Navy? (With wavering hand, *"Etsi-getsi."* So-so.) He answered them all quite seriously, the grin gone and—I guess—a slightly bewildered look, hanging above me, in its place.

Finally, though, he dropped a hand on my shoulder and bent to me. He'd come over to me, he explained, because he had something to show me. *No, no—it's all right. Let me show it to you. Here.* He went digging in his back pocket—for a moment I thought he was going to pull out his wallet to show me pictures. But when his hand came back around, he was holding a knife. *No, don't be afraid. Don't be afraid—I just want to show you something.* I pulled back, but, by the shoulder, he forced me forward—still smiling. *Here,* he said. *Here—go on. You take it. Go ahead. Take it. Hold it.* While he held the knife in his amazingly large hand, I saw the nails on his big fingers were clean, evenly clipped, with ivory scimitars over the crowns—under clear polish.

Like many Greek men, he wore his little nail half an inch or more long.

I hadn't noticed any of that, the night at DeLys's.

I took the closed knife from him and thought: Greek sailors don't usually have manicures. Briefly I wondered if he was queer himself.

He said: *"Orea eine . . . ?"* (Beautiful, isn't it . . . ?) He didn't make any other gesture to touch it but, with motions of two fingers together and the odd word, told me to open it up. *It isn't very expensive. It's cheap—but it's a pretty knife. Good. Strong. You like it? It's nice, yes? Come on, open it up. A good knife. That button there—you push it up. To open it. Yes. Come on.*

I pushed the button up, and the blade jumped out, a sliver of light, of metal, of sky.

Here! He laughed. *It's a good knife, yes?*

I nodded—that is, moved my head to the side, the Greek gesture for Yes. *"Ne,"* I said. *"Kallos to eine."* (Yes. It's a good one.)

He said in Greek: *You want this knife? You like it? Go on, take it. For you. You keep it. You like it, yes? I give it to you. For a present. For a present. Maybe you need it, sometimes. It's a good knife.*

"Yati . . . ?" I asked. Why are you giving this to me?

You want to kill me now. He gave a sideways nod, then added a chuckle. *Cut something of mine off, I bet. I wouldn't blame you.*

"No," I said. I shook my head (or rather, raised it in negation). *"Ochi."* I told him, *You take it.* I pressed the button. But it didn't close.

He took it from me now. There was another pressure point you had to thumb to make the blade slip in. With his big, manicured fingers, he thumbed it. The metal flicked into the silver and tortoise shell handle. Like that. *You sure? You don't want it?*

I said: *"Ochi—efharisto. Ochi."* (No—thank you. No.)

He put it in his back pocket again, and regarded me a little strangely, blinking his green-gray eyes in the sun. Then he said: *"Philli, akomi—emis?"* (We're friends, now—us?)

"Okay," I said, in English. "Just forget it."

"Esis. Ego. O-kay!" he repeated. *You. Me.* "O-kay. You like . . . I like . . ." With a flipped finger, he indicated him and me. "O-kay. Friend: me, you." He laughed once more, clapped me on

the shoulder, then turned to go back to the others. As he walked away, knife and wallet were outlined on one white buttock.

How, I wondered, were we supposed to be friends?

The other sailors were laughing—I'm sure about something else.

I watched them, wondering if I could see some effeminacy in any of their movements—queer sailors, camping it up on the station platform. Him . . . maybe. But not the others.

Just once more he caught me looking and grinned again—before the train came.

When we pulled from the station, his group was still talking out on the platform—so he wasn't on my train. I was glad about that.

That night, in my couchete, while we hurtled between Switzerland and Italy, in the dark compartment I thought about the two sailors; and when my body told me what I was about to do, I had some troubled minutes, when it was too easy to imagine the armchair psychiatrists, over their morning yogurt and rolls at the white metal tables in front of American Express, explaining to me (in three languages) how, on some level, I had liked it, that—somehow—I must have wanted it.

While I masturbated, I thought about the thick, rough hands on the squat one, but grown now to the size of the tall one's; and the tall one's hazel eyes and smile—but deprived of the Sen-sen scent; and about sucking the squat one's cock, with all its black hair—except that, for the alcoholic sweat and cologne, I substituted the slight work-salt of a stocky good-humored housepainter I'd had on the first day I'd got to Athens.

Once I tried to use the knife blade, as he'd held it, full of sky: Nothing happened with it.

At all.

But I used my waking up with the sailor beside me, his leg against my arm, his hand between his legs. I did it first with fear, then with a committed anger, determined to take something from them, to retrieve some pleasure from what, otherwise, had been just painful, just ugly.

But if I hadn't—I realized, once I'd finished, drifting in the rumbling, rocking train—then, alone with it, unable to talk of it, even with John or Heidi, I simply would have found it too bleak. I'd have been defeated by it—and, more, would have remained defeated. That had been the only way to reseize my imagination, let go of the stinging fear, and use what I could of both to heal.

Six

Unknown and alone, I have returned to wander through my native country, which lies about me like a vast graveyard . . .

—FRIEDRICH HÖLDERLIN, *Hyperion*

In London one night beside a neon-striped eating place, I'd stood outside plate glass, a triangle of blue sliding down at my eye, listening to a record on the jukebox inside, by a group that sang, in the most astonishing antiphony, about "Monday, Monday . . ."—as rich with pop possibilities as new music could be.

In France, for a day, I'd hitched north toward the Luxembourg airport through a stony landscape—sided with crumbling white walls, shuttered windows and planked-up doors that recalled so many of that country's warnings, from so many of its writers, about the meanness and a-sensuality of its strict, strict provinces.

And, in New York, three weeks later, I was sitting at the foot of my bed, when, after some argument that had to do with neither money nor sex, my wife walked in and slapped me, about as hard as I'd ever been hit, across the face—the only time either one of us ever struck the other. A week later, with her poems and the red clay casserole, she moved into another apartment, down on Henry Street. Which left me nothing but to plunge into the ending of the novel I'd been working on last fall and spring, full of Greece—but with no Heidi or Pharaoh, no Cosima or DeLys, no Trevor or Costas, no Jerry or [Turkish] John.

Two weeks after that I got a letter from Heidi—which surprised me: I hadn't written her at all. I sat on the bed in the back of my empty Lower East Side flat to read its more-than-dozen pages. The light through the window-gate made lozenges over the rumpled linen.

The return address on Heidi's letter was Munich, which was where her family lived. Its many beige sheets explained how she was with them now, how glad she'd been to see her mother once she'd arrived—and how the problems she'd sometimes cried to me about having with her father seemed, briefly, in abeyance. Had I gotten to the Deutsches Museum? (I had. And it had been quite as wonderful as she'd told me. But she seemed to think I'd probably missed it.) She hoped things were going well between me and my wife.

Then, in its last pages, she wrote:

Before I left Greece, I killed my poor Pharaoh—whom I loved more than anything else in the world. Even more than, for that little time, I loved you. But there was no one I could give him to. The Greeks don't keep pets. And the quarantine laws are impossible—they would have put him in kennel for six months; and that costs lots of money. Besides, he was just a puppy, and after six months more he wouldn't even have known me. But the day before I did it, I saw a dog—all broken up and bloody, with one leg and one eye entirely gone, and his innards—Oh, I don't want to describe it to you! But he was alive, though barely, in the garbage behind Kyria Kokinou's, because of what some boys had done to him. He was going to die. And I knew if I just let Pharaoh go, with the stones and the glass in the meat, and the Greek boys, he would die too. That's when I cried.

Since I was leaving Greece in two days, what I did was take my poor, beautiful Pharaoh out in the blue rowboat that David said I could use, with a rope, one end of which I'd already tied around a big rock (about eighteen kilos). I was in my bathing suit—as though we were going for a swim, back on Aegina. And while he looked up at me, with his trusting eyes—which, because you are such a careful writer, you would say was a cliché, but I could really look into those swimming, swirling eyes and see he did trust me, because I fed him good food every day from the market and took him for his walks in the morning and at night so he could make his shits and his pee-pees, and I had protected him all winter and spring from those horrid Greeks. I tied the rope around his neck, the knot very tight, so it wouldn't come loose. Then we wrestled together in the boat and I hugged him and he licked me, and I threw him over the side. He swam around the boat, as he used to when I'd take him out in the skiff on Aegina, with most of the rope floating in curves, back and forth, snaking to the gunwale, and back over. Once he climbed in again—and got me all wet, shaking. Then he jumped out, to swim some more.

He just loved to swim. And while he was swimming, sometimes he glanced at me. Or off at a sea bird.

When he looked away, I threw the rock over.

The splash wet me to my waist. Over the time of a breath, in and out, while the boat rocked up and down, all the curves in the rope disappeared.

And still paddling, Pharaoh jerked to the side—and went under.

There were ripples, moving in to and out from the boat.

There were the obligatory gulls—one swooped close enough to startle me, making me sit back on the seat. Then it flew away.

The paper mill squatted in its smelly haze across the harbor.

But it was over.

Like that.

I waited ten minutes.

I'd thought to sit there perhaps an hour or so, being alone with myself, with the water, with what I'd done—just thinking. But after ten minutes—because of the gull, I think—I realized I'd done it, and I rowed back to the Pasilimani dock.

Although I cried when I saw the poor dog out behind the house, I didn't cry with Pharaoh. I'm really surprised about that—about how little I felt. I suppose I didn't feel worse than any other murderer who has to do things like that daily for a living—a highway bandit; a state executioner. I wonder why that is?

Cosima thought I was just a terrible person, and kept saying that there must have been something else I could have done.

But there wasn't. And I hope she comes to realize that. I hope you realize it too.

I used to say the Greeks were barbarians, and you would laugh at me and tell me that people's believing they could deal with the world in such general terms was what made it so awful. And I would laugh at you back. But now I know that I am the barbarian. Not the Greeks who are too hungry to understand why anyone would keep a dog. Not the Germans who managed to kill so many, many Jews with their beautiful languages, Yiddish and Hebrew, and who, still, someday, I hope will let me into their country to study. Not the southern whites like Jerry and DeLys who lynch and burn Negroes like you. Not the

*Negroes like you who are ignorant and lazy and oversexed and danger-
ous to white women like me.*

Me—and not the Others, at all: not you, not them.

Me.

*I loved my Pharaoh so much. He's gone. My memories of him are
beautiful, though.*

*I hope someday you will write something about him. And about
me—even though you have to say terrible things of me for what I did.
And because of how little I felt when I did it. But, then, you haven't
written me at all. Maybe you'll just forget us both.*

That was her only letter.

*—Amherst
September 1990*

Signing Yourself:
An Afterword

Charles H. Rowell

I think I know something about the American masculinity which most men of my generation do not know because they have not been menaced by it in the way I have been.

—JAMES BALDWIN

One minute you're a person, the next moment somebody starts treating you as if you were not. Often it happens just that way, just that suddenly. Particularly if you are a black man in America.

—JOHN EDGAR WIDEMAN

The authors of the narratives collected in *Shade* are men of African ancestry who were born between the 1930s and the 1970s on three different continents: North America (and the Caribbean), Africa, and South America. Some of them are migrants from their native lands to other regions. Others, especially those born in the United States, have remained at home where they resist, along with those from other countries, and fight oppression of various kinds, and in doing so affirm their dignity and assert their rights as citizens. Although the majority of the twenty-two writers in *Shade* are North Americans, these gay men do not constitute an ideological or aesthetic monolith; they are a symphony of voices from three different generations, dating back to the 1930s, the decade during which Charles Wright (USA) and Severo Sarduy (Cuba, 1936–1993) were born. The second generation—K. Anthony Appiah (Ghana), Samuel R. Delany (USA), Melvin Dixon (USA, 1950–1993), Jaime Manrique (Colombia)—was born during the 1940s and 1950s. James Earl Hardy, Randall Kenan, Darieck Scott, Reginald Shepherd—these North Americans are but four of the sixteen writers representing the third generation, those bold and courageous young men who not only publicly affirm their gayness but also posit it as an asset central to their creativity and their daily lives. This third generation will not compromise their humanity; they cannot live a lie about their sexuality. In their bold honesty about themselves, the writers in *Shade*, like James Baldwin and Bruce Nugent before them, risk much: their lives.

Black heterosexual communities, like their European American counterparts, neither embrace nor sanction open gay living. In fact, there are many blacks throughout the African Diaspora, and even in Africa itself, who contend that homosexuality is not indigenous to Africa and is, therefore, a non-African phenomenon, which black people should avoid and reject. Once you make public your gayness, then, the impulse of black communities is to attempt to repress your voice, to define your life as an abomination before God, and to cast you as a threat to the black family and the collective struggles of black people. You in turn discover that your family, your church—most of the institutions you revere—ostracize you. You cease to remain a human being in the eyes of individuals policing and controlling these institutions. To be black and gay in the United States is to live or act overtly in accordance with your sexual identity and suffer or enjoy the consequences; or to allow yourself to be forced into the shadows, onto the margins, or within some other site that renders you invisible, unseen, and unheard.

As if all of that is not enough, to be black, gay, and male in the United States is to suffer at once the same negative forces that white gays confront daily and to endure an additional burden: to refight, with the community where you would expect to find refuge and brotherhood, the same old battles of domination and exploitation which all black people—gays, lesbians, and heterosexuals—wage daily against racism. That is, the white gay community maintains and acts on the same racist ideologies that its heterosexist counterpart continues to construct. And at the center of their collective racist ideologies is their representation of the black male, heterosexual and gay, as object or fetish—what James Baldwin describes as "a kind of walking phallic symbol: which means that one pays, in one's personality, for the sexual insecurity of others."

No wonder then that even during these post-Civil Rights and post-Stonewall (1969) years we discover the black gay literary text being ignored, excluded or, at best, marginalized. Black writing communities in the United States are all too familiar with white editors who question whether their writing is "good enough." Take for example George Stambolian and Felice Picano.

In his Introduction to *Men on Men 4: Best New Gay Fiction* (1992), Picano reveals his own racism and paternalism, as well as that of Stambolian, the editor of the anthology series:

> *If African-American gays and Asian-American gays and Latino gays were now writing good enough fiction for him to present, George [Stambolian] insisted that was because of the explosive growth of the gay male culture in this country, reflected and even stimulated by the previous three volumes of* Men on Men. *He wondered if the new work would have been written without the strong example, or even the existence, of the corpus he'd presented and, professionally, helped codify.*

Self-aggrandizement indeed, as if there were no African American culture, gay and straight, out of which gay black writers create. The tokenism (or total exclusion of black writers altogether) is representative of white editors of gay anthologies. One has only to browse the table of contents of recent gay white anthologies—*The Faber Book of Short Fiction, Waves,* and the *Penguin Book of Short Fiction*—to discover the editors' impulse to exclude or marginalize black writers. Would gay black writers be nurtured and encouraged by the work of editors or publishers who are hostile or disrespectful to them and other black writers? I think not.

Black gay writers are nurtured, encouraged, and supported by black individuals and art forms—and by those outside their communities—that speak to them. There is already a kind of renaissance in black writing in the United States, especially in fiction, which has not only found a mass market among general readers but also in college and university classrooms. New gay black writers have also profited from the work of gay writers of different races and ethnicities: Samuel R. Delany, Andrew Holleran, Yukio Mishima, to name only a few. The positive experiences that a few black writers undergo in creative writing courses offered at predominately white universities and the collective struggle and self-affirmation that are part of the Gay Rights Movement help to account for the sudden development of numerous gay black writers in the United States.

The purpose of *Shade*, then, is to record the development and to provide, for the first time, a collective forum for some of those engaging black fiction writers; the object of this anthology is also to call attention to an important, yet unexamined, component of black literature, and to add another dimension to the Eurocentric construction which, in the United States, is called "gay literature." Another purpose of *Shade* is to present the variety in gay black fiction writing, as currently represented in the work Larry Duplechan, James Earl Hardy, and Jaime Manrique, writers whose books are enjoying unprecedented popularity. In *Shade* there are narratives about identity, narratives of exile, narratives about coming of age and coming out, as well as stories about cross-dressing, sexual violations, and gay men marrying as heterosexuals. These and numerous other subjects are examined in a variety of linguistic and structural experimentations—a polyphony—in the diverse narratives of *Shade*.

Shade is an international project. In fact, it was its international scope which made our work as co-editors very difficult. The difficulty arises from this question: Who in the Black World is willing to sign or identify himself as gay, much less as a gay writer? As co-editors living in the United States, Bruce Morrow and I are very much aware of the acts of violence against gay people in this country. We are aware that despite the political activism of the Gay Rights Movement and the achievements made since Stonewall, as well as the cautious support gay and lesbian communities receive from the Clinton Administration and progressive sectors of the clergy and educational institutions, there is still entrenched homophobic opposition from public officials who seek to deprive gays and lesbians of their dignity. Although certain progressive state and local governments have gone so far as to institute laws that protect the rights of gays and lesbians, there remains, since the recasting of extreme right wing ideologies during the Reagan Administration, a small group of homophobes who shriek their homohatred from the nation's capital. Most vituperative among these hate mongers is Jesse Helms, the strident senator from North Carolina. But it was not North American gay bashing that made difficult our tasks as co-editors of *Shade;* the institutionalized and personalized homophobia and homohatred in parts of the Third World paralyzed our efforts, making it impossible to gather materials from some regions of the globe. Our intention was to assemble an international gathering of fiction by gay men the world over. We have done so but not with the number of texts from outside the United States that we had originally hoped to collect. Why? In the Caribbean, South America, and Africa, very few individuals are brave enough to sign or identify themselves gay to the public. The consequences of doing so are grave: They result from state-sponsored homohatred or from anti-gay cultural practices, which threaten the life of the individual. This terrorism has been underscored by certain political and cultural activities on the African continent and in the Caribbean. The homophobic pronouncements of Zimbabwe's President Robert Mugabe, and the recording of anti-gay lyrics by popular Caribbean musicians, such as Buju Banton and Shabba Ranks, are ample testaments confirming the terrorism to which gay men and women are subjected.

In a November 7, 1995, National Public Radio news segment, Michael Skoler reported on Mugabe's campaign against gay and lesbian people in Zimbabwe. Two months before the report aired, Mugabe banned a group of gays and lesbians from participating in an international book fair in Harare, the nation's capital. Skoler reported that the President referred to gays and lesbians as " 'perverts, people who are worse than dogs and pigs' . . . hinting that homosexuals should be attacked and thrown in jail." Americans, Mugabe insisted, should "keep their sodomy, bestiality, stupid and foolish ways to themselves." He topped off his remarks by insisting that "homosexuality is foreign and repulsive to African culture, an immoral import brought to Zimbabwe from white society." This tyranny gives us pause, and yet reminds us as co-editors that, in other parts of the African Diaspora and in Africa, writing is at once a luxury and a need. This virulent homophobia toughened our resolve to assemble an international anthology which would include gay voices from various parts of the Black World.

It is not easy to live the life of a gay person outside or inside the United States. Couple that with being black and male, and you discover a disturbing world fraught with complexities.

What does it mean to be a black male in the Untied States of America? This is a complex question whose answer demands changes in the ways we read the American past. A balanced answer requires nothing short of a reexamination of the psycho-history of North America and its evolving racial and sexual ideologies. As we continue in our attempts to answer this question, we will discover that we must carefully revise the history of the white American effort to construct a negative image of the African American male, and to use that image as a central instrument in prescribing a role for him—a shifting one indeed, dating back to the Middle Passage, a role nevertheless purposely designed to exclude, confine, and therefore, contain the black male. Once the black male is controlled, the white man has argued, the black population en masse becomes a subject people, a position that the white settlers in the Americas designed and implemented to ensure the advancement of the European project of domination and exploitation.

When James Baldwin comments on what it means to be a black male in the United States, he identifies and critiques one of the pivotal tenets of the European project in the Americas. Speaking with Nikki Giovanni in an extended dialogue, Baldwin argues that

> the situation of the black male is a microcosm of the situation of the Christian world. The price of being a black man in America—the price the black male has had to pay, is expected to pay, and which he has to outwit—is his sex. You know, a black man is forbidden by definition, since he's black, to assume the roles, burdens, duties, and joys of being a man. In the same way that my child produced from your body did not belong to me but to the master and could be sold at any moment.

This erodes a man's sexuality, and when you erode a man's sexuality you destroy his ability to love anyone, despite the fact that sex and love are not the same thing. When a man's sexuality is gone, his possibility, his hope of loving is also gone.

Another component of the answer to the question I raise entails an examination of how the white female colludes in the efforts of the white male to dehumanize and control black men and black women. These and other issues related to the workings of the White World and its continued efforts to dominate, exploit, and ultimately to destroy people of color are vital in our efforts to read the meaning of being black and male in the United States.

Although we must acknowledge and examine how, and the extent to which, the political and social machinations of the White World impinge upon the lives of black people, the meaning of being black and male in the United States is not simply a reactive phenomenon. That is, what it means to be a black male has also to do with individual self-construction and the community. What, for example, is *manhood*? This concept has its own complexities which range from how the black male presents himself to the world to issues of social, economic, political, and cultural responsibilities to self, family, and community. Related to the subject of manhood are issues of *maleness* and *masculinity*, concepts which not only inform the black male's relationship to other males but to women as well. We should remember, however, that each of these issues, as they manifest themselves in the lives of black males, is informed by socioeconomic class and cultural exposure, by certain values and experiential knowledge. To be black and male in the United States is not only to live complexities of another's making but also to attempt to construct a self and chart a life, however difficult, of one's own.

The question about the meaning of the black male takes on added dimensions when one introduces it to gay male identities. What does it mean to be black and male and gay in the United States? To answer this amplified version of my original question, we must revisit the concerns the question evokes, and we must also address issues of identity as they manifest themselves in African American and European American communities. We must also examine the dynamics of the intersection of race and gay sexuality in gay and lesbian culture in general. If we interrogate these issues with the thoroughness they require, we will discover that to be black and male and gay in the United States is to live in a state of perpetual siege: either to endure, in silence, the debilitating circumstances which threaten to destroy the very core of your humanity, your selfhood; or, as the result of living publicly as a gay black male, to risk physical and psychological violence from both black and white heterosexist communities.

Yet, in spite of the heterosexist threats and the tragic toll which AIDS has taken on black and white gay communities, being gay in the United States is not all "doom and gloom," particularly, for example, if you live in or near a large urban center (New York, Atlanta, Chicago, Washington, San Francisco, etc., where there are substantial supportive gay communities), if you have the economic means to live apart from the immediate dangers of the homohatred of heterosexists, or if you possess the educational preparation, the intellectual bearings, and the will to confront or transcend what I have described as "a state of perpetual siege." Under these circumstances and with these accoutrements for survival, the North American authors contributing to *Shade* have managed to do so; and as artists they, first fighting, have, in the words of a poem by Gwendolyn Brooks, civilized "a space / Wherein to play" their "violin[s] with grace." They have given the black gay voice agency in narratives which eloquently inscribe one of the "unspeakables" of the American experience.

The authors in *Shade* have also deliberately signed themselves gay, and in doing so they have liberated and prepared themselves to bear witness to the various facets of the meaning of being black, gay, and male. Actually, they not only bear witness to this phenomenon in their writing in general, they interrogate it—not as a curiosity, or an exotic or deviate existence of an "other." Rather, like the filmmakers Marlon Riggs and Isaac Julien, the authors in *Shade* represent being black, gay, and male with the same interest and integrity as Ernest J. Gaines represents being black, straight, and male in Louisiana; or Ellen

Douglas represents being white, straight, and female in Mississippi. Like these two Southerners, the authors gathered in *Shade* write about what they know, and much of what they know has long been deemed the unspeakable. They narrate, lyricize, and interrogate "the unspeakable"; they speak it. And when they speak, they affirm their gayness as a legitimate way of living, loving, and thinking in the world; they subvert the homophobic ideology—and its accompanying linguistic apparatus—which dehumanizes gays and other oppressed people. In their texts, the authors in *Shade* present gay experiences as metaphors for reading the world.

—*Charlottesville, Virginia*

Author Biographies

K. ANTHONY APPIAH was born to a Ghanian father and a British mother, and raised in Kumasi, Ghana. He received his Ph.D. in philosophy at Clare College, Cambridge University, and is now professor of Afro-American Studies and Philosophy at Harvard University. He is the author of a number of philosophical books—most recently *In My Father's House: Africa in the Philosophy of Culture* (1992)—and three novels, *Avenging Angel* (1990), *Nobody Likes Letitia* (1994), and *Another Death in Venice* (1995).

BENNETT CAPERS has published stories in several literary magazines, including *Gettysburg Review*, *Poughkeepsie Review*, *Allegheny Review*, *South Carolina Review*, and *Fiction Magazine*. He has received the First Book Award (Terry McMillan, Judge) and the Open Voice Award (David Bradley, Judge). He lives in Brooklyn.

SAMUEL R. DELANY is the author of more than thirty fiction and nonfiction books, including *The Mad Man*, *Atlantis: Three Tales*, and *Silent Interviews: On Languages, Sex, Science Fiction, & Some Comics*, a collection of essays. A four-time winner of the Nebula Award from the Science Fiction Writers of America, he is a professor of Comparative Literature at the University of Massachusetts at Amherst.

MELVIN DIXON who died of AIDS in 1993 at the age of forty-two, was a professor of English at Queens College in New York. He is the author of two novels, *Trouble the Water* (1989) and *Vanishing Rooms* (1990), the poetry collection *Change of Territory* (1983), and a book of literary criticism, *Ride Out the Wilderness: Geography and Identity in African-American Literature* (1987). He translated from the French *The Collected Poems of Léopold Sédar Senghor* (1991).

LARRY DUPLECHAN Larry Duplechan is the author of three novels, *Eight Days a Week* (1985), *Blackbird* (1986), and *Tangled Up in Blue* (1989).

JAMES EARL HARDY is the author of *B-Boy Blues* (1994), the first Africentric gay hip-hop love story, which has become one of the best-selling titles ever published by a small press. He is also the author of a biography of filmmaker Spike Lee and of a portrait of the pop group Boyz II Men. An honors graduate of both St. John's University and Columbia University's Graduate School of Journalism, his byline has appeared in the *Washington Post, Entertainment Weekly, Newsweek, Essence,* and *The Advocate.* He was born and raised in Bedford-Stuyvesant, Brooklyn, and lives in New York City.

CHARLES HARVEY has published stories in *The Ontario Review* and *Story*. His story "When Dogs Bark" is included in *Dispatches from the Front,* which will be published in 1996. He lives in Houston and is finishing a novel, *The Road to Astroland.*

GREG HENRY was born in Antigua, West Indies, and raised in East Elmhurst, Queens. A 1993 graduate from the Utica campus of Syracuse University, he has written for Gannett newspapers.

A. CINQUÉ HICKS was born in Los Angeles, California, and grew up in Altadena, California. He studied literature at Harvard University and currently lives in Somerville, Massachusetts, where he works as a publicist for a family policy research film.

BRIAN KEITH JACKSON is a graduate of Northeast Louisiana University and has received fellowships from Art Matters, Inc., and the Jerome Foundation for his play *After Thoughts*, and was a 1995 finalist for the Frederick Douglass Fellowship for Young African-American Fiction Writers. His first novel, *The View from Here*, is forthcoming from Pocket Books in 1996. He lives in New York City.

G. WINSTON JAMES is Performance Coordinator for Other Countries: Black Gay Expression, Managing Editor for the organization's upcoming literary anthology, and former coeditor of *Kuumba*, the African-American Lesbian and Gay poetry journal. His poetry and prose has appeared in numerous anthologies, including *Waves: An Anthology of New Gay Fiction* (1994), *The Road Before Us* (1991), *Sojourner* (1993), *Milking Black Bulls* (1995), and *Words of Fire* (1996).

JOHN R. KEENE, JR. is the author of the novel *Annotations* (1995). His poetry, essays, and short stories have appeared in numerous publications, including *Callaloo* and the *Kenyon Review*. A graduate of Harvard College, he is a member of the Dark Room Collective. From 1993 to 1995, he was managing editor of *Callaloo*. He is currently studying at New York University.

RANDALL KENAN is the author of the novel *Visitation of Spirits* (1989) and the short story collection *Let the Dead Bury the Dead* (1992), which was nominated for the National Book Critics Circle Award and won the Lambda Award for best gay men's fiction. For his exceptional promise as a fiction writer, he received one of the 1994 Whiting Writer's Awards.

JAIME MANRIQUE is a Colombian-born writer. His first volume of poetry received Colombia's National Poetry Award. His most recent novel is *Latin Moon in Manhattan* (1992) and the poetry collection *My Night with Federico García Lorca* (1995). He has just completed *Twilight at the Equator,* a collection of novellas and short stories. His young adult biography of Federico García Lorca is forthcoming from Chelsea House. He teaches in the Spanish Department at Mt. Holyoke College.

BRUCE MORROW is the recipient of the 1995 Frederick Douglass Fellowship for Young African-American Fiction Writers. His work has appeared in the *New York Times, Callaloo, aRude,* and the anthologies *Speak My Name: Black Men on Masculinity and the American Dream* and *Ancestral House: Short Stories from the African Diaspora.* Morrow lives in New York City and can be reached via e-mail at bmorrow@panix.com.

ROBERT E. PENN is currently a member of the Board of Directors of Other Countries. His poetry, essays, and short fiction have appeared in a number of anthologies and periodicals including *Sojourner* (1993), *The Road Before Us* (1991), *Essence, Thing, COLORLife, The Portable Lower East Side* and *Art & Understanding,* to which he is also a contributing editor. His story "Uncle Eugene" was written in loving memory of his father, Robert E. Penn, Sr., Th.D., 1916–1976.

L. PHILLIP RICHARDSON has been a member of the Other Countries collective almost from its inception in 1986. His poetry and fiction has appeared in Other Countries' Black Gay Voices issue and *The Road Before Us.* He lives in New York City.

CHARLES H. ROWELL is a professor of English at the University of Virginia and the founder and editor of *Callaloo.* His poetry, prose, and interviews have appeared in a variety of periodicals and anthologies including *The Southern Review, The Harlem Renaissance Reexamined* and *Conversations with Ernest Gaines.* He lives in Charlottesville, Virginia.

SEVERO SARDUY (1936–1993), a writer of Afro-Cuban and Chinese heritage, left his native Cuba for France in 1960, never to return. He is the author of six highly acclaimed novels, several volumes of poetry, essays, and plays. A painter and radio host, he was an editor of Editions du Seuil, where he introduced contemporary Latin American fiction to European readers.

DARIECK SCOTT is the author of the novel *Traitor to the Race* (1995). He is currently pursuing his Ph.D. at Stanford, after receiving an M.A. in Afro-American Studies from Yale and a J.D. from Yale Law School. His work has appeared in *Ancestral House*, *Christopher Street* and *Callaloo*. He lives in San Francisco.

REGINALD SHEPHERD has studied at Bennington College, Brown University, and the University of Iowa's Writers' Workshop. His collection of poems, *Some Are Drowning*, won a 1993 Associated Writing Program's Award. His poetry and prose have appeared in numerous periodicals and anthologies including *The Antioch Review*, *The Kenyon Review*, *Nation*, *The Paris Review*, *Poetry* and *In the Life*.

BIL WRIGHT, a recipient of a 1995 Millay Fellowship, is a fiction writer, playwright, and poet. His fiction and poetry have appeared in *Men on Men 3*, *Art and Understanding*, *The Road Before Us*, *The James White Review*, *The Name of Love*, and many other anthologies. His plays have been produced in the United States and Germany, and published in the anthology *Tough Acts to Follow*. As a 1994 Jerome Award Winner and Mabou Mines Resident Artist, he adapted and staged Audre Lorde's *Zami, a New Spelling of My Name*. He lives in New York City.

CHARLES WRIGHT was born in Franklin, Missouri, in 1932. Early on, he worked at his writing under the direction of Lowney Handy in Marshall, Illinois. He is the author of two novels, *The Messenger* (1963) and *The Wig: A Mirror Image* (1966); a nonfiction work, *Absolutely Nothing to Get Alarmed About* (1973); and a variety of uncollected short stories.